Praise for the work of Ch

M000202468

"This is a terrific book. I can't ~~...~~ ~~....~~ ~~....~~ ~~.......~~ I have seen fiction, especially science fiction, put so richly in context. *It Walks in Beauty* introduces us to a remarkable man, gives us insight into the American science fiction community of the 1940s and '50s, and reminds us how much damage the McCarthy era of red hunts did to ordinary human lives and to American civilization. Among the stories, I especially like 'The Names of Yanils,' a thoughtful consideration of the relation of people to tradition, and 'It Walks in Beauty,' an utterly creepy and true description of sex roles in '50s America. I was there. I remember those sex roles, just as I remember the red hunts. We have not recovered yet. Nor will we recover until the ideas and integrity of people like Chandler Davis are incorporated into our history and culture."

— Eleanor Arnason, author of *Ring of Swords* and
A Woman of the Iron People

"Although Chandler Davis has published less than a score of science-fiction short stories, some of us have long treasured them as brilliant gems. Josh Lukin's thoughtful collection of Davis's fiction and nonfiction offers 21st-century readers a fine introduction to the work of this neglected and invaluable writer."

— H. Bruce Franklin, author of *War Stars: The Superweapon in the American Imagination* and *Vietnam & Other American Fantasies*

"This is a wonderful and unusual selection of science fiction and political/psychological non-fiction, a collection of writing by Chandler Davis. Informed by his personal life, his unwavering political activism over the last half century, his professional life as a mathematician, Davis's work provides invaluable insight and direction about what is to be done—and always with wit, clarity, tolerance, and dissent. Whether writing imaginatively or factually, he shows how narcissism so destructively gets in the way of seeing others as real people and how it works against acknowledging what is unknown. Chandler Davis relates to past, present, and future times, always open to decipher the whole picture and to speak up."

— Judith Deutsch, President of Science for Peace

About the Aqueduct Press Heirloom Books

Aqueduct Press's series of Heirloom Books aims to bring back into print and preserve work that has helped make feminist science fiction what it is today — work that though clearly of its time is still pleasurable to read, work that is thought-provoking, work that can still speak powerfully to readers. The series takes its name from the seeds of older strains of vegetables, so valuable and in danger of being lost. Our hope is to keep these books from being lost, as works that do not make it into the canon so often are.

∼ L. Timmel Duchamp

It Walks in Beauty

Selected Prose
of Chandler Davis

Published by Aqueduct Press
PO Box 95787
Seattle, WA 98145-2787
www.aqueductpress.com

9 8 7 6 5 4 3 2 1

ISBN: 978-1-933500-37-9

Library of Congress Control Number: 2010904003

Cover Illustration by Anna Tambour
Book Design by Kathryn Wilham
Illustration on p. 347: The Davis family home on Shawm Hill by Quentin Brown, 1986, by permission of H. Chandler Davis

Printed in the USA by Thomson-Shore Inc.

Heirloom Books

1

IT WALKS IN BEAUTY

SELECTED PROSE
OF CHANDLER DAVIS

Edited and with an introduction by

Josh Lukin

To my parents:
"The teaching of your mouth is better to me
than thousands of gold and silver"
– *Josh Lukin*

To my family:
"So *that's* what the future's like.
Now I know."
– *Chandler Davis*

Contents

INTRODUCTION

History, Heresy, Hegemony:
  On the Relevance of Chandler Davis by Josh Lukin ... 3

ESSAYS AND LETTERS

Critique & Proposals, 1949 ... 52

…From an Exile ... 63

Two Open Letters
  Violence & Civility ... 86
  Imprisoned Mathematician: J.L. MASSERA ... 91

The Selfish Genetics ... 96

From Science for Good or Ill ... 106

The Untimely Rhetoric of Chandler Davis's Essays
  by Josh Lukin ... 120

STORIES

Last Year's Grave Undug ... 141

Adrift on the Policy Level ... 167

It Walks in Beauty ... 194

The Statistomat Pitch ... 229

The Names of Yanils ... 241

SPEECH

"Shooting Rats in a Barrel": Did the Red Hunt Win? ... 271

INTERVIEW

"Trying to Say Something True":
  The *Paradoxa* Interview with Chandler Davis ... 290

AFTERWORD

Alternatives to Reverence ... 348

ACKNOWLEDGMENTS ... 359

INTRODUCTION

History, Heresy, Hegemony:
On the Relevance of Chandler Davis

Josh Lukin

"CHANDLER DAVIS!!"

It was early in 2002, and the author of the email with that subject heading was David R. Willingham, a dapper retired linguistics professor living near Seattle and the General Editor of *Paradoxa: Studies in World Literary Genres*. I'd been struggling for a few years as Guest Editor of an issue of that journal, to be entitled "Fifties Fictions" and dedicated to finding rebels and iconoclasts in overlooked literature of a decade widely stereotyped as "conformist": the issue included scholarship on lesbian fiction, African-American satire, EC Comics' parodic treatment of the Cold War, and women's Beat literature. The usually sarcastic and blunt Dr. Willingham was moved to use two exclamation marks and thirteen capital letters by my proposal to interview Horace Chandler Davis, who as a victim of the House Committee on Un-American Activities *and* a Red Scare exile *and* a science fiction writer *and* an advocate of recovering "lost" aspects of cultural history was tailor-made for the issue's theme. Professor Davis, when I visited him in Toronto, gave me four hours of his time; and the published interview, reprinted at the end of this volume, was praised by the handful of scholars and intellectuals who read the small-circulation journal.

Professor Willingham's excitement over the inclusion of Chandler Davis in "Fifties Fictions," at that time, was both apt and vindicated; I wonder whether the reasons for Aqueduct Press's interest will be as clear. *It Walks in Beauty: Selected Prose of Chandler Davis* is the first male-authored book to be published by Aqueduct; it includes three stories with all-male casts; and its articles most often focus on male victims of oppression. Its aptness for a feminist press is, then, not immediately apparent; so I hope to make a case for it on biographical, literary, political, and theoretical grounds. Davis's feminist life and the strategies he developed in his battles with the Red Hunters could be of particular interest to feminist readers; a look at his work is also important to more general issues of ideological struggle and of recovering ideas and texts from progressives of the past — hence my emphasis on the fact that US Communism from 1935-1955 was a fruitful source of feminist thought, which provided a milieu that supported Davis's values. The relevance of Davis's work to several present-day political battlegrounds will also, I believe, become evident in the course of my argument.

Biographical:

Chandler Davis lives a feminist life. The feminist blogger Bellatrys, denouncing Harlan Ellison in 2007, wrote that Ellison's age was no excuse for his sexism, as was evinced by the life of the much older Chan Davis. But to eschew sexism in one's life and thought is no small feat for a man born in 1926: the best-known US writers among Davis's contemporaries include Robert Bly, Neal Cassady, Hugh Hefner, J.P. Donleavy, and Tim LaHaye, none of them celebrated opponents of the patriarchy.[1] Indeed, Natalie Zemon Davis has explained that her mentor at Smith College

> feared my marriage tolled the knell of my history career, though she never said it right out. Her generation had taken a different path; how could I ever be a scholar if I were traipsing after my husband amid the clutter of children? On the other hand, I had a husband early along who truly believed in women's careers and who was genuinely committed to sharing household tasks and parenting. We began a lifelong conversation about politics, history, science, and literature. (1997)

Such gender equity is rare enough in the present day; for many in the twenty years after World War II, it surpassed the limits of the thinkable. In perhaps the sole critical essay to date that analyzes Chandler Davis's work, L. Timmel Duchamp writes that

> Natalie Zemon Davis broke all the social and ideological rules binding US women in the 1950s. She and Chandler Davis shared domestic and child-care duties. Such accomplished professional women as Davis were so rare in

---

1 Notable US women born in 1926 include Marilyn Monroe, Harper Lee, Gina Berriault, and Carolyn Heilbrun, all casualties of the patriarchy to some extent.

> the mid-1970s that although I knew her only
> by reputation, as a graduate student I took her
> as a role model and worshipped her from afar.
> ("Old Pictures" 74-75)[2]

Davis's sister Mina Davis Caulfield and his daughter Simone Weil Davis have also done influential feminist scholarship: the former is an anthropologist who brings a Marxist perspective to the study of imperialism, the discourses of oppression, and the cultures of resistance; the latter is a literary scholar and prison educator whose work has addressed the impact on women of advertising and commodity culture.

Davis's support of feminist activism extends beyond home and family: as a trustee of the Davis-Putter scholarship fund founded by his father, the board of which also includes his three sisters, he helps to administer need-based grants to "students actively working for peace and justice," particularly in opposition to sexism, imperialism, corporate tyranny, racism, poverty, and homophobia. Recent years have seen dozens of women activists benefit from the fund: Sora Han, now an assistant professor at UC Irvine, is a scholar and activist who addresses cultural images of femininity and incarceration, feminist interpretations of Western Marxists, and Asian-American women's prison narratives; poet and educator Eneri Rodriguez has been a program director at the Women's History Museum

---

2 Such admiration did not end when feminist pressures increased the presence of women in intellectual fields; three days ago as I write this, Renaissance historian Anthony Grafton remarked online, "When faced with any complex problem, scholarly, pedagogical, or moral, asking yourself what Natalie Zemon Davis would do is always the right thing to do" (2008).

and studies the ongoing massacre of women in Juarez; and Tiffany King co-founded Resistahs, a community education collective in Wilmington, Delaware, that works on transformative education for African-American women, among them public housing residents, Vo-Tech students, and survivors of domestic violence.[3]

Gender equity was a Communist issue. It has for some time been a commonplace that US Communists, despite their spectacular misconceptions concerning the horrors of Stalin and the USSR,[4] were ahead of the curve on many social justice issues in their own country; but it is most often the anti-racist struggle that is held up as an example of such a cause. Only recently have scholars paid extensive attention to Communist advocacy of gender justice. Chandler Davis says that his feminist and homophilic views were initially fostered by his parents, whose values on that front were informed "more by Greenwich Village freedom than by the Third International." But, whereas other circumstances of mid-century life might have discouraged the retention of such interests, the Communist discourse was one of the few that, however sporadically, endorsed an interest in gender equity. Most surveys of gender politics in that era acknowledge that US Reds could have done much more for women; Alan Wald observes

---

3   Some of the more famous recipients of Davis-Putter grants have included Robert Moses and Margaret Burnham of the civil rights movement and Mumia Abu-Jamal, whose great *We Want Freedom: A Life in the Black Panther Party* (2004) owes its existence to Davis-Putter.

4   Although he had long criticized aspects of the Communist line in private, Chandler Davis first took a public stand against Soviet policy at the time of the 1968 invasion of Czechoslovakia, for reasons he details in his essay "The Purge."

that "pro-Communist women writers were part of a political movement that devoted only limited theoretical
attention to the origins and dynamics of women's oppression" (2002, 252). Yet in 1957, Carl Marzani[5] wrote that
American Marxists must examine themselves to determine how much they had absorbed of such hegemonic
values as "pragmatism, male supremacy, chauvinism, facile optimism, and so on, which are endemic in our society" (18). The fact that "male supremacy" could by then be
routinely inserted on a list of sins against Marxist values
owed much to the labors of gender theorists on the Left
from 1935 on.

Although anti-patriarchal[6] stories and articles appeared in the Communist press earlier in the thirties, the
watershed seems to have been the 1939 appearance of
Mary Inman's *In Woman's Defense*, perhaps the first book-
length work by a US Communist to analyze the cultural
and social aspects of patriarchal oppression. Inman delivered a thorough critique of gender essentialism, conclud-
ing that "Human nature, manufactured characteristics,
and falsified characteristics have all been lumped together
and labeled female nature" (306). She anticipated recent

---

5   A Red Scare victim whom Davis much admired – see the interview
    that concludes this volume.

6   I try to avoid the anachronistic use of the term "feminist" in this part
    of my discussion, since Communists disavowed the term: they saw
    "feminism," which had been denounced by Lenin himself late in his
    life, as a right-wing individualist movement that sought to empower
    women within the norms of bourgeois society. While my descriptive
    use of "anti-patriarchal" and even "gender" is anachronistic inasmuch
    as those terms were not available to mid-century writers, some forms
    of the ideas they convey were present.

analyses of the way the patriarchal system oppresses both genders, starting by tracing the transmission of oppressive ideology:

> Men are trained to guard women, especially those of their immediate family, and to a considerable extent women not of their family, and women also receive training to act as guards of other women. But in the background of these men and women who function as guards is a group of mercenary propagandists, novelists, newspaper columnists, and speakers... So, when all is said and done...we get back to the same old formula of [1920s Danish sociologist K.A.] Wieth-Knudsen's, wherein men are to oppress women and then a small group of rich men is to oppress them all, including women of their own class. (312, 314)

Inman's analysis of the social reproduction of male supremacy— of how the standards of child-rearing "manufacture femininity," how society implements such oppressive tools as "overemphasis of beauty," and how literature, movies, fashion, and language perpetuate a "culture of women's subjugation" — are also striking in their insights, as is her argument that the tropes of women's liberation risk denigrating the value of traditional, domestic "women's work" (Weigand 2001, 33, 59).

Systematizing and transcending the insights of earlier Communists on gender, Inman's work influenced a substantial cohort of Red activists after World War II to mobilize on women's issues. The Congress of American Women, founded in 1945 by Susan B. Anthony II and

Mary van Kleeck, was redbaited out of existence in 1950; nonetheless it was instrumental in raising Left awareness of the gender issues Inman and earlier feminists had analyzed (Weigand 48-64). In 1948, thanks in part to the success of Canadian Auto Workers (CAW) leader Betty Millard's pamphlet "Women against Myth," the Party published an article under the name of chairman William Z. Foster that codified a remarkably progressive stand on gender. The article denounced "stubborn and dangerous male chauvinist ideas" concerning the inferiority of the female intellect; it bemoaned "the aggressive role played by the man in the sexual act with the woman"; it insisted that "an ideological attack must be made against the whole system of male superiority ideas which continue to play such an important part in woman's subjugation" (180, 181, 86). In 1949 and 1950, grassroots pressure led the Communist papers — *Daily Worker* and *People's World* — to eliminate content that presented women as sex objects or domestic servants to their spouses and instead celebrate their history and political agency (89).

Kate Weigand's research on "Red Feminism" reveals that Communist emphasis on gender justice had a real impact on everyday life and culture in the US Communist world.[7] Weigand's interviewees speak of many husbands who eagerly shared domestic and child-rearing tasks.

---

7   The impact of these changes varied greatly from place to place and from person to person: Kathlene McDonald observes that "the Party's official position did not necessarily filter down to the rank-and-file membership" (Lukin 2008, 43). Around 1991, a septuagenarian ex-Communist friend who had been close to the Party from 1944 until 1949 asked me, "How did these feminists and homosexuals end up on the Left? It used to be a movement for minorities and working

State and local CP chapters "investigated and intervened in numerous cases" alleging male chauvinist behavior or speech: "Typically, the CP charged such men with male supremacy, subjected them to the criticism of their peers, and sentenced them to 'control tasks involving study on the woman question' so that they might unlearn the poisonous ideology of male chauvinism" (130). In the arts, Weigand reports, "Communists made a conscious effort to create new cultural artifacts that portrayed women as strong and intelligent" (115). The Red press often printed critiques of misogynist culture: Weigand presents as typical David Carpenter's 1951 complaint that

> ...the capitalist overlords of US imperialism increasingly defile women. The entire cultural power of the capitalist class — movies, books, magazines, radio, schools, churches, etc. — attacks women, particularly of the working class, almost from birth, to destroy their minds and creative social abilities. Every word, every picture, is aimed at making women accept sexual and kitchen slavery as their destiny. (119)

The fight for gender justice, by then, could no longer be dismissed as a bourgeois project, nor could the critique of culture be minimized as contrary to historical materialist principles. Domestic relations and cultural representations of gender were generally acknowledged objects of Communist critique.[8] The Davises' feminist heroism is in

---

people." In the face of Communists' complex and contradictory attitudes on gender equity, Davis's consistent progressivism is notable.

8   In the face of my focus on Communist culture, Davis wants to emphasize that he did not confine himself to that intellectual milieu. He

no way an inevitable consequence of the fact that Natalie and Chandler were Reds — many Communists only paid lip service to gender equity — but the particulars of their political allegiances are relevant to their work.

Literary:

Chandler Davis wrote several feminist stories. Society exerts its ideological pressures subtly; and, as Stephen Ball has famously said, "We do not speak the discourse. The discourse speaks us" (1990, 18). It is possible, then, and indeed not rare, for a writer leading a feminist life and versed in anti-patriarchal arguments to fall into the most clichéd and conservative narrative conventions when writing fiction. There is no guarantee that an author with the critical tools that were available to Chandler Davis would have been able to use them in writing fiction; and it is to his credit that he was.

The most overtly feminist piece in Davis's oeuvre is "It Walks in Beauty": philosopher John Holbo has characterized the story as "a veritable Butlerian jihad," suggesting that its message prefigures Judith Butler's ideas on gender-as-performative by thirty-six years (2004). L. Timmel Duchamp has written vividly of how, in the context of mainstream 1950s gender discourse, the norms

---

writes in a 2008 email:

> I was open to ideas from across the Left, though we were exhorted not to be: to anarchist & Trotskyist ideas most commonly. This made me welcome the New York SF crowd, mostly ex-socialist rather than socialist, but vertiginously open-minded. It was the same liberating mood I felt in the New Left in 1965-67, when Kirkegaard, Lenin, & Emma Goldman could be cited with approval in the same small bull session.

of the story's setting, which a reader today would see as wildly dystopic, were not very far from the "natural" gender prescriptions of US society (2004). But the story's insights have precedents in the Red Decade; in 1935, some of the ideas entailed in its critique appeared in Rebecca Pitts's critique of sex and male supremacy in bourgeois society, "Women and Communism," which was published in *New Masses*. Pitts characterized "the two chief functions of mankind" as work[9] and sex, and decried social norms that thwarted people's potential and distorted their lives by unduly focusing on one of those functions at the expense of the other. She argued that, under the regime of private property, sexual behavior among most people had become purely egocentric:

> *Sex* has been transformed into *sexuality*: from an impersonal end (participation in life) it has become a personal means. Sometimes, transmuted by an elaborate ritual of romance, this ego-sexuality becomes the "in love" state so characteristic of our culture: naïvely greedy in popular songs and screenplays; subtly disguised in the lamentations of a Byron or a De Musset. Whether "in love" or not, however, each sexual partner desires in the other the mirror and gratification of his own self-love. So widespread

9   Like much good sf, and like the kind of fiction socialists have long admired and sought, Davis's stories often pay close attention to work and the workplace, demonstrating that artisanship and meticulous attention are part of even the most routine jobs and sometimes modeling what more-or-less unalienated, creative labor might look like. This kind of focus seems to have fallen out of fashion for some time in "mainstream" literary fiction.

13

> is this personalism that we crown it with social
> approval and call it "normal." (323)

Pitts's hope that the relations between people based upon
sex, like those based upon labor, could be humanized and
purged of their alienating forms so as to confer value and
dignity upon their practitioners bears some resemblance
to the hope expressed by Paula in "It Walks in Beauty."

I have argued elsewhere[10] that, in an era in which
the grossest misogyny in life and literature passed un-
remarked or celebrated, even small anti-sexist gestures
were worthy of notice. Chandler Davis was in the minority of sf writers who sought consistently to create female
characters with competence, authority, and agency. In the
stories for *Astounding Science Fiction* that first made his
reputation, we see a female Congressional staffer whose
competence and quick thinking helps avert nuclear holo-
caust ("To Still the Drums," 1946), a revolutionary cell on
Ganymede in which men and women have equal authority ("The Journey and the Goal," 1947), a female leader
of a revolt against a eugenicist autocrat ("The Aristocrat,"
1949), and a planetary research team in which men and
women collaborate as scientific peers ("Share Our World,"
1953). But Davis's most penetrating anti-sexist statements
are his later works set in patriarchal societies — not only
"It Walks in Beauty" but also the oft-reprinted "Adrift on
the Policy Level."[11]

---

10 In "Cold War Masculinity...." For accounts of misogyny in sf, see
   Larbalestier (2002) and Franklin (1980).

11 Even Davis's most androcentric stories have anti-sexist moments:
   "The Names of Yanils," for example, insists on the fact that the

Jean Smith, in a tribute to Davis, characterized "Adrift on the Policy Level" as "about scientific advice getting shuffled aside in a corporation" (1993), which suggests that the story's theme is bureaucratic incompetence in the world of commerce. While broadly true, that characterization elides the story's most innovative social, psychological, and political attributes. Politically, it matters that the setting is not "a corporation" but "The Corporation," a quasi-governmental entity that not only runs on marketing but administrates large geographic regions; psychologically, the story's satirical punch owes much to the way in which The Corporation has by the end imposed a blissful false consciousness on the protagonists; and socially, the story offers a novel depiction of how an oppressive society uses gender to further its ends.

The subtleties of the story's approach to gender may not be immediately clear to a reader today, inasmuch as the piece plays with three commonplaces that are rooted in the era of its creation, *viz*:

1. The fifties (and indeed the preceding and following decade) saw a huge expression of anxiety that managerial jobs were emasculating or feminizing men, both because they were not rugged individualist forms of self-assertion and because they entailed "emotional labor" and attention to the minutiae of pleasing others, tasks that were thought of as more appropriate to women.

Fishers are the most patriarchal society in their region, and also leaves a reader feeling that they're the most retrograde.

2. Sf of the fifties (and the forties and the sixties) had rigid conventions in which women were allowed authority. Luise White famously observed in 1975 that "...active, vigorous women characters [in sf] invariably worked either directly for the state, or for some male-run institution that controlled so much power and revenue, it might as well be the state itself" (Delany 1994, 167); she noted that these women included the heroes — Kathy in *The Space Merchants*, Rydra Wong in *Babel-17*, and many others — as well as the monsters, such as Hedy in *The Space Merchants* and Olivia in *The Stars My Destination*.

3. Mainstream literature was less ambivalent: women with authority in political or bureaucratic milieux were pretty consistently monsters along the lines of *The Manchurian Candidate*'s Eleanor Shaw, *One Flew over the Cuckoo's Nest*'s Big Nurse, *The Ugly American*'s Marie MacIntosh, and (from Humbert's point of view) *Lolita*'s Miss Pratt. Such women, however, were unsexed or sexually grotesque. Historian Robert Dean points out that *The Ugly American*, for example, "warned [that] women could subvert the imperial project from two directions: from within, as indolent luxury-loving 'Moms,' and from without, as alien sexual temptresses" (1998, 29).

The Communist line on gender may also be relevant to an understanding of the story, because Communists regarded female empowerment within the constraints of capitalist institutions as no success at all, a goal of bourgeois feminism (today we would call it a Third Wave approach). An attentive Communist would also have been aware of (albeit not necessarily in agreement with) Popular Front era arguments about "sexual servility" like Rebecca Pitts's, which is also relevant to "It Walks in Beauty":

> To get a husband (even lovers, even admirers), [woman under capitalism] must please the dominant male — "normally" an undeveloped egotist who regards her as a means to his own pleasure. It becomes her business, therefore, to arouse desire; to play by means of sex-allurement, dress, and personal charm upon male ego-sexuality. Instead of being a rounded, creative personality, she is warped and twisted… It is proof of a strong urge in woman that so many really do — in spite of this terrific pressure from bourgeois society — lead creative lives. (1987 [1935], 324)

Pitts does not use the word "business" casually; she is consciously in a tradition of criticizing the commodification of Sex Appeal.[12] And while Chandler Davis seems loath to depict any woman as unconsciously "warped and twisted," his work is remarkably aware of the sexist pressures that Pitts and other thoughtful Reds described.

So "Adrift on the Policy Level" is the work of an author whose stories have begun, perhaps thanks to the political persecutions or social changes he is observing, to grow

---

12 As Brecht had done in *Die Dreigroschenoper* and *Happy End* a few years earlier.

more caustic and satirical; and it is the product of a creative mind that has already, in "The Aristocrat" and "Share
Our World," shown the ability to circumvent sf conventions concerning the position of empowered women. Unlike Davis's earlier stories, "Adrift" cannot offer a character
who is conscious of its society's problems and points the
way toward freedom. The premise of the satire — that The
Corporation is a total institution, exercising all of its hegemonic powers to preserve the status quo — obviates the
possibility of a liberating figure.[13] Instead, the story does
its political work by burlesquing the ideological norms of
mid-century US society and fiction. If the emotional labor
and inauthentic "other-directed" poses that the managerial world requires are "feminizing," it asks, wouldn't the
perfect corporation have them done by women using the
skills of "manufactured femininity"? If the tools of the
sexual temptress are so powerful, wouldn't female agents
of authority use them, rather than being starchy and
schoolmarmish termagants? Isn't gender and the ability
to perform it in the hope of manipulating one's superiors
something that men have also, such that Mr. Demarest's
style of masculinity can change "from Viking to Roman"
as the occasion demands? And, *pace* sf traditions, how
likely is it that a corporate-political functionary under

13 The great risk in satire, as Randy Newman well knows (consider
various sentimental recordings of "Sail Away"), is that it will be interpreted as endorsing or claiming the inevitability of the conditions
it is decrying. I suspect that the popularity of "Adrift on the Policy
Level" owes something to readers who think that the subaltern female characters *are* Big Nurse figures and see the story as endorsing
the conservative trope that "Women are Society" and must be over-
thrown.

capitalism can use her "active, vigorous" character and her suasive powers for anything other than being a Company Woman and maintaining the institution's homeostasis?

Political:

In the wake of recent controversies, both in the sf world and in the feminist blogosphere, as to whether feminism is necessarily a movement of the Left, it may be a bold suggestion that various anti-conservative political agendas are in fact integral to feminism and vice-versa. Nonetheless, although the US political map was different thirty years ago, the Right, as manifested in movement conservatism, is at present in opposition to substantial tenets of feminism; and Chandler Davis's advocacy and analysis of various Leftist agendas (some of them quite compatible with the goals of liberals and even of those Libertarians who have grown disillusioned with the Right) are of use to feminist thought and highly relevant to present-day conflicts. I offer three propositions to that effect.

Diversity in Representation is a Feminist Issue. Dismayingly, this was a point of contention in the 1860s and is still contested as I write in mid-2008. In June 2008, the *Washington Post* ran an article by Linda Hirshman bemoaning how feminism has changed since *The Feminine Mystique*, denouncing "intersectionality" and attempts by progressive feminists to include the concerns of women of color, women in prison, and women victimized by war and pollution. Characterizing feminism as "fragmented" and "sclerotic," blaming black women for Clarence Thomas's presence on the Supreme Court, and fearing that feminism has become a "social-justice-for-everyone" movement, Hirshman accused contemporary feminists of "shedding potential allies" — presumably allies for whom the presence of goals not prioritized by affluent white women is a deal-breaker.

Of course, Hirshman's nostalgia for the feminism of Friedan stops at a convenient point in history: *The Feminine Mystique* focused on the experience of affluent white women as a strategic move to avoid being redbaited, a risk of which labor activist Friedan was acutely aware. Ninteen -fifties Red critiques of male chauvinism, whether by women of color such as Claudia Jones and Alice Childress or by white women such as Martha Dodd and Ruth Seid (aka Jo Sinclair), took for granted the need to address and include women "triply oppressed" by race, class, and sex. I have written recently (2008, Introduction) of conflicts in 1950 over "inter-group representation" in textbooks and of how some on the Left ridiculed "pressure groups" who opposed racial stereotyping: these issues of recognition and inclusion were not invented by Alice Walker in the seventies, as Hirshman comes close to suggesting.

The earliest Chandler Davis essay herein, "Critique & Proposals, 1949," is a manifesto for diversity in representation, addressing the problems of racial and ethnic stereotyping in science fiction. As I note in the interview, Davis consistently practiced what he preached, populating his stories with characters of diverse ethnicities and ancestry. One of the characters in "The Individualist" is a black man; the hero of "To Still the Drums" has a Jewish surname; and the heroine of "Share Our World" is the brilliant Chang Kwei-T'ao, whose beauty from the point of view of the deuteragonist (Tim Balch, whose physical descriptions suggest that he is black or Maori) differentiates her from the cold, repressed Susan Calvin type of female scientist who haunted earlier sf. Again, featuring characters with non-WASP but non-stereotypical origins put Davis is in a small minority in the fifties — possibly Robert Heinlein (himself an ex-Leftist) was the only major sf writer attempting the same. Ray Davis (no relation) has observed of the piece's continued relevance that

> [w]hat was controversial in 1949 remained, in some large and powerful circles, controversial in the 1990s, when Davis's reasonable suggestions would be labeled "political correctness." The unpopular being lost to history, a worthy concern only becomes widely recognized once it's widely held, when it can be attacked for shallow trendiness. (2004)

I would suggest that the unpopular is not so much "lost to" history as exorcised from it, resulting in such attacks as Hirshman's on such presumably newfangled and ephemeral ideas as inclusiveness.

Peace is a feminist issue. Chandler Davis's peace activism, evident in his earliest stories as well as "Last Year's Grave Undug" and the essay "Science for Good or Ill" that he wrote for the Nuclear Age Peace Foundation, mobilizes some subtle analyses of the political and ethical issues entailed in anti-militarist work. The connection of peace with women's issues, like the other progressive associations I have discussed, has a history in Communism; unfortunately, it's not a very useful history for the present day. Weigand's history of "Red Feminism" reports that in 1947

"The CAW's Peace and Child-Care commissions asserted that because women bear and rear children, they are the best, most committed fighters for peace" and acknowledges that, in contrast to its other programs, "the Congress of American Women's approach to the issues of peace and child-welfare tended to reinforce traditional assumptions about women's 'natural' roles…" (56). To my mind the term "roles," even when modified by "natural," has voluntarist connotations that tend to mischaracterize the era's *norms* as *options*: Duchamp observes of the 1961 Women Strike for Peace that

> [t]hey understood that their credibility as moral persons hinged on their representing themselves as good mothers… [Presenting themselves as mothers and housewives] did not just legitimize their dissent to the world; it legitimized their dissent to *themselves*. Because they were good mothers and good housewives, they had to try to stop nuclear weapons testing. The "feminine mystique," that is to say, was not a screen for their behavior but an internalization of their society's values. (2004, 63-64)

These were not "roles" from which one had the option of adopting "role-distance," much less shedding in favor of other "roles"; they were subject-positions based on a rigid and essentialist view of gender, a view that history and anthropology have utterly discredited. For all the great work that bereaved mothers such as Cindy Sheehan and Celeste Zappala have done for peace in recent years, such arguments as the CAW's and the WSP's have at the very least to be modified if they are to be compatible with present

-day feminism. Motherhood and traditionally female care-giving roles can certainly be one model for extending one's compassion; but they are not the only such model, nor should they be used to prescribe what the "proper" subjectivity of women must be.

More contemporary arguments for feminists' engagement with peace activism rest upon inclusiveness and upon ideology. A policy of inclusiveness, as I have noted, is widely interpreted by feminists as necessitating attention to women and girls victimized by war and to their distinctive sufferings and modes of resistance. Attention to gender ideology has revealed how what one might call "manufactured *masculinity*" has been central to warmaking in history: Robert Dean has explained how, in the Cold War, gender was "part of the very fabric of reasoning employed by officeholders" (1998, 30); K.A. Cuordileone has traced the impact of Cold War masculinity in the broader mid-century culture (2005). Recent evocations of the masculine imperative against peace are even less subtle than Arthur Schlesinger's depiction of fifties Leftists as feminized: we have of late seen *National Review* editor Jonah Goldberg's "Every ten years or so, the United States needs to pick up some small crappy little country and throw it against the wall, just to show the world we mean business"(2002) and Thomas Friedman's early 2003 argument that America's belief in an open society necessitated that we pick a country in the Muslim world and send our troops door to door in every town therein to say "Suck. On. This." By virtue of its suspicion of "traditional assumptions" about what's "natural," feminist *anti*-essentialism has excelled at seeing through and refuting militarist ideology.[14]

Women's movements committed to peace may welcome newly recovered anti-war polemics such as "Violence and Civility" and "Science for Good or Ill." A possible objection might arise to the effect that their points are ones that feminists are already aware of; but there's value in that too. Davis's essays, some of which Ray Davis has aptly styled "beautiful examples of 'plain speaking' rhetoric" (2005), offer not only pedagogical tools for approaching people as-yet unaware of the issues they raise but rhetorical options for cutting through conservative arguments made *en mauvaise foi*. The late William F. Buckley Jr., for example, built a career on non sequiturs that rendered his liberal interlocutors slack-jawed with incredulity — on abortion, "If it's just a clump of cells, why kill it?" and on nuclear proliferation, that people at risk of instant death "ought, then, to live more joyously." Plain speaking might help bring the discussion back into a register more connected with reality.[15] And if Davis's first two stories for

---

14 The late Iris Marion Young was a shining example of such an analyst. Her "Logic of Masculinist Protection" and other writings on the post-9/11 security regime are also of great relevance to Red Scare studies.

15 A similar case might be made for Chandler Davis's writings on incarceration: the plain-speaking account in "So You're Going to Prison!" of the irrational prison bureaucracy, psychological preparation for prison, Davis's relations with his fellow prisoners, the hacks, and his sweatshirt...all may be accused of outdatedness in the face of the "Prison Literary Renaissance" of 1967-77 or of being insufficiently theorized. But the essay's cheery simplicity makes it ideal for a number of audiences, including those unconverted to the views that some deeper accounts assume readers already possess.

Astounding[16] and "Last Year's Grave Undug" make long-familiar points, political art that helps reinforce or validate already-developed counterhegemonic beliefs can still be moving and valuable in the face of a dominant order that wants us to forget or relinquish those convictions.

Academic freedom is a feminist issue. Thanks to the overwhelmingly male populations of university faculties and the widespread assumptions about women's lack of agency, the academic Red Scare seems to have claimed few female victims as such: none of the lengthy histories of the era on my shelves mentions more than eight female professors who were investigated by Congress. Blacklisted women educators were more often drawn from public school faculties, where the issues at stake differed somewhat from those at research universities. In the current climate of academic intimidation, however, women and feminists are targeted regularly and often with special vitriol: Oneida Meranto, after having been singled out by conservative propagandist David Horowitz for condemnation, received many emails of the "Die Commie bitch" sort and took measures to ensure her physical safety; Anahid Kassabian left Fordham University after harassment for her criticisms of the Israeli Right; and Mehrene Larudee was denied tenure by DePaul for supporting the tenure bid of her militant and controversial colleague, Norman Finkelstein. Horowitz's online journal contains scores of articles attacking Women's Studies, all of which attract the

---

16 Both published in 1946, when US triumphalism was dominant: "The Nightmare" is one of the earliest warnings about the perils of nuclear proliferation, while "To Still the Drums" is a suspense story about nuclear escalation written years before the arms race began.

zealous support of commenters. Many graduate students, lecturers, adjuncts, and junior faculty are in too tenuous a position to go public with their stories of oppression or lack the resources to propagate their stories of resistance. But many scholars among the tenured, such as Sophia McClennen, Joan Wallach Scott, Barbara Bowen, and Lisa Duggan, have courageously spoken and acted against legislative, judicial, and fiscal threats to academic freedom.

Under such circumstances as we face today, any account of the tactics, interpretations, feelings, and perceptions of our predecessors in the struggle against authoritarian repression is valuable, however different the attackers' tactics and targets. Davis writes in "The Purge" about such strategizing: "Knowing we might soon face the same form of harassment a friend — or a stranger — had faced at another campus, we would read the transcripts: Now, would that response work here? How might I do that better?" (414). Davis's work on the international scene is also instructive. An exemplary piece of human rights work herein, drafted for an occasion on which threats to academics were far graver than any so far in the US, is the letter, "Imprisoned Mathematician," which Davis researched and wrote with anonymous collaborators, typed and mimeographed himself, and handed out by the hundreds to colleagues attending the Winter Mathematics Meetings (1976). The letter led not only to Math Society action in support of Uruguayan political prisoner José Massera but also to the Society defensively creating a Committee on Human Rights of Mathematicians, which over the years stuck up for many other prisoners of oppressive regimes, regardless of political orientation, including Vaclav Benda

(Czechoslovakia), Tayseer Arouri (Palestine), Anatolii Shcharanskii (USSR), and Sion Assidon (Morocco).

On a more theoretical level, Davis's analysis of what academic freedom is for in "…From an Exile" has a cogency and accessibility that, I think, outdoes even the best work of Timothy Burke and Michael Bérubé (both tireless and articulate critics of Horowitzian pressures) on that theme. And as in "So You're Going to Prison!" Davis's accounts of psychological, or internal, approaches to oppression are also worth considering: his reluctance (in "Shooting Rats in a Barrel") to succumb to bitterness toward others in his profession is of a piece with his general strategy — evident, as the interview mentions, in his advocacy for Kin-Yip Chun[17] — of maintaining a results-oriented approach to political negotiations and refusing "to turn any political discussion into an argument about motives," thus refuting Saul Bellow's famous characterization of his era's Communists. "The Purge" also allows for commiseration across fifty-odd years: those humanities departments that are spending a great deal of energy, energy which they'd prefer to apply to research, defending themselves against lawsuits that the Alliance Defense Fund initiates (on behalf of conservatives whose complaints are too extreme for even David Horowitz to take seriously) will understand Davis's asking in that essay, "[w]hen was progress to find a place on the agenda alongside avoidance of disaster?" (414). And its theme of approaching struggles against oppression

---

17 An unjustly-treated physics researcher at the University of Toronto: see his Wikipedia entry and <http://www.caut.ca/uploads/chun_report_final.pdf>

with a *forsan et haec olim meminisse iuvabit*[18] attitude can be quite moving; for some temperaments, Chandler Davis is good for the soul, and reading his essays offers a healing message akin to coming home after a day's confrontation with oppressive forces and listening to the Weavers or Tracy Chapman or Pat Humphries.[19]

Theoretical:

As a fiction writer, Chandler Davis, as early as 1947 (in "Letter to Ellen," his fourth published story) and for thirty years thereafter, was a theorist of ideology, exploring what convictions, misconceptions, commitments, or hegemonic beliefs led people to act against their own interests or to lower the quality of their own lives. In these times, when the idea of "false consciousness" is widely rejected by theorists as patronizing or discredited, reflections such as Davis's are particularly valuable. I offer several aspects of ideology his challenges to which might be of use to feminist thought.

---

18 Virgil: "Even this [experience] may someday be good to have remembered."

19 I derive this image from the great Kay Boyle who, after her husband was fired from US government service for having continued to pursue Nazis in postwar Germany rather than going after Communists, found herself blacklisted as well. She recalled,

> when we were having our hearing, which lasted three days, we'd come back to our apartment in the American enclave and I would open the windows — it was summer — I'd open the windows and I'd put on Paul Robeson...(Fariello 1995, 337).

I have listed the music of the following generations; presumably KRS-One or Rage Against the Machine or Flobots can play the Robeson role among people younger than myself.

Individualism. Some readers may find it painfully evident that anti-individualist thought is a feminist resource and ask, Isn't DIY individualism obviously an anti-feminist position, as is clear from the likes of *National Review* author Kate O'Beirne and her argument that she'd still be a high-priced lawyer with as many female colleagues and peers even if second-wave feminism hadn't happened (Traister 2006, 3)? But individualist thought takes more insidious forms. Throughout the 1990s, Susan Bordo was contesting the voluntarist/individualist claims of the US Cultural Studies theorists, trying to explain to them that feminism was not trying to condemn individuals for their choices but to criticize "the complex and densely institutionalized *system* of values and practices" in which some choices, often the most "rational" ones, were in fact decisions to submit to hegemonic forces and not bold assertions of individual agency. "I should not deceive myself," Bordo wrote memorably, "into thinking that my own feeling of enhanced personal comfort and power means that I am not servicing an oppressive system" (1993, 32, 31).[20]

I have used the term "hegemonic" anachronistically: Chandler Davis was not aware of Antonio Gramsci's work on hegemony until the 1960s, after he had written most of his fiction. But there are illuminating parallels between the two Marxist thinkers' work. In "The Individualist," the title character, a mercenary working for a pair of thugs who aspire to an interplanetary trade monopoly, is captured by his enemies. They accuse him of anachronistic thinking and of adhering to an ideology that might serve his bosses

20 A more recent and notably acute critique of the mystifications of "choice" appears in Simone Weil Davis's oft-reprinted "Loose Lips Sink Ships."

for a short while longer but that he and his bosses can no longer survive by:

> "Look, Nick, the Beldens have no chance of win-
> ning on Callisto. No chance. Men had to learn
> to cooperate before they could get to the planets
> at all, and by this time they've learned good and
> thoroughly. The individual who's out for him-
> self is an anachronism. You and the Beldens — a
> hundred years ago you'd have felt right at home.
> Then everybody was 'out for a fast buck,' as they
> used to say. In this century everybody works
> together, and darn near everybody likes it that
> way." (1951, 28)

Gramsci's concise suggestions that unless a person has worked at a coherent world view he or she will suffer from "remnants of parochial prejudices from past historical epochs" and will routinely follow a world view borrowed from another class (in Marzani 1957, 17, 21) are relevant here. As an alternative to seeing "man as an individual prisoner of himself," Gramsci argued that,

> [w]e must conceive of individual man as a series
> of active relationships, a process, in which his
> individuality is not the only element to be con-
> sidered, though it is of the greatest importance…
> [We may address the centrality of the individual's
> self-consciousness] provided that the individual
> is always conceived not as isolated, but one full
> of the possibilities offered to him by other men
> and by nature. (in Marzani, 47-48)

Davis presents just such a conception optimistically in the creative collaborations of "Share Our World," and with more ambivalence in the disrupted collectivity of "Hexamnion." In "The Selfish Genetics," he offers a spirited defense of the possibilities of communal thought against the everyone-for-himself individualist ideology of the sociobiologists.[21]

Historicide and Naturalization. All of the Davises I've mentioned are committed to recovering the "suppressed" or the "written out of history," as is this essay and indeed this volume. Chandler Davis discusses the fact of such suppression in the interview and some of its causes in "Shooting Rats in a Barrel." His most explicit fictional statement on historicide is "The Names of Yanils," which thirty-odd years ago concluded his sf career like a door slamming on a cell. Now, "The Names of Yanils" cannot be read as a political argument like his earlier works can: it stacks the deck by describing the loss of history in a pre-literate culture, making its applicability to our world less than obvious. But read in conjunction with "Shooting Rats in a Barrel," the story provides something like an objective correlative: it offers the reader a sense of how it *feels* when one turns on the radio one day and asks, Hey, when did *that* obvious idea get purged from the public discourse?

Indeed, an aspect of historicide is the dominant order's ability to declare certain values and ideas passé, which is part of the discursive tactic Jacques Derrida identifies in *Specters of Marx* as "exorcism." Davis wrote in "The Purge"

21 Mina Davis Caulfield has offered a more extensive rebuttal of the sociobiologists' retrograde prejudices in her "Sexuality in Human Evolution: What Is 'Natural' in Sex?" (1985).

of how quickly Reagan's military adventures became popular once he'd initiated them: "So easily, without resorting to reason or even to coercion, can the powerful change opinions, just by having the power" (425). The fact that opinion was ever otherwise may be obscured—Terry Eagleton in *Ideology: An Introduction* notes that "An ideology is reluctant to believe that it was ever born, since to do so is to acknowledge that it can die" (1991, 58). A traditionalist society such as that of "The Names of Yanils" will follow this convention; a society that prides itself on Bold Innovation will, as in "The Statistomat Pitch," make claims for the scientific and technical superiority of its ideas over the stale relics of the past (the New Deal, in the case of that story). The norms of "The Statistomat Pitch" thus illustrate a thesis of *The German Ideology*:

> For each new class which puts itself in the place
> of one ruling before it is compelled…to repre-
> sent its interest as the common interest of all the
> members of society…it has to give its ideas the
> form of universality, and represent its ideas as
> the only rational, universally valid ones. (68)

"The Statistomat Pitch" shows how such universalized ideas can present themselves not as the eternal truths of a culture but as its recently-discovered "natural" laws.[22]

---

22 What makes "The Statistomat Pitch" especially chilling is that the norm of its setting is the merger of state and corporate power, which (in a maxim that folklore falsely attributes to Mussolini, but which in fact more resembles Dimitrov's 1935 claims about "dictatorship of the most reactionary…elements of finance capital") is a core principle of fascism, and a norm that our legislative and judicial systems seem ever more comfortable with in the real world. As might be expected of a Leftist in his era, anti-fascism is one of the

There is, however, a difference between a "This is everywhere and always the case" argument and a "This is the *natural* way" argument: fifties misogyny, for example, acknowledged that there were and had been cultures that sought female equality but assured Americans that we were beyond that or that sex equality was one of the vices of the Soviet Union. According to *Look* magazine in 1954,

> A woman in Russia has a chance to be almost anything—except a woman. Even today, in a relatively cosmopolitan Moscow, a good-looking, well-dressed girl wearing make-up is one of three things: a foreigner, an actress or a prostitute...there are just two beauty parlors which by Western standards deserve the name. (Barson 1992, unnumbered pages)

Eagleton characterizes naturalization as the process in which "a ruling ideology does not so much combat alternative ideas as thrust them beyond the bounds of the thinkable. Ideologies exist because there are things which must at all costs not be thought..." (1991, 58). Such a process is evident in the impasses encountered by the characters in "Letter to Ellen" and "It Walks in Beauty," wherein people's experience encompasses what their world's ideology has declared unthinkable; the farmer in "Last Year's Grave Undug" is also unable to fathom the "unnatural" goals and interactions among the story's heroes thanks to his attachment to parochial prejudices from past historical epochs.

---

unifying principles behind Davis's writing—note also his equation in "Critique & Proposals, 1949" of patriarchal values with a Nazi principle: "the *Kinder-Küche-Kirche* line."

"Adrift on the Policy Level" is harder to categorize. The legitimation process in that story conforms to Eagleton's observation that a "mode of domination is generally legitimated when those subjected to it come to judge their own behavior by the criteria of their rulers" (55); but are those criteria universalized, naturalized, or neither? I propose that one might distinguish the two forms of legitimation in part by the tone used by their victims: universalization is more often expressed in a rational or cognitive register, while naturalization has a more emotional or affective thrust in its expression. This distinction occurs because the persuasive tactics of universalization can operate within the language of argument, whereas naturalization must mobilize the disciplinary emotions — disgust at the "unnatural," shame at the possibility of having been mistaken in accepting the natural, dread of the chaos that lies outside the natural categories, fear of being in the minority that rejects the natural.[23] By those criteria, "Adrift on the Policy Level" is a story of naturalization: the heroes upon surrendering to The Corporation feel the ecstasy

---

23 Gramsci writes of how the "average man" meets with a challenge to his convictions:

> The average man feels that so many people cannot be as wrong as his ideological opponent would like him to believe... He may not remember the argument [that informs his current views] concretely, and he couldn't repeat it, but he knows it was true because he heard it and was convinced. The permanent reason for the permanence of a conviction is to have been strikingly convinced once. (in Marzani 1957, 37)

This mode of rationalization was astutely parodied by the late Douglas Adams, whose satirical novels and lectures were brilliant at skewering all kinds of antirational practices and habits.

34

that characterizes Davis's characters when they are in a profound state of false consciousness.

Idealism and Transcendence. I use the term "false consciousness" in its contemporary sense, to mean ideas and goals held by the oppressed that, without their conscious acknowledgment of the fact, serve and empower the system that oppresses them. When Engels introduced the term, however, he was speaking of a more specific error, one that even the most astute and well-intentioned progressive thinkers can make:

> Ideology is a process accomplished by the so-called thinker consciously, indeed, but with a false consciousness. The real motives impelling him remain unknown to him, otherwise it would not be an ideological process at all. Hence he imagines false or apparent motives. Because it is a process of thought he derives both its form and its content from pure thought, either his own or that of his predecessors...he does not investigate further for a more remote process independent of thought; indeed its origin seems obvious to him, because as all action is produced through the medium of thought it also appears to him to be ultimately based upon thought. (Letter to Mehring, 14 July 1893)

Similarly, Eagleton explains that "Ideology can denote illusory or socially disconnected beliefs...which, by distracting men and women from their actual social conditions (including the social determinants of their ideas), serve to sustain an oppressive political power" (83-84). The thinker in the grip of ideology is not only mistaken about his or her motives, he or she sees "thought" as the origin and ground of ideas, rather than attending to the material facts of history, asking who pays or who benefits, or addressing what "more remote process" might facilitate, discredit, or determine certain trajectories of thought. "The Names of Yanils" is a great monitory tale of what happens when ideas become detached from practical human endeavors and the roots of those ideas, in geological changes and in human egotism that arises from social organization, are obscured. Engels's argument is an elaboration on *The German Ideology*'s challenge to the idealism of the German philosophers: "The production of ideas, of conceptions, of consciousness, is at first directly interwoven with the material activity and the material intercourse of men — the language of real life… Men are the producers of their conceptions…" (42). Hence I shall revert to calling this problem "idealism" and retain "false consciousness" for its present-day connotations, such as misidentifying one's opponents and embracing one's oppressors.

Eagleton believes that he has found an insurmountable weakness in Marx and Engels's account of the idealism/materialism binary — to him, that schema suggests an interiority that cannot account for ideology's "active social force":

> Ideology here is essentially *otherworldliness*: an imaginary resolution of social contradictions which blinds men and women to the harsh actuality of their social conditions. Its function is less to equip them with certain discourses of value and belief relevant to their daily tasks, than to

> denigrate that whole quotidian realm in contrast
> with a fantasized metaphysical world. (77)

Why such an "imaginary" perspective is incompatible with "active social force" is perplexing. Perhaps living in the secular UK, Eagleton was unaware of the extent to which "otherworldliness" motivates active social forces in Earth's more spiritual nations such as the United States, where, for example, the idea that the State might help people in their material lives has for many passed beyond the thinkable, leaving them with a commitment to activism on behalf of what the press calls "moral values." The manifesto of the Prairie Muffins, a society of submissive housewives who oppose women's suffrage, includes as its third and fourth points:

> 3) Muffins are aware that God is in control of their ability to conceive and bear children, and they are content to allow Him to bless them as He chooses in this area.

> 4) Prairie Muffins seek to conform themselves to the image of God by not chafing at the trials and afflictions which He brings to them, but thankfully submitting to His loving providence as He makes them fit for heaven.

There is little distinction here between the otherworldliness of "He makes them fit for heaven" and "discourses of value and belief relevant to their daily tasks." The emulsifier by which the socially contradictory values are mixed together is what Stuart Hall has called the New Right's powerful ability "to constitute new subject positions from which its discourses about the world make sense" (1988, 49)—

hatcherites, dittoheads, security moms, Swift Boat Veterans, Concerned Women for America, Prairie Muffins, premillenial dispensationalists.

God does not appear directly in the "fantasized metaphysical world" in Chandler Davis's stories; but the ecstatic feelings of fulfillment experienced by the protagonists of "Adrift on the Policy Level" and "The Statistomat Pitch" have a religious feel to them, as they involve the sense of having pleased and earned the recognition of a transcendent other; the gender economy of "It Walks in Beauty" runs on a promise of such recognition, as does the competition for leadership in "The Names of Yanils." A passage in Gramsci suggests a partial explanation of how some of these characters' misguided loyalties operate:

> However, because of social and intellectual subordination, this class *borrows* a world view from another class and asserts this borrowed world view in words… This "verbal" consciousness is also responsible for actions. It is tied to a given social group which influences [a person's] ethical behavior, the direction and exercise of his will. (In Marzani 1957, 21, 29)

The "false consciousness" of characters in "Adrift on the Policy Level" and "The Statistomat Pitch" is indeed manifested in hackneyed language that corresponds to Gramsci's formulation. But "verbal consciousness" in Davis's fiction is not only the work of mistaken propositions such as "Our society certainly rewards its most deserving members." The feeling of spiritual elevation that makes "false consciousness" so alluring has other sources.

In particular, the metaphysical world by whose rules Davis's characters try to operate works via *transcendent signifiers*. In "Letter to Ellen" and "It Walks in Beauty," it is individual words that acquire an imaginary aura into which individuals project their entire ethical selves — "Human" in the former story and "Love" in the latter.[24] It was these transcendent signifiers that Christopher Caudwell, a scholar Davis admired, had in his sights when he wrote of the undertheorized abstractions that constitute "bourgeois illusion." For example:

> Liberty does seem to me the most important of all generalised goods — such as justice, beauty, truth — that come so easily to our lips. And yet when freedom is discussed a strange thing is to be noticed. These men — artists, careful of words, scientists, investigators of the entities denoted by words, philosophers scrupulous about the relations between words and entities — never define

---

24 Attempting to defend the possibility of "false consciousness" against the claim that people can't be *that* substantially mistaken about the world that is the case, Eagleton makes a vivid point about such signifiers:

> Imagine, however, a society which uses the word "duty" every time a man beats his wife. Or imagine an outside observer in our own culture who, having picked up our linguistic habits, was asked by his fellows on returning home for our word for domination, and replied, "service." (1991, 14)

Eagleton unfortunately styles these uses of language "distortions" or "deviations," as though there were some "correct" way of using such value-laden, abstract terms as signs for more or less unambiguous referents, upon we all could be expected to agree. There isn't: their only use is in strictly-defined contexts, where their ambiguity is reduced, or as multivalent signifiers, where their ambiguity is exploited.

> precisely what they mean by freedom. They seem
> to assume that it is quite a clear concept, whose
> definition every one would agree about. (1938)

Sadly, even seasoned theoreticians of the present day will invoke Love or Meaning or National Security as though such terms were so specific as not to need rigorous elaboration.

Gramsci optimistically predicts that when the contradictions between the "borrowed world view" and a people's experience become too great, they will act in accord with more practical values; and both "Letter to Ellen" and "It Walks in Beauty" present a man who, in a dialogic relationship with a woman, takes action contrary to what reverence for the transcendent signifier would seem to prescribe. Davis's nonfiction, notably his 1979 essay "What Might Sex Mean?", is also hopeful about demystifying the shibboleths of "verbal consciousness."[25] But being enamored of such signifiers — "I love Luana too!" or "You're a real friend; you're human" — so consistently leads in Davis's stories to self-destruction that, by the time a reader reaches "I take the name of Yanils" in Davis's final story, one shudders with the realization that "Yanils" has become a new emblem of mystification and anticipates the damage that will ensue.

Theories of ideology are, as I say, particularly necessary in these pragmatic times when one risks hearing on every

---

25   Kenneth Burke and Maxim Gorky, by contrast, believed that transcendent signifiers — "word magic" to the former, "myth" to the latter — were inevitable and had to be mobilized on behalf of Communism (for Burke, see Denning; for Gorky, see Eagleton). I don't think that strategy worked out in a productive way.

street corner, "Whaddaya mean, 'false consciousness'? You think the people are passive dupes, you pompous elitist?" As often as not, that accusation is a *ressentiment* move that translates to "How dare you adhere to your views and not mine?"[26] But taking the trouble to theorize ideology is the opposite of elitist condescension. For all that Chandler Davis admires the short fiction of Cyril Kornbluth, many of that anti-Communist author's short stories taken together — "The Little Black Bag," "The Marching Morons," "The Luckiest Man in Denv" — convey (to my mind) a Célinesque disgust with humanity that feeds the highly undertheorized "Most people are stupid" explanation of human self-destructiveness. They're comforting to read after a day of dealing with incompetence in one's work environment or one's shopping adventures — "It's just the Marching Morons again, darling." But a formal commitment to such an attitude comes perilously close to victim-blaming, ignoring the culpability of the powerful and condemning those who, as Plekhanov[27] observed in his 1891 critique of Ibsen, have less agency:

26 Michael Bérubé is a noteworthy exception: he takes the term "false consciousness" to imply a simplistic model of desire according to which, once the contradictions of capitalism lift the scales from the eyes of the masses, they will achieve "class consciousness" and join the revolution (2004). While such 1930s fantasies are worth criticizing, I still find the term "false consciousness" useful in the definition I have given for it and think my differences with Bérubé are disagreements over denotation.

27 Davis says that he does not recall having thought of Plekhanov as a big direct influence upon him; however, he was a fan of Marxist historian and archaeologist Vere Gordon Childe, whose thought seems to have been influenced by Plekhanov.

> Who actually constituted this "compact major-
> ity" with whom our hero [in *An Enemy of the
> People*] found himself at odds? First, there were
> the shareholders of the Municipal Baths; second,
> the landlords; third, the newspapermen and pub-
> lishers, and lastly, the townspeople — who were
> under the influence of these three elements and
> followed them blindly. In proportion to the first
> three groups the townspeople naturally formed
> the "compact majority." But if Dr. Stockmann
> had bothered to observe this, he would have
> discovered that the majority against whom he
> thundered (to the great glee of the Anarchists)
> are not really enemies of progress; rather it is
> their ignorance and backwardness, which are
> products of their dependence upon a financially
> powerful minority. (Plekhanov 1891)

The anti-elitist position, explicit in most of Chandler Davis's stories, thus demonstrates *how* in the absence of overt
threats people might come to find the pursuit of their oppressors' interests the most attractive, the least daunting,
or the only conceivable approach to life.

Chandler Davis's fiction is, like his accounts of Red
Scare survival and his nonfictional broadsides against
conservative views of human nature, a model of hope-
fulness. Demystifying the processes by which oppressive
structures are naturalized and legitimized exposes those
structures as contingent and reversible. If history has
been purged by human beings, it can be recovered by human beings; if we have lost sight of the human origins of
ideologies, we can regain it; if the forces of reaction cre-

ate alluring new subject positions for people, so can the forces of liberation; and if subjection to ideology does not mean that people are stupid, they can change their minds. Furthermore, if the ecstasy of being at one with the transcendent signifier or winning the gaze of approval from an authority is seductive, so are the pleasures of mutuality and communal endeavor among peers; the real world no less fulfilling than the world of mystification. L. Timmel Duchamp has observed that "hopeful" fiction is, to her, necessarily counterhegemonic and anti-voluntarist:

> When I don't call bits of "common sense" into question, I am tacitly either valorizing or declaring it a hopeless "fact" of ineluctable human existence… A "happy ending" would insist that there is no problem or contradiction that a sufficiently strong individual can't overcome. A "happy ending" would subscribe to the notion that humans are not social creatures, mutually dependent in every way imaginable, but monads living separate existences in which everyone always has the choice of doing the Right Thing. (And that of course there always *is* a "right" thing to be done.) (1998)

Hopeful stories, to Duchamp, offer intellectually galvanizing perspectives on the way things ought not to be and the possibility that they might be different: they challenge the doxa that we continually hear telling us that it will be all right later this year if it isn't already, or that it's always been this way, or that it's naïve to want things to improve. The great radical sf writers of today — among them Rebecca Ore, Carolyn Ives Gilman, Andrea Hairston, and

Nisi Shawl—simultaneously model and argue for a world view in which we can overcome our fear of challenging those doxa, showing that it's possible, desirable, and needful to fight the conditions that we've been told we might as well meet with gratitude or resignation. And Chandler Davis is one of the many heroes whose lives and work can remind us that nothing and no one is as immutable as the dominant order would have us believe.

> *The release of this volume will be accompanied by the launching of a website, located at <http://writing.chandavis.com>, that offers links to several Chandler Davis pieces for which this book lacked space: "The Purge," "So You're Going to Prison!," the complete version of "Science for Good or Ill," and "What Might Sex Mean?" appear there, along with selected works of fiction.*

Works Cited

Ball, Stephen. 1990. *Politics and Policy Making in Education: Explorations in Policy Sociology.* London: Routledge.

Barson, Michael. 1992. "*Better Dead than Red!*" New York: Hyperion.

Bellow, Saul. 1994. *It All Adds Up: From the Dim Past to the Uncertain Future.* New York: Penguin.

Bérubé, Michael. 2004. Friday Frank Blogging. *Le Blogue Bérubé.* September 24. http://www.michaelberube.com/index.php/weblog/comments/459/ (accessed June 18, 2008).

Bordo, Susan. 1993. *Unbearable Weight: Feminism, Western Culture, and the Body.* Berkeley, CA: University of California Press.

Caudwell, Christopher. 1938. Liberty. A Study in Bourgeois Illusion. *Marxists Internet Archive.* http://www.marxists.org/archive/caudwell/1938/liberty.htm (accessed July 1, 2008).

Caulfield, Mina Davis. 1985. Sexuality in Human Evolution: What Is "Natural" in Sex? *Feminist Studies* 11.2: 343–363.

Cuordileone, K.A. 2005. *Manhood and American Political Culture in the Cold War.* New York: Routledge.

Davis, Chandler. 1949. The Aristocrat. *Astounding Science Fiction* Oct: 6-38.

——. 1970. Hexamnion. In *Nova 1,* ed. Harry Harrison, 39-53. New York: Delacorte Press.

———. 1951. The Individualist. As Blind Play. *Planet Stories* May: 24-31.

———. 1947. The Journey and the Goal. *Astounding Science Fiction* May: 99-115.

———. 1947. Letter to Ellen. *Astounding Science Fiction* June: 42-53.

———. 1946. The Nightmare. *Astounding Science Fiction* May: 7-24.

———. 1988. The Purge. In *A Century of Mathematics in America, Part 1*, ed. Peter Duren, 413-428. Providence, RI: American Mathematical Society.

———. 1953. Share Our World. *Astounding Science Fiction* August: 55-98.

———. 1960. So You're Going to Prison! *The Nation* Dec 3, 1960: 435-437.

———. 1946. To Still the Drums. *Astounding Science Fiction* Oct: 159-172.

———. 1979. What Might Sex Mean? Samizdat circulation.

Davis, Natalie Zemon. 1997. A Life of Learning. *American Council of Learned Societies*. http://www.acls.org/Publications/OP/Haskins/1997_NatalieZemonDavis.pdf (accessed June 15, 2008).

Davis, Simone Weil. 2002. Loose Lips Sink Ships. *Feminist Studies* 28,1 (Spring): 7-35.

Davis, Ray. 2004. "Critique & Proposals, 1949" by Chandler Davis. *Pseudopodium* August 22, 2004. http://www.pseudopodium.org/ht-20040822.html#2004-08-22 (accessed July 9, 2008).

———. 2005. Three Ways of Looking at a Blacklist. *Pseudo-podium.* December 1, 2005. http://www.pseudopodi-um.org/ht-20051106.html#2005-12-01 (accessed June 27, 2008).

Davis-Putter Scholarship Fund. http://www.davisputter.org

Dean, Robert D. 1998. Masculinity as Ideology: John F. Kennedy and the Domestic Politics of Foreign Policy. *Diplomatic History* 22: 29-62.

Denning, Michael. 1996. *The Cultural Front: The Laboring of American Culture in the Twentieth Century.* London: Verso.

Delany, Samuel. 1994. *Silent Interviews: On Language, Race, Science Fiction, and Some Comics.* Hanover, NH: Wesleyan University Press.

Duchamp, L. Timmel. 1998. What Makes Fiction Hopeful? *L. Timmel Duchamp.* February 1998. http://ltim-mel.home.mindspring.com/hopeful.html (accessed 2 July 2008).

———. 2004. Old Pictures: The Discursive Instability of Feminist SF." In *The Grand Conversation: Essays.* Seattle, WA: Aqueduct Press.

Eagleton, Terry. 1991. *Ideology: An Introduction.* London: Verso.

Engels, Friedrich. 1893. Engels to Franz Mehring. *Marxists Internet Archive.* July 14, 1893. http://www.marx-ists.org/archive/marx/works/1893/letters/93_07_14.htm (accessed June 12, 2008).

Fariello, Griffin. 1995. *Red Scare.* New York: Avon.

Franklin, H. Bruce. 1980. *Robert A. Heinlein: America as Science Fiction.* New York: Oxford University Press.

Friedman, Thomas. 2003. Suck. On. This. *Charlie Rose*, May 30, 2003. Public Broadcasting Service.

Goldberg, Jonah. 2002. Baghdad Delenda Est, Part Two. April 23, 2002. *National Review Online.* http://article. nationalreview.com/267340/baghdad-delenda-est-part-two/jonah-goldberg (accessed January 27, 2010).

Grafton, Anthony. 2008. Blog comment. June 21, 2008. To Potter, Claire B. What Would Natalie Zemon Davis Do? A Few Meditations on Women in History and Women's History. *Tenured Radical.* June 19, 2008. http://tenured-radical.blogspot.com/2008/06/what-would-natalie-ze-mon-davis-do-few.html (accessed June 24, 2008).

Hall, Stuart. 1988. The Toad in the Garden: Thatcherism among the Theorists. In *Marxism and the Interpretation of Culture*, eds. Cary Nelson and Lawrence Grossberg, 35-57. Urbana-Champaign, IL: University of Illinois Press.

Hirshman, Linda. 2008. Looking to the Future, Feminism Has to Focus. *Washington Post*, June 8, 2008. http://www.washingtonpost.com/wp-dyn/content/article/2008/06/06/AR2008060603494.html (accessed June 20, 2008).

Holbo, John. 2004. It Came From the 1950s. *john & belle have a blog.* January 12, 2004. http://examinedlife.ty-pepad.com/johnbelle/2004/01/it_came_from_th.html (accessed June 16, 2008).

Inman, Mary. 1987. Selections from *In Women's Defense.* 1939. In *Writing Red: An Anthology of American Women Writers, 1930-1940*, eds. Charlotte Nekola and Paula Rabinowitz, 304-315. New York: The Feminist Press.

Larbalestier, Justine. *The Battle of the Sexes in Science Fiction.* Middletown, CT: Wesleyan University Press, 2002.

Lukin, Josh. 2006. Cold War Masculinity in the Early Work of Kate Wilhelm. In *Daughters of Earth: Twentieth Century Feminist Science Fiction*, ed. Justine Larbalestier, 107-129. Middletown, CT: Wesleyan University Press.

———. 2008. *Invisible Suburbs: Recovering Protest Fiction in the 1950s United States.* Jackson, MS: University Press of Mississippi.

Marx, Karl Heinrich, and Friedrich Engels. 1845. *The German Ideology.* Amherst, NY: Prometheus Books, 1998.

Marzani, Carl. 1957. *The Open Marxism of Antonio Gramsci.* New York: Cameron.

Pitts, Rebecca. 1987. Women and Communism. 1935. In *Writing Red: An Anthology of American Women Writers, 1930-1940*, eds. Charlotte Nekola and Paula Rabinowitz, 316-328. New York: The Feminist Press.

Plekhanov, Georgi. 1891. Ibsen, Petit Bourgeois Revolutionist. *Marxists Internet Archive.* http://www.marxists.org/archive/plekhanov/1908/xx/ibsen.htm (accessed July 1, 2008).

Prairie Muffin Manifesto. http://buriedtreasurebooks.com/PrairieMuffinManifesto.php (accessed June 24, 2008).

Smith, Jean. 1993. This Scientist Is Not Neutral. *Peace Magazine* Jan-Feb: 24-25.

Traister, Rebecca. 2006. My Lunch with an Antifeminist Pundit. *Salon.com.* January 17, 2006. http://www.salon.com/mwt/feature/2006/01/17/o_beirne/ (accessed June 20, 2008).

Wald, Alan. 2002. *Exiles from a Future Time: The Forging of the Mid-Twentieth Century Literary Left.* Chapel Hill, NC: University of North Carolina Press.

Weigand, Kate. 2001. *Red Feminism: American Communism and the Making of Women's Liberation.* Baltimore, MD: Johns Hopkins University Press.

Young, Iris Marion. 2003. Feminist Reactions to the Contemporary Security Regime. *Hypatia* 18: 223-231

———. 2003. The Logic of Masculinist Protection: Reflections on the Current Security State. *Signs* 29: 1–25.

Essays and Letters

From the 1870s until the rise of the Internet, and in some quarters to this day, Amateur Press Associations were a significant medium of communication for widely dispersed groups of aficionados to discuss a common interest. They reduced the cost of self-publication and promoted community, through a democratic system of centralized collation, subscription, funding, and mailing. The Vanguard Amateur Press Association (VAPA) was the second APA in the US science fiction community: it existed from 1945 until 1950. Prominent "Vapans" included James Blish, Russell Chauvenet, V.K. Emden (later Virginia Blish), Bob Lowndes, Larry Shaw, John Michel, Robert Bloch, Don Wollheim, and Judy Zissman (later Judith Merril). "Critique & Proposals, 1949" first appeared in Vanguard Amateur Press Association. Of the work's context, Professor Davis wrote in 2004, "my hindsight, and even Hubbard's testy reaction, are less germane than a little characterization of the group it went to: essentially, a microcosm of Greenwich Village intellectuals in and about science-fiction, some of whom had been through a lot together including formation and rupturing of political alliances. My article's tone presumes some intellectual-ethical commonality, plainly, but it doesn't perhaps hint that the readers mostly had already discussed politics with each other, sometimes including me, a lot. I was introducing a thesis, but I wasn't introducing it to strangers."

Note: A couple of the twenty-three-year-old author's terms might be seen as politically insensitive: "Eskimo" and, applied to Puerto Ricans, "foreign-born"; the editors retain them for historical fidelity. APA house styles were very condensed, not unlike today's Instant Messaging ("enuf," "wd," "cd," "frends," "thotlessness"). "ASF" is *Astounding Science Fiction;* a "slip-stick" is not an erotic practice but a slide rule, which tool was the engineer's badge of office prior to the advent of the pocket calculator.

CRITIQUE & PROPOSALS, 1949

THE SUBJECT OF stereotyping in pulp fiction has been discussed enuf to be almost as dull as the stereotypes themselves. & it doesn't really matter too much. So we meet in every other story the megalomaniac genius or the clean-cut, woman-chasing slipsticker. So what? It just means we're reading mediocre fiction, which after all is our prerogative.

But sometimes — all too often — you run into stereotypes which are of more concern. Take L Ron Hubbard's recent "The Automagic Horse" [*Astounding Science Fiction*, October 1949]. In this story appear the following: a ruff-hewn, stingy, r-rolling Scot; an uneducated, tuff, wise-speaking Italian-American; & a Jew who peddles insurance to his uncle's employees. If I remember rite, each is the only character of his population group to come on the scene. In the same story (this is so usual I need hardly mention it) we have the handsome, carefree engineer hero, who one assumes is Irish-American, & the sexy wench, apparently Yankee.

Pretty routine sort of casting, that's all — or so you mite say. & I'll stipulate rite away that it's not the kind of consciously fascist racism you find in John Buchan. I'm sure that if there was a conscious thot in Hubbard's mind while he wrote "The Automagic Horse," it has not found its way into print. It's farthest from my mind to accuse him of ill-will toward anyone in writing the thing.

What I'm charging him with is his very thotlessness. Readers who are convinced that all Italians talk like gangsters & follow the races will give an internal uh-huh reading Hubbard's words; readers who habitually assume that an Italian they haven't met yet is going to turn out to have those same stereotyped characteristics will be reinforced in the habit; readers who are Italian will quite possibly be insulted. All of these reactions will be below the conscious level in most readers; that doesn't matter. They're still there. They still will make it harder for Italians in this country to get the marks they deserve from nominally unprejudiced high-school teachers, or to get the jobs they need from nominally unprejudiced employers. "The Automagic Horse" is one more straw on the back of an overladen camel which, if this were a cartoon, I wd label "Democracy."

My complaint isn't only against Hubbard. If it was, it'd be gratuitous & malicious for me to do my complaining publicly. But also, if he were the only offender there wd be no offense. It's exactly because reams of this stuff are written that they are dangerous. & it's for the same reason that Hubbard, casting about randomly for cute characters for his story, picked a collection of stock types as the easiest to handle, & picked these particular ones as about the easiest & most familiar of all. It's for the same reason again that very few readers, even those who wd bristle at the word "kike," will bristle when they read "The Automagic Horse." To summarize — it's because these characters are stereotypes that they're stereotypes. & it's a serious matter;

character-typing of this sort does a lot more harm than just detracting from the interest of a story.

What's to be done about it? Well, if I didn't have ideas on that I wdn't bother vapans with discussion of a problem whose existence most of them have probably heard about.

Lowndes gave part of the anser in vapa a few years back. He said that as editor of a Western magazine he wd accept no story with a Negro, Indian, or Mexican villan unless in the same story there was a member of the same group who was sympathetic & unstereotyped. That's an exellent rule of thumb for weeding out the worst cases, tho I think it shd be extended to weeding out a story like Hubbard's (which has no villan), or stories like A.B. Chandler's in which all the British enlisted men (tho not villains) speak with Cockney accents & limited vocabulary. It's still only a rule of thumb, & only a palliative at best; & few editors follow it.

The best place to look for a remedy is to the writers. What's the trouble there? Usually, as I say, thotlessness. The chances are Hubbard has Italian frends who speak the same dialect he does & Jewish frends who are neither businessmen nor nepotists; the chances are Chandler didn't change his pronunciation of the initial "h" when he himself left the enlisted ranks. They just didn't think about the effect of what they write.

They *cd*, perfectly well. & even editors who wdn't follow the Lowndes Rule wd not *reject* stories which *avoided* the stereotypes.

But writers can go farther than mere avoidance. After all, the easiest way to avoid direct offense is to name all your characters Farnsworth or Dodd, & let it go at that.

Which is no good either, for my money. A writer has the opportunity to do something positive: to illustrate in his stories the trivial & unobtrusive fact, still worth pointing out as often as possible, that Flannery & Sarafian can be buddies. It adds verisimilitude, too. I remember I read the works of one prolific ASF author for years before I realized how monochromatic his engineers were; when I did realize, I saw also that it had been bothering me all that time. Were this author's frends really so uniform that he cast his stories this way automatically? I've learned since that they aren't, but the stories remain the same. Myself, I've rarely been in schools or jobs where my associates didn't include Negros, Jews, & what have you; when I have been, I've known why & I haven't liked it.

But leave verisimilitude aside. To the readers we're most concerned about it may *not* seem natural that Flannery & Sarafian drink beer together. It may even stick out like a sore thumb: the reader has after all been presented for years with even more segregation in his pulp fiction than he's likely to have seen in his daily life. That doesn't matter. Slug him with it. Let your slipstick-ing hero be Negro; let his buddy be Chinese or East Indian. Why not? After a while the reader will get used to it — *which is exactly the object.*

What's more, don't forget that Flannery & Sarafian can be buddies even if Sarafian speaks with an accent. This is something that's often forgotten by those who wd agree perfectly with the rest of what I've said. The movie *Gentlemen's Agreement* [1947], for example, conveyed strong indignation at discrimination against Jews; but it considered only Jews who look, talk, & act like Yankees. Now I have Jewish frends who "look Jewish": I have Jewish frends who speak with one accent or another. For that matter, practically all Negroes "look like Negroes," & most of the Puerto Ricans in this country are forein-born & show it in their speech. The case against discrimination does not rest on the fiction that people are all alike. Nor does rejection of such a stereotype as the Italian fruit-vendor mean that all Italians holding fruit-stand concessions shd sell them to Yankees. However, if an author needs a fruit stand in a story I don't think he shd make its proprietor a Verdi-singing Italian, even tho there's nothing rong with such a person's having such an occupation; the reader will have met the character previously in a disproportionately large number of stories.

In short: Complete stereotypes are very harmful even when handled as sympathetically as in H.L. Gold's "Trouble with Water" [1939], but it may be desirable sometimes to give a non-Yankee character some traits (such as a forein accent) which have been unfairly represented as objectionable by the stereotypers.

You may have been bothered a few paragrafs back by a suspicion that my suggestions were departing from the realm of the immediately feasible. I'll settle that rite now. They are. A Negro hero wd not be tolerated by many editors, & I suppose practically all editors wd prefer that you make him white. I don't know any market exept for leftist magazines or arty ones where a Negro hero wd be allowed to get the girl if she was white. There's an instance from my own writing experience: a (sympathetic) character in one of my stories was a Negro fysicist. In manuscript; in the story as published it was not mentioned that he was

Negro. In breaking this resistance down, readers as well as writers shd help. Letters criticizing chauvinist stories wd go a long way tord persuading editors to accept positive ones. (I shd add that already *ASF* has had many stories with sympathetic, unstereotyped characters who were East Indians, Italians, Jews, or even Negroes. No major reform is necessary for this precedent to be followed.)

I haven't said anything yet about the specifically science-fictional aspects of the question. In s-f you're not writing about the world of 1949, which, as far as inter-group harmony goes, stinks. You're writing often about the distant future, when we hope the present divisions & oppressions will be eliminated. This makes a difference. Example: In a story about the near future you shd include Negro scientists, even tho tragically there are few of them in fact; in your 24th-century America there shd be Polynesian & Eskimo scientists as well, because you can be darn sure they'll be around when the 24th century arrives. Second example: Character who you mite name Iso Yukawa or Selma Hirschman in the 20th century, mite in a time more remote be named *Vassily* Yukawa or *Christiana* Hirschman; you want to assume that all population groups will participate in future civilization, but you also want to recognize that they won't remain as separate as they have been. (The once-oppressed Welsh are still a distinct group, yet no Englishman wd forbid his dauter to marry an otherwise qualified Welshman.) Third example: In the 24th century, Parker Hollister will be as likely to speak with a non-American accent as Karel Kowalewski, or almost as likely.

There's one type of stereotyping which I haven't discussed in spite of the fact that it raises problems similar to those of nationality stereotyping. I mean the Kinder-Küche-Kirche line, which, is followed appallingly often in American popular literature & has occasionally appeared quite blatantly in s-f. The reason I haven't discussed it is that here s-f (or at least *ASF*) is way ahead of most pulps, & still improving. Women in s-f are frequently educated (even the stock hero-marrying dauters of professors); they're also frequently dominant characters, important to the story as more than love-objects. It is unfortunate that, as illustrated recently in *ASF*, doctors of the future all are male & are assisted by female nurses. But on the whole s-f authors invent women who are people almost half as often as they invent men who are people, which is more than you can say for mystery writers.

I hope the recommendations I've made will be taken seriously—especially by those of you who are editors &/or writers. To go along with the tradition that Negroes, Jews, & Italians can be admitted into fiction only in minor roles as stereotyped comic-relief is to reinforce in readers' minds the prejudice, which I assume is abominable to all of us, that Negroes, Jews, & Italians can't be admitted to equal positions in American life. It's not enuf to refrain from expressing bias; it's necessary to counteract the bias present in practically every page now read by Americans. The criterion of your success in the next story you write will not be your adherence to my suggestions; they're only my suggestions, & I'd like to have discussion of their correctness. The criterion will be the reactions of your readers. Write a story that will give a few bigots the jolt they need. Write a story that will open the eyes of the unconsciously bigoted. Write a story that will compensate, for some Negro reader, for the insults he's taken from white people in just the day preceding.

Remember that the large majority of your readers — the *large majority* — either discriminate or are discriminated against; keep that in mind all the time. Then write a story that satisfies your conscience.

Original manuscript of Critique & Proposals, 1949

by Chan Davis
1949

CRITIQUE & PROPOSALS

The subject of stereotyping in pulp fiction has been discussed enuf to be almost as dull as the stereotypes themselves. & it doesn't really matter too much. So we meet in every other story xxxxxxx the xxxxxxxxx megalomaniac genius or the clean-cut, woman-chasing slipsticker. So what? It just means we're reading mediocre fiction, which after all is our prerogative.

But sometimes --all too often-- you run into stereotypes which are of more concern. Take L Ron Hubbard's recent THE AUTOMAGIC HORSE. In this xxxxxxxxxxxxxxx story xxxxxxxxxxxxxxxxxxxxxxxxxxxxxxxx appear the following: a ruff-hewn, stingy, r-rolling Scot; an uneducated, tuff, wise-speaking Italian-American; & a Jew who peddles insurance to his uncle's employees. If I remember rite, each is the only character of his population group to come on the scene. In the same story (this is so usual I need hardly mention it) we have the handsome, carefree engineer hero, who one assumes is Irish-American, & the sexy wench, apparently Yankee.

Pretty routine sort of casting, that's all-- or so you mite say. & I'll stipulate rite away that it's not the kind of consciously fascist xxxxx racism you find in John Buchan. I'm sure that if there was a conscious thot in Hubbard's mind while he wrote THE AUTOMAGIC HORSE it xxxxxx has not found its way into print. It's farthest from my mind to accuse xxxxxx of ill-will toward anyone in writing the thing. him

What I'm charging him with is his very thotlessness. Readers who are convinced that all Italians talk like gangsters & follow the races, will give an internal uh-huh reading Hubbard's words; readers who habitually assume that an Italian they haven't met yet is going to turn out to have those same stereotyped characteristics, will be reinforced in the habit; readers who are Italian will quite possibly be insulted. All of these reactions will be below the conscious level in most readers; that doesn't matter. They're still there. They still will make it harder for Italians in this country to get the marks they deserve from nominally unprejudiced high-school teachers, or to get the jobs they need from nominally unprejudiced employers. THE AUTOMAGIC HORSE is one more straw on the back of an xxxxxx overladen camel which, if this were a cartoon, I wd label "Democracy".

My complaint isn't only against Hubbard. If xx xxx, it'd be xxxxxxxxx gratuitous & malicious for me to do my complaining publicly. But also, if he were

-2-

the only offender there wd be no offense. It's exactly
because reams of this stuff are written that they are dangerous. & it's for the same reason that Hubbard, casting
about randomly for ~~material~~ cuts characters for his story,
~~~does~~~ picked a collection of stock types as the easiest to handle,
& picked these particular as about the easiest & most familiar of all. It's for the same reason even those who wd
few readers, even those who wd bristle at the word "like",
will bristle when they read THE AUTOMAGIC HORSE. To sum-
marize-- it's because these characters are stereotypes that
they're stereotypes. & it's a serious matter; character
typing of this sort does a lot more harm than just detracting
from the interest of a story.

What's to be done about it? Well, if I didn't
have ideas on that I wдn't bother vapans with discussion
of a problem whose existence most of them have probably
heard about.

Lowndes gave part of the anser in vapa a few
years back. He said that as editor of a western magazine
he wd accept no story~~xxx~~ with a Negro, Indian, or Mexican
villan unless in the same story there was a member of the
same group who was sympathetic & unstereotyped. That's
an excellent rule of thumb for weeding out the worst cases,
tho I think it shd be extended to weeding out a story like
Hubbard's (which has no villan),or stories like AB Chandler's
in which ~~all~~ the British enlisted men.(tho ~~~stereotype~~ not villans)
~~xxxxxxxxxx~~ speak with Cockney accents & limited vocabulary.
It's still only a ~~xxxxxxxxx~~ rule of thumb, & only a palliative at best; & few ~~editors follow it~~.

The best place to look for a remedy is to the writers.
What's the trouble there? Usually, as I say, thotlessness.
The chances are Hubbard has Italian ~~frends~~ who speak the
same dialect he does & Jewish frends who are neither businessmen nor~~x~~ nepotists; ~~xxxxxx~~ the chances are Chandler didn't
change his ~~pronunciation~~ of the ~~letter~~ initial "w" when he
himself left the enlisted ranks. They just ~~a~~dдn't think~~xxx~~
about ~~xxxxxxxxxxxx~~ the effect of what they write.

They ~~o~~d perfectly well. & even editors who
wдn't follow the Lowndes Rule wd not ~~reject~~ stories which
~~avoided~~ the stereotypes.

But writers can go farther than mere avoidance.
After all, the easiest way to avoid direct offense is to
name all your characters Farnsworth or Dodd, & let it go
at that. Which is no good either, for my money. A writer

[partial text from sheet edge, right side:]
lustrate
l worth
Sarafian
member
ars before
hen I
; me all
niform
I've
emain the
or jobs
& what
aven't liked it.

[lower sheet:]

have you, ---

But leave verisim~~xxx~~
we're most concerned about it may ~~xxx~~
that Flannery & Sarafian drink beer together. It may even
stick out like a sore thumb: the reader has after all been
presented for years with even more segregation in his pulp
fiction than he's likely to have seen in his daily life.
That doesn't matter. Slug him with it. Let your slipstick-
ing hero be Negro; let his buddy be Chinese or East Indian.
Why not? After a while the reader will get used to it--
which is exactly ~~xxxxxx~~ the object.

he readers
seen natural

What's more, don't forget that Flannery & Sarafian
can be buddies even if Sarafian speaks with an accent.
This is something that's often forgotten by those who wd
agree perfectly with the rest of what I've said. The movie
GENTLEMEN'S AGREEMENT, for example, conveyed ~~xxxxxxxxx~~
strong indignation ~~against~~ at discrimination against Jews;
but it considered only Jews who look, talk, & act like
Yankees. Now I have Jewish frends who speak with one accent or another.   Puerh Riss
For that matter, practically ~~all~~ Negroes ~~look like Negroes."~~
~~xxxx~~ & most of the ~~Italxxx~~ ~~xxxxxxxxxx~~ in this country are forein-
born & show it in their speech. ~~The point is~~ ~~xxxxxxxxxxxx~~
~~xxxxxxxxx~~ The case against discrimination are alike,&
~~xxxxxxxxx~~ does not rest on the fiction that people are all alike,&
~~xxxx The xxxxxxxxxxxxxxxxxxxxxxxxxxxxxxxxxxx~~
~~xxxxxx Negro xxxxxxxxxx forbid any Negro xxxxxxxxxxxxx~~
~~xxxxxxxx Similarly xxxxxxxxx~~. Nor does rejection of
~~olding~~ such a stereotype as the Italian fruit-vendor mean that
all Italians a ~~xxxx~~ fruit-stand ~~xxxxxxxxx~~ concessions
shd sell them to Yankees. However, if an author needs a
fruit stand in a story I don't think he shd make its proprietor ~~Italian~~ ~~xxxxxxxxxxxx~~ a Verdi-singing Italian,
even tho there's nothing rong with such a person's having
such an occupation; the reader will have met the character

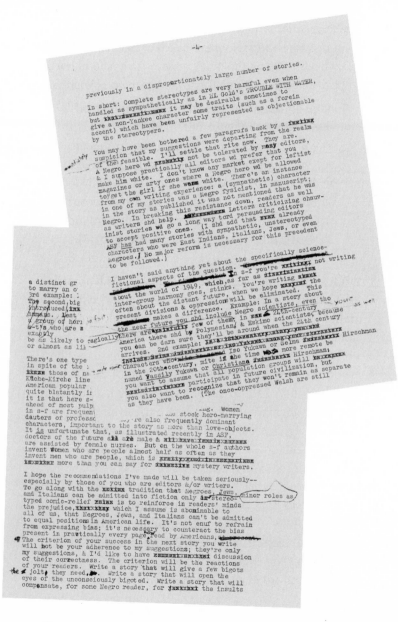

-4-

previously in a disproportionately large number of stories.

In short: Complete stereotypes are very harmful even when handled as sympathetically as in HL Gold's TROUBLE WITH WATER, but ~~this sometimes~~ it may be desirable sometimes to give a non-Yankee character some traits (such as a forein accent) which have been unfairly represented as objectionable by the stereotypers.

You may have been bothered a few paragrafs back by a ~~feeling~~ suspicion that my suggestions were departing from the realm of the feasible. I'll settle that rite now. They are. A Negro hero wd ~~probably~~ not be tolerated by many editors, & I suppose practically all editors wd prefer that you make him white. I don't know any market exept for leftist magazines or arty ones where a Negro hero wd be allowed to get the girl if she ~~were~~ was white. There's an instance from my own writing experience: a (sympathetic) character in one of my stories was a Negro fysicist, in manuscript; in the story as published it was not mentioned that he was Negro. In breaking this resistance down, readers as well as writers shd help. ~~Letters~~ Letters persuading editors to accept positive ones. (I shd add that ~~even~~ already ASF has had many stories with sympathetic, unstereotyped characters who were East Indians, Italians, Jews, or even Negroes.) No major reform is necessary for this precedent to be followed.]

I haven't said anything yet about the specifically science-fictional aspects of the question. ~~The trouble~~ In s-f you're ~~writing~~ not writing about the world of 1949, which, as far as ~~discrimination~~ inter-group harmony goes, stinks. You're writing ~~about~~ often about the distant future, when we hope ~~most of~~ the present divisions & oppressions will be eliminated. This ~~naturally~~ makes a difference. Example: In a story about the near future you shd include Negro scientists, even tho there are ~~relatively~~ few of them, ~~in~~ ~~the~~ 24th-century America there shd by Polynesian & Eskimo scientists, because you can be dam sure they'll be around when the 24th century arrives. 2nd example: ~~In the 24th-century,~~ ~~names like Selma Hirschman or~~ Iso Yukawa or Selma Hirschman Characters ~~who are~~ ~~named~~ ~~Iso Yukawa or Christiana~~ will ~~be~~ ~~the~~ more remote be in the 20th century, mite if the time ~~Iso~~ ~~Yukawa~~ ~~or~~ ~~Selma~~ ~~Hirschman;~~ named ~~Vassily~~ Yukawa or Christiana. ~~will~~ in future civilization, but you want to assume that all population groups will ~~participate~~ ~~will~~ participate in future civilization, but you also want to recognize that they won't remain as separate as they have been. (The once-oppressed Welsh are still

a distinct gr
to marry an o
3rd example:
The second, big
introduced ~~ink~~
humans. Lest
a group of hori
~~b-t's~~ who ~~are~~ ~~a~~
exactly
be as likely to ~~racially~~
or almost as lik

There's one type
in spite of the ~~kl~~
~~those~~ those of ~~na~~
Küche-Kirche line
American popular
quite blatantly in
it is that here s-
ahead of most pulp
in s-f are frequent
dauters or professo
characters, important to the story as more than love-objects.
It is unfortunate that, as illustrated recently in ASF,
doctors of the future ~~are all~~ ~~are~~ male & ~~all have female nurses~~
are assisted by female nurses. But on the whole s-f authors
invent women who are people almost half as often as they
invent men who are people, which is ~~sadly~~ ~~more than you can say for~~
~~better~~ more than you can say for ~~detective~~ mystery writers.

~~... Women~~
~~... re~~ also frequently dominant

I hope the recommendations I've made will be taken seriously--
especially by those of you who are editors &/or writers.
To go along with the ~~extion~~ tradition that Negroes, Jews,
and Italians can be admitted into fiction only ~~in~~ stereo- ~~(minor roles as~~
typed comic-relief ~~relax~~ is to reinforce in readers' minds
the prejudice, ~~which I~~ which I assume is abominable to
all of us, that Negroes, Jews, and Italians can't be admitted
to equal positions in American life. It's not enuf to refrain
from expressing bias; it's necessary to counteract the bias
present in practically every page read by Americans, ~~and present~~
The criterion of your success in the next story you write
will not be your adherence to my suggestions; they're only
my suggestions, & I'd like to have ~~intelligent~~ discussion
of their correctness. The criterion will be the reactions
of your readers. Write a story that will give a few bigots
the ~~x~~ jolt they need. ~~Jx.~~ Write a story that will open the
eyes of the unconsciously bigoted. Write a story that will
compensate, for some Negro reader, for ~~jxxxxxi~~ the insults

"...From an Exile" first appeared in *The New Professors*, ed. R.O. Bowen (Holt, Rinehart, & Winston 1960). The volume was reviewed by one John McCormick in a piece memorably titled "Five Twitterings, Three Songs, and One Roar from the Academy," (*Kenyon Review* 22 [1960]: 686-690), which offered the highest praise for Dr. Davis's prose and argument. The review is replete with dyspeptic musings on what a state the academy must be in if these are its "New Professors"; but Mc-Cormick repeatedly includes such qualifiers as "always excepting Chandler Davis" and "Chandler Davis alone..." McCormick ultimately avers that Davis "sets in painful, wonderful perspective the shallowness, the whining, and the smugness of most of his fellows in this curious bed that Mr. Bowen has contrived. Underlying Davis's polemic is a respect for students and for human life that only a few of the contributors share" (690).

...From an Exile

I AM NOT a professor. Maybe I never will be one.

My apprenticeship was honorable, as a teaching fellow at Harvard, where I got my PhD in mathematics, and as an instructor at the University of Michigan. I loved the university life. Not that it occurred to me at the time to compare it to any other; I had never seriously considered leaving it.

However, it happened that one summer, ten distinguished members of my faculty convened (five at a time) and unanimously declared me guilty of "deviousness, artfulness, and indirection hardly to be expected of a University colleague." I had refused, first before the House Committee on Un-American Activities and then before these juries of professors, to answer yes or no to the question, was I a Communist. The juries could assume (with that background and in the year 1954) that their recommendation that I be fired would mean my complete expulsion from the profession.

In fact my life as a mathematician, though attenuated, is not extinguished. I have managed to get a certain amount of research done. I show up at Math Society meetings. My fellow mathematicians, who stood up for me most gratifyingly when distinguished juries were telling them I was not fit for their company, still welcome me to their company. They gave me the pleasure and honor of a year's fellowship at the Institute for Advanced Study. Currently I have an editorial job with our reviewing journal — a position of, at any rate, responsibility.

But the universities — the universities of America — have so far opened only their back door to me, only a crack, though I knocked at their front door, politely but unmistakably, for years.

So now, under their window what song do I raise? A howl of grief? Have I risen to haunt you, displaying my shocking wounds to wrench your conscience? Not precisely.

To prove that I am fit to teach would be too easy to be interesting. I was exiled from academe, not as an incompetent, but as a heretic. To prove that my heresies meet your standards of tolerability or your dean's (though it might be difficult enough, all right) would be uninteresting because too special. There is a considerable fraternity of academic exiles these days, and there is no need to single me out from it.

I propose to give an account of the fraternity. Especially its admission procedures. I will ask you to consider what the exiles were and how they were removed from the universities; and exactly how easily they can be spared.

First, though, an evaluation in general of the dissenter's contribution to the university. This is the right decade for it. In a time when selection of academic personnel had been operating smoothly, the evaluation I mean to make might seem harmlessly truistic; today, my claims may seem tall claims indeed. The case for expelling the dissenter has been so much repeated recently; the notion that the dissenter is at any rate not important has offered such welcome consolation to the reluctant accessories to his expulsion; even the dissenter's defense has so often fallen back on the opportunistic argument that he is just like everyone else. I argue the importance of having colleagues who differ from you.

I

The dissenter's main contribution he makes only if his heresy is valid. Any university should aspire to recognize and encourage a modern Copernicus, in any field of thought. Recognition and encouragement might come too late if they waited for the innovation to be acknowledged correct by the department chairman (let alone the trustees).

This homily seems vulnerable when you think about it. If a truth is so obscure that we can't perceive it, we professors who are specialists in perceiving truths, then isn't the burden on its advocates to lick it into better shape? Why should they be granted academic rewards for a seedling theory, on credit against its eventual maturation?

Well, of course, the burden is on its advocates to advocate it. But in the nature of things a really significant innovation is likely to be hard to appreciate, or even understand, in the old terms. Its advocates themselves may not understand it too well. Their easily stated tenets may seem self-exposing falsehoods to normal people (particularly if they deny something economically or emotionally precious) and may, indeed, be wrong. The new generally resembles the old in one respect anyhow: not being perfect.

A valuable innovation may appear, yet its adherents remain an uncelebrated minority (even among the enlightened) for some time.

Furthermore it may need, more than an accepted doctrine, patient service by full-time acolytes. Not only because they will be better able to see its correctness; not only because their painstaking work can gather material for convincing the unconverted; but also because the main value of the innovation may consist in its application as a method of detailed analysis. What would the theory of evolution be today if there had nowhere been freedom to do anything more than believe it? It would still be, as in Erasmus Darwin's time, an intellectually attractive fancy.

It became part of science only thanks to its rich elaboration in the nineteenth century.

Here I have to distinguish between the "amateur dissenter" who believes a heresy while making his living at an orthodox vocation, and the "professional dissenter" who devotes his main intellectual effort to the heresy. What I have been saying leads to the conclusion that the universities should welcome professional dissenters, even though some of them (one can't tell except in hindsight which ones) will turn out not to have had anything of distinctive value to contribute. This is so important that if at the moment no first-class candidates are on the market, the universities should welcome even somewhat dubious ones — just to advertise the existence of a demand for professional dissenters! The penalty for keeping these people around is small: at worst their heresy may be altogether wrong, but even in that unlikely extreme case it may, confronting truer competing ideas, help generate new and still truer ideas.

Does this mean embracing the angle-trisecting mathematician and the hollow-earth cosmologist? And if not, how can we draw the line? By what criterion should a department executive committee decide, among prospective appointees whose specialties seem absurd, which one to prefer? Should everyone competent to teach freshman courses become thereby the judge of the value of his own work?

The department should not, I would say, attempt to draw a boundary around the respectable portion of its field, maintaining within the boundary a "balanced department" in which rewards are dispensed even-handedly.

This would lead to mechanical judgments where sensitive ones are called for. Let the department follow its own judgment as to where the greatest value lies. Let anyone adopting deviant standards resign himself to being judged by accepted ones and accordingly expect to see himself somewhat underrated. Only let him be judged fairly and not resented. Thus A. M. Turing at Manchester — in the years before the economic importance of large digital computers made his interest in algorithms a widespread one — was accepted and respected for his excellence by standards other than his own, and supported in pursuing his lonely specialty. A less extraordinary talent might have been forced to switch to a fashionable specialty, and even Turing earned less respect than he gets in hindsight. But you can't hope to reward a man for being ahead of his time more highly than you reward the man who is on a wrong track when you can't tell them apart; so, determine the amount of the reward by averaging the possibilities. Remember to be fairly generous in your guesswork: the number of beginning scholars is expected to increase fast, and more and more can be spared for the byways, if they're drawn to them.

All this pertains primarily to the professional dissenter. I suppose I am an amateur dissenter myself: most of my peculiar convictions, certainly including those I was fired for, have no tendency to reflect themselves in unconventional mathematics. Still I take them seriously — as, say, a Catholic may take God seriously although he is not a priest. Let me not understate the case for the amateur dissenter.

It is a strong one. If we desire to prepare the soil for an unpredicted innovation, we have no way of providing that it lies within one of the narrow plots which are the accepted disciplines. The innovation may attract disciples long before it is recognized as a possible way to make one's living: then it will have to begin as a hobby. Similarly, a new art form may be fun for its aficionados long before they dare to propose taking it seriously. In general, the universities can put up with much more fantastic deviation on the part of the amateur dissenter, because they lay no wager at all that he is right; having seen to it that he earns his keep, they can afford to leave his off hours up to him; thereby they are able to extend an invitation to progress further into the future.

Progress is the universities' business; their function is not merely custodial. And I maintain that just as innovations in ideas should be fostered in the universities more than outside, so should innovations in values. In some departments (literature and philosophy, at least) this is in the nature of the announced subject matter. But as a long-time lover of the bull session let me state the case more broadly. University students are a large group of active people, at the age for deciding what they want. Regardless of how material the subject matter of their specialty may be, they are concerned with values: they have to choose one goal for their lives above another. Their parents' choices may be, for them, wrong. They need, so that they can choose independently, an environment permissive toward the unexpected and rather charmed by it. To provide this environment is part of the universities' function; and one ingredient is professors who, while varying widely in their professional aspect, vary still more widely extracurricularly.

The universities are hotbeds of heresy. At least they usually are; it is characteristic for them to be; they should be. They should be teeming with intellectual doctrines some of which the majority find useless or even false, and with moral doctrines some of which the majority find unattractive or even evil. And the diverse parties should dwell side by side, not with the tolerance of indifference, but embattled and cherishing each other: each should know that in its quest the contest with those who disagree will bring faster progress than would an unobstructed route.

The description does not fit the status quo. It does not ideally fit the status quo ante either. But if there is a shortage of active doctrinal challenge in the universities today, it is in order to give at least a brief, anxious look at the most conspicuous blow to academic freedom of recent years: political firings of professors.

II

The exiles, then. Who should I mean by "exile"? Those who were fired from university teaching jobs for their politics, surely, or forced to resign. But also it seems natural to include those who for the same cause simply were not able to find a job, or were obliged to accept jobs far below their qualifications, to accept non-academic jobs, or to emigrate. I will include anyone who qualified on any of these counts at any time during the current Red-hunt — say, from 1947 (Truman's first "loyalty" program) to 1959 (when I am writing).

We exiles have not been systematically studied. Eminent social scientists with foundation grants have studied academic freedom by surveying random samples of working professors (which, if it is not convenient wilful blindness, is at any rate a very different approach). One professor set out to write a book on the exiles, but became one before it was finished, which interfered seriously with its progress. We have been treated, sometimes misleadingly, by a few novelists.

What I can tell you in a few pages is told from knowledge (even though I have made no survey, and will cite few names). We exiles know each other pretty well — partly because some of us shared political contacts in the forties for which we were all punished subsequently, and partly because our shared predicament now draws us together.

To give you an idea — I sat down the other night and listed all the exiles I could think of. (I arbitrarily excluded people who lost their jobs by refusing to sign generally required oaths, as at the University of California, although a good many of them would qualify.) In about fifteen minutes I ran the list up to eighty! Not all the eighty are known to me by name, but thirty-seven of them I have met, and these include several of my close friends.

This is a good many exiles. Altogether there must be something between a hundred and a thousand — smaller, for illustration, than the number of women teaching in co-ed colleges, but much larger than the number of Negroes teaching in other than Negro colleges. Loss of a group this size is significant, at a time when universities are hard up for faculty; and some of the exiles are a good deal more than minimally competent.

But these sacrifices to the "loyalty" revival are far from a random sample. How were we selected?

Many were non-co-operators before Congressional committees. If such testimony was public, it was often followed, as in my case, by a strictly academic inquisition. These hearings provided a semblance of independence for the administration's eventual decision to fire; for, though caused by and roughly patterned after the Congressional ones, they were carried on by university people, often the victim's own colleagues. This very feature made them incomparably more painful. Of the two professors I can think of who went through such hearings in public universities without being fired, one quit anyhow, in disgust at the humiliating lack of confidence in him which the hearings expressed!

The majority of us became exiles more gently. An agent from the Un-American Committee or the FBI would speak to a dean, who would then reach agreement with the fingered professor that it would be best for both parties if the firing was unpublicized. Or more gently yet—a thesis adviser would include in his letters of recommendation the hint that a fresh PhD was "much concerned with social problems," and with or without further inquiry, employers would pass him by. Such practices are quite general. I know of instances among our mightiest private institutions. Unquestionably, since they are secret, there are many times as many instances as I know of; and it is reasonable to assume, by extrapolation, that still milder discrimination against left-wingers, carrying too light a sentence to make them exiles, must happen still oftener.

The whole gamut of methods continues in use, too. Several of the exiles joined us with full newspaper accompaniment within the last two years; and a number of professors have been convincingly threatened with exiling during 1959-60.

Many of the exiles succeeded in returning to academic status comparable to what they lost; but most have not. This story, well worth telling, I must skip.

What sort of people were exiled? In the first place, it should be understood that among them were Communists. I know it is cried that the Red-hunters aim at a much broader target than just the Communist Party; and most of them do seem to. But if one of them aims at a peace committee, say, his attack will get more co-operation if he can find a Communist in the committee on whom to concentrate it. I know it is cried that some of the Red-hunters are plain liars and that most of them will admit fantastic "evidence" in support of a charge of Communism; and this is true, too. But the standards of evidence in these cases, though shamefully low, were at any rate such that Communists were much more likely to be fired as Communists than anti-Communists were.

Along with the Communists, the exiles include many more people who, even to objective eyes, rather resemble Communists: former Communists, members of organizations which had Communist support, former members of such organizations, non-Communist Socialists, theoretical Marxists, etc. It makes sense to class most of these in a single group, and to say that, though mostly not Communists, they were accurately accused of the heresy of leftism; for they share certain ideological tendencies which the

Red-hunters systematically attempt to suppress as "communistic." There are non-left-wing exiles who were accurately accused of such heresies as pacifism or (in the South) anti-segregationism, and exiles who were inaccurately accused of one heresy or another. But the non-left-wing exiles, however important, are not very numerous. For the sake of simplicity I will usually, from here on, discuss the exiles as if there were only the left-wing exiles, of which I am one.

My first conclusion is that not one of us (left-wing or other) should have been fired—indeed, that there was no prima facie suspicion that any of us should be; hence that many distinguished juries not only arrived at wrong answers but concerned themselves with preposterous questions.

If Marxism was so crackpot a doctrine that it prevented sound scholarship, one might well investigate whether a colleague had contracted it. I have pointed out that the champion of an unrecognized doctrine must face some extra burden to establish his competence. But this is irrelevant here because the left-wing scholars I am talking about were not attacked by colleagues for professional unsoundness. Our competence was either unmentioned by our attackers or (as in my case) conceded.

We were accused of being under intellectual discipline which hindered open-mindedness. Now the fact is (I know these people, remember) that sure enough! some of us are almighty cocksure; some can irritate me even when I agree with what they're cocksure of. I have also known cocksure conservatives, but nobody has proposed that they be fired, much less that all conservatives be fired because some are cocksure. We exiles are not subject to a

single discipline; the diversity of our opinions would surprise you; more to the point, we are most of us, I would
say, a more independent, contentious, and open-minded
lot than the professors who survived us. But even if we
were on the whole much more dogma-tied, this would be
no call to single us out from the other dogmatists. Particularly since diehard adherence to a heresy is in general less
menacing to free inquiry than matter-of-course adherence to orthodoxy: because the heretic, being constantly
challenged, is deprived of the illusion that his rut is the
whole road.

Then also, we were accused of influencing students.
A shocking thought! Well-meaning friends sometimes
defended us with pleas that, of course, we kept our poisonous ideas to ourselves. But to us, our left-wing ideas
seem true, and therefore not poisonous. We would want
to avoid putting undue pressure on our students to accept
them, but not to avoid even submitting them to students!
In practice most of us did go to the extreme of concealing
our left-wing ideas from our students—but from realistic
fear for our own security, not from fear of corrupting the
students. Even if our views are all wrong, it would not cor-
rupt any thinking person just to hear them advocated.

The professional dissenters among us had not merely
the right to "influence" students, but the responsibility. A
philosophy professor who accepts dialectical materialism,
for instance, will have difficulty in speaking honestly if he
tries to speak as a philosopher without speaking as a dialectical materialist. Herbert Phillips, in this predicament, set
an example of courage and fairness to shame many of his
fellow Marxists as well as his enemies: presenting various

positions but avowing plainly which was his. The colleagues of such a man, if they think Marxism is not good philosophy, may then regret that their Marxist is not too good a philosopher, and think to improve him by converting him; but they should remember that it will not improve him to intimidate him into donning Thomism or empiricism.

We amateur dissenters had it easier. Our only real responsibility in this regard was to avoid wasting class time on irrelevant expositions of our heresies. Most of us held to this scrupulously; perhaps if the incentive of fear had been absent, we might have produced more counterparts of those conservative colleagues who larded their lectures with irrelevant anti-WPA or anti-Soviet jokes.

Then, too, we were accused of belonging to a conspiracy to commit espionage or armed revolution. A very few were actually accused of spying; but almost all of us were not, I think, even suspected of overt acts of this nature. What was the accusation, then? Merely that we supported organizations which somewhere and sometime engaged in espionage or furthered revolutions? This charge was true of some of us. A telling charge, perhaps — if it had been brought, say, by our pacifist colleagues. But a laughable charge when brought by people who consider the professor's role perfectly consistent with supporting espionage by the CIA and revolution in Guatemala.

I am not saying that Russian power politics and American power politics are mirror twins, but only that the university should not be an agent of either. It should be impartial on matters where individuals, or even the freest state, can not be impartial. However anti-Soviet some of you are, however strongly you suspect foul treason among us, you should not involve the university in fighting that non-academic battle. Counterespionage is not the dean's job. He's probably not much good at it anyway.

I'm afraid I have been belaboring the obvious for a couple of pages now. The standard rationalizations for firing Reds have the transparency of the emperor's new clothes. They are never invoked against conservatives, though logically applicable; they are rarely bothered with in the quiet firings. I can't believe that such poppycock persuaded many of our colleagues that we deserved exile. I do believe that many of our colleagues were persuaded, by seeing the poppycock most solemnly received, that they could not afford to defend us.

The only essential charge against us was heresy. From outside the universities came a clamor to dress the anti-Communist ranks; we were charged with being out of line. To fire us for this was wrong.

But I said it was wrong in every single case. Do I really mean to be so sweeping? Surely there were some incompetents among those fired? Quite likely, by chance, a few; but none, I dare say, whose incompetence was proved in the course of deciding to fire them for heresy. But surely there were some cases of political immorality? Particularly, people who falsely denied that they were Communists? Yes, a few; it saddens me that some people diminished themselves by lying in an effort to save their positions; but I remember that the test they failed most of their colleagues did not face; I think of the far more numerous people, now snug in their academic tenure, who began much earlier in response to much less severe threats to conceal and even suppress their own dangerous thoughts;

and I think of Galileo; and I decide that the universities, and morality, would be best served by a lenient view of forced recantations.

My second main conclusion about the left-wing exiles is that we do not now constitute a thriving heresy. What has been banished from the campuses in us is a collection of rather like-minded individuals, not a coherent ideological movement. For agreement on political and economic matters we may turn to each other, but for interesting new contributions we turn to the universities. We have the numbers and the talent to provide the nucleus of an intellectually creative heresy — why don't we?

1. Being exiled has hurt our output. Unaccustomed jobs, emotional stress, separation from scholarly surroundings — it is hard to keep plugging. But a lot of us do.

2. Too few of us are professional dissenters, too many amateurs. Maybe this is because full-time left-wing intellectuals were already largely excluded from universities at the beginning of the period 1947-1959 (witness, e.g., Scott Nearing, Morris U. Schappes, and Paul Sweezy) and throughout the period faced much higher barriers. Radical students felt a bread-and-butter pull toward politically neutral vocations.

3. We lack the sectarian spirit. I have mentioned that our opinions vary widely, but I am now making a different point. Even considering only left-wingers of some single species, a left-wing mathematician has closer affinity to a conservative mathematician,

in many respects, than he has to a left-wing sculptor or lawyer. Well, naturally. But this is becoming more and more the case, during the decades of suppression of the left, because we left-wingers as individuals choose to make it so. We do not accept the fate of a pariah group. Most of us yearn for the masses, for the mainstream; and lack the patience to guard a peculiar flame through generations of persecution. (Contrast the pacifists!)

4. I must add that a healthy school of Marxist thought in the Communist countries, if there was one, might be a valuable stimulus to American left-wing thought. A serious Marxist tradition does survive in those countries, but elevation to the status of official doctrine has not helped it: it has been entangled with governmental expediencies, and most enfeebling of all, it has been deprived of confrontation by active dissenters. Caveat victor.

III

My friend E. E. Moïse (a tolerable maverick, no exile) remarked while the political purges were in full swing that the universities would not suffer if the victims were simultaneously and mysteriously to disappear, but would suffer seriously from the act of firing them. He should not be held to account for literal interpretation of his rhetorical statement. I have pointed out that losing our services was not a negligible loss quantitatively. I would demur more strongly that the loss of a healthy heresy is much more serious than the loss of so many individual scholars; and though I have confessed that we can't claim to be a thriving heresy today, we might be if we hadn't taken such a beating. The ideas we were prevented from developing may not all be developed by the unpurged, who lack our odd slant.

But let me get to the point of Moïse's remark. We were not pruned hygienically from the academic tree but wrenched from it in violation of its orderly growth. It should be inspected for damage.

Most obvious (though not most important), and most obviously intended by the Red-hunters, is the demoralization of the unexiled left. The lesson that they'd better watch their step or they may be next is too obvious to be ignored. Those who have not in the past approached the left are likewise well-taught that they had better not. This, as much as the failings of the exiles, accounts for the recent decline in the left-wing intellectual movement or movements. Thousands of professors are revisiting conservatism this season, and I wonder how many of them would have been impelled to make the tour by its intrinsic charm.

A more general lesson has been taught, perhaps less consciously. It has been demonstrated that the universities cannot afford to shield a few faculty members if it means hurting the whole institution by jeopardizing bequests (this is dean's talk; a pamphleteer would say equipollently, the universities sacrifice academic freedom to the big money). In the long run this is ominous; even immediately it may occasion perfectly realistic uneasiness in any professor, his administration being what administrations are today. Your job security is rightly envied, professors, but it is contingent on your not irritating too far (even unintentionally) too many rich.

In this direction are grave effects of the purges. But how far do they go?

In the social sciences, certain types of research motivated by Marxist or related theories, are discouraged. But far from abandoned! In sociology particularly, the development of the previously active lines of research, even apparently "dangerous" ones, has been thwarted gratifyingly little. (So, at least, I gather from rumors reaching me; I speak as an outsider to the field.) This is partly because some people are courageous; partly because the dangerousness of an idea can be camouflaged sometimes by jargon; partly because a line of research previously pursued by two hundred investigators may lose half of those without being fatally undermanned.

Gross stifling of research has resulted here and there from the firings, but only in fields obviously related to the Communist Party or to current governmental policy.

(I want to mention in passing the proliferation of social-scientific work frankly and more or less directly in the service of current governmental policy. I have suspicions that these government-screened political scientists are taking over from the more academic thinkers in their departments by force of numbers; that opposition to the trend has been deterred by the sacrosanctity of the Established Economic System and the Bipartisan Foreign Policy; that this sacrosanctity, on the campus, owes much to the firings. This is perhaps an instance, not of gross stifling, but of gross imbalance.)

The subtle inhibitions are more widespread. I call them subtle, but only in the sense that they're petty and pass without much notice — not in the sense that they're sophisticated. They act in little spasmodic avoidances. A professor recoils from discussing economic influences on ideology; or from detecting a pecuniary motive in the policies of a corporation president or diplomat; or from publishing an appreciation of Sean O'Casey unredeemed by a peck at his politics. Poor timid thing! You can nibble the edge of one of our ideas without obligation to accept the whole cake! But the timid things are not tempted, and circle far around. These automatic avoidances are so taken for granted that they have been made the basis of a familiar polemic technique: one sketches wittily an analogy between a Communist slogan and the formulation of one's opponent — the latter being thereby demolished without the trouble of refuting it. The response to this technique's effectiveness, in turn, is for formulations vulnerable to it to be suppressed in advance by their author even if there is no genuine similarity to anything left-wing at all.

Left-wing ideas are being stamped out, but by a terribly broad boot.

The subtle inhibitions are pervasive, but not omnipresent. Do they act against boldness of invention in fields far from politics? I have been observing mathematicians, and, less extensively, physicists, throughout these years. As far as they go, I venture a definite answer: No. Limitation in social thinking has not caused limitation of invention in general. I can conceive of such a relationship, but so far I have not observed it.

And I venture to favor, among possible explanations, this as the main one: Even in social thinking, the heresy-hunt does not punish originality per se, and is not perceived as threatening originality. At the instant of conception or even of first public expression, an idea is not "dangerous." The thought-controllers are afraid only of organized heresy; likewise for scapegoat purposes an organized heresy is most attractive; and an organized heresy probably has a stabilized core of doctrine. Its adherents take the doctrine as basis for their further thinking; whether or not they take it as the exclusive basis, they may proceed to thinking of brilliance and daring, or of utter passive repetition. This will not decide their punishment. To the extent that they are punished for their ideas, it will be for their acceptance of the basic doctrine, which is not original with any of them. If the doctrine is by and large true, then the heresy-hunt will have punished wisdom, but not originality.

Of course a successful heresy-hunt, once it has dispersed organized heresy, may turn to striking at anything unexpected. Then, indeed, all experimenting with ideas is risky, and if one is to survive, one's protective inhibitions must be more confining. The governmental "loyalty-security" programs have no doubt entered this stage; but the university aspect of the Red-Hunt, my subject here, has not.

And suppose it never does. And suppose that the general paralysis infects the universities no worse than it has. And suppose that the exiles become no less dispensable than now and not much more numerous. Can you then consider the episode closed, speak of McCarthyism (and of us) in the past tense, and relax in the knowledge that your universities are fairly free (at least for everybody but the exiles, who weren't perfect anyway)?

This is the general view. Opposition to a firing is rapidly engulfed, once the firing is concluded, by impatience to forget about it. One of the distinguished colleagues who found me fireable was elected president of the local AAUP chapter less than two years later (while the national AAUP was still in process of duly censuring my firing). Almost no administrations guilty of excluding teachers for their politics have reversed themselves. Exceptions: a very few quietly excluded scholars have subsequently been just as quietly admitted; several University of California non-signers were reinstated, of course; and there was one college which pretty explicitly repudiated a political firing quite like mine, though without offering the victim his job back. One of my friends said fervently that he would not want me to get my job back, that it would be too unpleasant for everybody concerned. Unpleasant—that I grant. Most of the exiles have made it easier for the academic world to forget them by dropping out of sight to avoid unpleasantness and to avoid drawing more fire.

But it won't do. For your own sake, for the universities' sake, you must face what happened. More than you need the exiles in particular, you need dissent in general, a profusion of ideas richer than you have seen before. You must welcome dissent; you must welcome serious, systematic, proselytizing dissent—not only the playful, the fitful, or the eclectic; you must value it enough, not merely to refrain from expelling it yourselves, but to refuse to have it torn from you by outsiders. You must welcome dissent, not in a whisper when alone, but publicly so potential dissenters can hear you.

What potential dissenters see now is that you accept an academic world from which we are excluded for our thoughts. This is a manifest signpost over all your arches, telling them: Think at your peril. You must not let it stand. You must (defying outside power; gritting your teeth as we grit ours) take us back.

"Violence & Civility" first appeared in *The New York Review of Books* Volume 15, Number 5: September, 24 1970. This letter was a response to an article by the Anglo-Catholic essayist James Munro Cameron (1910–1995), "A Special Supplement: On Violence," in that newspaper. The relevant content of Cameron's piece is clear from Professor Davis's letter. Cameron, in turn, wrote a brief reply that appears in the same issue, in which he denounced "revolutionary chatter" and expressed skepticism of "disruption" but explained, "when I speak of 'not inviting the violence...of our society to enter the world of the university' I have the Pentagon in mind as much as the Panthers. I suspect Mr. Davis missed this and I am sorry if I didn't make it plainer" and noted his admiration for the martyred Catholic war resister, the Blessed Franz Jägerstätter (1907–1943).

Asked for context on the "Violence & Civility" letter, Professor Davis wrote in 2009, "At about the same time, I wrote a piece for New Universities Conference on the same subject. I said that when the crazies are threatening the university library and the establishment is repressing them, our position must not be with either. The establishment is aiming to preserve the university as it is, the crazies are aiming to destroy it, but we are aiming to transform it. Thus our position is not either of their positions; it also is not intermediate between them.

"That last point may be peculiar to me. In mathematical terms, if the establishment stands at point P and the crazies at point Q, then we are not even in the convex hull of P and Q. People in NUC had been in SDS only a few years before and didn't relish appearing to be compromising with the establishment; I was reassuring them that a genuinely transformative program is not a mere blend of their former radicality with their deans' conservatism. It is not a matter of titrating the proper admixture of two reagents, it is a matter of striking out in another direction..."

Violence & Civility

TO THE EDITORS:

The key concept in J.M. Cameron's essay "On Violence" [*NYRB*, July 2] is not violence but civility. At least it is the key to further analysis of his argument. The word "violence" he perversely makes even more elusive than it is for non-philosophers by trying to get it to carry all its secondary meanings and connotations around all the time. What a relief that he does not similarly encumber the word "civility"! The confusion could have been comical, what with courtesy of manner, Roman law, and bridge and highway construction. Sparing us the irrelevant referents, he assigns to "civility" a meaning which, while subtle, he intends to be unitary and constant throughout his essay:

> The goods of civility are what Hobbes took them to be: the sociability which is made possible by the general reliability of those with whom one lives (men are predictable in their daily lives and keep their promises and don't lie too much), literature, history, and the arts…the cultivation of the earth with the enjoyment of its fruits, technology applied to making us comfortable and delighting the senses, and so on.

The closest he comes to specifying a meaning for "violence" is assigning it the role of antithesis to civility:

> ...where there is violence there is that much less
> civility, and where there is a great deal of vio-
> lence civility tends to vanish.

I can willingly accept Mr. Cameron's civility as a useful primitive concept in a discussion of political morality.
But only by understanding his emphasis to be on the first
three operative words of his definition: "sociability," "reliability," "predictable." That is, I take Mr. Cameron's civility to mean stability of society, but more particularly, that
stability which gives him comfort, confidence in his social
milieu, and enjoyment of a continuing culture. As to "literature, technology, and so on," they must be in the definition merely to illustrate aspects and conditions of the civil
life — otherwise, disruptive examples of literature or technology would make his concept embrace its opposite.

Mr. Cameron's essay, rich though it is in detail and
even in wisdom, has a simple conclusion. He admonishes
us, the left, that "as a whole...the universities remain en-
claves of civility," and that consequently we had better not

> ...invite the violence that comes from the in-
> justices of our society to enter the world of the
> university.

Now I agree that reliability and continuity in our social relations and language are essential to all our life. We
must understand their relatively invisible function before
we can cope (as increasingly we must) with the more conspicuous roles of novelty and disruption. I am not able to
give an adequate discussion of the importance to the left
of the defense of civility; I wish I were. But let us be clear
that Mr. Cameron is not fit to do it either.

His psychology ascribes honesty, generosity, all the basis for mutual confidence to inherited, traditional social norms. Once the "institutions and traditions" are allowed to change, once we throw traditional "moral and intellectual paradigms" into question, Mr. Cameron is sure that the "world of human action" whose connective fabric is language will be "replaced by the warm volitional world of *I want! I want!*"

Most of us have experienced situations in which tradition dictated hypocrisy, selfishness, or isolation, and in which honesty, generosity, or mutual confidence was achieved by innovation. At least we think we have. Transcending of the inherited morality may be much less common and less significant than we Pollyannas on the left think. But it is significant, even if rare; understanding and fostering it are urgently dictated by the objective of transforming — or even saving — human society.

Now whenever one demands things which the entrenched don't feel like granting, and brings the demands in ways they hadn't expected, they call it violence. Mr. Cameron generally accepts their usage of the word, though he understands the conservative bias involved. He is tolerant of the demanders, and if they are weak and oppressed he is even sympathetic. But his tolerance and sympathy are *in spite of* the ingredient of social innovation. Any breach of the traditional norms of behavior, being a breach of predictability and hence of civility, is for him a sacrifice of social value — possibly to be excused by a sufficient concomitant gain of justice, but still a sacrifice. He would never see a positive value to a suspension of the traditional expectations, like the French students'

May events (*Tout est possible*), conferring permission to innovate. He would never speak of such a lapse of decorum as "liberation."

No doubt it would be antirational of us to use our word "liberation" loosely — as a synonym for "lapse of decorum," say, or for "disruption." And no doubt there are situations, on campuses and off, which however conducive to innovation fail to give birth to any; it would be antirational of us to view them as other than a missed opportunity. But there is no rationality to Mr. Cameron's denial that liberating situations can exist. Indeed he avows such profound agnosticism as to the consequences of political action that he should be embarrassed to chide us or anyone else for lack of rationality in politics.

Disruption is sometimes liberating and sometimes not. Mr. Cameron disqualifies himself from drawing these distinctions. We must find the courage and understanding to make them ourselves.

Professor Davis co-authored "Imprisoned Mathematician" and handed out mimeographed copies in person at the Winter Mathematics Meetings of 1976. Massera (1915–2002), possibly his country's most celebrated mathematician, was released in 1984, as the military dictatorship prepared to relinquish power. Most of the letter's readers would have been aware of the US-engineered coup three years earlier that had ended Chile's long tradition of democracy and suspected that the US ambassador's claims regarding Uruguay were hardly disinterested; indeed, it has recently been established that the Nixon administration, fearing another Leftist victory like that of Allende in Chile the year earlier, tried hard to influence the 1971 Uruguayan elections. From 1969 and perhaps earlier until 1977, a year after the military takeover, the US provided "security assistance" to Uruguay, replacing police officers with US-trained torturers and counterinsurgency fighters.

Imprisoned Mathematician:
J.L. MASSERA

JOSÉ LUIS MASSERA has been a leader of Uruguayan mathematics. He was Professor of Mathematics in the Faculty of Engineering of the University of Uruguay from 1943 to 1973, and for most of that time also in the Faculty of Humanities and Sciences. He has done important research in stability theory of differential equations, and is co-author with J.J. Schaeffer of *Linear Differential Equations and Function Spaces* (Academic Press, 1966). With Rafael Laguardia, he founded in 1942 the Institute of Mathematics and Statistics in Montevideo, where all the active mathematicians of Uruguay have studied, including Schaeffer, Gunter Lumer, Enrique Cabaña, Marcos Sebastiani. Many North American mathematicians remember him personally, from Montevideo visits or from his fellowship year 1947-48 at Stanford, Princeton, and NYU.

Professor Massera is a long-time member of the Communist Party of Uruguay, and became a member of its Executive Committee in 1955. He was a Communist representative in Parliament 1963-66 and 1967-71.

Uruguay had a long tradition of parliamentary democracy, dominated by two parties, the Blancos and the Colorados. After World War II, economic problems, attributed to the contraction of British markets for beef, led to wide unrest. Urban terrorism broke out, and President Jorge Pacheco turned "the country into something of a temporary police state. He declared a state of emergency (still in effect) in 1968, imposed stiff wage and price controls, and cracked down on demonstrating students, striking workers, and suspected guerrillas" (*LA Times*, Dec. 5, 1971). For the 1971 presidential elections, "A great mass movement was created — the Frente Amplio, an alliance of reformist parties with a general at their head — that sought to follow the Chilean example and bring socialism to Uruguay through the ballot box" (*Guardian-LeMonde*, August 16, 1975). Juan María Bordaberry of the Colorados took office with a slight plurality over the Blancos; the Frente Amplio, joining Communists and Christian Democrats behind retired General Líber Seregni Mosquera, polled less than a fifth of the vote but held the balance in both houses.

Then in June 1973 Bordaberry, with the support of the armed forces, disbanded Parliament and banned all political activities. According to a former student of J.L. Massera who has recently written us, the staff of the Institute of Mathematics and Statistics was discharged at this period, and a warrant issued for Massera's arrest.

In November 1975, apparently in anticipation of the scheduled 1976 elections, mass arrests began. "The Uruguayan government says it has arrested about 100 persons in recent days for 'dissent'" (*Miami Herald,* Nov. 20, 1975). "Former presidential candidate Wilson Ferreira Aldunate has claimed in Caracas that there are 8000 political prisoners in Uruguay.... Large numbers of alleged Communists have been arrested recently" (*Latin America*, Dec. 12, 1975). We have heard from the former student cited before, from Geza Stary (the head of the Uruguayan National Federation of Professors), and from others that Professor Massera was arrested in November and has been held incommunicado. The former student reports that Massera is presently in the Military Hospital and is believed to have a broken leg resulting from beatings by his captors. The authorities announced Massera's imprisonment only in December.

Though there is no first-hand testimony that Massera has been maimed, this is a natural and realistic fear. Torture of political prisoners has become common in Uruguay, and Amnesty International names four political prisoners who died there under torture between April and September 1975 (*Amnesty International Newsletter*, Dec. 1975).

Individual mathematicians and organizations have been asked by Professor Massera's friends to cable the Uruguayan authorities expressing concern for his safety and human rights. Many individuals have done so. Last month, the Fourth Interamerican Conference on Mathematical Education, Caracas, sent an appeal to the Uruguayan government, as did the Council of the Canadian Mathematical Congress, meeting in Montréal.

Lipman Bers, President of the American Mathematical Society, inquired about Massera to the Ambassador of Uruguay to the US; the Ambassador replied that Massera at the time of his arrest was "the military and political leader of the outlawed Communist Party," which had weapons and was preparing armed insurrection. However, Amnesty International has adopted Massera as a prisoner of conscience — a designation it never gives to prisoners it believes to have been engaged in violence.

Appeals should be directed to

> Sr. Presidente de le República Oriental del Uruguay
> Sr. Juan Maria Bordaberry
> Casa de Gobierno
> Montevideo, Uruguay

and to

> Sr. Presidente de la Suprema Corte de Justicia
> Dr. Remule Vago

Ibicuy y San José
Montevideo, Uruguay.

It is requested that information of such appeals be sent to

Prof. Geza Stary
Casilla de Correo NO 4332
Correo Central
Buenos Aires, Argentina

so that word will reach Massera's defenders within Uruguay.

— — — — — — — — — — — — — — —

We urge representation on behalf of J.L. Massera by the American Mathematical Society and other professional organizations.

— Felix Browder, Chandler Davis, Henry
Helson, J.L. Kelley, George Pólya, Steve Smale,
Gabor Szegö, Peter Szegö

"The Selfish Genetics" was published in the University of Toronto *Varsity* in 1979 on the occasion of Richard Dawkins's visit to campus: it addresses his then-recent book, *The Selfish Gene*. The sidebar was printed separately and distributed by Professor Davis and his colleague C.K. Fong as a flyer to people entering Professor Dawkins's lecture. Professor Davis characterizes these pieces as "colloquial" expressions of the ideas he was later to elaborate in "La Sociobiologie et son explication d'humanité." (*Annales, E.S.C.* 36 [July-August 1981: 531-571]).

The Selfish Genetics

THE TROUBLE, MR. Dawkins, is in the first place with your use of the word "should." As indeed you recognize. In what sense *should* I be selfish, or be partial to others presumed to share genes with me? What is your aim in writing a book to tell me I should?

You put yourself in the tradition of evolutionary theory — of Charles Darwin, J.B.S. Haldane, R.A. Fisher, and Robert MacArthur — a tradition I also honor. Your title suggests different antecedents: the nineteenth-century capitalists who, being caught with their hand flagrantly in the cookie jar, said in effect, "Sure, I grab. Everybody grabs, it's human nature. Don't condemn me for it, admire me because I do it so well." But no — you don't profess to admire selfishness, and you ask that your "should" not be taken as exhortation. Apparently you would distinguish yourself from the crude rationalizers of dog-eat-dog individualism. Then why the "should," and why the insistent cleaving to their phrase "nature red in tooth and claw"? The main thing seems to be to refute any assertion of an evolutionary basis for group loyalty. Even Edward O. Wilson falls under suspicion of being soft on altruism!

Now I am going to argue that there is more wrong with your account than just choice of words; so let me state some portion of it without any "should." First: that which natural selection selects is, primarily, the gene. Thus evolutionary explanation of any aspect of behavior must consist in connecting the behavior, on the part of an organism, with preferential survival of a gene the organism carries. If the behavior is "altruistic" — works for survival of another individual at one's own expense — then it can be favored by the evolutionary process only insofar as a benefiting individual carries the gene in question. It is in this sense that you call selfish even the gene which directs unselfish behavior by the organism.

Second: you suppose that observed altruistic acts will be adequately explained by their tendency to benefit individually those, such as close kin, who are likely to share one's genes. This supposition involves, on the negative side, rejection of alternative modes of action such as group selection. You deny that a gene instilling an impulse to aid one's fellows would tend to proliferate, even by the mechanism of making the generous individual's tribe a tribe likely to prosper, because its benefits would redound as much to neighbors lacking the gene and hence not reciprocating. And the supposition entails on the other hand confidence in the effectiveness of kin selection and such mechanisms — confidence that the shuffling of genetic material is rapid enough and geological time long enough that even slight advantages in survival value will be manifested in increased frequency of a gene.

Let's agree not to phrase the evolutionary study of altruistic behavior in terms of selection of "a gene for altruism." Altruistic genes, selfish genes, spiteful genes…these are figments, at best a *façon de parler*, at worst downright confusing. One gene never made a complex strategy of behavior. If one new gene does introduce a new way of defending an organism's survival, it must do so by modifying an already complexly coded strategy. Its effect must be mediated by specific modification of perception or response. Thus it is reasonable to suppose that a new gene may make a mother turkey less prone to eat her offspring by altering her notion of what sort of small moving object to peck at, but it is not reasonable to suppose that it may change her strategy across the board, enhancing care for progeny and only that. The force of W.D. Hamilton's calculations of the effectiveness of kin selection is not to show that altruistic genes can be selected, but to show conditions for one simple mechanism by which genes for more specific behavior may be selected. The program then is to hypothesize these specifically acting genes in an effort to explain the behavior.

I don't have to inform you that this is the program: you know it; you exemplify it. I do want to insist on stating it properly, because some of my arguments depend on this. You should be willing. To project a selection mechanism which may cause a gene to survive back onto the gene itself, as if it had purpose, is a teleological fallacy as destructive as any.

If you agree this far, it would seem to oblige you to retreat somewhat from your thesis that selfishness "comes natural." Just as a reflex suitable to deter the mother turkey from eating her own offspring might deter her from eating her neighbor's too, so the impulses which make most of us want to care for our natural children make us want to care for other children as well. A rigorous selfish-gene theorist would reproach real-life genes for their inaccurate aim, perhaps. I ask you to reconsider that attitude. Isn't it more appropriate to say that (in such a way of life and reproduction as the turkey's) reluctance to eat small moving objects which may be turkey chicks is a trait that leads to higher reproductive success for the strain having it — and this undiminished by the fact that, to be sure, it also leads to higher reproductive success for neighbors of those having it.

Summarizing my first point — selfishness, or restrictions on the scope of one's altruism, can't be selected for as such because that's not the sort of thing there are genes for. Modes of behavior that can be selected for are not so discriminating as to make favoritism for genetic relatives feasible. The mechanisms of selection which favor care for kin will likely favor care for fellows generally.

Theorists who reject this argument may be over-influenced by social-Darwinist rhetoric. I hope you concede that survival does not require rivals' demise — that dog does not eat dog. This is fortunate indeed, for adaptation. Survival of a species often requires diversity in the gene pool, and this would be lacking if successful genes regularly wiped out their competitors.

You may cling to the notion that, even though helpfulness to non-kin may accrue as a by-product to care for kin, it is only a by-product — that in evolution, generosity itself never pays off. I challenge that too. I am not going to leap to the defense of group selection, though I do think its defenders have a case. Neither am I going to plead the special importance for evolution of brief periods of expansion of a new strain, in which you would admit an organism has least to lose from working for the good of its species. No, I'll take the more competitive situation of a stable population not divided into well-isolated breeding groups. Even there, there is a mechanism tending to select generous behavior. Let's call it the "well-built-nest effect."

It works like this. The society in which I live is likely to be that in which my children and other kin will grow up. If that society is viciously competitive, they will have a harder time growing up, and that gives me a Darwinian stake in making it harmonious. Just as a mosquito which chose to lay eggs in dry sand would leave fewer descendants, so will a social animal which behaves so as to set up, as the ambience for its progeny, a laissez-faire Eden of each against all. Any gene enabling me to render my community more co-operative, less destructive, is giving itself, through my children, a better chance of survival.

Again, this is only a mechanism by which some particular co-operative tendency may be selected; it does not mean there must be a gene "for" cooperativeness. Further, for any gene to be favored by this mechanism, the organism must be social in a sense somewhat like the human.

My second point against your thesis is that you omit mention of the well-built-nest effect. You may counter that

WHAT DOES BIOLOGY
HAVE TO TEACH US ABOUT SOCIETY?

A lot, one hopes. After all, social groups are built of people, who are indeed animals.

But if sociobiology announces it can explain only such behavior as is directed to the benefit of ego and close kin — if to sociobiology all altruists are impatient for their reward and all group loyalties subordinate to self-serving — then sociobiology disqualifies itself as a basis of social science, or even as a new insight. It denies too much of the human behavior we all observe and live.

Adam Smith and Milton Friedman have spread the slander that each "rational man" is selfish. A convenient doctrine, for some: But not thereby a datum for science.

We observe, and rejoice in, the fact that PEOPLE CAN PULL TOGETHER. People of different families. Different races. It even feels good.

In this we differ from termites. Granted.

you and other sociobiologists do mention the effect, under the rubric of "reciprocal altruism," and state a case against its importance. You may even think this is a particularly tenuous sort of reciprocation, in the next generation. But it is not a matter of reciprocation at all. I am saying that habitual unreciprocated generosity on my part, or simply sociality, may be pro-survival in evolutionary terms, by helping provide for my children a favorable environment.

Without venturing to conjecture specific traits which the well-built-nest process has furthered, let me generally recommend it for a major problem area: how our species acquired, presumably very rapidly, such an elaborate kit of hereditary social skills. A special center in the brain for analysis and generation of language, another center specialized for recognizing individuals by their faces, and more: we may perhaps properly count as social that proudest human talent, our conceptual treatment of things not present to the senses. Skills almost useless in an atomistic, territorial way of life, and unimportant to life in a small band whose members stay near each other, but essential to life in the simplest human society, and more essential the more complex it becomes. Skills less helpful to seizing one's fellows' crop than to helping them reap it.

Because such skills are more relevant the more important interactions between people become, it is plausible that their genetic equipment evolved in the same part of humanity where the cultural component was proliferating, and this enhances the plausibility of selection mechanisms which can operate in a complex society. The usual theory of group selection requires small competing groups isolated from each other (dog-pack-eat-dog-pack, shall we say?). My claim is that within a large melting pot, social behavior can be selected, even behavior which a classical economist would stigmatize as altruistic.

I trust you will go along with this broadening of the scope of the discussion. To me, all the social skills, to the extent that they are heritable, pose exactly the same sort of problem for evolutionary theory as apparent altruism does.

You agree, on the other hand, that we must narrow the discussion in another respect: One does not have to explain much of human sociality by genetic evolution, indeed one must not try. That we have the genetic materials with which to construct social relations is what the evolutionist may succeed in explaining. What social construction ensues, must be explained from different causes. If this were not clear from general considerations, it would be forced on us by the spectacle, throughout history, of social institutions and morals changing much faster than genetic composition of the population could change — and of contemporaneous tribes presumed similar in genetic make-up which nevertheless order their societies very differently.

Thus I do not at all argue "nurture versus nature" against you. Happily, there is no occasion to, for you yourself drastically limit the explanatory power you claim for genetics.

You do this, however, in a curious way. After painting your horribly bleak picture of how we "should" act, to suit our genes, you admit that nothing compels us to act that way. A loophole for morality that not all your compeers leave: You make this admission very hastily — rather like the Renaissance philosopher who, after devoting a whole book to the teachings of reason, retracts it all in a paragraph on the contrary teachings of faith. But I take you at your word, and examine your concession. What departures from the tyranny of the gene do you leave us hope for? You pay most attention to our capacity to restrict procreation; but presumably if pressed you would include all our social skills, our capacity to feel responsibility and guilt, empathy, respect and self-respect…. How do we become suddenly able thus to defy the dictates of billions of years of evolution? Your answer to this apparently tough question is exceedingly offhand, and amounts to this: Now we know better. Society and culture, following laws of their own and progressing at a faster pace than genetic control of behavior does, have put all these discrepant ideas into our anti-social heads.

Well, certainly, culture puts at our disposal repertories of concept and behavior which we would not have if our only inheritance were our genetic inheritance. The question is, what do we do with them! Why do most of us feel really bad when we've displeased our fellows? Why does it seem to be harder for a politician to learn to lie than for most people to learn the commoner's habit of truthfulness? Why does it seem to be so hard to learn to love the grasping "economic man," even in that exceptional culture (our own) which officially extols him? Somehow humanity seems to be more amenable to an ethic of generosity than is consistent with its whole biological nature being selfish.

This, then, is my final point. While welcoming your recognition that social development calls for non-genetic explanation, I reproach you with, in a sense, giving away too much. Though all the elaboration of spoken and written culture be the province of social scientists, the knack of speech is in the animal; though religion, custom, and law be the province of social scientists, the power to live by social codes is in the animal; you must not renounce the challenge of accounting for their appearance.

The existence and importance of human historical development does not justify calling our social proclivity an invention, superficially grafted onto rugged-individualistic basic natures. Our speech is processed by neural structures as natural as those for coordinating our walking. Our pangs of guilt or sympathy are conveyed by hormonal secretions as natural as those for our pangs of hunger or lust. If our self-preservation is natural, so are our sociality and our human decency.

"Science for Good or Ill" was published as Booklet 26 in the Waging Peace Series of the Nuclear Age Peace Foundation in 1990. As of this writing, information on and resources from that organization can be found at www.wagingpeace.org.

SCIENCE FOR GOOD OR ILL

(excerpt)

SCIENCE, SEEN FROM outside, may seem like a free lunch: a source of unexpected wealth and cures for what ails us. Or it may seem like a dangerous juggernaut, generating appalling weapons, out of control. From the inside, to us who practice it, science as a whole is scarcely visible; it is simply there as the context for our lives. Only with a special effort can we ask ourselves the big questions.

Clearly, both the simple outsider's views are right. Science offers the possibility both of great benefit and of great damage. **Those who practice science should admit, however reluctantly, that our work can have consequences with huge moral implications that we are not being invited to control. I am one of those who cannot duck the responsibility. We recall that the defendants in the Nuremberg War Crimes Trials were not exonerated on the plea that they were only following orders, and we** feel in the same way that we can't evade the issue on the grounds that we were only following where science led.

Let me give a few examples of efforts by scientists to move toward taking a common moral position. There are many. I'll start with one in which I was involved.

Hundreds of mathematicians signed a statement that appeared as an ad in the *Notices of the American Mathematical Society* in 1967, right next to recruiting ads from Lockheed, Litton, the National Security Agency, and so on. The statement read:

> **Mathematicians**: Job opportunities in war work are announced in the *Notices*, in the Society's Employment Register, and elsewhere. We urge you to regard yourselves as responsible for the uses to which your talents are put. We believe this responsibility forbids putting mathematics in the service of this cruel war.

It is considered quite bad form in our society to blow the whistle on any activity for which money can be paid. Making such a public statement, we put ourselves on the spot. Some of the objections come from outside; some from other scientists. Here are a few of those objections.

OBJECTION #1: "What are you, anti-science? anti-progress? Science is knowledge, knowledge is power. How could you be against knowing more?"

When they say anti-science, I know what the word means. Hostility to rational knowledge is rife today, and the harmful fallout from technology may feed it. Time was, several centuries ago, that there was an anti-scientific ideology of some importance even among the learned. People sometimes blamed scientists (in the image of the arrogant Dr. Faustus) for trying to understand things that God did not intend mortal humans to understand. Still, I don't see that the call for social responsibility in science is of this nature. I think this objection is, therefore, simply off the subject.

We are not anti-science in general. We do believe that science can be the expansion of our understanding, and if the use of science raises problems — of course I *am* saying that it raises problems — we'll have to deal with them by understanding them, using *more* knowledge not less.

Those who label anyone anti-scientific who questions science are demanding that we give science *carte blanche*. But we mustn't. **Science is a human product, and people must control it for human purposes.**

A further, subtler point: there's a hidden bias in this objection. If we exempted science from criticism we would be giving *carte blanche* not just to science in general — something which might be arguable — but to science as it stands! We may agree science is on the whole good, but we must be careful not to suppose it is perfect. Even if every answer scientists think they have now were just so (which is too much to hope), one might still wonder whether they have always chosen the best questions to investigate: **even true statements may be criticized as trifling or irrelevant.**

OBJECTION #2: "You can't reverse progress. It might have been better not to discover nuclear fission, but you can't undiscover it."

Well, no, although sometimes detailed knowledge is almost completely forgotten. If the nations could get their governments to agree that nuclear bomb technology should no longer be used, they might want to stop educating bomb technicians. Practical techniques might become very rusty in one generation. But the principles are very likely to remain available—just as historians who wonder about the crossbow can find enough in the historical and archeological record to build a pretty good working reproduction. And again, we didn't suggest undiscovering; **criticism of some of science's products doesn't imply a demand to abolish knowledge**.

Still there's something to it. The fear of science expressed from ancient legends up to today often includes this warning: you can't put the djinni back in the bottle; you can't put the lid on Pandora's box. True. Our choice of research directions affects what we find now, and moreover, it also affects what is available to our successors.

OBJECTION #3: "There's no such thing as responsibility in scientific research, because when you do the research you can't foresee what its uses may be."

This sort of objector points gleefully to the case of Godfrey Harold Hardy. Heartsick to see his fellow mathematicians streaming into war work—I'm talking now about the First World War—Hardy became a total pacifist. He declared later in life that he was glad that none of his scientific results had ever been of the slightest use to anyone. (A paradoxical stance indeed for this passionate humanitarian: you'd think he would have wanted to be of use.) He was ignoring, perhaps because it is mathematically so simple, the Hardy-Weinberg Law, which he contributed to population genetics. He was also ignoring a more spectacular exception, which he didn't foresee and which few people could have imagined before the 1940s:

the so-called Hardy spaces, whose theory he founded in the 1920s, are now so central to what we call linear systems theory that whole conferences are devoted to them, paid for largely by Air Force grants, and populated in considerable part by military researchers.

What do I have to say about Hardy's guilt in the military uses of his ideas? He would have regarded these applications as entirely deplorable, and on the whole he might have been right. They do not, however, illustrate the impossibility of knowing ahead of time the applications of one's research: granted, Hardy didn't foresee any application of these spaces, but *he didn't try*. **One of our duties as scientists is to try to perceive the relations between different ideas; it's not a duty we should be reluctant to carry out, because much of the excitement of science comes right there, in the richness of the connections that appear.** I think this point is important and too seldom made, but it's only a small part of my answer to Objection #3.

If Hardy had understood that one of his spaces had potential practical application by way of linear prediction theory, it might have soured *him*, but most of us don't share his extreme rejection of applications. When linear prediction theory was developed in the late 1930s, by Andrei N. Kolmogorov in the Soviet Union and Norbert Wiener in the United States, they did see the connections, from Hardy spaces through probability theory to communication and missile detection. The applicability was intrinsic to their investigation. What's more, they were willing participants in military research against the Nazis. Though they broke relations with the military after the Second World War — Wiener in a drastic open letter in the *Atlantic Monthly*—the military didn't break relations with the ideas they had given it. The djinni was not put back into the bottle.

One can imagine Hardy saying to these two gentle, democratic men, as concerned and humanitarian as he was, "You see, my point is proved. You gave your ideas knowing they had uses, but you couldn't restrict them to non-military uses. When the generals got them, you couldn't restrict the generals to using them only against the Nazis; and they used them for each of your countries against the other." If he happened to notice me, I would come in for sharper reproach because I had the benefit of more hindsight. Some mathematical results I got in the 1970s—after so much had been written on scientific responsibility, after the ad against war work that I just proudly quoted—are also often cited at those same military-supported conferences.

Actually, some of the signers of that 1967 war work ad were simultaneously working on military contracts! Two of them made the newspapers at the time, when the generals threatened to cut off their contract money in reprisal for signing the ad. This outraged many professors as an interference with their freedom of expression. In the end, the threat to cut their support off was not carried out. We might ponder also whether they were being consistent. They undoubtedly believed there would be no serious military uses of the research they were doing on weather modification. The military command, however, thought weather modification was a directly military topic, and indeed attempted to turn cloud-seeding into a weapon against the Vietnamese.

OBJECTION #4: "You have no right to censor science anyway. What are we scientists? Just the employees who do the work. Decisions on what to do with the results of scientific work are made by society at large; it would be elitist for us to claim exclusive rights to them just because we have this special role of generating the ideas."

This line has annoyed me for years. It bothers me because it's wrong, morally and factually, and at the same time it's so close to right that I hate to have to oppose it.

It's morally wrong, in the first place. If my work, or some part of it, is cruel and anti-human, that touches me more closely than it touches anybody else because I am doing it; and that gives me a special responsibility that nobody should try to get me to pass off. This is not an elitist attitude: it applies to every participant in an anti-human project.

The objection is factually wrong, in the second place. Scientists are *not* censoring science or the uses of science, in practice, but others who have less to do with creating it *are*. Let's keep them in mind.

The owners of the Johns Manville Corporation decided to keep on marketing asbestos products for decades after they knew it was causing thousands of cancers; on a larger scale, the owners of RJR Nabisco (whoever owns it this week!) continue to push tobacco decades after they knew it was causing hundreds of thousands of cancers (and as the American consumer begins erecting a defense against it, the tobacco corporations line up diplomatic pressure from the Bush administration to induce Asian governments to import the stuff). For a third example, the decision to obliterate Hiroshima and Nagasaki was not made by the scientists (many of them were vocally against it, even Edward Teller), but it wasn't made by society at large, either: it was made *secretly* by President Harry Truman and his cabinet, and even long afterward, it remains hard to get a straight account of their motives.[1]

And yet something about the objection is right. Decisions on the allocation of research resources, decisions on science education, and decisions on the course of technology really ought to be made by society at large. I agree with that. Only it is no argument against my raising the problem of social responsibility of science. Quite the reverse: it's an argument for talking about it *more*. In this essay, I'm going out of my way to raise it with non-scientists as well as scientists. If scientists are more intimately involved than the rest, it doesn't follow that I want to exclude the rest. I don't.

Even if decisions about supporting and using science were concentrated outside the scientific community, we may perhaps legitimately insist on our right to negotiate as a group with our paymasters. When relations with the military came up in the American Mathematical Society in 1987, it was in this form. Hundreds of individual members

---

1 If the motive had been to shorten the war by demonstrating the power of the new weapon, the bomb could have been exploded in an unpopulated area in sight of Tokyo, and this was Teller's recommendation. Secretary Stimson's diaries and other sources threw some light on the decision in later years. See P.M.S. Blackett: *Fear, War, and the Bomb: Military and Political Consequences of Atomic Energy*, Whittlesey House, New York, 1948. Len Giovanetti and Fred Freed: *The Decision to Drop the Bomb*, Coward-McCann, New York, 1965. For a fascinating analysis and guide to bibliography, see chapter 9 of H. Bruce Franklin: *War Stars: The Superweapon and the American Imagination*, Oxford University Press, New York, 1988.

petitioned for a policy statement (1) calling on the Society to seek more non-military funding for the nation's mathematical research and (2) directing the Society's officers to do nothing to further mathematicians' involvement in the Strategic Defense Initiative. The proposal was submitted to a referendum of the Society's membership in 1988. With over 7000 voting (about twice the number usually participating in election of officers), the statements passed by votes of 4034 to 2293 and 5193 to 1317 respectively. Now, if only the officers of the Society can be brought to act accordingly.

Is it clear that such group stands are legitimate? Perhaps the only proper form of resistance to misuse of science is exercise of individual conscience. This is sometimes said directly as in Objection #5 below, but more often implied.

OBJECTION #5: "Those of you who don't think you can conscientiously do certain scientific work certainly have a right to freedom of conscience. No need to mount campaigns, just vote with your feet. You can just change your field of science, or even change to non-technical employment."

Well, sure we can. A lot of us do. John Gofman left his job in nuclear medicine so he could publish freely his own estimates, not his employers', of radiation damage. Robert C. Aldridge quit as a missile design engineer in order to publish strategic weapon analyses for all of us to share. Molecular biologists leave the lab to organize agronomical stations for Central American farmers much too poor to pay for them.

Less extreme cases abound: many of my colleagues and students have switched from one "normal" position to another to reduce their involvement with destructive technology or increase the constructive utility of their work. I mentioned the mathematicians' ad of 1967; one of its signers moved from Lockheed to a university, one moved from Sandia Corporation to another university. Recently one of the X-ray laser whizzes left the Lawrence Livermore Labs in search of less bellicose research topics.

And yet, I wouldn't accept the notion that responsibility in science should mean only for some individuals to opt out. That would be an artificial limitation. Nevertheless, our campaigns are often to disseminate individual statements of conscience, and this may have the virtue of clarity. I'll give a few more examples of such statements.

An organization called the Committee for Responsible Genetics, led by the MIT biologist Jonathan King among others, has been circulating this statement internationally:

> We, the undersigned biologists and chemists, oppose the use of our research for military purposes. Rapid advances in biotechnology have catalyzed a growing interest by the military in many countries in chemical and biological weapons and in the possible development of new and novel chemical and biological warfare agents. We are concerned that this may lead to another arms race. We believe that biomedical research should support rather than threaten life. Therefore, WE PLEDGE not to engage knowingly in research and teaching that will

further the development of chemical and biological warfare agents.[2]

Bearing in mind the Hippocratic Oath traditionally
taken by medical doctors, we might put such statements
in broader terms. If physicians state their obligation to
use their specialty only for the good of humanity, why not
other professions? Consider the following oath proposed
at an international conference in Buenos Aires in 1988 by
Guillermo Andrés LeMarchand:

> Aware that, in the absence of ethical control, sci-
> ence and its products can damage society and
> its future, I,_____, pledge that my own scientific
> capabilities will never be employed merely for
> remuneration or prestige or on instruction of
> employers or political leaders only, but solely
> on my personal belief and social responsibil-
> ity—based on my own knowledge and on con-
> sideration of the circumstances and the possible
> consequences of my work—that the scientific
> or technical research I undertake is truly in the
> best interest of society and peace.

This statement has been signed by, among others, a large
majority of the 1988 graduating class in Buenos Aires and
many scientists internationally.

The following statement was disseminated at Hum-
boldt State in California in 1987, and subscribed to since
then by large contingents at graduations there and at many
other universities:

2   186 South Street (4th Floor), Boston, MA. 02111.

> I, _____, pledge to thoroughly investigate and
> take into account the social and environmental
> consequences of any job opportunity I consider.

A number of prominent scientists have publicly subscribed to the following Hippocratic Oath for Scientists,
Engineers and Technologists:

> I vow to practice my profession with con-
> science and dignity;
>
> I will strive to apply my skills only with the
> utmost respect for the well-being of humanity,
> the earth and all its species;
>
> I will not permit considerations of nationality,
> politics, prejudice or material advancement to
> intervene between my work and this duty to
> present and future generations;
>
> I make this Oath solemnly, freely and upon my
> honour.[3]

What is really meant by such pledges? Is it enough for
those who feel that way to move to a different job?

It's not enough. **The reason we raise the issue in scientific societies, many members of which may already be
doing clearly constructive work, and in graduating classes of students, and in general audiences, is that science
and technology are social products.** The technology of
Zyklon-B for the Nazis' gas chambers, or of binary nerve
gas for today's weapons, is a product of scientific lore built
up by an intellectual community. The social responsibility

---

3   The Institute for Social Inventions, 24 Abercorn Place, London
    NW89XP.

of the biological scientists is not merely to get somebody else's name rather than one's own attached to the job! **Just as the Hippocratic Oath should make each doctor repudiate Nazi-style experimentation on human subjects by all doctors, biological responsibility should mean that each biologist refrains from misuse of the science and gets others to refrain too. Responsibility should be applied collectively.**

Unrealistic — sure. The level of mutuality I'm imagining here is unattainable now. The vision is of a process of deepening a community code of ethics over many stages. As the need is felt more widely, it can happen. Right now we see medical ethics being reworked, with great attention from thousands of specialists. Scientific and engineering ethics can be developed the same way: publicly and worldwide. So far, it is lagging way behind.[4]

Works Cited and Suggested Readings

Blackett, P.M.S. 1948. *Fear, War, and the Bomb: Military and Political Consequences of Atomic Energy*. New York: Whittlesey House.

Giovanetti, Len and Freed, Fred. 1965. *The Decision to Drop the Bomb*. New York: Coward-McCann.

Franklin, H. Bruce. 1988. *War Stars: The Superweapon and the American Imagination*. New York: Oxford University Press.

Unger, Stephen H. 1982. *Controlling Technology*. New York: Holt, Rinehart & Winston.

4   For discussion of existing codes of professional ethics, see Unger (1982) and Frankel (1987).

Frankel Mark S. (ed). 1987. *Values and Ethics in Organization and Human Systems Development.* Washington, DC: American Academy for the Advancement of Science.

Cover of original publication.

THE UNTIMELY RHETORIC
OF CHANDLER DAVIS'S ESSAYS

Josh Lukin

THE DECEPTIVELY SIMPLE register of Chandler Davis's essays, as well as their straightforward, step-by-step mode of reasoning, may obscure the fact that he is a powerful and unconventional author of nonfiction.[1] With the exception of "Imprisoned Mathematician" and "The Selfish Genetics," all of the nonfiction contained here, as well as "So You're Going to Prison!" and "The Purge," attempts the difficult task of invoking Davis's personal experience or action in the course of making a broad societal argument. Each makes generous use of the first person singular, as does "The Selfish Genetics" — both in his one-on-one style of argument with Dawkins ("What is your aim in writing a book to tell me I should?") and in the metadiscursive statements he uses to organize his argument ("I do wish to insist on stating it properly, because some of my arguments depend on this."). Such rhetorical

---

1   More straightforwardly: it took time and the repeated expressions of awe on the part of Ray Davis and others for *me* to recognize that fact, so I want to make it easier for others.

decisions are challenging, courageous, and, when done well, uniquely effective for several reasons.

First, Davis's uses of the first-person tend to emphasize the distinctiveness of his views and experiences, defying the essayistic convention of universalism. The essay genre, as Jeffrey Cane Robinson has explained, "presupposes an ideal community of intimates who know and share without essential dispute and disagreement" (quoted in West 1986, 399). Essays in that tradition invoke an Aristotelian "we" who can be expected to have identical responses and sensibilities: as Cornel West has written of Trilling, this "we" possesses an "authority [that] is unearned because no rational or moral case has been argued and defended, only asserted and assumed" (400). Davis, on the other hand, is always quite clear on who his "we" (and his "you") are: the science fiction community, the mathematical community, humanity considered as a species. And most of his prose is devoted to arguing rational or moral cases.

Second, the ideal of impersonal disinterest that the invocation of one's own experience violates has long been a standard, in some quarters, for what constitutes serious thought. A few years ago, I received the following in an email from a publisher concerning a feminist essay that I wanted to anthologize, a piece in which the author's experience was used as exemplary of what societal pressures were exerted upon women of her class and era: "Make sure that the memoir aspect is not the main thrust. It must contain the same scholarly rigour and backbone as the other essays in the collection. In this vein, I prefer that you not introduce personal notes into your work either." I wonder whether the essay would have received the same response if the essayist had, instead of claiming her own experience as a data point, cited that of a published memoirist. How much distance is necessary for "rigour and backbone"?

Third, it is indeed possible for an essayist either to deflect criticism or to engage in a veiled form of universalization by using the authority of experience. Invoking experience to shut down discussion with an implicit "You can't tell me that I'm drawing the wrong conclusions from my own trauma!" is a common move in some political circles; and, although the "View from Nowhere" — the implicit claim that one transcends the personal — is sometimes recognized as an attempt to universalize the view of an able-bodied white male professional, one still encounters bold and unsubstantiated claims that a writer's experience speaks for, or is necessarily evidence of, the lives of large classes of people in the same social category. For an essayist, then, to use the personal and make it persuasive is a task that requires *more* "rigour and backbone" than do mandarin, "detached" styles of argument.

So much for the challenges. The effectiveness of Davis's rhetoric at criticizing the naturalizations and universalizations of ideology comes in part from the acknowledgment (not surprising in someone who works in such a collaborative profession as mathematics) that, as Nietzsche observed, there is no "pure, will-less, painless, timeless subject of knowledge" (1994 [1887], 92): everyone has a perspective and a standpoint, such that a claim on the part of an individual to represent the sole source of objectivity is often a screen for the grossest attempts to impose one's arbitrary personal prejudices. The post-structuralist revolution and the feminist critique of "The View from Nowhere" have made that insight common in recent years; but long ago, Chandler Davis neither took claims of pure disinterest at face value nor expected that his own readers would accept such claims. Davis's brief letter on "Violence & Civility" is an exemplary demolition of the "View from Nowhere." The letter has in addition to its lucid argument and powerful prose style a perspicacity that only becomes clear in light of a close look at the rhetorical and intellectual tradition to which it was responding. The author Davis's letter targets, J.M. Cameron, has a set of values that may seem notably eccentric[2] forty years after the debate in question; but he was a presence in North American journalism for over thirty years, and the supposedly "objective" attitudes on his part that Davis dissects still cast a shadow over intellectual discourse.

A present-day reader, seeing in Davis's letter a critique of an author who opposes "civility" to "violence," might reasonably infer that the letter was occasioned by a conservative author who thought social change was generally indecorous. But in fact, J.M. Cameron in his "A Special Supplement: On Violence" (1970) and elsewhere throughout his long journalistic career self-identified as a man of the Left. Cameron (1910–1995) was an enthusiastic supporter of the US civil rights movement, gun control, the Second Vatican Council, and "the authority and powers of the federal government" ("Reaction to Goldwater") as a means to fight racial and economic injustice (1964, 564); he had opposed and would continue to decry nuclear escalation,

---

2   Humanistic scholars of my generation and younger might recall Eve Kosofsky Sedgwick's witty analysis of Cameron's taste in *Epistemology of the Closet* (1990, 141-3).

the "filthy and barbarous war" in Vietnam ("Cardinal Spellman, Charles Davis" 1967, 418), the "spiritual vulgarity" of the Catholic Right ("Nuclear Catholicism" 1983),[3] anti-immigrant legislation, and those who would tolerate white supremacy in Rhodesia. Cameron's heroes included Medgar Evers, the Blessed Franz Jägerstätter, Saint Maximilian Kolbe, Archbishop Oscar Romero, and Benigno Aquino—all martyrs killed by right-wing regimes. And in an era when scholars begrudgingly allowed one or two women into the literary and historical canons, Cameron expressed high regard not only for the safely canonized Jane Austen but for George Eliot, Rebecca West, and Charlotte Brontë; for the Victorian feminists Josephine Butler and Florence Nightingale; and for such "lowbrow" novelists as Ellen Wood, Susan Warner, Margaret Kennedy, Daphne DuMaurier, and Harriet Beecher Stowe.

Much of the conservatism in Cameron's later writing hinges on issues of sex—he opposed what he saw as such newly-acceptable practices as birth control, sodomy, gay liberation, and abortion, in accord with the doctrines of two popes.[4] It is in his work on this theme that the short-

3   Online archives of *The New York Review of Books* are not paginated.

4   I have not seen any articles wherein he says so directly, but Cameron's views on sex are likely connected to the 1968 appearance of *Humanae Vitae*, issued by Giovanni Mantini (Paul VI) and written in large part by Karol Wojtyla (John Paul II). Cameron had strong opinions on which aspects of Catholic doctrine issued directly from the Holy Spirit: in the sixties, he harshly denounced conservative critics of Vatican II for opposing that divine force; in 1975, he wrote,
    It strikes me as idiotic that Catholics should solemnly discuss, as matters on which the Church could change, the traditional teaching about homosexuality, continence outside marriage, the killing of the unborn, the indissolubility of Christian mar-

comings of the "View from Nowhere" are most apparent: in order to maintain his rhetorical distance, he disavows the first person singular whenever it threatens to intrude upon his argument, as in his 1976 explanation of what marriage is for:

> In the Biblical tradition, including the New Tes-
> tament, marriage is above all a permanent sexual
> union, and also, for those who are fortunate and
> work hard at it, a union of friendship… What I
> call gnosticism rests on the view, unknown to
> the Old Testament and cogently argued against
> by Aristotle, that man is a spirit with a body,
> whereas in my view — that it is *my* view is of
> course absolutely unimportant — man is a body
> with distinctive capacities. (Letter to *NYRB*)

This perspective on Christian views of the human body is worthy of attention, and has an interesting lineage (I would include Hawthorne and Pater among Cameron's philosophical antecedents); but the style of argument is disconcertingly close to "This is not my opinion: it's God's!" Contrast the generous and unselfconscious use of the first person, and the dearth of argument from author-ity, in most of Chandler Davis's essays.

"A Special Supplement: On Violence" initiated ten years of writings by Cameron on the subject of universi-ties. His doctrines on those institutions tend to issue not from divine authority but from the prophets John Henry Newman, Matthew Arnold, and Lionel Trilling. Hence he

---

riage, as though these were matters of human devising, like clerical celibacy or the traditional restriction of the priesthood to males. ("Christians, why…" 103)

is repeatedly alarmed by changes in the self-image of students and scholars in the contemporary university: in 1972, he writes of activist professors, "Nothing quite like this has ever been known in the world before"; he laments that

> The notion of a humane education resting upon an appreciation of the long historical development of our culture and upon the study of letters…is now derided, not so much by the obvious louts and bullies who reach for their revolvers when they hear the word "culture," but by such members of the intelligentsia as the 1971 president of the MLA. ("Trilling, Roszak, & Goodman")

Cameron here is alluding to Louis Kampf, who, three years after having been punched and arrested by the Chicago police for putting up "radical posters" at a Modern Language Association convention, gave a Presidential Address urging social engagement in the teaching of the humanities. Kampf argued against the seductive power of Arnoldian claims that the life of the mind transcends the social; he averred that academic humanists are performing alienated labor; that being increasingly uncertain about one's employment, tenure, and political freedom can be inimical to the life of the mind; that universities, far from being autonomous realms, serve the interests of power; that academics must unionize; and that composition class size must be kept small.

All of Kampf's priorities seem to have scandalized Trilling; his epigone, Cameron, could not get his head around the idea that mental laborers in the academy were employees, noting in 1978 that

[i]t isn't surprising that undergraduates should
feel themselves members of an external prole-
tariat, and take appropriate action, if the members of the faculty themselves take their position
to be that of employees of a large corporation.
But here the nature of the university has been
forgotten. ("Doing Poorly at Doing Good" 440)

in the course of bemoaning "The decline of authority in
state, school, and family" (438), a phenomenon he also connects to racism and birth control. Two years later, in the
course of discussing curricular reform in higher education,
Cameron asserted that an ethos of pleasure, exemplified by
sexual freedom, was inimical to the values associated with
academic study because "it is quite plain that to be a liberal-
ly educated man, in the nineteenth-century sense, involves
years of what seems to be unrewarding toil at subjects not
always at the time very exciting, a limitation of choice…"
("The Idea of a Liberal Education" 1980, 201).

If Cameron were simply a grumpy old man who needed to be told, "Just because these things elicit the same
feelings in you, James, that doesn't mean they're connected," the details of his oeuvre would be of limited interest.
But his world view has a history and affiliations that make
them worthy of analysis and of the challenges Chandler
Davis offered. Norman Mailer's views on sex,[5] without the
direction of the Vatican, approached the conservatism of

5 Mailer, another opponent of second-wave feminism and contracep-
   tion, had compared masturbation to the bombing of civilians in
   Vietnam. I have written ("Cold War Masculinity…") of how, although progressives today may regard his views on gender and sex
   as highly eccentric, Mailer in the sixties and seventies was hardly an
   outlier.

Cameron's; another *NYRB* contributor, a widely influential public moralist who divides the world in a manner
similar to Cameron's, is Christopher Lasch. Lasch's work
of the seventies also tends to posit a segment of society
that can and should be walled off from history and politics, focusing not so much on The University as on The
Family, but viewing that institution, like "liberal education" in Cameron's analysis, as having reached its summit
in the nineteenth century and been sliding downhill ever
since. Cameron's view of the domestic scene is more generous than Lasch's: he lacks that worthy's gynophobia and
is acutely aware that child abuse, for example, has long
been a social issue of some gravity. But some of the arguments that Lasch used to naturalize an ideal of the family
as a milieu into which political struggle had only recently
intruded have analogs in Cameron's arguments on higher
education: Cameron's condemnation of Kampf, for example, shares with Lasch's opposition to feminists an eagerness to blame the messenger for the problems s/he is in
fact accurately reporting. And both attribute social change
in their hitherto stable havens on "narcissism."

Only toward the end of "A Special Supplement: On Violence" does it first become clear that Cameron regards The
University as a realm of purity that should be sequestered
from politics: specifically, he asserts the imperative that

> the universities remain enclaves of civility. To
> invite the violence that comes from the injus-
> tices of our society to enter the world of the
> university is a piece of folly; for the university
> is capable in some degree of that impassioned

detachment from which cures for some of our
injustices may be hoped for.

The assumptions that violence, when it reaches the
university, enters by invitation and that detachment is that
institution's normal condition are striking claims to make
in mid-1970; and they come as a surprise after a good deal
of rhetoric in which Cameron manages to acknowledge
the horrors of State-sponsored violence that the "moder-
ate" voices of his time tended to naturalize.

Indeed, the third part of the essay begins promisingly,[6]
taking issue with Max Weber's views on power. Weber,
Cameron tells us, believed that violence was necessary in
politics and could not in practice be hampered by individual morality: it was

> the business of statesmen to have regard to the
> general and distant consequences of what they
> do. A statesman may have some natural revul-
> sion from, say, a massacre of civilians (for exam-
> ple, the inhabitants of Hiroshima and Nagasaki);
> but he sets this aside and stiffens his resolution
> for the sake of what he takes to be the general
> consequences of the horrid deed.

Cameron objects to this ethos on the grounds of the impossibility of knowing the consequences of our actions and

6   The first part of the essay is dominated by a meandering historical-
     philological exploration of the term "violence," which Chandler Davis
     gently ridicules in his response; in the second part, Cameron's "View
     from Nowhere" becomes more tendentious, as he explores why
     violence unsettles "us" in the present day with generalizations about
     the emotional reactions of a hypostatized "we," an undefined inter-
     pretive community that seems to share all of Cameron's mores.

makes an observation, sadly apt in the present day, about overconfident political leaders in the Vietnam war: "Never before in history have statesmen been so hubristic as they are today; and never has hubris been so swiftly punished. Commonly the punishment for hubris falls not upon the leaders, but upon their people." Cameron advocates adherence to the ethics of personal virtue, then takes an odd turn and condemns the "cult of spontaneity and the vogue of such writers as Marcuse and Norman O. Brown and the apocalyptic McLuhan." His conclusions seem to be that we are no longer at a juncture in history when civility can be compatible with injustice, but that revolution is a bad idea and the counterculture suffers not only from millenarian illusions but from infantile narcissism, so we should eschew violence and seek Aristotelian virtue.

Davis's generous evisceration of Cameron's "On Violence" pinpoints the very moments of disingenuousness that ally Cameron with the Reasonable Left of his time and characterize some of the quasi-progressive mandarins of our own day. Davis, acknowledging the wisdom present here and there in Cameron's article, makes his first argument a version of "What do you mean 'we,' white man?" The necessity of that argument in that era can hardly be overstated. Matthew Arnold's "disinterestedness," reincarnated as Trilling's claim to be "outside ideology," was soon to evolve into Lasch's "detachment" and Todd Gitlin's "common dreams." The only objective values are those articulated by the cultivated elite: others are pathological, "special-interest groups," or the understandable but resentment-fueled moans of wounded subjectivities. In recent times, norms that treat reformers and dissidents as in need of therapy, such as Lasch used in criticizing Randolph Bourne and Jane Addams, have evolved into erudite dismissals of consciousness-raising and "identity politics" as distractions from the *real* goals of social equality.[7]

Davis's insight, that Cameron is arguing in favor of "that stability which gives him comfort, confidence in his social milieu, and enjoyment a continuing culture" (88), kicks Cameron off of the Olympian heights[8] from which he pronounces his judgments and raises the question of just who, to use Cameron's description of the counter-culture's language, "is not unlike young children crying with delight or in pain." To Cameron, civility arises when infantile "willfulness is cured by the establishment of habits through our incorporation into institutions and our induction into a cultural tradition, hitherto one in which there has been a set of moral and intellectual paradigms"; if those traditions are "in flux," there is a danger of regression to the infant's unregulated desire, manifested in hippies and campus protests. Cameron's distress at the student movement's "willfulness" prefigures Lasch's 1979 *Culture of Narcissism* and even the Good Sixties/Bad Sixties dichotomy promoted by Gitlin; Davis's language of "comfort" and "enjoyment" shows exactly how subjective and culture-bound Cameron's feelings of alarm are and evokes an image of the aging English critic yearning for

---

7   See Duggan (2004) and Mardorossian (2002) for challenges to analogous dismissals in the present day.

8   I adopt the adjective used by Peter Steinfels, who in a sharp critique of Cameron's views on sex says that he writes "from an Olympian distance" (1976, 638).

the plenitude of the womb, or perhaps the cradle, while fearing that the hippies will take away his rattle.

There is no harm in having a disposition that yearns for the comforts of tradition; but, as Davis indicates, there is nothing useful in claiming that history, humanity, and ethics show that disposition to be the correct, objective one. Yet Cameron's tactics — the Olympian distance and the pathologizing of an opposing position — were widespread in his era. 1970 was the year in which Shulamith Firestone gave the title "The Personal Is Political" to an article by Carol Hamisch arguing for community and communication among diverse women's groups; Firestone's point, in a time when feminist consciousness-raising was derided as "navel-gazing" or at best "therapy," was that such issues as the division of domestic labor, abortion, child-care, appearance, and sexuality were not the problems of screwed-up individuals but the results of widespread power relationships that could only be addressed by changing objective conditions. This insight would not have been news to Rebecca Pitts, but it took many years for the women's liberation movement to make it intelligible to the bulk of progressives. Even at the end of the seventies, Chandler Davis felt he had to explain in his discussion of sex that

> [j]ust as in economics we find a social ethic truer than individualist liberalism, we will have to think socially even in this sphere so often called private. After all, we speak of the women's *movement*, of the gay rights *movement*. We organize marches and boycotts.... It's a social issue, we meet it socially, then of course we should think

and talk about it socially. ("What Might Sex Mean?" 1979, 3)

By then, Davis could reasonably expect that his readers would understand his argument — such may not have been the case ten years earlier. The tradition of claiming Arnoldian "disinterestedness" or Arendtian "heartlessness" had by 1970 created a discourse in which the personal could never be political, because the personal was a polluting or distorting influence on the political, and in which domestic violence, for example, could never be a political issue. To conceive of the domestic realm as open to political reform would have been to endorse the very bureaucratic intervention that Lasch and his fans agreed was destroying our once-comforting social institutions.

It is no longer possible for an educated writer to survive unchallenged upon making the specific generalizations that sustained Cameron: his claim that the Judeo-Christian world has always respected Biblical guidelines on sexual relations, for example, has even been denied by the US Supreme Court. But the general impulse to define a comforting realm as outside of society, impervious to the buffetings of politics or history, retains its allure. A physicist colleague, Vandana Singh, writes to me from Massachusetts that

> the detachment/disinterest thing comes up in science too, and is considered a necessary part of the attitudes that a good scientist must have... But that has been extended to imply a cold detachment from the consequences of one's inquiry into nature and ultimately a cold detachment

from Nature herself. It's an excuse for not taking responsibility… (2009)

Chandler Davis, unbeknownst to Dr. Singh, elaborated a related point twenty years ago, enumerating in "Science for Good or Ill" the many objections he had seen raised to scientists' claiming social responsibility. Against the views that would leave "society" and "science" in distinct and distant categories, Davis argued that

> [s]cience is a human product, and people must control it for human purposes… If my work, or some part of it, is cruel and anti-human, that touches me more closely than it touches anybody else because I am doing it; and that gives me a special responsibility which nobody should try to get me to pass off. (108, 112)

Many scientists have lived according to such principles; many others, however, believe that their work can and should be done independently, or without consideration of, such obstacles to "detachment" as culture, politics, or the survival of the human species.

For some, it is still The University that should retain its imagined purity: Dean Catharine R. Stimpson, a famed opponent of graduate assistant unionization, in 2000 denied that graduate assistants are employees,[9] ascribed the

---

9   Samuel Delany addressed this argument in 2009, explaining its "detachment" from history:

> Sixty years ago, when graduate education was an overwhelmingly privately financed affair, and there were only four or five graduate students per department, the best students were rewarded with a special class in their own area of expertise (or a TAship working with a full professor already teaching in that

allure of the union to the "appeal of identity politics," and added in a flourish of Cameronian rhetoric:

> The union efforts also summoned up the modern myth of liberation, of freedom and power for individuals won through the collective struggle against an intimidating but defeatable bully. In contrast, the myth of graduate education is more austere. It is the story of the quest for truth, of the beauty and power of advanced learning and teaching, of the nobility of Aristotle's opening of the *Metaphysics*…

Over twenty years separate Cameron's "For the faculty to negotiate with 'the university' is to admit that the faculty is not the university…in effect to abandon the entire university tradition and to accept the term *university* as denoting an employing authority, like Bell Canada…" (*On the Idea of a University* 78–9) and Stimpson's "my feminism, with its emphasis on collaborative methods of working, made me doubt that the adversarial process of collective bargaining, in which the United Auto Workers would be

---

area), in which to try out presenting their ongoing research. At that point, at least an argument could be made for not treating graduate students who taught as full employees of the university. But this practice grew into what we have today: over fifty per cent of the universities' classes—virtually all the elementary courses—taught by an army of graduate students. Without them, the university would collapse and be unable to do its job. Not to acknowledge that graduate students are, today, indispensable employees of the institution—and to go on pretending that their classes are just select plums doled out only for academic excellence and that they need not secure for the graduate student teaching them the full rights of a university teacher—is to be willfully blind and morally imbecile.

involved, was the best way to resolve differences." But both make a claim for the university as a comforting, pastoral realm where conflict can be wished away.

As for the tendency to pathologize the desires of the marginal, as Cameron does both in his universalizing approach to sex and in his condemnation of the counterculture, that practice has become a minor industry. Tobin Siebers astutely observes that

> [t]he academic Right and Left often share the tendency to view psychological flaws as underlying the desire to form political identity groups, with the result that critics of identity politics often reproduce the descriptions of political minorities used by their oppressors, labeling them as wounded, resentful, power hungry, or narcissistic. (2008, 206)

Cameron's belief that we must be wary of ready access to gratification in sexual or academic life has faint echoes on the "austere" Left; there are still social critics who are deeply suspicious of world views that valorize pleasure. Ellen Willis observed in 1994 that even progressives tend to "share the traditional view of morality as the disciplining of desire" and as such ignore the possibility that "genuine goodness — empathy, respect for others' rights, a sense of responsibility" is allied with, rather than at odds with, being happy and fulfilled in life, and that evil comes from oppression and domination rather than failure to regulate desire (122, 121).

The austere determination, which Willis sees among liberals, to police the Left for crimes against altruism seems alien to Chandler Davis, whose descriptions of political resistance never stigmatize self-advocacy as selfishness or decry pleasure as narcissistic. Yet Davis, unlike Willis, does not oppose "individualism" to that austerity: while invoking pleasure in his arguments, he never minimizes the importance of communal endeavor. In "What Does Biology Have to Teach Us about Society?" for example, Davis did not take Cameron's tack of appealing to Hobbes (!) for an endorsement of virtue but instead announced, "We observe, and rejoice in, the fact that PEOPLE <u>CAN</u> PULL TOGETHER. People of different families. Different races. It even feels good" (101). In "The Purge," he wrote "After my release from prison, it was relaxing to go on an anti-Bomb march with my wife again" (423). It is not "narcissism" or an abandonment of the search for truth to mention, in the course of advocating certain ideas, that socially valuable insights and activities bring about personal enjoyment. It is not necessary to claim "detachment" in order to pursue intellectual work or political change with rigor and honesty. And it did not come as news to the author of "It Walks in Beauty" that the personal is political.

Works Cited

Cameron, J.M. 1970. A Special Supplement: On Violence. *The New York Review of Books* 15(1) July 2, 1970.

——. 1967. Cardinal Spellman, Charles Davis. *Commonweal* Jan 20, 1967: 417–419.

——. 1978. Doing Poorly at Doing Good. *Commonweal* July 7, 1978: 438–441.

——. 1980. The Idea of a Liberal Education. *Commonweal* April 11, 1980: 201–207.

——. 1976. J.M. Cameron Responds. *The New York Review of Books* July 15, 1976.

——. 1983. Nuclear Catholicism. *The New York Review of Books* Dec 22, 1983.

——. 1978. *On the Idea of a University*. Toronto, ON: University of Toronto Press.

——. 1964. Reaction to Goldwater. *Commonweal* August 21, 1964: 563–564.

——. 1972. Trilling, Roszak, & Goodman. *The New York Review of Books* Nov 30, 1972.

——. With Robert Coles, Eugene McCarthy, Garry Wills, Michael Novak, William F. Buckley, George E. Reedy, and Anne Jackson Fremantle. 1975. Christians, why do you still believe in God, in the promise of the Cross? *Harper's* April 1975: 94–103.

Davis, Chandler. 1979. What Might Sex Mean? Samizdat circulation.

——. 1988. The Purge. In *A Century of Mathematics in America, Part 1*, ed. Peter Duren, 413-428. Providence, RI: American Mathematical Society.

Delany, Samuel. 2009. Personal communication with the author. Jan 9, 2009.

Duggan, Lisa. 2004. *The Twilight of Equality?: Neoliberalism, Cultural Politics, and the Attack on Democracy*. Boston, MA: Beacon Press.

Gitlin, Todd. 1987. *The Sixties: Years of Hope, Days of Rage*. New York: Bantam.

———. 1995. *The Twilight of Common Dreams: Why America Is Wracked by Culture Wars.* New York: Henry Holt.

Lasch, Christopher. 1979. *The Culture of Narcissism.* New York: Norton.

———. 1977. *Haven in a Heartless World: The Family Besieged.* New York: Basic Books.

Mardorossian, Carine. "Toward a New Feminist Theory of Rape." *Signs* 27 (2002): 743-775.

Nietzsche, Friedrich. 1887. *On the Genealogy of Morality.* Trans. Carol Diethe. Cambridge, UK: Cambridge University Press, 1994.

Sedgwick, Eve Kosofsky. 1990. *Epistemology of the Closet.* Berkeley, CA: University of California Press.

Siebers, Tobin. 2008. *Disability Theory.* Ann Arbor, MI: University of Michigan Press.

Singh, Vandana. 2009. Personal communication with the author. Jan 17, 2009.

Steinfels, Peter. 1976. Second Thoughts on Sex. *Commonweal* Sept 24, 1976: 636–638.

Stimpson, Catharine R. 2000. A Dean's Skepticism about a Graduate Student Union. *Chronicle of Higher Education* May 5, 2000.

West, Cornel. 1986. Lionel Trilling: Godfather of Neoconservatism. In *Lionel Trilling & The Critics: Opposing Selves*, ed. John Rodden, 395–403. Lincoln, NB: University of Nebraska Press.

Willis, Ellen. 1994. Beyond Good and Evil. *Tikkun*, May/June. Reprinted 1999 in *Don't Think—Smile! Notes on a Decade of Denial,* 114-127. Boston, MA: Beacon.

STORIES

"Last Year's Grave Undug" was written in 1953 and first published in *Great Science Fiction by Scientists,* ed. Groff Conklin (Collier, 1962).

LAST YEAR'S GRAVE UNDUG

A STRANGER STEPPED into the clearing where Andy, Dom, and the old man had camped.

The stranger had a full beard and long hair, like Andy and his partners, but he wasn't nearly as well dressed. Denim shirt and pants, very worn. Instead of shoes, soles of rope or vine, tied on with thongs over the ankles. His eyes were pale blue and staring.

He stood with his back to an oak, facing the clearing, a gun under his arm; a cold and unknown person. The three travelers got to their feet. The gun, an old .22 apparently in pretty good condition, was pointed at Andy's belly.

It had been a long road from Akron, and on the way Andy had got used to guns. He kept his hands in the air and faced the stranger, but let his eyes stray over to the left to watch for a signal from the others.

The stranger was saying something. Andy didn't pay much attention; it was the kind of thing he'd heard before. "What are you doing around my land? If you have women and want to clear some land, there's all you could want downstream from here, t'other side of the creek. If you're just wandering and looking for what you can find, pass right on through. We got no room around here for your kind. A lot of city fellows who can't work for their board…" and so on.

Andy watched Dom's face. The lower lip drew down till the tips of Dom's front teeth were just visible under his black mustache. Andy repeated the signal to show he'd seen.

The stranger hadn't noticed anything. He was saying, "So I don't care what your reason is, you just—"

A corner of Dom's tongue appeared at the right side of his mouth.

Instantly Andy dropped full length on the ground to the right of where he'd been standing. The stranger's finger pressed the trigger—nothing happened. At the same time Dom crashed into the stranger's shoulder and twisted his right wrist behind his back. The stranger whirled all the way around, getting free, but now he was off balance, staggering into the bushes, and Pop had the rifle, the stock raised as a club. The stranger gathered himself to rush the old man, but with Andy back on his feet the three of them made too much to tackle. He stood looking from one to another of them, waiting.

Pop opened the rifle's breech. "Loaded," he said, and closed it again. "I think here's what we'll do. When we're ready to leave our camp here, we'll throw this squirrel gun of yours off into the brush where it'll take you a while to find it; then we'll start walking. We won't steal your gun, that might be hard on you."

The stranger said nothing. Pop went on, "You're safe from us, because we don't want what you've got. At least," his voice got sad, "I'm pretty sure you haven't got what we want, and if you have I don't know what to do about it. We're going to do just what you said: pass right on through. We just don't want you watching us with a gun in your hand, because we don't know you. Fair enough?"

They couldn't tell if he'd even been listening. Andy put out his hand; the stranger made no attempt to do anything but shake hands.

"All set?" asked the old man.

Dom looked around the clearing, verified that the fire was out, and shouldered the pack. "All set."

"Okay, let's go." He handed the rifle to Andy, who seized it at the balance and heaved it javelin-style out of the clearing. A good toss. The stranger followed it with his eyes to where it crashed in a thicket of maple saplings. Andy and his companions were toughened for walking, and this would give them as much lead as they wanted.

"Good-by, stranger," said Andy. "Good luck to your farm or whatever you've got." But the stranger had already turned in the direction of the gun.

The old man led the way upstream along the river bank, walking fast away from unfriendliness. At this point upstream was almost due east, and the early morning sun stared them straight in the face through a screen of maple and willow leaves. The trail was still good.

After a few minutes Andy spoke in a low voice. "His rifle was on safety?" he guessed.

"Right," said Dom. "I could see it from where I stood."

It was a common mistake these days. The safety catch was twice as important now as it used to be. Not only so you wouldn't hurt anybody with an accidental shot, but also so you wouldn't waste cartridges: you might not be able to get more.

Andy trudged on, looking at Pop's back in front of him, but seeing the blank blue eyes of the stranger above the loose beard that hid the expression of his mouth. What did he really know about him? Very little.

He was startled when Dom spoke behind him. "I bet that guy's following us. I didn't like the look in his eyes. I don't know if we should have given back his rifle."

"We did what we decided to do every time," answered Pop firmly. "If we'd taken his gun, he might have another one, and we're in trouble sure. If we leave the gun with him, he probably trusts us and we're that much safer."

"Yeah, he trusts us," said Andy, thinking of those eyes. "Did he look as if he'd ever trusted anybody?"

"He said we could settle if we wanted to, didn't he?" replied Pop. "Just another farmer. Andy, you never knew any farmers, before. It's you who don't trust *them*."

"Oh, I don't know.... How many farmers did *you* know before?"

"A good many." This was too vague to be convincing. Even coming from the old man, and in a good solid tone of voice, didn't go far. Pop answered Andy's silence: "I was in the Army in World War II, after all. I never knew a guy was a farmer there unless he told me. Of course I might not have had the luck to run into such a hillbilly as our buddy back there. But I figure they're pretty much like you city kids."

Dom said, "Oh, there's some difference, for sure, because of the different conditions of life. A farmer sticks to one ace. A guy from the city moves around, or at least he talks to somebody who's been around, and he'll *think* about switching jobs or moving. That guy back there was probably just like all the rest: more than anything else, he just didn't want anybody to mess with anything. For that matter, you can see how he feels."

Andy decided Dom had got this opinion from a book. There had been some of Dom's crew in his union, before, and sometimes Dom was just like them. He meant well, but he was too stubborn about his ideas. Besides…

He said, "I don't know if farmers are so different. They used to read the same newspapers we did."

He was stopped by the realization that Dom and he had now switched sides in the argument, still disagreeing. He was mildly disgusted with both Dom and himself. His last sentence hung in the air, and he might have sent braver ones after except that ahead of them their trail ended.

A road cut across at right angles, leading to the ruins of a bridge sinking in the stream on the right; straight ahead, another road continued their own path. Faster walking, they could hope.

They skirted a great mound of earth covered with yard-high underbrush, then scrambled up the embankment through more of the same purple-leaved bushes to the road. The old man sat on one of the few concrete roadside posts that remained upright; Dom and Andy stood beside him. Dom rested the pack on the next post. They looked around.

Downstream they couldn't see as much as they would have liked: the height of the embankment wasn't enough to lift them above the trees they'd walked under. To the south, across the river — more trees, telling them nothing. On their own side of the stream the road halved a wilderness of waist-high shrubs; only the frequent six-foot puffs of birch kept them from seeing miles of the stuff. A couple of houses and barn rose above the screen not too far away. Closer to, a billboard and a route sign decayed quietly: The Dowell Advertising Company and the State Department of Highways ignored them, and it was easy to do the same.

"Nobody here," said the old man, and looked eastward instead. That road was pleasanter. Little fences of brown grass marked the cracks in the pavement, ruling off rectangular plots of concrete, and in some of the plots there were pools of softer grass. There was shade, and the stream alongside; and the road pointed at the hills.

"All right to take this way?" Dom asked, a little afraid the suggestion would sound soft.

"Safe enough," agreed Pop. He hoisted himself to his feet, and they started, walking side by side now.

"Okay," said Andy, "but if we're going to be walking out in the open this way, let's be sure to make decent time."

"Right," said the old man, and he stepped up his pace before Andy could go on complaining.

They hiked on along the green road. The grade was steadily upward. Oven birds puttered in the underbrush and red squirrels overhead. After several miles of such a nice day, Andy said, "It's a nice day."

"Nice day and a nice road," said Dom. Pop was encouraged to try asking Dom, "You decided you think that character was okay, huh. Why? Because he had his safety on?"

"No, that was a mistake. He was a guy who could be mean to somebody who was interfering with him…or if he thought somebody was. He wants things to go on the way they're going. Probably a few families farming together back there. Guy's probably got a wife and kids…."

His voice was getting wistful. Andy interrupted him. "With a daughter for you, huh? Think we should have stayed there with him?"

Pop cut in, "How about you, Andy? Do you?" It was the same old topic—the Destination—and Pop was always willing to crank up the discussion.

"Not on your life," was Andy's answer. "I'll stick to the plan we started with: get far enough south so it won't be too cold to last through the winters, far enough up in the hills that the armies from the cities won't get to us. Find a few other people who are willing to try to live a decent life."

"So?"

"What do you mean, so?"

"I mean, you're right, that's the plan, we're with you—but how do we know where to stop? How are you so sure that character didn't have exactly the place you're talking about?"

"You know he didn't, Pop."

The old man smiled. "I asked you, Andy."

"Well, I don't know—it's obvious. For one thing, he was too eager to get rid of us. The place I want has got to want me. I don't mind if people ask me some questions first, but they should at least hope I answer right! They can't ask me to produce a wife at the entrance gate, cause I haven't got one; also they can't cuss the goldurn city slickers, cause that's what I am. Was."

"Right," said Dom. "I think they'll probably be city slickers themselves."

"Oh yeah? You want to go back to Lexington maybe?"

"Lexington's hell," Dom agreed. "Louisville's worse. I thought for a while there was no chance anywhere *but* towns like Lexington. You know, supply of cartridges, et cetera."

"They've got the ammo all right, and they use it on each other."

"Yeah, and all the towns are probably in the same loused-up condition. No more of that for me." No need to cover up the horror in his voice. In more than one basement hiding place this group had stayed alive only by silence and luck; by now they didn't expect of each other any poses of fearlessness. Dom said, "All I meant was, I think the people we ran to the hills to look for are people who ran to the hills to look for us. See my point? City kids like us, with the same plan."

Pop said, "There better be some hayseeds around somewhere. I don't know about you, but I'm useless on a farm unless somebody tells me what to do."

"If we run into a farmer who'll feed us for a few months' work, maybe we ought to take it," said Andy.

"No good! I've done that. But does that mean I've got twenty pounds of seed corn? Does it mean I'm *really* sure what I'd do with it next spring if I had it?"

Dom said, "My grandfather grew up on a farm, but I don't know if we can get by on that either."

"And yet it's more city slickers you're looking for!"

"I just say they're the likeliest. Your hillbilly is likely to be too ready to stay in his rut. Nothing changes his life too much, and he's agreeable."

It was the same thing he'd been maintaining a while back, and Andy's irritation was revived. "How'd you figure this out? Principles of Marxism-Leninism?"

"Could be," said Dom. "What have principles of Marxism-Leninism got to do with it?" But he couldn't pretend to have missed Andy's needling tone. "What the matter, Andy? Afraid I'm going to overthrow you by force and violence?"

This was meant to put Andy off balance, and it did, long enough for Pop to step in. "Andy, some things aren't important enough to fuss over. Didn't you ever make any mistakes in your life?"

Just the same, Dom was still on the defensive (so many years of the newspapers' attacks, and after that the death-faced Loyalty Legions hunting "saboteurs"). He said, "Mistakes? I don't know about that. I thought I had things pretty well figured out, before. I didn't want a war, and I guess I was right on that, okay. And — well, Marx and Lenin didn't predict anything like this mess, and neither did old Dom. The things I had figured out don't help much now."

"So forget them," said Andy.

"So don't fight about them," Dom came back.

"You're right of course." But Andy had decided too late to put a friendly tone on this, and it sounded grudging.

Dom said, "I might think *you* have a hole in your head sometimes, too."

"Even there you could be right."

Pop was perhaps chuckling but wasn't admitting it. He said, "Dom, you have a lot of your figuring out to do over again, huh? But it'll take a while. You haven't got anybody to talk to who's any help except Andy and me, and I don't help much. When you've got a roomful of people to bang the table and argue with, you can begin to get somewhere. Until then, there's one thing we *have* figured out: if we don't stay with each other, we'll be alone. We're like a family, in my language."

Dom watched his foot dribble a loose rock along the concrete. Then he said "Yeah" hastily, as if he'd just noticed an answer was called for. His face was serious. "I might have disagreed with you and Andy if I'd met you before, but I know we agree now on everything important. We're all in the same boat. If only Andy would pull his weight in the pack-carrying…"

He grinned. Andy agreed, and took the pack from him, hitching it up onto his shoulders. It was also his turn to make a pledge of allegiance.

He said to Dom, "I love you like a brother." He had said that to people sarcastically a hundred times in his life and was embarrassed to find himself meaning it. So he added, "Of course back in Akron, you know, I never got along too well with my brother."

The old man let out the laugh he'd been hoarding. "How about your father, Andy?"

"He used to whip me in the back entry." They all laughed.

"Well, we start fresh now," Dom said cheerfully. "We'd better." Andy's mood had changed again; he felt like the pictures of Atlas.

"We better had. There's nothing else we can do."

The edge of the universe might be fifty miles back of them and crumbling, but if he kept the pack on his shoulders and didn't slip, the sun would rise tomorrow.

Dom kicked another loose rock. It skidded off the road, and he found still another handy to his toe to continue the game. He said suddenly, "Gee, there's a lot of rubble on the road. Where'd it all come from? The bank to the left isn't that steep."

Pop said, "Flood, maybe. You probably didn't notice the cabin we passed back there, you were too busy being kids."

"Sure," Dom protested, "old ruined frame house, on the right, all fallen to the ground."

"Yeah, except it wasn't all that old, and it was very ruined. The roof wasn't in sight."

"Flood then, I guess. It can't have been this spring, though, or we'd see more signs."

Andy added, "This road is pretty high to be flooded." He looked down through the bushes to the sunny stream bed.

"It would have to be some flood," Dom agreed. "Say, remember that shambles at the bridge we passed? Could it have done that?"

"*Some* flood."

The next half mile showed clearer and clearer signs, though the road still rose high above water level. Finally they ran up against a roadblock — several giant trees which had fallen from the left across their way. The trunks were black and crumbling, except for one steely oak, and tiny new trees were sprouting from the wreckage.

Beyond the dark barrier the road rose steeply to a village. Following an agreed procedure, they left the road and crept among trees to try to enter the village by the back way. They scrambled on all fours up a steep bank covered with loose shale that made silence difficult; then they stood, several yards apart, looking over a board fence at a two-story frame house. The back yard had gone back to weeds, the windows were broken, inside they saw a large walnut table lying on its side. Still the shingle roof, yellow clapboard walls, and cellar door were the same as if people lived here. They watched a long time before slipping around to the street and walking two more blocks to the center of town.

There it was even harder to believe they were alone. They could count the proofs; but the whole pattern of buildings, fire hydrants, and "Chili" signs made no sense without people. You still believed that if you dropped an envelope addressed to Chicago into the mailbox it'd be delivered—otherwise why was the mailbox there? Not that you were sure you knew anybody in Chicago, by now.

A one-story brick building was labeled "US Post Office" in stone letters, while crayon-on-cardboard letters labeled it "Loyalty Legion HQ." Under new management. But now it was under *no* management.

"What's the name of this place?" asked Dom.

Andy read a sign: "Danciger."

"Danciger, K-Y, what got you?…"

"Suddenly I don't like small towns."

The healthy sun baked silence out of the town like pus out of a wound. They wanted to leave. Dom said, "Let's leave."

"Got to look around for food," said the old man. "Where should we try? The grocery store?"

Andy hesitated. "If we knew why everybody left, we'd know better where to try. Were they afraid of an attack or just starved out, or what?"

"They probably went back to their cousin on the farm someplace — carting all the canned goods with them."

"They weren't flooded out," Andy realized. "There hasn't been any flood here." Everybody nodded.

"Well, the grocery store?" the old man asked again.

Dom stood as if he was fascinated, pointing at the ex-post office and its two obsolete signs. "Let's try here." Nobody felt like arguing.

The revolving door was jammed; they stepped through the broken glass. Inside the building it smelled the way the street outside had looked. Breathing through their mouths, they still had no trouble following the smell. It led to the office labeled "Postmaster" and "Legion Commandant — Keep Out," which was where the dead men were.

The travelers didn't look at the six dead men or at each other while they searched rapidly for food. It'd be here if it was anywhere; these late thugs with black holsters and olive-drab armbands outside their overcoats would have sifted the town for everything edible; but there was nothing, only a pile of empty cans in one corner.

Still they stayed a minute longer. The office looked as if desks and everything had been thrown from one wall to the other at least once, but the six bodies were laid out fairly regularly on the floor, as if they'd died in their sleep.

"How old are these, do you think?" asked Andy. "Last winter's?… Funny they have those armbands — same thing Beatty's Loyalty Legion wore in Lexington before Hickman's took over."

Pop suddenly bent over the nearest body and opened a few of its pockets with his left thumb and forefinger. From one of them he drew a crumbling sheet of paper, which he opened in front of Andy without looking at it. Andy smiled sourly and began to read, mimicking Beatty's accent: "I pledge loylty to d'Constitooshn of d'United States of Americar an' to d'Way of Life f'r which it stans, an' to defend her against all enmenies foreiga an' dmestic. I *am not now* an' *haven never been*—"

Dom snorted. "Beatty's Way of Life!" He shook his head, miserably. But Pop just smiled.

"I *thought* they were from Lexington. How would there be that many black holsters in Danciger?"

"I follow you," said Dom. "But what were they doing up here? They couldn't convince people in Lexington they were loyal by chasing saboteurs *this* far. Starving to death up in the hills — what were they bucking for, the Congressional Medal?"

"I doubt if they starved," said Pop quietly. "The holsters are empty. And if you look at the side of this guy's head—"

One look and they could see he was right. Which direction had these six men been shot from? The door? They looked around. The side windows? The back window?

Dom said for the second time, "Let's leave."

They left; gunfire over the snow in a deserted village was behind them, warm spring sun on glittering maple leaves ahead. But the old man said, "Somebody caught up with them, took them by surprise. Who was it? What do you think, Dom?"

"Not Hickman's Legion. They haven't been chasing *any*body *this* far. I don't know. Geez, I thought we'd got away from the cities.…"

Andy needled him — "Those good old cities you like so much —" but sympathetically.

"Used to like so much."

"Yeah."

A side road cut off to the right, downhill. It was macadam, and it'd get them back to the river, so they took it without stopping to look at the toppled road sign. If they had, they'd have known what they were coming to a little sooner. As it was, they were in the middle of a discussion of when to eat lunch when they rounded a curve and Andy gasped, and they all stopped.

It started below them and a little to the right, and ran massively on across the valley: concrete, who could tell how many tons of concrete? A dam. A tremendous sheer face of dam. Beautiful.

Andy was not too stunned to notice things. Why was the concrete so stained most of the way to the top? Oh golly — we're looking at the *upstream* side. No water in the reservoir. That gap in the middle of the dam: dynamite must have started that, and the lake had done the rest while it vanished. Good-bye, good-bye.

He said, "Yep. It was some flood, all right. And it wasn't this year; there wouldn't be anything but grass on the bottom of the reservoir if it had been."

"Who would have done this, Andy?" asked Pop.

Dom laughed absentmindedly. "Must have been Red agents — ask any Loyalty Legionnaire."

Andy tried to answer, though, because the old man had asked him to. "Who did it? Maybe we can figure out, at that. The Danciger patriots decided somebody downstream was an invader, and let the water loose against them…. Then Beatty heard about the flood and decided here were some *real* saboteurs, so six sincere jerks came up and cleaned out the town of Danciger. And after they weren't there any more, nobody had any reason to come back to the town of Danciger: no traffic on the road and no power from the dam for the better part of a year." It all made sense, but it didn't matter much.

He was looking at the dead dam. Beside the dam, all the futile history of the Beattys and the Hickmans looked as minor and temporary as the stories that gangster killings used to get in the newspapers, before.

The dam, now, made him feel really bad. It was big, and all one single thing you could see at once, and it was gone. It was a tremendous monument to the past, but not at all to the future — just to the past.

He didn't want to believe it. "There must be a power station on the other side." While he spoke, he and Dom were starting on down the road again, with Pop following. "If it was above flood level, there might still be some power there — storage batteries. No, I guess not."

Dom left the road to skip down the steep bank to the left. Andy followed more gingerly because of the pack. They were below the former water level; the rocks were mossy but not slimy; they ran skidding down loose gravel to the bottom. It was like a Sunday picnic when you were a kid, except for everybody having a full beard and nobody laughing.

They waited while the old man caught up. He walked to their right, and to his right was the shoulder of the dam. The land here had been undistinguished farmland, then had carried a lake for a decade or two; the lake had moved on, and now it was scrub and grassland again.

The little pool behind the breach in the dam was all the water the reservoir could hold now. A row of three island boulders lay across it just this side of the dam, but the pool didn't really end till you got to the gap in the concrete. There the stream spilled into dodging rapids — a lot like the ones upstream that fed the pool, except that here the rock they drenched was man-made.

In front of that tragic ruin, what could you say? Snap your fingers, "Oh heck," as if it was a cracked dish?

Andy tried picking up the pieces again. "Most of the dam's still here. Those piles of concrete will last as long as any hill; there isn't so much to patch here in the middle."

Dom burst out, "Oh sure, Andy, the *things* are mostly still here. The concrete's mostly still here, and the power station may not be wrecked too bad; as far as that goes, some of the dynamite may have been left over from this job and still be sitting in a basement up in town. A lot of good that does us."

"Well at least when somebody wants to dam this stream again he'll have a pretty good start."

"Yeah. When there's somebody to do the repairing, somebody to haul their cement…somebody to use the power from the station."

"Now, everybody's too busy looking for mythical invaders. Tearing apart the country looking for the saboteurs who are supposed to be tearing it apart."

"The invasion wasn't mythical," said Pop deadpan, sitting down on the rock. "The US invaded itself." The other two just stared until he smiled, and they caught on. Beatty had invaded Danciger, Hickman had invaded Lexington, and one each a hundred per cent more American than the one before.

Andy looked at the pool and swore quietly. "Shadow boxing, and we broke our neck."

Dom said, "I wonder what guys like Hickman did before. Some kind of cop, probably."

Andy answered in spite of himself. "Hickman was a union president." He bit his lip.

"No kidding! In Akron?"

"Yeah." Why hadn't he kept his mouth shut?

"I suppose he specialized in cleaning the left-wingers out of the union."

"That's right."

Andy thought, Don't ask it! But Dom did: "And I suppose when Hickman ran for local president, you voted for him."

"…Yes. Well listen, Dom, I didn't know then what was going to happen—what's more, neither did you. And the guy that was running against him had a Taft-Hartley indictment—" He abandoned that sentence in absolute confusion.

Pop soothed him. "That union election's over long since."

Dom had to say something. "Hickman's still Hickman."

"And there are lots more like him. How long can he keep it up? Five years?"

Andy snorted. "As long as Beatty did; until a bigger liar shows up with a bigger arsenal."

"But with the same lie? How long will their lie go over? How long can they keep people excited about this 'enemy' when nobody ever sees the enemy?"

"Not much longer," Dom announced. "Ideas like that don't start from nothing. This subversive scare was made up by the corporations to keep the workers divided (guys like Andy)." Andy had something about Stalin on the tip of his tongue, but he missed the moment and Dom went on. "Now that there's no more capitalist class there's no reason for the Red scare to keep going." He didn't feel playful, but he gave Andy a dig in the ribs and said, "There's your principles of Marxism-Leninism."

The old man was thinking. "There may be no reason for it to keep going, but I wish I saw the good reason for it to stop. Everybody just has to look around him to see the truth, huh?"

"No more bosses' newspapers to fill them full of lies. Why should people be anti-Red, after they calm down? What harm are the Reds doing them?"

"Well now," said Pop, "most people think plenty of harm. Things are going lousy, and the lousier they go the more Reds there must be to cause it all, so get out a new Loyalty Legion and have another rat hunt."

"But it's such a fraud, they'll see through it. Andy saw through it."

"So did I, but —"

Andy broke in, "It wasn't such a fraud at the start. After all, places *were* atom-bombed. The newspapers didn't make that up."

"I guess there must have been a few ICBMs landed in this country. I don't think they made that up. But how do you know which side started firing them first? And if there was supposed to be a Red invasion, how come we don't see any signs of it, now that the US is in no shape to defend itself?"

"Hah!" Andy was ready for that one. "Your Russian buddies are probably in the same snafu we are. They're probably all busy executing each other as agents of Wall Street. Much too busy to invade anybody even if they want to."

Dom was *not* ready for that. He had never thought of it before, and it was a crushing thought; yet already he almost believed it. There was nothing he could say.

Pop said to Andy, "All the more reason not to get bitter about who started the war. *Dom* didn't start it, for sure."

"And neither did I."

"Right. You know, if things had gone a little bit differently, the two of you might have been in different armies, fighting each other."

Silence. Dom thought about Andy, "He was a dupe, but it doesn't matter now."

Andy had thought the same thing about him many times.

Andy said, "If they left it to guys like Dom and me there wouldn't be any wars."

"Anyhow as long as there were guys like Pop around…" Dom kidded, his hand on the old man's shoulder.

Pop laughed. "Okay, no more wars."

Dom said wryly, "Watch that radical talk."

Pop got to his feet. "Well, enough Monday-morning quarterbacking, huh? Let's get this show on the road." The world is dead, long live the world. "Dom, how about crossing over those three rocks to the other side? It looks like a good place for lunch, and we ought to get a few more of these trout before we leave the river."

So Dom skipped from one boulder to the other across the lip of the pool; he found the footing okay and the others followed him. It wasn't until Dom had the net spread in the pool and Andy and Pop had a reluctant fire of reeds going that Andy asked shyly, "Say Dom, did you ever work building a dam, before?"

"No. I never worked but in the one plant."

"You, Pop?"

"Yeah, I did once." He didn't volunteer to go on.

"It must have been something."

"Like any other job, then. I was in construction work for several years when my kids were small: various buildings, one factory, and then this one dam. Oh, I guess it was more exciting than being a parking-lot attendant, but it was more dangerous too."

"Imagine building a dam or a factory."

"Yeah. Or trucks, eh Dom?"

"Trucks," said Dom, finding it ludicrous. "I was superman. Now nobody can make a truck." He pulled up the net, took out three good-sized trout, then spread the net again.

Andy jiggled the frying pan, which contained a couple of fish from this morning's catch and half a left-over can of baked beans. He said, "Well, some day…"

The old man began to sing:

> *Oh when I was a little lad*
> *With folly on my lips,*
> *Fain was I for journeying*
> *All the seas in ships;*
> *But now I cross the southern swell*
> *Every dawn I see*
> *The little streams of Doone are running free,*
> *The little streams of Doone are running free.*

Dom said, "Where do you get your songs, Pop?"

Andy wished the old man would sing some more. Andy didn't know many songs himself. He sang:

> *Waiting and wishing*
> *For the day when no more I'll roam;*
> *Waiting and wishing,*
> *For the day when I'm turning home —*

The words sounded phony, maybe because he'd heard them too often; he went on for a few lines just humming the wistful tune.

Pop absently sang a couple of the lines he'd left out:

> *Though we won't live*
> *In luxury,*

We'll be so happy,
Just you and me, when I'm through
Waiting and wishing —

The old man chuckled, nibbling the edge of a mint leaf he'd picked. "I knew the guy who wrote that."

"You knew him?"

"Not to talk to. He lived on the same street I did in Detroit (it was a long street), and we used to see him ride by in his Buick. After that song came out, we saw him ride by in his Cadillac. Hm. He also wrote "True to You Forever," and he divorced two wives. We all sang the songs."

"Well…it was a funny old world all right. But I'm not feeling picky. How about it, Dom? I'd give a lot to have it back, phonies and all."

Dom said very quietly, "You know I agree. Phonies, capitalists, and all."

"Yep. I'd take it back even if it had to be Hickman who gave it to me."

"If he would — you know I agree."

"Or," said Andy, "if it took a rescue expedition from Brazil. I even wish your Red invasion would show up to rescue us, Dom, even if it is a little behind schedule."

"No," said Dom, "it looks as if it's up to us." He roused himself with difficulty and pulled up the net again.

Andy came to himself a little too. He got up and went over to the water by the three boulders, to get a drink. He was still seeing the pool and the living day and responsibility through a misted pane of nostalgia. When he saw a man right beside him, standing in the gap in the dam, he spoke in innocent surprise: "How long have you been there?"

The man answered the same way, "I just got here."

It was the man with the squirrel gun who was perhaps not the same as the city kids but had read the same newspapers. He was wet to the knees from the spray of the rapids, but the gun was back in his hands and his blue eyes were the same as this morning.

The stranger recovered first. Without taking his eyes off Andy, he called down to the bottom of the concrete canyon, where he'd come from, "Stay back there till 1 give the word, fellows."

Andy couldn't see anybody down there. A bluff? or were there reinforcements? The stranger walked out beside the pool; Andy backed up. The stranger looked at the three of them and said, hardly opening his mouth, "I've been here long enough to hear those last couple of remarks."

(Now, let's see — what *had* they been saying?) He turned eyes and gun on Andy. "You're a Communist."

In a sudden delirium, Andy believed in the stranger's reinforcements. Ghosts of FBI men peered from behind rocks, ghosts of Loyalty Legionnaires marched on the hillside He whispered, "*No — not me.*"

The stranger's gun was on safety again! Andy saw it, and in a moment, in just a moment, he'd — but the stranger wasn't alone this time, he had his friends with him now.

"I got an idea you fellows are Communists like those six who came up from Lexington last winter."

This insanity drew the ghosts closer. "*Not me, stranger.*"

Eyes and gun swung to Dom. "How about you?"

"Look, friend," said an impossibly calm voice, "what difference does that Communist malarkey make now?"

Maybe he was going to go on to say something perfectly reasonable and convincing, maybe Pop had something to say, but Andy did not move and the stranger snapped the safety off and fired. Dom fell.

Andy cried, "No! No!" Andy roared, and wept, and threw the stranger into the pool, and using the rifle butt as a threat chased the stranger up onto the boulders and down the rapids. Andy shouted, killing the ghost army, "Move! Move! Go! Faster! Run!"

The stranger twisted and danced over the tumble of water. It caught him and flushed him out violently at the bottom. Andy watched him crawling stiffly out onto the bank down there, and shouted, pointing at the ruined dam, "*Your* fault — not ours!"

That was a pointless thing to say, he realized as the stranger disappeared. Was it even true?

He put his hand to his forehead. Blame! How could he blame anything on the fools who didn't know any better?

He climbed back out of the concrete canyon. Pop was washing the wound in Dom's side. He had taken their service revolver out of the pack and laid it beside him. Dom's face was screwed up in pain, so he must be conscious at least.

Andy stood there looking at him. Blame! Blame! Did it mean anything to call it the stranger's fault? There Dom was, and Andy could have saved him.

Andy said, "Dom counted on us."

The old man spoke soothingly; the tone was mostly for Dom, the words mostly for Andy: "That character just put one shot into the side of the waist here and out the back. That .22 wasn't made to kill a man in the first place. Dom should be all right." He turned toward Andy a bleak face, and Andy knew he was a long way from confident.

"Son, don't feel bad. Living is hard recently. Next time Dom will be wiser too. Do what you can now. Make sure that character is really gone, then come back, and we'll see about some bandages, also some lunch."

Do what you can now....

Andy would stick with Pop. They would save Dom. It would be hard; but Andy would be able to stand it, because he was already used to living on so many improbable hopes and so much guilt.

"Adrift on the Policy Level" was written in 1954. It first appeared, in a slightly altered version, in *Star Science Fiction Stories* in May 1959. The author's preferred version first appeared in *Above the Human Landscape: A Social Science Fiction Anthology*, eds. Willis E. McNelly, Leon E. Stover (Goodyear Publishing, 1972).

ADRIFT ON THE POLICY LEVEL

I

J. ALBERT LARUE was nervous, but you couldn't blame him. It was his big day. He looked up for reassurance at the burly bass-voiced man sitting so stolidly next to him in the hissing subway car, and found what he sought.

There was plenty of reassurance in having a man like Calvin Boersma on your side.

Albert declared mildly but firmly: "One single thought is uppermost in my mind."

Boersma inclined his ear. "What?"

"Oxidase epsilon!" cried Albert.

Cal Boersma clapped him on the shoulder and answered, like a fight manager rushing last-minute strategies to his boxer: "The one single thought that *should* be uppermost in your mind is selling oxidase epsilon. Nothing will be done unless The Corporation is sold on it. And when you deal with Corporation executives you're dealing with experts."

LaRue thought that over, swaying to the motion of the car. "We do have something genuinely important to sell, don't we?" he ventured. He had been studying oxidase epsilon for three years. Boersma, on the other hand, was involved in the matter only because he was LaRue's lab assistant's brother-in-law, an assistant sales manager of a plastic firm…and the only businessman LaRue knew.

Still, today — the big day — Cal Boersma was the expert. The promoter. The man who was right in the thick of the hard, practical world outside the University's cloistered halls — the world that terrified J. Albert LaRue.

Cal was all reassurance. "Oxidase epsilon is important, all right. That's the only reason we have a chance."

Their subway car gave a long, loud whoosh, followed by a shrill hissing. They were at their station. J. Albert LaRue felt a twinge of apprehension. This, he told himself, was it! They joined the file of passengers leaving the car for the luxurious escalator.

"Yes, Albert," Cal rumbled, as they rode up side by side, "we have something big here, if we can reach the top men — say, the Regional Director. Why, Albert, this could get you an assistant section managership in The Corporation itself!"

"Oh, thank you! But of course I wouldn't want — I mean, my devotion to research —" Albert was flustered.

"But of course I could take care of that end of it for you," Boersma said reassuringly. "Well, here we are, Albert."

The escalator fed them into a sunlit square between twenty-story buildings. A blindingly green mall crossed the square to the Regional Executive Building of The Corporation. Albert could not help being awed. It was a truly impressive structure — a block wide, only three stories high.

Cal said, in a reverent growl: "Putting up a building like that in the most heavily taxed area of Detroit — you know what that symbolizes, Albert? Power. Power and salesmanship! That's what you're dealing with when you deal with The Corporation."

The building was the hub of the Lakes Region, and the architecture was appropriately monumental. Albert murmured a comment, impressed. Cal agreed. "Superbly styled," he said solemnly.

Glass doors extending the full height of the building opened smoothly at the touch of Albert's hand. Straight ahead across the cool lobby another set of glass doors, equally tall, were a showcase for dramatic exhibits of The Corporation's activities. Soothing lights rippled through an enchanted twilight. Glowing letters said, "Museum of Progress."

Several families on holiday wandered delighted among the exhibits, basking in the highest salesmanship the race had produced.

Albert started automatically in that direction. Cal's hand on his arm stopped him. "This way, Albert. The corridor to the right."

"Huh? But — I thought you said you couldn't get an appointment, and have to follow the same channels as any member of the public." Certainly the "public" was the delighted wanderer through those gorgeous glass doors.

"Oh, sure, that's what we're doing. But I didn't mean *that* public."

"Oh." Apparently the Museum was only for the herd. Albert humbly followed Cal (not without a backward glance) to the relatively unobtrusive door at the end of the lobby — the initiates' secret passage to power, he thought with deep reverence.

But he noticed that three or four new people just entering the building were turning the same way.

A waiting room. But it was not a disappointing one; evidently Cal had directed them right; they had passed to a higher circle. The room was large, yet it looked like a sanctum.

Albert had never seen chairs like these. All of the twenty-five or so men and women who were there ahead of them were distinctly better dressed than Albert. On the other hand Cal's suit — a one-piece woolly buff-colored outfit, fashionably loose at the elbows and knees — was a match for any of them. Albert took pride in that.

Albert sat and fidgeted. Cal's bass voice gently reminded him that fidgeting would be fatal, then rehearsed him in his approach. He was to be, basically, a professor of plant metabolism; it was a poor approach, Cal conceded regretfully, but the only one Albert was qualified to make. Salesmanship he was to leave to Cal; his own appeal was to be based on his position — such as it was — as a scientific expert; therefore he was to be, basically, himself. His success in projecting the role might possibly be decisive — although the main responsibility, Cal pointed out, was Cal's.

While Cal talked, Albert fidgeted and watched the room. The lush chairs, irregularly placed, still managed all to face one wall, and in that wall were three plain doors. From time to time an attendant would appear to call one of the waiting supplicants to one of the doors. The attendants were liveried young men with flowing black hair. Finally, one came their way! He summoned them with a bow—an eye-flashing, head-tossing, flourishing bow, like a dancer rather than a butler.

Albert followed Cal to the door. "Will this be a junior executive? A personal secretary? A—"

But Cal seemed not to hear.

Albert followed Cal through the door and saw the most beautiful girl in the world.

He couldn't look at her, not by a long way. She was much too beautiful for that. But he knew exactly what she looked like. He could see in his mind her shining, ringleted hair falling gently to her naked shoulders, her dazzling bright expressionless face. He couldn't even think about her body; it was terrifying.

She sat behind a desk and looked at them. Cal struck a masterful pose, his arms folded. "We have come on a scientific matter," he said haughtily, "not familiar to The Corporation, concerning several northern colonial areas."

She wrote deliberately on a small plain pad. Tonelessly, sweetly, she asked, "Your name?"

"Calvin Boersma."

Her veiled eyes swung to Albert. He couldn't possibly speak. His whole consciousness was occupied in not looking at her.

Cal said sonorously: "This is J. Albert LaRue, Professor of Plant Metabolism." Albert was positively proud of his name, the way Cal said it.

The most beautiful girl in the world whispered meltingly: "Go out this door and down the corridor to Mr. Blick's office. He'll be expecting you."

Albert chose this moment to try to look at her. And *she smiled*! Albert, completely routed, rushed to the door. He was grateful she hadn't done *that* before! Cal, with his greater experience and higher position in life, could linger a moment, leaning on the desk, to leer at her.

But all the same, when they reached the corridor, he was sweating.

Albert said carefully, "*She* wasn't an executive, was she?"

"No," said Cal, a little scornfully. "She's an Agency Model, what else? Of course, you probably don't see them much at the University, except at the Corporation Representative's Office and maybe the President's Office." Albert had never been near either. "She doesn't have much to do except to impress visitors, and of course stop the ones that don't belong here."

Albert hesitated. "She *was* impressive."

"She's impressive, all right," Cal agreed. "When you consider the Agency rates, and then realize that any member of the public who comes to the Regional Executive Building on business sees an Agency Model receptionist—then you know you're dealing with power, Albert."

Albert had a sudden idea. He ventured: "Would we have done better to have brought an Agency Model with us?"

Cal stared. "To go through the whole afternoon with us? Impossible, Albert! It'd cost you a year's salary."

Albert said eagerly: "No, that's the beauty of it, Cal! You see, I have a young cousin — I haven't seen her recently, of course, but she was drafted by the Agency, and I might have been able to get her to —" He faltered. Boersma was looking scandalized.

"Albert — excuse me. If your cousin had so much as walked into any business office with makeup on, she'd have had to collect Agency rates — or she'd have been out of the Agency like that. And owing them plenty." He finished consolingly, "A Model wouldn't have done the trick anyway."

II

Mr. Blick looked more like a scientist than a businessman, and his desk was a bit of a laboratory. At his left hand was an elaborate switchboard, curved so all parts would be in easy reach; most of the switches were in rows, the handles color-coded. As he nodded Cal to a seat his fingers flicked over three switches. The earphones and microphone clamped on his head had several switches too, and his right hand quivered beside a stenotype machine of unfamiliar complexity.

He spoke in an undertone into his mike, then his hand whizzed almost invisibly over the stenotype.

"Hello, Mr. Boersma," he said, flicking one last switch but not removing the earphones. "Please excuse my idiosyncrasies, it seems I actually work better this way." His voice was firm, resonant, and persuasive.

Cal took over again. He opened with a round compliment for Mr. Blick's battery of gadgets, and then flowed smoothly on to an even more glowing series of compliments—which Albert realized with a qualm of embarrassment referred to *him*.

After the first minute or so, though, Albert found the talk less interesting than the interruptions. Mr. Blick would raise a forefinger apologetically but fast; switches would tumble; he would listen to the earphones, whisper into the mike, and perform incredibly on the absolutely silent stenotype. Shifting lights touched his face, and Albert realized the desk top contained at least one TV screen, as well as a bank of blinking colored lights. The moment the interruption was disposed of, Mr. Blick's faultless diction and pleasant voice would return Cal exactly to where he'd been. Albert was impressed.

Cal's peroration was an urgent appeal that Mr. Blick consider the importance to The Corporation, financially, of what he was about to learn. Then he turned to Albert, a little too abruptly.

"One single thought is uppermost in my mind," Albert stuttered, caught off guard. "Oxidase epsilon. I am resolved that The Corporation shall be made to see the importance—"

"Just a moment, Professor LaRue," came Mr. Blick's smooth Corporation voice. "You'll have to explain this to *me*. I don't have the background or the brains that you people in the academic line have. Now in layman's terms, just what *is* oxidase epsilon?" He grinned handsomely.

"Oh, don't feel bad," said Albert hastily. "Lots of my colleagues haven't heard of it, either." This was only a half-truth. Every one of his colleagues that Albert met at the University in a normal working month had certainly heard of oxidase epsilon—from Albert. "It's an enzyme found in many plants but recognized only recently. You see, many of the laboratory species created during the last few decades have been unable to produce ordinary oxidase, or oxidase alpha, but surprisingly enough some of these have survived. This is due to the presence of a series of related compounds, of which oxidases beta, gamma, delta, and epsilon have been isolated, and beta and epsilon have been prepared in the laboratory."

Mr. Blick shifted uncertainly in his seat. Albert hurried on so he would see how simple it all was. "I have been studying the reactions catalyzed by oxidase epsilon in several species of *Triticum*. I found quite unexpectedly that none of them produce the enzyme themselves. Amazing, isn't it? All the oxidase epsilon in those plants comes from a fungus, *Puccinia triticina*, which infects them. This, of course, explains the failure of Hinshaw's group to produce viable *Triticum kaci* following—"

Mr. Blick smiled handsomely again. "Well now, Professor LaRue, you'll have to tell me what this means. In my terms—you understand."

Cal boomed portentously, "It may mean the saving of the economies of three of The Corporation's richest colonies." Rather dramatic, Albert thought.

Mr. Blick said appreciatively, "Very good. Very good. Tell me more. Which colonies—and why?" His right hand left its crouch to spring restlessly to the stenotype.

Albert resumed. buoyed by this flattering show of interest. "West Lapland in Europe, and Great Slave and Churchill on this continent. They're all Corporation colonies, recently opened up for wheat-growing by *Triticum witti*. and I've been told they're extremely productive."

"Who is Triticum Witti?"

Albert, shocked, explained patiently, "*Triticum witti* is one of the new species of wheat which depend on oxidase epsilon. And if the fungus *Puccinia triticina* on that wheat becomes a pest, sprays may be used to get rid of it. And a whole year's wheat crop in those colonies may be destroyed."

"Destroyed," Mr. Blick repeated wonderingly. His forefinger silenced Albert like a conductor's baton; then both his hands danced over keys and switches, and he was muttering into his microphone again.

Another interruption, thought Albert. He felt proper reverence for the undoubted importance of whatever Mr. Blick was settling, still, he was bothered a little, too. Actually (he remembered suddenly) he had a reason to be so presumptuous: oxidase epsilon was important, too. Over five hundred million dollars had gone into those three colonies already, and no doubt a good many people.

However, it turned out this particular interruption must have been devoted to West Lapland, Great Slave, and Churchill after all. Mr. Blick abandoned his instrument panel and announced his congratulations to them: "Mr. Boersma, the decision has been made to assign an expediter to your case!" And he smiled heartily.

This was a high point for Albert.

He wasn't sure he knew what an expediter was, but he was sure from Mr. Blick's manner that an unparalleled honor had been given him. It almost made him dizzy to think of all this glittering building, all the attendants and Models and executives, bowing to him, as Mr. Blick's manner implied they must.

A red light flicked on and off on Mr. Blick's desk. As he turned to it he said, "Excuse me, gentlemen." Of course, Albert pardoned him mentally, you have to work.

He whispered to Cal, "Well, I guess we're doing pretty well."

"Huh? Oh, yes, very well," Cal whispered back. "So far."

"So far? Doesn't Mr. Blick understand the problem? All we have to do is give him the details now."

"Oh, no, Albert! I'm sure *he* can't make the decision. He'll have to send us to someone higher up."

"Higher up? Why? Do we have to explain it all over again?"

Cal turned in his chair so he could whisper to Albert less conspicuously. "Albert, an enterprise the size of The Corporation can't give consideration to every crackpot suggestion anyone tries to sell it. There have to be regular channels. Now the Plant Metabolism Department doesn't have any connections here (maybe we can do something about that), so we have to run a sort of obstacle course. It's survival of the fittest, Albert! Only the most worthwhile survive to sec the Regional Director. Of course the Regional Director elects which of those to accept, but he doesn't have to sift through a lot of crackpot propositions."

Albert could see the analogy to natural selection. Still, he asked humbly: "How do you know the best suggestions get through? Doesn't it depend a lot on how good a salesman is handling them?"

"Very much so. Naturally!"

"But then — Suppose, for instance, I hadn't happened to know you. My good idea wouldn't have got past Mr. Blick."

"It wouldn't have got past the Model," Cal corrected. "Maybe not that far. But you see in that case it wouldn't have been a very important idea, because it wouldn't have been *put into effect*." He said it with a very firm, practical jaw line. "Unless of course someone else had had the initiative and resourcefulness to present the same idea better. Do you see now? *Really important ideas attract the sales talent to put them across*."

Albert didn't understand the reasoning, he had to admit. It was such an important point, and he was missing it. He reminded himself humbly that a scientist is no expert outside his own field.

So all Mr. Blick had been telling them was that they had not yet been turned down. Albert's disappointment was sharp.

Still, he was curious. How had such a trivial announcement given him such euphoria? Could you produce that kind of effect just by your delivery? Mr. Blick could, apparently. The architecture, the Model, and all the rest had been build-up for him; and certainly they had helped the effect; but they didn't explain it.

What was the key? *Personality*, Albert realized. This was what businessmen meant by their technical term "personality." Personality was the asset Mr. Blick had exploited to rise to where he was—rather than becoming, say, a scientist.

The Blicks and Boersmas worked hard at it. Wistfully, Albert wondered how it was done. Of course the experts in this field didn't publish their results, and anyhow he had never studied it. But it was the most important field of human culture, for on it hinged the policy decisions of government—even of The Corporation!

He couldn't estimate whether Cal was as good as Mr. Blick, because he assumed Cal had never put forth a big effort on him, Albert. He wasn't worth it.

He had one other question for Cal. "What is an expediter?"

"Oh, I thought you knew," boomed Cal. "They can be a big help. That's why we're doing well to be assigned one. We're going to get into the top levels, Albert, where only a salesman of true merit can hope to put across an idea. An expediter can do it if anyone can. The expediters are too young to hold Key Executive Positions, but they're Men On The Way Up. They—"

Mr. Blick turned his head toward a door on his left, putting the force of his personality behind the gesture. "Mr. Demarest," he announced as the expediter walked into the room.

III

Mr. Demarest had captivating red curly sideburns, striking brown eyes, and a one-piece coverall in a somewhat loud pattern of black and beige. He almost trembled with excess energy. It was contagious; it made you feel as if you were as abnormally fit as he was.

He grinned his welcome at Albert and Cal, and chuckled merrily: "How do you do, Mr. Boersma."

It was as if Mr. Blick had been turned off. Albert hardly knew he was still in the room. Clearly Mr. Demarest was a Man On The Way Up indeed.

They rose and left the room with him to a new corridor, very different from the last: weirdly lighted from a strip two feet above the floor, and lined with abstract statuary.

This, together with Mr. Demarest, made a formidable challenge.

Albert rose to it recklessly. "Oxidase epsilon," he proclaimed, "may mean the saving of three of The Corporation's richest colonies!"

Mr. Demarest responded with enthusiasm. "I agree one hundred per cent — our Corporation's crop of *Triticum witti* must be saved! Mr. Blick sent me a playback of your explanation by interoffice tube, Professor LaRue. You've got me on your side one hundred per cent! I want to assure you both, very sincerely, that I'll do my utmost to sell Mr. Southfield. Professor, you be ready to fill in the details when I'm through with what I know."

There was no slightest condescension or reservation in his voice. He would take care of things, Albert knew. What a relief!

Cal came booming in: "Your Mr. Blick seems like a competent man."

What a way to talk about a Corporation executive! Albert decided it was not just a simple faux pas, though. Apparently Cal had decided he had to be accepted by Mr. Demarest as an equal, and this was his opening. It seemed risky to Albert. In fact, it frightened him.

"There's just one thing, now, about your Mr. Blick," Cal was saying to Mr. Demarest, with a tiny wink that Albert was proud of having spotted. "I couldn't help wondering how he manages to find so much to do with those switches of his." Albert barely restrained a groan.

But Mr. Demarest grinned! "Frankly, Cal," he answered, "I'm not just sure how many of old Blick's switches are dummies."

Cal had succeeded! That was the main content of Mr. Demarest's remark.

But *were* Mr. Blick's switches dummies? Things were much simpler back — way back — at the University, where people said what they meant.

They were near the end of the corridor. Mr. Demarest said softly, "Mr. Southfield's Office." Clearly Mr. Southfield's presence was enough to curb even Mr. Demarest's boyishness.

They turned through an archway into a large room, lighted like the corridor, with statuary wilder still. Mr. Southfield was at one side, studying papers in a vast easy chair: an elderly man, fantastically dressed but with a surprisingly ordinary face peeping over the crystal ruff on his magenta leotards. He ignored them. Mr. Demarest made it clear they were supposed to wait until they were called on.

Cal and Albert chose two of the bed-sized chairs facing Mr. Southfield, and waited expectantly.

Mr. Demarest whispered, "I'll be back in time to make the first presentation. Last-minute brush-up, you know." He grinned and clapped Cal smartly on the shoulder. Albert was relieved that he didn't do the same to him but just shook his hand before leaving. It would have been too upsetting.

Albert sank back in his chair, tired from all he'd been through and relaxed by the soft lights.

It was the most comfortable chair he'd ever been in. It was more than comfortable, it was a deliciously irresistible invitation to relax completely. Albert was barely awake enough to notice that the chair was rocking him gently, tenderly massaging his neck and back.

He lay there, ecstatic. He didn't quite go to sleep. If the chair had been designed just a little differently, no doubt, it could have put him to sleep, but this one just let him rest carefree and mindless.

Cal spoke (and even Cal's quiet bass sounded harsh and urgent): "Sit up straighter, Albert!"

"Why?"

"Albert, any sales resistance you started with is going to be completely gone if you don't sit up enough to shut off that chair!"

"Sales resistance?" Albert pondered comfortably. "What have we got to worry about? Mr. Demarest is on our side, isn't he?"

"Mr. Demarest," Cal pointed out, "is *not* the Regional Director."

So they still might have problems! So the marvelous chair was just another trap where the unfit got lost! Albert resolved to himself: "From now on, one single thought will be uppermost in my mind: defending my sales resistance."

He repeated this to himself.

He repeated it again.…

"Albert!" There was genuine panic in Cal's voice now.

A fine way to defend his sales resistance! He had let the chair get him again. Regretfully he shifted his weight forward, reaching for the arms of the chair.

"*Watch it!*" said Cal. "Okay now, but don't use the arms. Just lean yourself forward. There." He explained, "The surface on the arms is rough and moist, and I can't think of any reason it should be — unless it's to give you narcotic through the skin! Tiny amounts, of course. But we can't afford any. First time I've ever seen that one in actual use," he admitted.

Albert was astonished, and in a moment he was more so. "Mr. Southfield's chair is the same as ours, and he's leaning back in it. Why, he's even stroking the arm while he reads!"

"I know." Cal shook his head. "Remarkable man, isn't he? Remarkable. Remember this, Albert. The true salesman, the man on the very pinnacle of achievement, is also — a connoisseur. Mr. Southfield is a connoisseur. He wants to be presented with the most powerful appeals known, for the sake of the pleasure he gets from the appeal itself. Albert, there is a strong strain of the sensuous, the self-indulgent, in every really successful man like Mr. Southfield. Why? Because to be successful he must have the most profound understanding of self-indulgence."

Albert noticed in passing that, just the same, Cal wasn't self-indulgent enough to trust himself to that chair. He didn't even make a show of doing so. Clearly in Mr. Southfield they had met somebody far above Cal's level. It was unnerving. Oxidase epsilon seemed a terribly feeble straw to outweigh such a disadvantage.

Cal went on, "This is another reason for the institution of expediters. The top executive can't work surrounded by inferior salesmanship. He needs the stimulus and the luxury of receiving his data well packaged. The expediters can do it." He leaned over confidentially. "I've heard them called backscratchers for that reason," he whispered.

Albert was flattered that Cal admitted him to this trade joke.

Mr. Southfield looked up at the archway as someone came in—not Mr. Demarest, but a black-haired young woman. Albert looked inquiringly at Cal.

"Just a minute. I'll soon know who she is." She stood facing Mr. Southfield, against the wall opposite Albert and Cal. Mr. Southfield said in a drowsy half-whisper, "Yes, Miss Drury, the ore-distribution pattern. Go on."

"She must be another expediter, on some other matter," Cal decided. "Watch her work, Albert, You won't get an opportunity like this often."

Albert studied her. She was not at all like an Agency Model; she was older than most of them (about thirty); she was fully dressed, in a rather sober black and gray business suit, snug around the hips; and she wasn't wearing makeup. She couldn't be even an ex-Model, she wasn't the type. Heavier in build, for one thing, and though she was very pretty it wasn't that unhuman blinding beauty. On the contrary. Albert enjoyed looking at her (even lacking Mr. Southfield's connoisseurship). He found Miss Drury's warm dark eyes and confident posture very pleasant and relaxing.

She began to talk, gently and musically, something about how to compute the most efficient routing of metallic ore traffic in the Great Lakes Region. Her voice became a chant, rising and falling, but with a little catch in it now and then. Lovely!

Her main device, though, sort of sneaked up on him, the way the chair had. It had been going on for some time before Albert was conscious of it. It was like the chair.

Miss Drury moved.

Her hips swung. Only a centimeter each way, but very, very sensuously. You could follow the motion in detail, because her dress was more than merely snug around the hips, you could see every muscle on her belly. The motion seemed entirely spontaneous, but Albert knew she must have worked hard on it.

The knowledge, however, didn't spoil his enjoyment.

"Gee," he marveled to Cal, "how can Mr. Southfield hear what she's saying?"

"Huh? Oh—she lowers her voice from time to time on purpose so we won't overhear Corporation secrets, but he's much nearer her than we are."

"That's not what I mean!"

"You mean why doesn't her delivery distract him from the message? Albert," Boersma said wisely, "if you were sitting in his chair you'd be getting the message, too—with crushing force. A superior presentation always directs attention to the message. But in Mr. Southfield's case it actually

185

stimulates critical consideration as well! Remarkable man. An expert and a connoisseur."

Meanwhile Albert saw that Miss Drury had finished. Maybe she would stay and discuss her report with Mr. Southfield? No, after just a few words he dismissed her.

IV

In a few minutes the glow caused by Miss Drury had changed to a glow of excited pride.

Here was he, plain old Professor LaRue, witnessing the drama of the nerve center of the Lakes Region—the interplay of titanic personalities, deciding the fate of millions. Why, he was even going to be involved in one of the decisions! He hoped the next expediter to see Mr. Southfield would be Mr. Demarest!

Something bothered him. "Cal, how can Mr. Demarest possibly be as—well-persuasive as Miss Drury? I mean—"

"Now, Albert, you leave that to him. Sex is not the only possible vehicle. Experts can make strong appeals to the weakest and subtlest of human drives—even altruism! Oh yes, I know it's surprising to the layman, but even altruism can be useful."

"Really?" Albert was grateful for every tidbit. "Real masters will sometimes prefer such a method out of sheer virtuosity," whispered Cal.

Mr. Southfield stirred a little in his chair, and Albert snapped to total alertness.

Sure enough, it was Mr. Demarest who came through the archway.

Certainly his entrance was no letdown. He strode in even more eagerly than he had into Mr. Blick's office. His costume glittered, his brown eyes glowed. He stood against the wall beyond Mr. Southfield; not quite straight, but with a slight wrestler's crouch. A taut spring.

He gave Albert and Cal only half a second's glance, but that glance was a tingling communication of comradeship and joy of battle. Albert felt himself a participant in something heroic.

Mr. Demarest began releasing all that energy slowly. He gave the background of West Lapland, Great Slave, and Churchill. Maps were flashed on the wall beside him (exactly how, Albert didn't follow), and the drama of arctic colonization was recreated by Mr. Demarest's sportscaster's voice. Albert would have thought Mr. Demarest was the overmodest hero of each project if he hadn't known all three had been done simultaneously. No, it was hard to believe, but all these vivid facts must have been served to Mr. Demarest by some research flunky within the last few minutes. And yet, how he had transfigured them!

The stirring narrative was reaching Mr. Southfield, too. He had actually sat up out of the easy chair.

Mr. Demarest's voice, like Miss Drury's, dropped in volume now and then. Albert and Cal were just a few feet too far away to overhear Corporation secrets. As the saga advanced, Mr. Demarest changed from Viking to Roman. His voice, by beautifully controlled stages, became bubbling and hedonistic. Now, he was talking about grandiose planned expansions—and, best of all, about how much money The Corporation expected to make from the three colonies. The figures drooled through loose lips. He clapped Mr. Southfield on the shoulder. He stroked Mr. Southfield's arm; when he came to the estimated trade balances, he tickled his neck. Mr. Southfield showed his appreciation of change in mood by lying back in his chair again.

This didn't stop Mr. Demarest.

It seemed almost obscene. Albert covered his embarrassment by whispering, "I see why they call them backscratchers."

Cal frowned, waved him silent, and went on watching.

Suddenly Mr. Demarest's tone changed again: it became bleak, bitter, desperate. A threat to the calculated return on The Corporation's investment — even to the capital investment itself!

Mr. Southfield sat forward attentively to hear about this danger. Was that good? He hadn't done that with Miss Drury.

What Mr. Demarest said about the danger was, of course, essentially what Albert had told Mr. Blick, but Albert realized that it sounded a lot more frightening Mr. Demarest's way. When he was through, Albert felt physically chilly. Mr. Southfield sat saying nothing. What was he thinking? Could he fail to see the tragedy that threatened?

After a moment he nodded and said, "Nice presentation." He hadn't said that to Miss Drury, Albert exulted!

Mr. Demarest looked dedicated.

Mr. Southfield turned his whole body to face Albert, and looked him straight in the eyes. Albert was too alarmed to look away. Mr. Southfield's formerly ordinary jaw now jutted. His chest swelled imposingly. "*You*, I understand, are a well-informed worker on plant metabolism." His voice seemed to grow too, until it rolled in on Albert from all sides of the room. "Is it *your* opinion that the danger is great enough to justify taking up the time of the Regional Director?"

It wasn't fair. Mr. Southfield against J. Albert LaRue was a ridiculous mismatch anyway! And now Albert was taken by surprise — after too long a stretch as an inactive spectator — and hit with the suggestion that he had been *wasting Mr. Southfield's time*…that his proposition was not only not worth acting on, it was *a waste of the Regional Director's time*.

Albert struggled to speak.

Surely, after praising Mr. Demarest's presentation, Mr. Southfield would be lenient; he would take into account Albert's limited background; he wouldn't expect too much. Albert struggled to say anything.

He couldn't open his mouth.

As he sat staring at Mr. Southfield, he could feel his own shoulders drawing inward and all his muscles going limp.

Cal said, in almost a normal voice, "Yes."

That was enough. just barely. Albert whispered, "Yes," terrified at having found the courage.

Mr. Southfield glared down at him a moment more.

Then he said, "Very well, you may see the Regional Director. Mr. Demarest, take them there."

Albert followed Mr. Demarest blindly. His entire attention was concentrated on recovering from Mr. Southfield.

He had been one up, thanks to Mr. Demarest. Now, how could he have stayed one up? How should he have resisted Mr. Southfield's dizzying display of personality?

He played the episode back mentally over and over, trying to correct it to run as it should have. Finally he succeeded, at least in his mind. He saw what his attitude should have been. He should have kept his shoulders squared and his vocal cords loose, and faced Mr. Southfield confidently. Now he saw how to do it.

He walked erectly and firmly behind Mr. Demarest, and allowed a haughty half-smile to play on his lips.

He felt armed to face Mr. Southfield all by himself—or, since it seemed Mr. Southfield was not the Regional Director after all, even to face the Regional Director!

They stopped in front of a large double door guarded by an absolutely motionless man with a gun.

"Men," said Mr. Demarest with cheerful innocence, "I wish you luck. I wish you all the luck in the world."

Cal looked suddenly stricken but said, with casualness that didn't fool even Albert, "Wouldn't you like to come in with us?"

"Oh, no. Mr. Southfield told me only to bring you here. I'd be overstepping my bounds if I did any more. But all the good luck in the world, men!"

Cal said hearty goodbyes. But when he turned back to Albert he said, despairing: "The brushoff."

Albert could hardly take it in. "But—we get to make our presentation to the Regional Director, don't we?"

Boersma shrugged hopelessly, "Don't you see, Albert? Our presentation won't be good enough, without Demarest. When Mr. Southfield sent us on alone he was giving us the brushoff."

"Cal—are you going to back out too?"

"I should say not! It's a feather in our cap to have got this far, Albert. We have to follow up just as far as our abilities will take us!"

Albert went to the double door. He worried about the armed guard for a moment, but they weren't challenged. The guard hadn't even blinked, in fact.

Albert asked Cal, "Then we do still have a chance?"

He started to push the door open, then hesitated again. "But you'll do your best?"

"I should say so! You don't get to present a proposition to the Regional Director every day."

With determination, Albert drew himself even straighter, and prepared himself to meet an onslaught twice as overbearing as Mr. Southfield's. One single thought was uppermost in his mind: defending his sales resistance. He felt inches taller than before; he even slightly looked down at Cal and his pessimism.

Cal pushed the door open and they went in.

The Regional Director sat alone in a straight chair, at a plain desk in a very plain office about the size of most offices.

The Regional Director was a woman.

She was dressed about as any businesswoman might dress; as conservatively as Miss Drury. As a matter of fact, she looked like Miss Drury, fifteen years older. Certainly she had the same black hair and gentle oval face.

What a surprise! A pleasant surprise. Albert felt still bigger and more confident than he had outside. He would certainly get on well with this motherly, unthreatening person!

She was reading from a small microfilm viewer on an otherwise bare desk. Obviously she had only a little to do before she would be free. Albert patiently watched her read. She read very conscientiously, that was clear.

After a moment she glanced up at them briefly, with an apologetic smile, then down again. Her shy dark eyes showed so much! You could see how sincerely she welcomed them, and how sorry she was that she had so much work to do—how much she would prefer to be talking with them. Albert pitied her. From the bottom of his heart, he pitied her. Why, that small microfilm viewer, he realized, could perfectly well contain volumes of complicated Corporation reports. Poor woman! The poor woman who happened to be Regional Director read on.

Once in a while she passed one hand, wearily but determinedly, across her face. There was a slight droop to her shoulders. Albert pitied her more all the time. She was not too strong—she had such a big job—and she was so courageously trying to do her best with all those reports in the viewer!

Finally she raised her head.

It was clear she was not through; there was no relief on her face. But she raised her head to them.

Her affection covered them like a warm bath. Albert realized he was in a position to do the kindest thing he had ever done. He felt growing in himself the resolution to do it. He would!

He started toward the door.

Before he left she met his eyes once more, and her smile showed such appreciation for his understanding!

Albert felt there could be no greater reward.

Out in the park again he realized for the first time that Cal was right behind him.

They looked at each other for a long time.

Then Cal started walking again, toward the subway. "The brushoff," he said.

"I thought you said you'd do your best," said Albert. But he knew that Cal's "I did" was the truth.

They walked on slowly. Cal said, "Remarkable woman.... A real master. Sheer virtuosity!"

Albert said, "Our society certainly rewards its most deserving members."

That one single thought was uppermost in his mind, all the long way home.

"It Walks in Beauty" was written, under the title "The Star System," in 1954. A substantially different version, under the current title, was published in *Star Science Fiction* in January 1958: editor Frederik Pohl, without telling Davis, dramatically altered the story, changing its humane tone to one of misanthropic irony. In mid-2003, Josh Lukin noticed that legendary sf editor Ellen Datlow had announced the story's republication on the now-defunct website SCIFICTION. Lukin immediately alerted Davis to the fact, and sought out Datlow's contact information for him, so that he could assure that the preferred version was republished. Hence the author's original version first appeared on SCIFICTION in September 2003 and has been bootlegged elsewhere on the Internet. This volume marks its first print publication.

It Walks in Beauty

"I LOVE LUANA," said Max dreamily, leaning against the ladder that ran up the towering vat of Number 73.

Jim heard him and came over. "I love Luana, too," he said.

Max looked up, delighted. "You, too?" Jim nodded. If Jim had disagreed with him, Max would have cheerfully defended Luana all day, but it was even more fun for his friend to understand already. "That Luana," said Max, shaking his head in wonder at the strength of his own devotion.

"She's some kid," Jim seconded, shaking his head the same way. "That kid was made for loving, and does she know it!"

"That's the most important thing about a woman," Max assured him seriously. "She should want to be loved. With all her being she should welcome all the passion a man has to give." Max had never understood this before, because Luana was his first real love.

"That's right," said Jim, "and Luana fills that bill with plenty to spare."

They both chuckled gloatingly. Max hooked an elbow over a ladder rung, Jim sat on the bench in front of the indicator strip, and they got comfortable for a thorough listing of Luana's attractions. Luana's little scarlet mouth, Luana's mincing shoulders, Luana's little stretch and yawn, presenting her breasts — oh, yes, Luana's breasts, very important! They went through all these features, stopping to appreciate each one in detail, shaking their heads, grinning, and grunting: "Mm, mm."

They had got to Luana's snake-hips walk when the alarm had to go off on Number 71. Loud, unmusical, quickly-damped *bink bink bink*. Jim shrugged to his feet and walked down to 71, turning off the alarm. Max looked over his shoulder.

There were 144 tiny strands of synthetic protein fiber being extruded from jets at the bottom of each vat, solidifying as they hit the salt bath. While they shot fiber downward, the jets circled horizontally, twisting strands in sixes, then six sixes together, so that altogether from 144 strands came four ropes — threads, rather, of lanon, humming away down through the floor, driven by the friction of a series of delicate little rollers at the highest speed and tension they were likely to be able to take.

At Number 71 one of them had failed to take it. It had broken. A delicate little roller had sprung up a few millimeters with the release of tension, and before the upswing was completed electronic relays had triggered emergency measures: one circle of jets had stopped circling or extruding, so that now only 108 strands streamed from Number 71; wheels driving the snapped thread through tank after tank below them had adjusted their tension to guide the tag end through; the alarm bell had rung for Jim.

Jim checked the indicator strip. It showed nothing, so the trouble must be in the jets themselves. Jim drained off the bath around the stopped circle and reached in with a pair of needle-nosed tongs and a brilliant flashlight pointing at a 45° mirror, to find which of the jets had failed.

Max left. He was embarrassed about showing unnecessary interest in the lanon spinners in front of Jim.

He strolled down to Number 78, the end of their row, checking indicator strips. At the end of the row he looked both ways. Harriet happened to be doing the same at the end of the row next to his; they waved casually.

Max sat down in front of Number 73. He wanted Jim to finish with Number 71 so they could go on talking about Luana. It was the next best thing to seeing Luana herself. Jim was older than he was, two pay classifications higher, and a lot more experienced. Talking to Jim strengthened his confidence that Luana was the sexiest woman in the world, and that what he felt was genuine adult love.

When 71 was going again, Max asked first, "What was wrong?"

Of course Jim didn't answer, just pretended to spit behind him. He sat in the same place he'd been in before and squinted at Max. "So, young Max has started seeing Luana's show, has he?"

Max was stung. "*Started?* I've been there every night for a long time."

"I haven't seen you there."

"Say, that's right — I haven't seen *you* there more than twice. How long have *you* been going?"

"Off and on for —"

"Off and on!" exclaimed Max. "I don't go off and on! I go every night. I don't see how you can stand to go to any other dancer when you could be seeing Luana. For five weeks I've even been sitting up front. Man, I'm really hooked."

"I sat up front there for the first time last night," Jim admitted. "But I always enjoyed Luana. I've been seeing her off and on for longer than you've been at Lanon."

Max was not impressed. He kept his scorn to himself. Imagine seeing Luana for over a year before you fell in love with her! It had taken *him* only a few weeks before he was sure, and since then his loyalty had been absolute. He just said, "Anyway, you're going tonight, huh?"

"And how. Like to go down together? I'll meet you after dinner."

Max was flattered. "Sure enough." But he should tell Jim about his other plan. That wouldn't be easy. He might not even have made the other plan if he'd known Jim loved Luana. He hesitated.

Jim went on, "Am I going tonight, he asks. I'm just as hooked as you are, now. I'm not going to miss any chances to see that kid. Boy, would I like to —" He said what he'd like to do to Luana.

Max said that he would like to, too.

Jim began whistling. Max couldn't hear the tune above the hum of the spinners; neither could Jim, but it broke up the talk.

Max checked the indicator strips again. He stopped at Number 77.

The smooth column called simply "vat" concealed a continuous-flow protein-synthesis process in complex convolutions of tubing. The contents were sampled and analyzed continuously and automatically; the results were transmitted to the indicator strips, but also called for their own corrections at the reagent input valves. So the readings weren't supposed to vary much. The indicator also showed the rate of input of reagents; *that* sometimes did vary a good deal. As now on Number 77.

It was the hydroxyl input at Level 8. Normally this was a small rate, sometimes zero; now a good deal of dilute base was pumping in up there. Max pulled the chain which slid the hanging ladder to him, and went up. At Level 7 he passed the transparent deck known as the Supers' Walk. He pressed the button to signal the lab, then climbed up to Level 8 and opened a port in the side of the vat, revealing a tangle of tubing… No, there was nothing wrong mechanically with the input valve.

Paula appeared just below him. Paula wasn't a superintendent, just an analyst, but the lab was right next to the office, and analysts as well as supers had the run of the Supers' Walk.

"Hi," said Max. He was glad Paula had come out, instead of just talking into a mike, the usual way.

"Hi, Max, what's the trouble?"

"Hydroxyl input up to two point. Nothing else showing yet."

"Which analyzer is calling for more hydroxyl?"

"The pH at the same level. That's what I'm looking at now." He poked through a new port.

"Listen" (pointing to the tiny pipes running from Jim and Max's row to the lab). "Send us some of your input solution in line A, and some from the chamber in B." Paula smiled. "You're getting sharp, Max, to spot this thing so early."

"Oh, I'm doing okay." He smiled back. Jim would never have praised him, and Paula knew this stuff as well as Jim did.

He flipped the toggles that would send the samples Paula wanted to the lab, then closed up the port. "Shall I stay up here?"

"Suit yourself." Another smile over Paula's departing shoulder. Max wasn't allowed above Level 6 unless something was wrong or he had explicit permission. Now he had permission.

He watched the little figure walking in a businesslike way back to the lab. Paula wore a man's short haircut and a man's pants, like any career girl. It was a little ridiculous, like a man yet not quite a man; Max had to admit it.

But he didn't really feel it. Everybody respected Paula as a worker. In Max's case the word was *liked*. Paula had been his *friend*, almost from the first day he'd worked at Lanon, and he didn't care who knew it.

Since he had permission to stay up here, he looked around. He opened up the ports on Levels 7 and 8 and traced the connections without touching them. He could imagine the comment he'd get if Jim saw him: "Hey, youngster, don't you know your job yet? If you've still got valves to memorize, I guess I didn't drive you hard enough in your apprenticeship." But Max was just interested. He liked to go over things again. Paula understood.

He would have liked even better to follow Paula into the lab. He'd never been in there; to him it was only a wide, whitely lighted room whose door always closed before he saw more.

Partly to look busy in case Jim was watching him from below, he picked up tools and tested some of the analyzers at Level 8. He didn't find anything, of course.

Then he tested viscosity at a couple of points. He wouldn't find anything there either, of course. But he did! In the tank where the benzene solution of peptide derivatives sprayed in tiny bubbles into a water phase, the mixture acted wrong. Likely the bubbles were too big, giving too small a total benzene-water surface and throwing everything off from Level 9 down. This must have been the trouble all along, though he couldn't have guessed it.

He signaled the lab again, shut off the inputs, and went to work on the spray nozzles. For this job he should have called Jim. But Paula came out again, and this time Max was complimented even more, and Max was glad he had tackled the job himself.

The heck with Jim! Max felt good enough to go through with his plan for tonight, and never mind Jim. As he finished the job, he hung up his tools and said, "Say, Paula, would you like to go down to Luana's together? I'll meet you at your dormitory after dinner."

No answer. Paula's face was very serious and almost soft in an unfamiliar way.

To make it clear that this was an invitation to something that was very important to him, Max explained, "I love Luana."

Still no answer. Was seeing a dancer too unfamiliar a suggestion? Max couldn't remember seeing very many career girls in Luana's audience, as a matter of fact, and those hadn't come with men. He asked, "Have you ever been to a dancer's house before?"

"Oh, yes, I've seen dancers before." Now Paula smiled, and decided. "Max, it was nice of you to ask me. I'd like to go to Luana's with you. I'll meet you after dinner."

"Swell," said Max, and retreated down the ladder. But it hadn't been swell; it had been a disappointment, compared with the way any man would have reacted to the invitation, even if he'd turned it down.

Well, naturally, it wouldn't be the same as a man. But why had Paula hesitated that way?

"How have things been going, Jim?"

"All quiet. You sure took a long time up there."

"Yeah, the stream into the tank on Level 9 wasn't getting broken up. That doesn't happen too often, huh?"

Jim grunted.

This was a good enough explanation for Max's having taken so long. Max could have added that the only reason he'd found what the trouble was so early was curiosity, but it didn't even occur to him to do it. Some difficulties you avoid automatically, by habit.

But Max plunged right into another difficulty. "Say, Jim, how about Paula coming with us tonight?"

He was expecting Jim to look surprised, but not to look the way he did! Max had already begun to wince when Jim started: "Why not invite Harriet, too, and make it a *family party?*"

Max didn't say anything. It was true Harriet was a friend of Paula's, but he understood Jim's sarcasm.

Jim showed no mercy. "'How about Paula coming with us,' huh? What's *it* going to see in Luana?"

"Okay, Paula's not the same as you or me, obviously, okay; but it's a nice guy just the same."

"It's a nice guy at work," Jim said slowly and emphatically, "and at Luana's it is not a nice guy, it's a fifth wheel. Pants don't make a man."

Max shrugged his shoulders, even though he was suffering. He wasn't prepared to quarrel with Jim or anybody else on the subject. Without thinking about it he knew it was absolutely necessary to him that Paula's coming along should not be made a big issue.

And equally necessary to him that it should come.

What could he do? He thought of making a joke to calm Jim down, but that's all he thought, he didn't think of the joke.

He just said bluntly, "Calm down. It's not its fault it's not a man."

"No," Jim agreed in the same exaggerated tone, "that is true; I'm sorry for it, and all that; but at Luana's it's a fifth wheel."

Max shrugged his shoulders again and turned away. "I don't know," he said, wishing he could be casual. "Paula's always been very decent to me, and I think it's a nice girl, that's all."

Something else for Jim to pounce on. "'*Nice girl*'? It's grown up now! It's not a little girl any more, it's a full-grown career."

Max knew the career girls themselves didn't like to be called simply "careers," but he accommodated. He went back to, "It's a nice guy."

With the heaviest sarcasm yet, Jim said, "A *personal friend* of yours, no doubt." That was his clincher.

Max stopped breathing. How could he handle *that* one casually? He couldn't. "All I said was, it's a nice guy." He didn't look at Jim. He meant it when he said, "Unfortunately, I already asked it, and I can't just back out."

"Did you tell it I was coming?"

"No."

"Well, that's good at least. Listen, why don't you tell it you're sick?" Suddenly Jim was making helpful suggestions to a friend in a jam.

"I can't stay at the dormitory tonight; I have to see Luana."

"Come along and see Luana, Paula won't know."

"It might find out; it might even come and see me there."

"Not likely, and if it does, so what?"

But that was going too far for Max. "Paula's a nice guy," he repeated stubbornly.

With a sudden snort, Jim said, "Go with Paula, then, but not me." Subject closed.

Max made another routine check of the row, then sat down a couple of spinners away from Jim. He was confused. If he'd known this was going to happen, he wouldn't have — what wouldn't he have done?

Why did Jim have to be so intolerant, anyway?

He wished he was talking to Jim about Luana again, but he knew he couldn't now.

Jim strolled over and said charitably, "You'll change your mind." Then he strolled away again. Obviously that was as far as *he* was going to go.

Max sat thinking unhappily. Maybe he *would* change his mind and tell Paula he was sick — maybe.

Remembering Paula's efficient walk and the brave self-respect with which it looked up at men, he felt a sudden strong stab of affection. He excused the emotion to himself. After all, it was a very nice guy.

Someone was on the Supers' Walk in their row. An analyst? He looked up. No, it was gray-haired Superintendent Kees himself. Without seeming to hurry, Max got to his feet and started pacing the row, checking every spinner. Jim caught on, too, and did the same.

Mr. Kees didn't pay any attention to them. He was looking over Number 77, where Max had just done the job on the nozzles. When Max met Jim at the middle of their row he crossed his fingers, and Jim repeated the sign — both of them surreptitiously, as if Mr. Kees could see crossed fingers from almost thirty meters above them. As if Mr. Kees would be surprised if he did!

After five minutes or so the superintendent left, without having looked down.

Max breathed easier, and Jim grinned at his relief. "We're glad to see you go," Jim muttered toward the Supers' Walk, and added in falsetto, "old Husband Kees."

"Huh? Since when is Kees married?"

"A couple of weeks ago."

Max thought Jim might be inventing this for his sake, to build him up after being nervous about Mr. Kees. "Honest?" he said.

"Yep. Just got the word from Roland this morning."

"He's jaypeed, you mean."

"Nope." Jim made a mock-solemn long face. "This is no jaypee fling, this is a real old-fashioned *family* marriage."

"No kidding! I never would have thought it. With all the money he's got, he could keep playing the field till almost any age. Who did he marry?" Max expected to hear the name of some famous dancer. Now, if it was a question of settling down with somebody like Luana, Max could see something in marriage, no matter what Jim might say.

"*Hah.* You know who he married?" Jim, in his glee, was having trouble keeping his voice low. "Remember Frederika?"

"Sure. It used to be one of the office secretaries, left about a year ago."

"Less than a year."

"Yeah. So who did Kees marry?"

"Frederika," Jim exulted, "changed its name, let its hair grow, took one or two dancing lessons, and opened a house."

"And Kees married *it*." Max was stunned.

"Her, now. Kees married her almost the minute it became legal. Bought out her contract and married her."

Max wondered if maybe Roland had made the story up. Even if this thing had actually happened at Lanon, Max felt vaguely that it'd be better not to talk about it. But curiosity was overriding. "How old is it—how old is she, anyway? Must be thirty at least."

"Thirty-five, I bet."

"Imagine a woman not getting the urge until she was thirty-five," Max marveled.

Jim pretended to spit behind him. "Obviously if a girl hasn't felt the urge by thirty-five, it's going to be a career. It's not cut out for anything else, period."

"You mean Frederika never really had a woman's instincts at all?"

"Obviously. Frederika became a dancer just so she could get married! How much of an audience do you think she ever got at her house? Who beside Kees?" Jim's eyes were bright with suppressed laughter, and his voice was a jeer. "I bet she couldn't even get a promoter. I bet behind the scenes Kees financed the whole thing himself. It must have cost plenty."

Max still felt the conversation was indecent, but —"Why did he do it? Why would he even go to see her?" It was hard to understand.

"He went to see her dance because he loved her."

This, at least, was a joke, Max knew. "Oh, go on. How could he love her when he could see real women, like Luana, or even Marta? It isn't *natural* to love anybody except the most beautiful woman you've seen, obviously."

"You don't have to tell me." Jim whispered, winking, "Confidentially, Kees wanted to get married from the beginning. He likes children!" And Jim's derision overflowed in violent laughter, loud and long. It was okay; if the super heard, he wouldn't know what the joke was. Max joined in, laughing at old Husband Kees.

Jim was still his friend after all.

II

It wasn't only loyalty to Paula that made Max go through with taking it to Luana's, it was partly loyalty to the way he'd felt about the idea in the morning. He was too stubborn to give it up so far as to lie to Paula.

As he and Paula went down the plush winding stair into Luana's, Max heard the audio inside, beat, beat, beat, and a rolling melody. It was playing Luana's theme, though, so he knew the evening was just beginning in there. The familiar excitement made him feel like running down those last few steps. As soon as they were at the bottom, he turned toward Luana.

Luana was gorgeous tonight. (Luana was always gorgeous!) Her head was raised as she faced the audience, her heavily shadowed eyes were closed, her scarlet mouth pouted, glittering jewels swung on her waist-length braids. Luana was gorgeous.

Luana gave a little stretch and yawn, presenting her breasts. Max tingled all over. What a body!

It was easy to see why so few girls became dancers. How many of them had bodies like Luana's? How many of them had bodies even approaching Luana's?

Tonight Luana was wearing practically nothing above the waist, and you could appreciate her to the fullest. Below the waist, she was covered, the same as always, by a loose ankle-length skirt which swirled excitingly whenever she turned. (Max had been trying to decide the last few nights whether Luana was pregnant again yet. He hoped not, of course.)

Mabel came up to Max and Paula as they stood at the bottom of the stairs, to take their admission fees. Max was returned abruptly to his problem. Would Mabel notice in the dimness the slight extra length of Paula's jacket that signified it was not a man? Would she let them in if she did know Paula's sex? To be sure, Paula had said it had seen dancers before, so maybe it was okay.

Max paid his own admission. Mabel said, "Good evening, Max," and turned to Paula. "Are you with him?"

"We're together," said Paula calmly.

Mabel took its money, too. She said, "You'll have to sit in the back."

"Certainly," said Paula.

They took their seats — in the back.

This was terrible! Max had been up front for five weeks without missing a night, and he was sure Luana must have been stirred by his constancy. She must have begun to realize he was not just an adolescent fooling around. What would she think now when she didn't see him?

It was possible she might notice him even back here. But if she did, what would she think? That he had decided he didn't want to stay up front.

This was all a big mistake!

Here was Max in the back with the mere spectators, and up there, separated from him by a wide aisle, sitting right at the edge of the lighted area where Luana danced, were a dozen other guys. Tonight, as far as Luana was concerned, they were the devoted lovers. Max was sick with envy.

He recognized most of them. There was Jim, with Roland, the other Luana follower from Lanon. Most outstanding, there was Dan Sellars. Two weeks ago Luana, late in the evening, while dancing around the stage with Dan Sellars, had led him off- stage to be jaypeed, ending the show for the night. Max's throat choked up just remembering it, thinking of the sudden rush of delicious passion that must have filled Luana's lovely body, imagining himself in Dan Sellars's place!

But it had not been Max, it had been Dan Sellars, and he and Luana had stayed that way for two whole weeks — not bad! And here was Max, in the back rows. Tonight would not be the night Luana would jaypee with him; or even have her first dance with him; or even lean invitingly over his chair in passing, as she had done twice this week.

Beat, beat, beat, and the melody rolled languidly.

Max told himself that he couldn't stay bitter while he was at Luana's.

Luana spread her slender arms wide, and clasped her hands behind her head. Leaning her head way back, she slunk back and forth in front of the audience, panting audibly. Back and forth, over and over.

Max knew this was irresistible. He knew the effect that would hit him now, and he waited for it impatiently, like a man who has just chug-a-lugged two double whiskeys.

It hit. It rocked him. He kept his eyes on Luana, feeding the flame... He still loved that Luana, all right. Oh, it had hit!

But maybe not quite so strong as usual?

Of course, he was farther away from her now. He wasn't up front.

The audio changed tunes, and Luana changed moods. She swung gaily up to Dan Sellars and danced him around and around the floor. He was certainly a good man for her when it came to dancing. Luana looked so graceful and loving when he held her. In some ways it was even better than watching Luana alone.

Without warning Luana danced him through the curtains out of the room. The audio was hushed. Nobody moved from his seat; it was too early for Luana's evening shift to be over, but there was a little rustle of whispering, speculating. It died to total silence as the curtain stirred.

It was Dan Sellars, alone. Luana was unattached again! She had renoed him!

Dan Sellars walked deadpan to his seat; he was still going to sit up front at Luana's, then. Max approved.

The audio blared and Luana skipped through the curtains, her scarlet lips laughing unrestrainedly. She was wearing a new skirt, flaming red, and her shoulders were spread with tiny spangles.

Swinging the red skirt merrily, Luana began to sing. How many dancers could sing too? — let alone sing like Luana.

It was *The Call of My House*, a fairly new song. Max was disappointed. He loyally enjoyed it, but really he thought most of the new songs, even the serious ones like this, sounded inadequate for the emotions he felt for Luana. They sounded insincere. Now the old songs — the *really* old songs that were revived every so often — had the directness of true art. The words were usually inappropriate for a dancer to be singing to her audience, but he could allow for that. The sentiments might be from another time, but they were sincere. Songs like *Rosalie*, *K-A-L-A-M-A-Z-O-O*, or *I Wanna Love You*.

After the song Luana began dancing with one after another of the men up front. Everybody was unusually excited tonight, because of Luana's having renoed — Luana herself most of all. It had a stimulating effect. She danced with Roland and even with Dan Sellars, more gracefully, more yieldingly than she had the last few nights. It was something to watch. But the more Max enjoyed it, the more he longed to be up front.

Luana sang again. Just as if she had heard Max's wish, it was one of the old favorites. He even thought she seemed to be singing toward the one empty seat Mabel had left up front. And after the song was over she'd be dancing again! If it wasn't for Paula —

Paula. He'd actually forgotten it was because of Paula that he was back here.

Remembering startled him; he turned to face Paula. It met his eyes.

It said conversationally, "Max, you're pretty devoted to Luana, aren't you?" How could it be so calm?

Well, naturally, it wouldn't be the same as a man.

He said intensely, "I'd do absolutely anything for her — anything at all."

Paula stared at him thoughtfully. He didn't have anything to say to it, or any real purpose in having turned in the first place. He was even a little embarrassed. And Luana's voice caressing him.

Paula said quietly, "I have to stay in the back section, but you can go up alone if you want to and sit in your usual chair."

"That's right!" he said. "Why didn't *I* think of that?"

In the front row you heard Luana's voice much more intimately.

Luana must have noticed him taking his seat in the middle of a number, but she would know it was just from impatience to be near her. What would she think of his being so late, though? Had he ruined his chances?

When she had finished the song, Luana stood at one end of the row of seats. The audio was off, everything was quiet. She yawned and stretched tantalizingly. Then she walked slowly from one follower to the next, the length of the row. She was deciding which one to dance with next;

but she was considering her decision a lot more carefully than usual; it must be an important one.

Nobody moved. Max had to restrain himself consciously from squirming with suspense. Luana started back along the row, hesitating at each chair. She was in front of Max! She stayed there — longer than she ever had before!

And moved on.

And danced with Jim!

Jim, who had been up front only one night before! There was no justice in it. Max just couldn't understand women at all. Jim was a nice guy, but after all!

Then came the catastrophe. Luana and Jim danced two or three times around the floor — gracefully, Max had to admit; they danced well together — and through the curtains.

The evening was over, in an explosion of applause from the audience. Luana had jaypeed Jim. Jim!

Max got up blindly and left, ignoring Paula's hand in his, ignoring the cool night air, walking without a thought in his head that he could bear.

III

Max was confused, as if he was waking up from a long sleep. He sat down beside Paula.

They were in a familiar enough place, the entry to the Spinning Department at Lanon. Max clocked in here every morning when he came to work. Every time he clocked in he looked at the time. Automatically he looked at the time now: 23:25.

"Why'd we come here?"

"I asked Antonina at dinner tonight if it wanted me to take its shift for it. I go on at midnight. I thought you wouldn't mind if we walked over here early."

"Do you buy other girls' shifts often?" he asked without much interest. "How much do you get for them?"

"I didn't buy the shift."

"Oh, you're just taking it as a favor."

"That's right. I knew I'd be up tonight anyway, and Antonina always has a hard time with the first shift."

They sat in silence. Paula's regular chewing became audible, and simultaneously Paula said, "I've got chocolate mints. Want one?"

For the first time tonight Max realized that Paula was a remarkable girl. Mints, at this point — remarkable. He thanked it and chewed contentedly.

They were silent again. Max turned back to troubled thoughts of Luana. After a while he couldn't keep from saying it any longer: "I can't understand her."

Paula answered, "Stop thinking she's a mystery, Max, and you can understand her as well as you understand most people."

This time Max turned to it in astonishment. It still sat relaxed, leaning against the wall, one arm around a knee. It didn't even look at him.

Max was going to say, "What could you know about the subject?" but he toned it down to, "How do you know?" He waited, watching Paula.

It chewed away at the chocolate mint, but it seemed less relaxed. "True of everybody. People are funny, but

214

they're all just people — if you see what I mean." It was definitely a little flustered now. "Anyhow, I know Luana."

"*What?*"

"Sure. Now, why should that surprise you? We went to school together. Of course, her name wasn't Luana then." Max did not ask to hear her former name. "She was my best friend — one of my best friends."

Why was Max surprised? Mostly because it had never occurred to him that he would ever have a *friend* who was a *friend of Luana's*. Even in his daydreams he had never thought about being close to Luana in that way. It was hard to get used to. There was something else, though.

It was the ages. Luana seemed so magic and unattainable it was hard to think of her childhood's being within memory. But when he considered — Luana had been sixteen when she got her first contract, that he knew, and he knew she had had three pregnancies. She must be about twenty. That was just her chronological age, and it seemed like a terrible liar. Why, *he* was twenty, and it seemed as if Luana must have been Luana long before he was born… yet must have been under twenty-five the whole time.

"How old are you?"

"Just turned twenty-two."

"You were older than Luana!"

"A little."

"Gee, I wonder what Luana was like as a girl?" He didn't really want to know; it was just an idea that was new and curious. He always mentioned new and curious ideas to Paula.

"What was she like? You couldn't have told her from anybody else. She went to the same classes and played the same games. Slept in the same dormitory." Paula laughed tolerantly, and Max remembered how adolescent his question must have sounded: curiosity about life at a girls' school!

Still it was fascinating, and he was talking to Paula so it was okay. "You knew her. All through school?"

"From the time she entered till the time she left. I knew Marta, too; her name used to be Henrietta. And a couple of dozen other dancers. You see, I just can't think of them as particularly mysterious—any more than I could think of you as mysterious when I work with you every day. But then—" Paula blurted out, "You're a man, after all. Sometimes I think career girls are the only ones who can understand people!"

"What do you mean?"

"For instance—who else reads? Can you imagine anybody reading because it wanted to, except a career girl? Well, that's not fair: *you* read. You're unusual. You haven't had much time for it recently, though, have you?"

"No." For a man there were more important things. To most people Max wouldn't admit that he had read at all since leaving school.

"But the main thing is, you cut yourself off from too many people. Career girls are the only ones who don't lie to themselves, so they're the only ones who can understand people."

Max didn't follow this at all.

Paula mused, "Here I go, though, lying to *myself*. We're cut off from people, too…We don't get to take care of children, the way the women do."

It sounded actually unhappy! This stopped Max with surprise for a moment; but he went ahead and retorted, "Well, if you understand people so much better than I do, tell me: How does Luana choose who to dance with? Or… who to jaypee? Explain *that* if you can." He felt downright resentful. Of Paula or Luana?

Paula stood up and paced back and forth a couple of times; its face was worried. It spread its hands. "I think I understand, Max, but it's not simple."

"Well, just tell me this: What possible reason could she have for jaypeeing a guy who's been a follower only one night? If she wanted to choose him, at least she could have waited till he'd been up front a decent period — a couple of weeks anyway."

"Oh, Jim was a newcomer, was he?" She smiled faintly. "And you've been pretty devoted to Luana, haven't you?"

"You asked me that before. Answer my question."

"All dancers choose newcomers sometimes, Max. If they didn't, there'd be no excitement for men who had just started sitting up front. They'd know they wouldn't be noticed till they'd waited out a couple of weeks — at least with a popular dancer like Luana. They might even stop coming before the couple of weeks were up. A dancer has to keep attendance up, or the promoter will complain."

"But — how could Luana —"

"How could she be so calculating? She should choose by the passion of the moment, is that it? I thought you wanted to understand why she chooses who she does; now you want a reason you *can't* understand." Paula sat down again and added less combatively, "I don't know. Probably whim comes in, too. I wouldn't be surprised." It gave itself another mint.

Max was still arguing. "Have you ever seen Luana since she became a dancer?"

"Yes, once."

"When?"

"Three years ago."

"So she'd only started then. You're not such a friend of hers. If you went down there to talk over old times, I bet she'd have Mabel throw you out."

"Hm. As a matter of fact, she might. Luana didn't follow my advice. Maybe she feels bad about it, one way or the other."

Luana, follow Paula's advice? Naturally not. Max didn't even interrupt his argument. "So you've hardly seen her since she was a girl, and you couldn't even talk to her now — how do you know so much about how she thinks? After all, Paula, there's a whole area of experience that you don't have anything to do with, that's very important to Luana." Not to mention Max.

"That's true," said Paula in a very small voice.

"All right, then how can you say—" He looked at Paula's soft face and stopped.

"In a way, what you say is very true. A whole area of experience that's very important — that's true, Max."

He looked at Paula and couldn't speak.

Paula said, "Have another mint, Max," and sat chewing quietly.

Max sat looking at the quiet, efficient, self-respecting, unhappy face with growing sympathy. Poor girl! He hadn't been fair to Paula. When he'd learned that Luana had once been just another girl like Paula, and Paula's friend, he'd learned only half. Paula had once been like Luana, too, and Luana's friend.

That was a hard thought, too.

Paula must have dreamed of womanhood then, the same as Luana. But some girls—most girls—didn't have what it took.

It was really terrifying. What must it be like to be a schoolgirl? Always wishing your complexion would clear up, wishing your breasts would grow rounder, waiting to feel that uncontrollable desire that would tell you you were a woman. He hadn't thought about such things since he was in school, and of course he hadn't been old enough then to understand.

What must it be like to be a grown career girl!

"I guess career girls must feel sort of"—he hesitated a little—"envious of dancers."

"That is the usual attitude, I believe," Paula stated tonelessly.

There was a lot he hadn't understood, all right, Max conceded. How could he have considered himself Paula's friend before? Now he felt so much closer to it.

"*It*"—even the pronoun was a continual reminder of Paula's failure. In every sentence he spoke about career girls he was pointing out that they were the ones who didn't make it. He could imagine how Paula must feel about that. Used to it, maybe, but surely not happy about it.

Max made a resolution. Maybe he was a little peculiar, but he didn't think so. After all, the elderly women who had been his school teachers had always been "her." Paula was his friend. Max resolved always to refer to any career girl as "her" from now on.

At least when he was alone with Paula.

He resolved even to *think* of Paula as "her." It wouldn't come naturally to use that pronoun for a modified man's name like "Paula," when he was used to using "her" only for real women's names like "Luana" or "Clarissa." He'd do it, just the same. The way he'd been talking up to now sounded cruel.

He smiled happily and started to tell Paula his resolution. The words wouldn't come. He didn't know how to say it without sounding ridiculous.

Why? Because his resolution was a bad idea? No, not a bad idea; just pitifully inadequate. How much difference would a pronoun make to—her? If he talked as if it was saving her life, he'd sound very, very silly, and just as cruel as if he'd done nothing.

If only there was some way to tell Paula that (at last) he sympathized.

Paula glanced at the clock. 23:49. The first shift would start showing up about now.

Paula stood up without looking at him. It—she—yawned and stretched. Max felt let down: apparently she didn't have anything more to say to him and was going to leave him ten minutes early, and he hadn't communicated to her yet.

Instead, she said, "Tired?"

"No."

"Why don't you come in with me? The super won't be around this shift, or any of the office staff. Don't even bother clocking in."

Paula went straight to the lab, but Max loafed on the Supers' Walk.

It was the Spinning Department in a different hour from the Spinning Department he saw daily, yet it might as well have been in a different year, or country. The rows of vats were the same, exactly the same, but strolling around the Supers' Walk gave a new and godlike perspective; they had changed. The row where he worked in the midday shift was superficially the same; he could recognize it without looking at the numbers, by the drooling discoloration on Number 74, the same as in the day; but instead of looking *up* at Mr. Kees he was looking *down* at somebody or other. To find out whether it was Max or not he'd have to check the personnel records. Who was he? *He* had changed.

He had an anything-could-happen feeling that he hadn't had since he was a kid, except maybe at Luana's.

Luana — she seemed distant now. Time heals sorrows, and to Max there was a lot of time between an hour ago and now. He was still a Luana follower, certainly; his memory did not show the conspicuous event which stopping loving Luana would have made. He didn't worry quite as much about love, though. Love and curiosity didn't mix. Tonight Max was curious.

Which adventure should he choose?

This afternoon if he'd had an invitation to drop into the lab any time, with nobody to object, he'd have run all the way. Tonight it was hard to choose. Paula had changed everything: Luana, the Spinning Department, Paula herself. Max was itching to understand them all.

He chose the lab, though, partly because Paula would be there. For any adventure, Paula should be there. Paula and curiosity went together.

Max pushed open the door to the wide, whitely lighted room.

It wasn't quite as wide as he'd thought, and part of it wasn't lighted. That was the row of four desks along the left that were more likely computers. Accounting didn't work the night shifts. The rest of the room was a dazzling array of valves and tubes. Max threw his mind open to see what they could tell him. He let his eye wander over the maze, guided by hunches drawn from his apprenticeship outside there. Apprenticeship—that's what this was. Everything was new tonight. Tonight should have come after his first day at work, or his first week perhaps. But if it had, he wouldn't have had a friend, Paula, who could show him around the lab.

He didn't see Paula. There was only one person in the lab, working in the far right corner, ignoring him. He recognized the person. "Harriet!"

"Hi, Max."

"I didn't know you knew this job."

"I've qualified for assistant, not for analyst."

"You taking somebody else's shift, just for tonight?"

"That's right. How about you?"

"Paula just asked me if I wanted to stick around. Where is Paula, anyway?"

"Out on one of the vats; Number 58, I think."

"She'll be right back, won't she? I was hoping—"

Uh-oh.

Harriet smiled at his faux pas; but not too jeeringly, if at all. Max felt his face getting entirely red—all over—maximum. He hadn't blushed since he was in school.

Harriet said, "Paula should be back pretty soon. Would you like to sit down in the office? I'm pretty busy here."

"The office!"

"The Superintendent's Office, in there." The door on the dark side of the room. "The guys always use it on this shift. There usually isn't anybody around to check, and I'll be able to tip you off in time if there is."

Max pushed open the door and went through.

He wouldn't have been surprised to see a tropic garden.

It was dark. He ricocheted off a hard desk into a soft chair. Keeping one hand on the chair for a base, he groped across the desk till he found a switch.

It only turned on a desk lamp. The little light fell concentrated on the desk top and scattered vaguely about the room. Desks, chairs, and cabinets were irresponsibly acute-angled. Max could have turned on more lights and reduced them to normality, but he preferred not to. He relaxed, acclimating to novelty.

In the direction he was facing, he couldn't see to the end of the office. Maybe the office extended farther than he'd assumed. He sat staring into the darkness there.

For a while he saw only darkness. Then a new, dim light went on and something moved. Max sat staring.

If what he saw might just as well have been a dream, why should he complain?

He thought he saw Luana.

Luana couldn't be in this office, but then neither could Max, and nevertheless here was Max, all alone, and, all for Max, here was Luana! Dancing! Why should he ask questions?

Luana danced for him.

Her hands clasped behind her head, that snake-hips walk. The same as this evening.

But the evening had ended wrong, so Max didn't let himself compare now to the evening. Everything was new this midnight. No music, she didn't need any! No crowded house, all the better!

He tried the experiment of watching the dance as if he had never seen it before. That wriggling walk was new. He could feel the burning passion that drove those hips. Then she stopped — stretched, lithely turning her body to right and left — and yawned. What a body!

Max almost groaned aloud. Why didn't she come closer? How was he supposed to stand it this long? Still he was the audience, he didn't get out of his chair.

Gradually she came closer, and each step she took toward him was an act of surrender. Max couldn't stand it. He jumped from his chair. This was the love of his life!

She began to sing, a husky wordless croon that made him shiver and want to cry. This was the love of his life! And all for him!

But it wasn't Luana. He had never heard the voice before. He had to admit to himself now that it wasn't Luana.

He didn't care! Everything was new tonight. He could see and hear, couldn't he? Couldn't he tell that this was love? How could he think of Luana after this? This was true love! That husky voice said, "Dance with me," and the unbearably beautiful face turned up toward him. The light rested on her soft cheek, and Max adored her. He put his arm around her and his hand touched her back. "Oh, my darling!"

The beautiful face frowned, and said, "Now do you see, Max?" The voice was Paula's voice.

Max didn't move.

Warmth still throbbing through him like echoes after thunder...

What had happened? Eventually he had to know. It had not been a dream. His hand was still touching her back—Paula's back. He removed it; then he stood absolutely still again, trying to think.

The face was still close to his, Paula's pitiful, pleading face. He had to remember that even with the mouth painted over scarlet, even wearing the grotesque jeweled wig, even obscenely dressed in woman's clothes, this was his friend, Paula.

He whispered, "*Don't worry, Paula, I won't tell anybody.*"

She gasped.

Her frown dissolved.

Her face went soft again; for a moment he thought she had fainted. But she had sprung back away from him three or four steps, as graceful as a dancer. She said, in the husky voice, "You can see and hear, can't you? Can't you tell I'm a woman?" She danced again, and crooned.

Sure, he could see and hear. He could see and hear his friend Paula bouncing around in a preposterous costume, with a faked voice, and it embarrassed him. He was cramped and sobbing with embarrassment.

"Max, please." The faked voice was begging now.

On a whim he relented and let himself pretend, conjuring up another emotional kick for the sake of the kick. Pretend it's a woman! The body was gorgeous, the voice made him shiver, the face unbearably beautiful. Exactly the same as before. He felt his passion rising again —

Instantly wrung off in icy fear and guilt. Too late, too late; now he knew. The love of his life made him gag.

"Paula, stop it!" he shouted. "Paula!"

Her white shoulders drooped, her husky voice broke. She stopped. Paula fell across the desk, *crying*.

Max couldn't help her and he couldn't ignore her. He listened inertly while she wept, "I just don't get it. I just don't get it. Oh, Max, I'm not going to blame you for anything. What was I trying to do, anyway? I'm as messed up as you are… I just don't get it, that's all. The wig?" She dropped it on the floor and her hair was Paula's short hair. "If I were a dancer I'd wear one. Luana wears one. I could go out and open a house tomorrow and you wouldn't see anything wrong with me. I just don't —"

She waited for her sobbing to calm, then spoke wearily. "Oh sure, as if it mattered. I tried out at Clarissa's house the same time Luana did. I went over, too. Better than Luana, as if it mattered. I could find a promoter tomorrow and open a house."

He wished she could! "Why don't you?" He dreaded the answer.

She sat up on the desk, looking around him at the floor. She ignored his question. "My fifth night at Clarissa's I got unusually strong audience reaction, from practically everybody, even Clarissa's front row." There was no pride or tenderness in her voice, or anything else. "When I went offstage Clarissa came on and said, 'We'll have to put that juicy morsel in a package all her own,' meaning I should have my own house. The applause was tremendous. But I knew that if I did it I'd have to sign a five-year contract, because I had no money of my own. I peeked through the curtain at all those popeyed, yelling faces, and I thought, '*Five years.*'"

What an unwomanly reaction! He was coldly certain of the answer as he began, "What's wrong with five years of—"

"Of life like Luana's? I tried to talk Luana out of doing it too, and she may regret it."

Coldly, "But why does it disgust you?"

"Oh, I know what you mean—am I anesthetic? No. Plenty of girls are, your myth is right that far, but I'm not."

It was evidently true. Paula was tired and discouraged enough at that point to tell the worst of the truth, much too weary to lie. But then—

"Then why can't you—"

"I couldn't stand five years of that kind of contempt. 'Juicy morsel!' Everything those guys wanted from me they could have gotten from a hypodermic needle." Paula's unprotected shoulders trembled. "I'm not going to blame anybody!"

Max was too weak to respond, too weak to stand. He sat down on the desk beside Paula, drawing his shoulder in so there would be no risk of touching her. He looked at her for one more shivering glance.

His friend Paula…alias the love of his life.

Love! Paula wanted him to love her — *it*, a career — and then said that love was contempt.

Max was lost. What did he have?

His work? But that meant Paula.

Jim? He could not imagine himself telling Jim any part of what happened.

Luana? Luana? He sought in his soul for his first love, which he had denied tonight for a mirage. He sought prayerfully and found an image of Luana. The image removed its wig, peeked through the curtain of yelling faces, and wondered if it could stand five years as a dancer.

It wasn't true. Luana had made the other choice. Luana was a woman! But this was the image Max saw. Jim had Luana; Max knew he would never have her now.

Paula stirred and got to her feet, straight and brave, under streaked makeup the familiar face of Paula. "Max, Harriet can't double for me in the lab all night. I'll get my obscene man's clothes on, and we'll have a cup of coffee before I get back to work, okay?"

Paula had left him alone in the world with her…it… her. He had no choice. "Okay," he said with no emotion of any kind. "I'll wait for you in the lab."

"You're a nice guy, Max, and eventually we'll understand each other."

"The Statistomat Pitch" first appeared in *Infinity Science Fiction* in January 1958. Professor Davis lacks a record of its original date of composition, but it preceded 1955.

THE STATISTOMAT PITCH

THE LITTLE SALESMAN buzzed into my hotel room exactly at 10. He must have been waiting in the corridor, ambushing the second-hand.

I watched from my deep chair in the corner while he slid open his raincoat, lifted it neatly off his back (the casual shrug wasn't his style), and stood with it hanging from his forefinger. With a bright, apologetic smile he hung it up in the alcove behind the door. I decided not to object to his using the tie hook without asking; it'd just slow things up.

The salesman smiled again, ducked out into the corridor and back in with a flat 24x20 brief case and a large, oddly shaped suitcase. His presentation charts and a mockup of the computer, obviously. More apologetic faces, and he sat down.

He said, "It was *very* good of you, Mr. Borch, to give me this chance to tell you about our new, personalized Statistomat… I know you're a busy man—"

I raised my drooping eyelids just enough to see him properly.

"— with all your responsibilities, and I hope I'll be able to answer all your questions on modern estate planning. That's what I'm here for!" He smiled as if he were pausing for questions, but he didn't pause.

He intoned, "The man of wealth has a special responsibility in our society. He is the trustee of invested capital, on which our economy rests; his proud charge is to direct and build his holdings wisely; and natural economic laws have justly placed the nation's considerable estates in the hands of men equal to the charge.

"At the same time, such men owe themselves freedom from deprivation. And they owe themselves a financial plan adapted to their own–er — preferences and tastes in freedom from deprivation. This is why we speak of *personalized* estate planning. Maybe this will be still clearer, Mr. Borch, if we look at an example."

Here we go again, I thought, as he hauled a packet out of his briefcase, opened it out into a little stand on the table, and flipped up the first chart.

"Take the case of Robert Jones, who inherits $25,000,000 from his father. The inheritance taxes are all taken care of by investment — incentive deductions, so Mr. Jones has $25,000,000 in liquid assets to invest."

Right on the ball, I thought. The hypothetical twenty-five million was just about twice the publicly known size of the Borch estate, therefore right in the league he could figure I'd like to be playing in. And the hypothetical Jones on the chart, confidently facing the future, was handsome and dignified, but not *much* more so than I was.

"Mr. Jones has a wife and one young son." They appeared beside him on the second chart, and they looked very pleasant. The salesman knew Jed Borch was unmarried. "He has planned to his satisfaction a way of life appropriate to his standing." On the next chart the Jones family was backed up by a half-acre bungalow, a lake, and wooded hills.

"His desire is for security, to ensure this pattern of living to himself and his wife, and to his son. His personalized Statistomat plans his finances accordingly." On succeeding charts, Jones changed only in subtle lengthening of the firm lines in his face, his wife didn't change at all, but his son sprouted to a six-footer and the bungalow grew some too. A bar graph superimposed on the picture kept track of the investment. By the time the boy was full-grown it had risen to a modest $100,000,000.

"On the other hand, consider Michael Thompson. Starting with the same sum of $25,000,000, he may just as legitimately view different goals. Mr. Thompson is unmarried, and has not yet chosen to what station he will aspire." Chapter Two of the charts had just as admirable-looking a man (different color hair). I was curious how much Statistomat would finagle for him, but not curious enough to sit through another dozen charts. When the salesman said, "Naturally, he's willing to risk —" I interrupted:

"I don't want any risk. Can't afford to." I smiled slyly. "Responsibility to society."

"Of course, of course, but you might be willing, like Mr. Thompson, to — er — look beyond the more accepted channels of finance for the sake of the larger returns that can be realized by breaking new ground, as it were — participating in pioneering enterprises."

"Oh, sure. Don't want to miss any bets."

So far you couldn't see anything to complain about in his pitch, considering it alongside the pitch for General Computers' Incomac. In fact it essentially *was* a General Computers pitch, with the brand name changed. Let's get to the point, I thought. I pointed to the odd suitcase. "Uh… what's that?"

He was adaptable enough to give up the Michael Thompson story and open up the suitcase, promptly and proudly.

"Oh, the computer," I said, almost encouragingly.

But he didn't let that stand. "No," he admitted, "this is just a life-size facsimile of the new Statistomat. I'm afraid the real thing is too valuable and too heavy for me to carry around, even to such an important interview as this."

"How heavy?"

"I'd say about ten times as heavy as this one," he evaded neatly. "Now on this facsimile I can illustrate the ideas we've been developing. Here, you see this screen and these knobs. I'll turn this switch on and we can watch this part of it just as if this was the real computer."

My surprise was genuine. His demonstration mockup was a live one. I wished my brother could see it.

"On this screen we record your time-dependent utility function. For your convenience, the input is mechanical, but from this point on all the Statistomat's computing is performed digitally."

I said, "Huh?"

"Time-dependent utility function," he repeated brightly.

"Oh, I can't be bothered — all that technical stuff — leave it to the specialists," I muttered, making the trap nice and inviting.

But he knew he had to explain. "Naturally only the essentials need *your* personal attention," he said smoothly. "You express in the time-dependent utility function your financial policy — the broad, overall outlines of the course you want to steer. This must come from you. This makes the difference between a Robert Jones and a Michael Thompson. You have a possibility of doubling your investment in a year, let's say. How certain do you have to be of it before you prefer it to a more conservative investment? Even odds? Six to four? Or we might ask a similar question about a ten-year period. You see the point."

"Uh…but it depends on how much I've got." I kicked myself. My brother would not approve my helping the salesman along like that.

"Ah, yes! Certainly! When you have a hundred million, an extra million won't seem nearly as important to you as when you have twenty-five. We understand! Our technical expression for this is that the value of money to the investor is not a linear function of dollars. Logarithmic, some say — but that depends on the investor. Whatever relationship you select as a matter of fiscal policy. That is a part, a critical part, of the information which you give the Statistomat when you work out your time-dependent utility function, or risk function, as we call it for short."

"No risk! Can't afford risk!"

"Mr. Borch, I speak with confidence when I assure you that your estate can be subject to as little risk when its direction is assigned to the Statistomat as in any other way." I almost called him on that, until I reflected that he had really made only one specific claim: that you could feed just as excessively conservative a risk function into the Statistomat, if you were compulsively conservative, as you could into the GC Incomac. That might be true.

He went on, "Two of the soundest business research agencies in the country have been invited to inspect all our operations and have okayed us, not once but repeatedly: the SEC and the FTC."

Darn right they've checked you, I thought — by law. And don't think they'll stop.

But it didn't do any good to spot a steep slant in his formulations. He was a salesman, after all. Just so he stayed clear of demonstrable falsehoods and "fraudulent tendencies" (as defined by the 1978 Commerce Act), he was within his rights.

He was staying clear. Some of his claims a stickler might want to check up on; but I wasn't going to bother any more to watch for things like that. I thought the stickler would find in each case that he'd been wasting his time. This little salesman seemed awfully good at skating just at the edge. He really knew his profession.

I didn't let my bafflement show. I just looked at him dully and made noises as if I was about to say something. I was, but I didn't know what.

There just had to be something bad about this Statistomat venture. Without (apparently) any new gimmick, a small new company was producing just as good a product as one of General Computers' best-managed divisions. How could Statistomat hope to deliver a normal profit? It wasn't reasonable. There must be badly cut corners, if not in the product then in the sales program or the servicing of customers; or else the investors *weren't* hoping for a normal return. In that case there was something funny in their motives — a long-range scheme to undermine GC, or something. That might show up in this salesman's pitch.

So I switched to, "How do I know what stocks this thing'll tell me to buy?"

"Not *tell* you to buy," he corrected charmingly, "*buy* you. The machine can be connected by direct wire to the Exchange's computer."

"Yeah-yeah, but how do I know what stocks I'll be getting? I want General Computers preferred!"

He smiled. "Quite possibly you'll find yourself the owner of a considerable block of GC preferred — provided of course your time-dependent utility function dictates a policy which —"

"You mean," I said, with the very suspicious expression my brother always objected to, "you'd let your machine bid for GC stock for me?"

"Naturally. The Statistomat has often recommended purchase of GC stock. Let me explain to you an aspect of modern firm management which may be so specialized as to have escaped your attention.

"Each firm draws up what is called a preference function. It is somewhat analogous to the investor's time-dependent utility function. It gives exact expression to the objectives of the firm. For any conceivable economic position the firm might be in, it determines, let us say, the weight the board places on a dividend this year as against a larger dividend a year from now, or ten. And so on. It is the criterion for all the optimization computations which pattern the firm's activities.

"Under a 1978 law, every corporation offering stock on the Exchange must publish its preference function. All these preference functions are known to your Statistomat; in effect, it is as if they were all in Statistomat's memory, continuously updated, automatically. Naturally, for a particular kind of investor only certain kinds of stock are suitable.

"But Statistomat does more—and this is the point I think you'll find intensely interesting. After all, more than the firm's policy is important. Two firms may have identical financial policies but very different dividend rates, either due to different degrees of success or to different kinds of partial success. Statistomat also has available to it a sound estimate of the firm's expectations—"

"Who does the—uh—estimating?"

"Based entirely on Commerce Department reports. That's as impartial as you can get, Mr. Borch, and it's also one of the best-informed sources in the country. The information is processed at our home office on one of the largest automatic computers in the world. You see, Statistomat Incorporated is deeply conscious of its responsibility to give flawless service to the men who control and direct America's fortunes."

The little salesman sounded overconfident again, so I thought I'd shake him up. "What does General Computers use for their whatchamacallit?"

"The General Computers' Incomac uses exactly the same sources of information."

I said in a bored voice, "What do you do different?"

"The principles of investment planning are scientific principles, Mr. Borch, and anybody working in this field must follow them."

Let's hear you desperate, I thought, but my voice just got drier. "Guess I might as well get an—"

"Of course there are differences!"

"Uh—yeah?"

"Oh, yes, yes! You see, even though the principles are the same, still if only one company was offering this service to investors—"

"Then what? It'd jack up the prices?"

But that was over-eager. He backed away immediately: "Certainly not, Mr. Borch. Who could suggest such a thing? We all know General Computers' spotless reputation as one of the most heavily capitalized corporations in the country. Besides, by now we should be free of wild brain-truster theories about the evils of monopoly." He smiled sanctimoniously.

I drawled, "So what if only one company was selling these machines?" My brother would be grinding his teeth at this follow-up. But I thought I just about had this salesman boxed. I'd better! He was catching on.

He answered, "Even though the same principles are applied, there are bound to be individual differences in their application. If all users of estate planning computers had relations with the same firm, all these minor fluctuations would be in the same direction for all of them. Although the investment mixes would be far from identical, they would be more alike than economic principle requires. On the other hand, the investor who has the courage to associate himself with an alternate set of analyses may be comparatively alone in the course he chooses. Thus he may benefit, when this course chances to be better than expectations, by having to share the reward with relatively few others."

I had him! I said, "You mean this thing might buy me different stocks from what the GC whatchamacallit would?"

"Why, yes, it would be surprising if there was not at some point a difference in the two solutions. That was the point you raised so well—"

"And you mean your answer might make me more money?

"Why, yes, in the case—that is, in the way that I was discussing. Mmm-hmm."

"But then you think GC gives out wrong solutions."

"Not *wrong*—"

"Solutions that aren't the best—that *means* wrong, huh?"

"Why, yes, I mean, I suppose that—" He stopped.

I smiled. I dropped my Jed Borch personality (which the little salesman probably much preferred). "You know who you've been talking to?"

"FTC?"

"An FTC Investigator," I said, professionally. Without waiting for him to ask, I showed him my card, with the impressive embossed words across, the center: "Fair Trade Corps." Then I pressed a button and instantly two cops were in the door and at the salesman's shoulders.

The salesman said, "What's the charge?"

"You know what it is."

"The charge, please."

I shrugged. "Fraudulent tendencies: to wit, unfair, untrue, and scurrilous maligning of a competitive corporate body, individual, and/or product. Okay, boys."

They handcuffed him and hustled him out without even picking up his luggage and his raincoat. He tried to look confident, but I thought the law-abiding public wouldn't suffer much longer from the conniving of Statistomat, Inc. I settled back into the deep chair and turned with a triumphant grin toward the door of the room's closet.

It opened. My brother, dressed in the distinctive charcoal-green suit of a General Computers junior executive, stepped out, turning off the tape recorder as he came.

He was grinning, too. "You had me biting my lip," he admitted, "but you came through all right. It's a good thing, too. It always gives me a specially grateful feeling when I see society saved from a deviant like that… It's not that there was any danger they would have challenged Incomac's market leadership, but even if they had continued in existence as small as they are now they would have taken away *some* customers. Our responsibility to our stockholders is not just to make profit. It is to make the maximum possible profit — to optimize!"

Of course!

My brother's gaze was distant as his keen mind searched for the deeper lessons of the day's work. He said, "Maybe we should get the public release of those Commerce Department reports discontinued."

"The Names of Yanils" was written in the mid-1970s but first appeared in *Crank!* in Spring 1994.

THE NAMES OF YANILS

YANILS OWNED THE name of Trumpeter. That is not to say that the Fishers *called* him Trumpeter, except twice a year: at and after the Assembly, which he announced with a trumpet blast, and at Convention. With the Chief it was different, he was called no name but Chief of Fishers. Yanils and others who had been his friends had forgotten the Chief's birth name from the day he became Chief. Yanils owned the birth name Yanils, and the name of Trumpeter, and the name of Feather.

He kept the trumpet; and it was legitimate for him to look at it in secret even during the winter, though of course he would not want to blow it then even softly. He kept the dangerous headdress of porcupine quills which, when he wore it as Feather, gave him the crest of a giant kingfisher. It was dear to him that the Fishers were the most important and best of the people (though some disagreed) and that he had the most important and fortunate lot of any Fisher (though with this he might have had to go to some long-deceased Trumpeter to find agreement).

The Fishers lived along the coast, southward from the mouth of Benwal. All their farms were within trumpet-call. The hunters never stayed overnight any farther than that, either, except in the spring. They did not range northward toward the River at any time: the Badgers had a permanent territory there which other people did not hunt even for game the Badgers could not eat.

Each spring, toward the time of the longest days, a storm came from the western ocean to signal the time of Commencement. Some springs, when none of the storms was very violent, only the Feather could tell which was the signal. Commencement meant primarily conferring manhood on any boys who were ready for it. This lasted several days, which Feather ruled. All the men, not only the new ones, felt very strange indeed. Then a long sleep, and an extraordinary feast which the women served, made them new men and opened the new year. (For the Beavers' and Badgers' mid-winter New Year's festival, the Fishers had little curiosity or respect.)

If there was a challenge for the name of Chief, it was best held at New Year's. Most years there was not. Every year at New Year's, new Chief or no new Chief, the Feather's second function began. This he enacted alone, and his ceremonial crest of quills was replaced by a more manageable one of duck feathers. The sea was off limits at this season even for Fishers—even for Yanils if bare-headed. But Feather braved the taboo, as often as he was permitted.

The first condition was that the sun had to be visible. When its whole disk was in view, Feather lighted the fire he had ready at the altar. Looking directly past the fire at the sun, he must see the smoke rising to his left. If it did, the third test, which seldom failed, was to offer to the ocean a dugout canoe as long as his hand, containing an effigy kingfisher: this had to float south, away from

Benwal. Then Feather took his own canoe out to sea, paddling northward and keeping watch.

Only in this way would the great schools of fish come. The first Fisher to see one was always the Feather. During the weeks that he was invoking the fish, no nets were sewn—it was obligatory to have them finished before Commencement—and nobody spoke the word "fish." When Feather had seen a school, he flung his crest into the ocean and became Trumpeter. He paddled to the village and ran to blow the trumpet at the altar for Assembly.

The Fisher men dropped whatever they were doing and launched rafts on the ocean, which was full of fish. The Trumpeter ruled the fishing, and decided when it had gone on for enough days. Then he told the Chief to send messengers to call the other people to Convention.

All the people had a two-day feast of fish—except the Fishers, who could never eat fish, and who feasted on meats brought by the others. The Badgers and Halfmoons, the Beavers and Deer, brought many gifts, sometimes including a new wife for the Chief of Fishers; and they went away loaded down with dried salt fish and with fairly fresh fish wrapped in kelp.

The Trumpeter ruled the Convention. When it was done, he took on his birth name again until the next spring.

It was dear to Yanils that Trumpeter was the mightiest name any of the People had, and that Feather was the most mysterious.

The mysteries were private to him, but not quite secret. All defeated challengers for the name of Chief—quite young men, usually—became Feather's apprentices for a while and were supposedly made ready to take on the role. (Actually most of them feared nothing worse.) Nobody knew whether a Feather or Trumpeter could die, but everybody knew what happened when the owner of the names died or was incapacitated during the off-season. One of the apprentices took the porcupine headdress, assumed the identity of Feather in an absolutely secret transformation, and called the next Commencement.

Any man could become eligible to learn the role of Feather by losing a challenge for Chief, except the son of a Feather.

Yanils was a calm, dark man with sharp eyebrow ridges and a sharp nose. His eyes were usually lowered—but to study something. The night his predecessor had died, Yanils had had the headdress before the Chief could reflect on how the new Feather was to be selected. At Conventions Yanils bargained well.

His wife died when their son Emelas was nearly grown, and he did not remarry. He began to talk to the boy about the advantages of being Feather. Even when this was as far as he went, it was something he said to nobody else, and Emelas had to be sworn to secrecy. He listened and learned well, sitting at his father's feet. Although he was almost as tall as his father now, he was forever looking up at him. Where Yanils's sharp eyes were always down, leaving his brows to dominate his face, Emelas turned his large dark eyes upward, at his father, at the sky.

This man Yanils, different from all other people and having this single confidant, wanted to give understanding.

Emelas would have to become a man in a year or two, but there was no reason why he had to be afraid of it, Yanils told him. To prepare himself, he would watch the next Commencement from hiding.

Any Fisher able to imagine such a sin would recognize without pause for thought that the penalty for discovery would be death. Desperate courage was required to carry it through. All men hunted in the same woods with pumas and bears and had the proper sort of courage in reserve. Plainly none of them but Yanils could have called on it for this. He did not hesitate. Emelas kept the secret.

The third and crucial night of Commencement, the boy made his own way to an agreed niche between a boulder and a bush. Only the edge of the arena farthest from the altar could be seen from there, but he was not to put his head out to get a more complete view. Each of the men came in sight anyway in the course of their groggy dance, and so did each of the three boys being initiated. The firelight on their faces seemed violently bright, but Emelas knew he himself was safely dark.

He heard the formulas no boy was supposed to hear until his year had come. What he felt was not the customary terror, or a vicarious form of it, but a special terror all for him. He was not dazed by many hours of dancing; besides, he was not here seeking a spiritual ordeal as the initiates were; for him it was imperative to keep control.

It did not help that the loudest voice, and the highest, and the most uninterrupted, was his father's. It was an unfamiliar, powerful voice, swooping and fluttering like a gale, like a bird. When there were words they were often explanations, repeated over and over, of the interpretation of the next operation to be performed on the initiates. Some were interpreted in terms of kingfishers, some in terms of the other tribes, some in terms of sex. The men of the Fishers, who were well known to have the most sub- missive women of any of the people, secretly worshiped, at Commencement, the Mother of Fishers; also they were the most extreme in arranging that women had nothing essential they lacked. Boys not being equipped with any equivalent of a vagina, they had to be provided with one: a hole was dug in the flesh at the base of the glans by twist- ing in a sharpened, hot sliver of stone, in such a way that the hole would afterward be covered by the foreskin and could be kept secret from anyone not similarly marked.

"Mother of Fishers, fins of our Mother, gills of our Mother. Mother of the dark wave, Mother of the White wave, brother to our brother in the dark night wave…"

This was the last phase of the initiation, so the men were using up the last of their strength in the dancing which accompanied it, their thighs were trembling, their balance was about gone. One of them reeled against the other side of Emelas's boulder, then rolled around it and backed away looking the boy full in the face. If the dan- ger could have been fought by throwing a rock or stran- gling the man, Emelas would have done it silently; since he was helpless, he cried out in surprise. There passed between him and the man the crest of the Feather! The Feather's wail rose — "wind wings, night wings, woman of the day and night, woman of the mountain, woman of die ocean, Mother of the ocean, woman and man of the wind wings" — the other man floated back to the dance, and

Emelas knew that although he had been seen and heard, nobody but his father knew he was there.

After the Commencement feast, since there was no challenge, the invocation of fish began at once. It was a warm, drizzly spring, so that it almost seemed the season had already passed. There were several days in which the sun did not rise clear, then one in which the wind was wrong, then several more cloudy. At last the kingfisher effigy could be given to the ocean. This was done ten different days, separated by days of inauspicious weather, and each time the canoe drifted northward. The Feather never began his vigil on the ocean.

There would be no fishing this year. The occasional bonito and barracuda that foraged off these coasts would run into no nets—and not much prey. It was the Lame Year.

Yanils could remember the last one. It had been before he was Feather, but the procedures had been taught him in his apprenticeship, so he played his part smoothly. The day he was sure it was the Lame Year, he stood in the water at the beach—not in his canoe—and deliberately took off his crest. He stood motionless, holding it upside down in front of him, for half the morning. By that time the word had got around, and half the Fishers were standing watching him. He began the chant for the Lame Year, word for word as he had been taught it. Assembly was a protracted, solemn affair, because it called the Fisher men, not to leap to their boats, but to choose a girl to give away at the Convention. Both Assembly and Convention went off well, although, as usual on Lame Years, the Fishers contributed nothing to the feast but corn. Their prestige suffered. They would have to be munificent next year.

The only major consequence was that no initiations were possible at the following Commencement. They required a whole bass skeleton, to become the living presence of the Mother of Fishers, but, as usual following Lame Years, there was none.

Emelas would have to wait one more year to become a man. The two of them did not discuss his spying on Commencement, so that there was no one to suggest aloud that the sin had caused the Lame Year. This occurred to Yanils, though. He considered it calmly for several days, that fall. It seemed to him that the initiation, even though it occurred at New Year's, didn't have much to do with the ocean, and breaking its rules couldn't change the ocean's willingness to bring them fish. The invocation of the fish had been carried out impeccably, hadn't it?

To consider so was not hard, but to rest easy on such a conclusion, with nobody to support it, was very hard. The Feather's watch for fish the next summer was a lonely and anxious time. He sat day after day in his canoe, very close to the ocean for whose favor he waited, and drew no strength from the mystery of his name. At length the schools came; it was a good year. He was confirmed.

Now Emelas could become a man. Though in all these two years he did not discuss his advance knowledge of the ceremony with his father, and of course never expressed any reluctance, it was plain that the intended prevention of fear had not worked. The boy was afraid, only not mystified. His only comfort was his possibility of looking on the Feather, not as an ominous demi-god, but as his conspirator. Not being able to stand in awe of Yanils, he leaned on him. He became the only Fisher to have sustained that surgical pain with a clear head, without the anesthetic of delirium. He was saddened, but his eyes stayed wide and his back straight.

Yanils, he whose mind was his own, thought how he could make his son Trumpeter. (He inclined to the view that this name would have to be passed on first; breaking tradition with the more occult name of Feather would be harder to put over.) Plans filled his mind during the long days of waiting for sky and wind to allow his canoe to set out.

During the preceding winter, far up the coast to the north, an earthquake had partially blocked a once-deep channel between the mainland and a large island. The great cold current which used to sweep right down the coast was now steered a little more out to sea. This allowed the comparatively desert southern current to run permanently in a course next to the shore, where formerly it had flowed only in widely-scattered exceptional years.

The Feather, confident this year and preoccupied, was a long time accepting the fact of another Lame Year. When he had to, he did. It was too late for it to imply guilt to him; he accepted it matter-of-factly and followed the appropriate forms, never observing aloud that this Lame Year was uncommonly soon after the last.

However, he and Emelas began surreptitiously seining at night as soon as they could get away with it. It would be convenient to have a sea-bass skeleton hidden away, in case.

They did not catch one, and there were no initiations.

By the time there had been four consecutive Lame Years, the need was urgent. Emelas had duly challenged for the name of Chief and been repulsed. One of his friends had challenged the following year and become Chief. Perhaps it helped this Chief's serenity that the next crop of adolescents was not becoming eligible to challenge him, for lack of Commencements. Surely it helped Yanils's serenity to have a Chief who had been brought up from childhood to revere him. But Yanils was least able of anyone to look serenely on the plight of the tribe.

The number of girls the Fishers gave away had to be increased to keep the Conventions equitable. This did not mean a shortage of wives: in fact, girls were staying single longer, for lack of men. The decrease in the size of the tribe would be appreciable in a few years.

Their food supply seemed to be decreasing even faster: able-bodied fellows were kept from hunting because they were formally not yet men, and the women didn't seem able to produce the extra corn the Convention called for. The difficulty of satisfying the Convention feast was eased a little when Trumpeter persuaded the people to accept river fish; but Benwal offered only perch and sunfish in meager supply. Except at Convention these were no help, since Fishers could not eat them.

The main problem was to resume initiations. It was manifestly Feather's problem, and he was struggling with it; he was not yet desperate enough to admit outside the family the need for unblessed ocean fishing, and in any case he doubted that any number of Fishers could find bass in waters where there weren't any.

That summer at Convention the young Chief, wrung with humiliation at the Fishers' fifth failure in six years to serve the customary banquet, and anxious as to how their substitute gifts were being received, without warning saw in front of him the carcass of a large bass. He looked up at the face of the Chief of Half-moons, who was offering him it as a gift. It was incredible, because none of the other tribes fished, and in any case the Half-moons never came near the ocean except for Convention. The Chief of Half-moons waited.

Trumpeter and Emelas, standing by, knew that a crucial moment had arrived. Emelas might have accepted, or cued the Chief to accept, and shown his eagerness — thereby losing more of their scarce credit and also exposing their cult. Not the Trumpeter. He intervened, not as representative of his tribe but as ruler of the Convention. "Chief of Half-moons, when have any people given fish to Fishers?"

The Chief of Half-moons smiled very slightly; the Chief of Fishers, seeing in the offer for the first time a jibe at the poor job he had done in offering fish, glowered and made the conventional aggressive sign between Chiefs, hopping twice on his right foot with right hand raised.

Trumpeter said, "Chief of Half-moons, such a gift is not welcome in the Convention. Take it away. If you want to offer it to Brother Beaver, wait till afterward." The Chief moved off and made as if to throw the skeleton away. "Farther!" He dropped it carelessly, all the way outside the crowded arena.

Trumpeter noted the spot and went on with business. Late that night, unseen, he and Emelas found the skeleton.

It turned out to be practically complete and quite fit for trans-substantiation into the Mother of Fishers.

They said nothing about it through another tense winter, in which the complaints about shortage of hunters were vocal and bitter in the village. They said nothing until the wild rain was falling, which signaled the new year. Then Yanils, becoming Feather, revealed that in the next three nights nine new men would be made. The relief was almost hysterical. On the strength of this, and of the last of the Commencement frenzy, Feather got away with passing his headdress and name to his son, in front of all the men. The ceremony for this, which the two had composed and rehearsed, was recognized as wholly authentic.

In the general exultation, they were the only two who were not sure of a good fishing year. Even they hoped, when after a month, one day finally the signs were right. Everyone watched the new Feather paddle out from shore and north along the coast. And again half a month later when he put out again. He returned this time to become Trumpeter — but a Trumpeter of a Lame Year. He stood crest down in the gentle surf, and there was no need to wait for the Fishers to gather for the chant: most of them were already there.

The next day the Assembly heard what he and Yanils proposed to restore the Fishers' standing among the people. Beside offering girls in marriage to the other tribes, they would offer girls and young men in service, on the understanding that these would remain Fishers, and return after two years. The scheme was well worked out (it had to be, for it was not feasible to submit something like this to the men for amendment). Each loaned Fisher would bear a fish-shaped scar on his upper arm, as a reminder of his allegiance. To avoid the scar being taken as a brand of inferiority, the Trumpeter and his father proudly displayed the wounds newly cut on their own arms: all Fishers henceforth would have them.

Yanils was glad his son had replaced him for this venture. In the first place, the young man was a more impressive Trumpeter, with his dark, wide eyes and his head held high. And then, they seemed to have more authority this way: the authority of wisdom and the authority of a powerful name inhered in two different men, who agreed.

The young man was aware he was taking more of the risk in case the plan failed. He was willing.

Yanils helped to get the Fishers' unquestioning support for the scheme. At Convention, questions would be raised, by men skeptical of all Fisher names. Yanils left it entirely up to his son.

The young Trumpeter spoke nobly of the pleasure he would take in granting so generous a gift as he was about to reveal. There was no lack of confidence in his manner; indeed Yanils, listening, was afraid he was antagonizing them by his haughtiness. When Trumpeter set forth the offer, however, the Chief of Badgers greeted it with frank gratitude. After that, even if the other tribes had not taken a single servant, the Fishers would have been back in good standing in the exchange. In fact every tribe took some.

This was the way the Fishers lived for many years. Yanils could not see that the quality of the nets declined; but they got no use except for a few little river fish to eke out the

Convention feast. Rafts, with a floor of thin poles lashed over three dugout floats, were in repair and waiting each spring; but they were never used. The worry of finding a bass skeleton for Commencement recurred. Some years the secret ocean fishing was successful. There were fresh-water bass in the Half-moon Lake and in the River, it turned out. If Yanils and Emelas had known they were getting fresh-water bass from the Chief of Half-moons, they might have shrunk from making the substitution; but by the time they noticed the difference, it had proved its efficacy in the initiation. Though the Chief of Half-moons never repeated his insulting offer, a young Fisher once brought back a bass, still dripping, when he returned from service to the Half-moons. A round-headed stranger, whom Yanils took into his confidence, for several years secretly brought bass caught in the River; since he was not one of the people, it was permissible, and Yanils paid well; but then he stopped coming. Most of the Fisher men never asked themselves where Feather got the body of the Mother of Fishers.

The Fishers were prosperous. Grateful for the servants, the other tribes were generous. The returning servants were strange, and sometimes annoying to the Chief. They brought back new and sometimes confused ideas of how to hunt, how to make baskets, how to make love. They might not endorse the ideas, but they felt magnified by having them to report.

Yanils and Emelas intended Emelas's son Artals to continue the dynasty, and put him through the preliminaries—manhood, unsuccessful challenge, and apprenticeship—at an early age. Even before that, Emelas had begun telling him the secret epic of the achievements of Yanils. He had time to include many little problems as well as the large ones, and all were told and re-told. His account was impressive and dramatic; it was also scrupulously accurate and represented Yanils winning by discovering a strategy which would win, while other strategies would have lost. It was the only legend among the Fishers which was of this kind. Artals also (this Emelas did not think of) heard the rational solutions before he could see the complexity of the problems that implied them; he heard the breaks with tradition praised before he knew the tradition or the force it had among the people. Hearing an episode told just as Emelas saw it, he did not see it like Emelas, though he tried. One thing was transmitted intact: admiration for Yanils.

Emelas died of a fever one spring. Yanils handed over the symbols of office to Artals. The old man was suffering more grief than was proper, and concealing it, which made him impatient and off-hand about the transformation of Artals. (To every previous owner of the names, the transformation had been momentous.) Then Yanils took over the coaching.

His pupil, he concluded quickly, was a dense one. Yanils may have been too old to relish aggressiveness like his own in a youngster, or too far past the years when he and Emelas had developed the new ways to remember how uncertain they had been. The main thing was this: Artals reminded him of Emelas and was not. He looked like his father; also, since his mother had been expelled from the household, Yanils could talk freely with him all day, just as with Emelas when he was a bachelor. So whenever

Artals reacted to any passing matter differently from what Emelas would have done, Yanils was disappointed. He didn't show contempt, but he showed his disappointment. To Artals the difficulty of pleasing the old man reinforced his veneration.

"What are you doing telling your friends how we choose who goes into service?" he nagged one winter as they inspected nets. "I don't tell all my friends, grandfather. Just Omas and Yeters, who are eligible to take my names. Somebody has to be ready in case I die. You wouldn't want the names back, would you?"

"I'll be dead before you. Teach those two what the Feather and Trumpeter have to do. Don't teach them things that aren't in the ancient rules. Don't teach them our ways. I suppose next you'll be telling them where we got the body of the Mother of Fishers."

Artals was startled. "Why not, grandfather? That is part of the job now. What would you want the new Feather to do — make no new men until there was another good fishing year?" An unlikely event, his tone emphasized.

The old man had no answer. Artals puzzled over his meaning, but within a couple of months gave up. To the extent that he understood, he obeyed.

Yanils, now the oldest man in the tribe, died shortly after.

For a long time his directing hand was not missed. Artals took a wife and raised children. He was not carefree, indeed he was not in any way a very happy man. But he did not feel during these years that the fate of the Fishers hung on him as it had on Yanils. As he did not aspire to supplant Yanils's legend, which he quietly spread, so he did not aspire to supplant Yanils's judgment. His authority extended essentially only over initiating men and playing host at Convention; aside from that, he was not very different from other Fishers.

Then suddenly one night he was pressed into the role of sage. Something happened to him which had never happened to Yanils: the Chief appealed to him. He came one rainy autumn night, wearing his dress cape. Artals's wife and two younger children were sleeping in the house, and the door was shut against the weather, so the two men had to stand with their heads in the smoky top of the house and take counsel in whispers, deepening the strangeness of the situation.

The problem was one which had been discussed generally among the men (except the Chief, who did not chat). The young bachelors who had returned from service during the last few years were an unruly bunch. There were not enough wives to go around, and they were bored. They had had two years apiece of doing their neighbors' work without thanks; they knew their neighbors' customs and territories; and they had taken up celebrating their emancipation by sneak raids on the other tribes. These had been few and petty enough so far that dignity would not allow punishing them. What would happen if they continued? The men shook their heads and speculated. If they had sons or brothers who were involved, they tried to caution them. But risk was welcome to the bachelors.

It seemed the problem was up to the Chief, who was ruler of all legitimate forays outside the village. At the same time, Trumpeter was, even more than the Chief, the Fishers' diplomat, and besides, Artals was heir of Emelas, heir of Yanils; so the Chief had come to him. In all due gravity, not pleading or ordering, the Chief set forth the problem. He stated all names and details he knew. When he had done with the statement of facts, he took up the causes—ending with this one:

"The young men do not follow the Customs. They know it is the custom to respect the other people. They know it is the custom to make gifts to them, to give them corn and give them service in pride, and take their gifts in pride. They say that Yanils taught that all customs may be broken. When they cross Benwal into Badger territory, something Yanils never did, they say this is Yanilism."

The coined word meaning "Yanilism," or perhaps "skepticism," was compounded "Yanils-scar-headdress." Artals had heard it before, especially from his brash, round-faced son Okteis. Okteis, though a man, had not been in service and was not known to have raided. Still it was true that he talked like this. Artals being the extreme of unexpected frankness and the principal chronicler of Yanils's resourcefulness, Okteis had expressed these ideas more freely with him than the other bachelors had with their fathers. Even so, it was only in unintentional eavesdropping that Artals had heard Okteis's more startling suggestions: that the rafts were useless, that all years were Lame Years, that Yanils had kept up the ritual of looking for great schools of fish in the ocean only as an impressive show to increase the respect with which the Fishers listened to his guidance, and that if alive today Yanils would agree that such mystifications were no longer useful. Artals did not quote this to the Chief. He had not heard this still bolder conjecture of Okteis: that bass were not essential, that perch or carp from Benwal could confer manhood on a Fisher boy.

The Chief said. "The grandson of Yanils knows that Yanils would not fight with our Brother Badger. The grandson of Yanils knows that Yanils would not have Fishers running far through the woods without the Chief leading them."

Yes. There was a third reason the Chief appealed to Artals: to stop the perversion of the tradition of Yanils.

Artals stood silent a long time. He went through everything in internal dialogue with Yanils and accepted only what he could imagine Yanils accepting. Seeing the motionless face of the Chief by the dim glow of his hearth, the sense of incongruity caught him; he lost certainty that tomorrow would be like yesterday, and he was able to evoke Yanils's imagination and confidence better than he ever had in the old man's presence. He decided.

"Chief. I own the name of Feather."

"Yes."

"I own the name of Trumpeter."

"Yes."

"Chief, I own the name of Yanils. I will take on the name of Yanils at a council of all the men which you will call. In the name of Yanils I will give the bachelors a winter raid which you will lead, which will dare our Brother Badger but not harm him, which will help the Feather and all our people."

The Chief did not answer.

Artals stated the plan: an annual attempt to net freshwater bass for the following Commencement. This meant invading the territory of either Half-moon or Badger. Because Half-moon Lake was frozen all winter and its known fishing spots were in sight of the settlement, it would be better the first time to try the river.

The Chief did not answer.

Artals explained the problem of the Mother of Fishers carefully, assuming it was unfamiliar. He asked where bachelors would be found to go into service if there were no initiations for a few years. Okteis and a few others had not served, but they would all resent being chosen after being spared once. New bachelors were needed, hence bass were needed.

The Chief left convinced.

At the Council, the men stood solemnly in a circle as at Assembly. Artals stood at the altar. Without the dominating presence and the planned oratory Emelas would have had, his straightforward opening was unconsciously powerful.

"Chief, I own the name of Feather."

"Yes. Artals."

"I own the name of Trumpeter."

"Yes, Artals."

"Chief, I own the name of Yanils."

"Yes, Artals."

"I take the name of Yanils."

"Yes, Yanils."

The response was such that he might have successfully done what the Chief had first wanted: simply told the young men to stop their nonsense. But he stuck to the plan. There was perfect silence as he spoke about the foray, and as far as he could tell perfect agreement, until, when he was almost through, a voice broke in.

It was Yastuls, the Chief's son, a lean, heavy-browed bachelor just back from service with the Badgers. He spoke tensely: "Our people can not fish except in summer, ruled by the Trumpeter. Yanils never fished except as the Trumpeter."

Artals-Yanils knew this was false, but he also knew his grandfather had wanted it believed. He said. "Our people are the Fishers. The fish are our blood in all seasons. The fish, our Mother, waits for us."

Yastuls, with eyes wide, said, "The ocean brings the body of our Mother to the Trumpeter in the summer." If he had any support it was inarticulate, and probably among the older men. It was extraordinary for him to insist so long.

"I, Yanils, say that you are not the Trumpeter, you do not own the name of Trumpeter, and you have not been instructed in the ways of Trumpeter, since you have never challenged."

The young man had to be loyal to the authority and tradition he was appealing for. He cooperated with the rest of the preparations, even contributing a few recent reports on Badger routine.

Part of the plan was to slake the young men's thirst for suspense by protracting it. Artals waited until the first full moon after the first snow to set out. He and the Chief were the only married men along. It was the only time the name of Yanils commanded such unity.

Crossing Benwal, they continued north on foot, packing canoes and nets. They followed the shore at the foot of rock slopes and cliffs. Most of the way they would be out of sight of anyone at the top, and the muttering surf would do something to cover any noise they made.

As they passed below the Badgers' village, they listened for any sounds of activity. To their surprise, they heard low voices. Yastuls whispered to his father in anguish, "It must be their New Year!" The Chief didn't make out the words, thought he was demurring again, and hurried ahead disgusted. Yastuls hurried after, trying to get him to listen, then gave up. They were past the village now anyway.

At the river they spread three nets between canoes and the shore. They couldn't help being exposed to sight here, so they posted lookouts in a ring around the fishing. They got a pretty good haul; in a short time they took stock and found that three of the fish they had caught were suitable, so they started back. There was plenty of time to reach Benwal by day-break: the moon was a little more than halfway across the sky.

Yastuls, realizing the Badgers would be preoccupied with the most sacred part of their ceremony, decided not to try again to warn his father. As the Fishers passed the village, the Badger men jumped them. They wounded a few Badgers with half-hearted spear-thrusts before being surrounded and disarmed. The Chief and Artals, obviously the leaders, were killed, and the young men sent home empty-handed and naked. They arrived bewildered and in pain after fording the icy stream. They were put to bed beside blazing fires, and slept through the women's wailings until midday.

They wakened healthy enough, but as dizzy with humili-ation as if with a high fever. The wailing was still going on. Nobody disturbed them until late afternoon, when the women brought them some bread and some clothes and the men came to take them to a council.

Omas had taken charge. He said a few words about the disgrace of the Fishers, so obvious that he needn't have bothered. Okteis expected the disgrace next to be concen-trated on the bachelors. Nothing of the sort. Omas went on to say that since they must have a Chief and the Chief must be chosen by challenge, there would be a challenge immediately, with the loser, if he survived, to get the trum-pet and the kingfisher crest. In an ordinary challenge, if the incumbent Chief lost, he had to be killed; today this rule had no application, there being no incumbent.

The contestants would be Okteis and Yastuls. After the first shock, Okteis decided it made sense. It was taken for granted that he would lose. That would make both Yastuls and himself succeed their fathers. Also the old men may have been so subtle as to want candidates who were bach-elors, but not trouble-making raiders. Of course both he and Yastuls were technically unprepared to become Feath-er, but that technicality was being overlooked.

Well, all right, he thought, but what a headache it would be to work with such a traditionalist Chief as Yastuls!

Without delay Omas put into his hand the sharp wooden dagger as long as his forearm, and faced him off for the challenge. He and Yastuls circled. They were both shaky in the knees. Okteis did not feel like facing danger

263

this afternoon. The danger was not entirely sham. Even the most perfunctory challenge had to have some resemblance to a fight. Besides, if Yastuls was thinking what a headache it would be to work with such a Yanilist Feather as Okteis, he had the option now to try to kill him.

Okteis decided that he was too weak to maintain the caution required through a long fight. He'd have to miss with one thrust, and then take the first one from Yastuls, docking it with his arm if necessary to keep it from being fatal.

He charged clumsily, all his attention on his defensive left arm, and swung his dagger in a slow sideways path that would be easy to dodge.

Yastuls didn't dodge it. He crouched to take it on the left shoulder, then dropped to the ground with the conventional cry of "Mercy, Chief of Fishers!" He peered nervously at the hand he had pressed to his scratched shoulder; yes, there was a little blood, he was within his rights in quitting. He smiled tautly. The Chief, who had been Okteis, was appalled at the completeness of his defeat. He was now Chief for life!

"You have no right!" he howled, tears marking his round, childish cheeks. "You have no right to the names of Yanils!"

Yastuls, still on the ground, said, "My mother's mother was the daughter of Yanils. I will be the Feather who restores the ancient ways." His speech was stiff, as if rehearsed. "The Fishers have suffered for the sins of Artals. Now we —"

"We suffered for you — you betrayed us," screamed the Chief. "You knew the Badgers. You knew we'd be caught!"

264

Now Yastuls was on his feet shouting too. "You think I wanted to lose my father? You think I wanted to be beaten by the same people who have been walking on me for two years?" His sincerity was clear, and the sympathy of the men watching swung to him. But he went on wildly, "We were punished for the sins of Artals. We will reform. We will follow the old ways, and the ocean will again bring us the body of the Mother —"

He was interrupted by several of the older men. He had forgotten: it was day, and though the women were not supposed to be near the arena, they might have heard the secret name, the way he was shouting.

This small victory calmed the new Chief, and by the next day he was cheerful again and joked with his friends about old-fashioned young Yastuls. For now, the old ways were entrenched, but it was mostly the old men who supported them. In a few years Yanilism would be nearly universal. Yastuls, meanwhile, rejecting bass from unhallowed sources, would be unable to create more men: a calamity, but one which would only discredit Yastuls the faster.

The Chief had a sense of humor but also a taste for movement: he would not have waited patiently if he had not seen other problems.

Irresponsible raiding was not one of them. He did organize a second poaching trip to the River. It was successful; he presented a bass to Yastuls with plenty of witnesses. Yastuls refused to touch it, and he took it away. But the problem that worried him was the Badgers.

They were taking too many girls in service and treating the men they took too badly. Artals had given away a girl Okteis liked last year; it hadn't been tragic to him, for he was not eager to marry yet, but it was fresh in his mind. All the tribes were demanding a lot, but this year the Badgers would have a special claim. There would be no new men. The Fishers would have only girls to send.

The first thing he did was to plant more corn. It meant putting men on women's work; but he explained that the extra corn was for Convention, where the other people brought meat, therefore was honorable—and perhaps should properly be entirely raised by men. The crop was not what he hoped, but he looked for further improvement the next year. As it was, the Fishers were able for the first time to make appreciable gifts of corn for the others to carry home.

It was not enough. The gifts of the others were generous. He offered no men, two girls for marriage, and one girl for service. It was clearly not enough.

The Chief of Badgers raised his right hand, hopped twice, and growled, "The Fishers take, without asking, the gift of crossing our territory. Surely they mean to return large gifts for this." It was fortunate he was not free to tell the non-Badger chiefs that his rites had been interrupted.

The Chief of Fishers said quietly, "The Badgers take, without asking, the blood of our fathers."

"The Badgers offer you, beside our other gifts, three canoes—and no nets."

The other chiefs seemed to feel accounts had at least been squared by this. But they all reminded the Fishers of the traditional obligation of service, "Why do you send no men this year?"

The Chief of Fishers looked up at Trumpeter, who stood stilly beside him. "The men are delayed by the will of the Feather."

"Who is the Feather?"

"The Feather is not here at this season. The Chief of Fishers, to show his great friendship and desire to appease his Brothers Badger, Beaver, Half-moon, and Deer, gives them a gift he has never given, by naming this mysterious name."

They were at once satisfied—especially the Badger, whose grievance of sacrilege had, in a sense, been repaid in kind.

The Chief of Fishers smiled at the Trumpeter, not in friendship but in challenge.

Yastuls could not last many more years. That winter the Chief again offered him an unblessed fish carcass, and again he refused. The Chief put new effort into the corn planting, but more corn, even in quantity to make up for the reduced offers of servants, would not satisfy the demand of the Fishers themselves for new initiations.

Yastuls thought that the failure to bring the fish his first year, in spite of his rectitude, might be due to insufficient rectitude. Had the nets been made according to ancient formulas? He was not really sure. His instructions had not been from a Feather, but second-hand through Omas and other contemporaries of Artals. They were sure of the preparations for launching Feather's canoe, and of all details of Commencement, but they did not agree very well on other things. They were not at all clear, for instance, on how often the blessed Yanils had suffered Lame Years. Some said, never two successive Lame Years while Yanils was Feather. Yastuls told himself, never two successive Lame Years while Yanils was alive, though none of the old men was that optimistic.

The Chief and his friends watched with open amusement the daily preparations of Feather. He awaited the sunrise at the altar, lighted his fire with full ritual. North wind. He walked back home stony-faced. He watched for another sunrise. Clouds. He walked back home, his cheeks sucked in, not looking to right or left for anyone. He had no doubt of his own ability to keep this up all season, five seasons; but he doubted the Fishers would wait.

The next morning nobody troubled to watch him. The sunrise was clear, the wind gentle from the south. He launched the kingfisher effigy. It was swept away to southward! He could begin his watch for fish! Last year he had never got this far.

In the afternoon, having drifted back close to the village, he noticed there were a few Fishers watching. Were they impressed? He wasn't close enough to see their faces.

That night nobody spoke to him. If they believed in his approaching triumph, they thought it better not to rush it.

The next morning the signs were all favorable again. He paddled out, and when he stopped he saw the current was bearing him rapidly southward. The sea was not choppy, but a breeze ruffled the surface. He strained his eyes in all directions. It would be easy to mistake a wavelet for the splash of a jumping fish.

Some months before, an eruption of an underwater volcano had directed the great cold current into a new channel — more strongly shoreward than ever. Today it brought the fish from the subarctic. The Feather saw hundreds leaping all around him. He sprang to his feet in the unstable canoe, in ecstasy, and flung his crest into the sea.

He was vindicated. The ways of Yanils would be preserved, and false Yanilism refuted.

Feather, his teeth chattering with triumph, ran to become Trumpeter in the old way, a long joyful peal not heard before in his time. The Fisher men ran to the rafts, even the unmanned Chief, and Trumpeter ruled the fishing.

They worked until the rafts were glittering with their catch. Trumpeter selected the coming year's body of their Mother, held it above his head in exaltation a moment, and wrapped it up to hide it from the women.

Then they dumped the rest of the fish back into the sea and returned home, saved.

SPEECH

"Shooting Rats in a Barrel" was given as a speech to the American Association for the Advancement of Science's February 1995 meeting in Atlanta. Although, as Professor Davis notes herein, Canada "refrained from having a Red Scare," there were blacklists and persecutions of alleged Communists there, albeit on a smaller scale and in a less systematic manner than in the US: see James L. Turk and Allan Manson, eds. *Free Speech in Fearful Times*. Toronto: Lorimer, 2007.

"Shooting Rats in a Barrel": Did the Red-Hunt Win?

I

THE ACADEMIC RED-HUNT was an episode some of you are old enough to remember and may not have forgotten. Episode? Surely it wasn't an isolated episode. There has been a systematic pressure against the academic Left, present for as long as there has been an academic Left. It intensified and took new forms during some episodes: the early 1920s was one, the late 1960s was one, but the one I am recalling was the major Red-Hunt of 1947-1960.

I was young (I turned twenty-one in 1947), I was academic (a graduate student in mathematics), I was on the Left life-long, as were my parents, so you can be sure I followed most alertly the developments I'm about to summarize.

The opening gun was not directed at professors; it was the campaign to rid the federal service of Communists and other Soviet sympathizers. Soviet sympathizers included much more than just us Left-thinking intellectuals: it included, for example, hundreds of Tsarist émigrés who retained nationalistic loyalty to their homeland. Soviet sympathizers of whatever sort had happily supported the Allied war against the fascist Axis. The constant pressure to expel the Left did not vanish during the alliance, but it abated. Thus my father failed a loyalty check for the OSS (predecessor of the CIA), but many of his fellow left-wingers passed it, and retained positions of responsibility in sensitive government agencies right into the post-war period. The US government was then retargeting its efforts. A fellow US Naval officer (breaking secrecy regulations) told me in summer 1945 that his orders to the Pacific Theater were for the purpose of "beating the Russians to Port Arthur." Winston Churchill announced in his Fulton, Missouri, speech in 1946 that the world was divided into two camps, Western and Soviet—a thesis which Stalin soon took up in even balder terms.

This realignment, dubbed the Cold War, was no doubt a disaster, and I am not defending it. I do say that, given the realignment, it was to be expected that many people welcomed by the government in the years 1942-45 would become unwelcome. The loyalty purge was unstoppable. It came in the form of President Truman's Executive Order of 1947. The loyalty hearings that followed purged the government service not only of policy advisers who would harmonize badly with the new Cold War policy theme; in much greater numbers, the civil servants who were expelled were clerical or other employees who had or were thought to have left-wing tendencies in their off-job lives. A pattern was set which would be imitated.

Right-wing legislators joined in. Congressional Red-Hunting, sometimes related to legislation flimsily or not at all, had erupted briefly before World War II and was vigorously revived in 1947. Public hearings were held for the announced purpose of proving that the Truman government was sheltering Communists instead of purging them; that Hollywood contained a powerful conspiracy to inculcate communist values in the movie-goer; and that left-wing scientists had leaked nuclear secrets to Soviet agents.

These years, 1947-1950, established the ground rules that remained in force for the decade that followed. Most institutions, from the government through the unions and universities to the American Civil Liberties Union (yes, I said the American Civil Liberties Union), declared Communists unwelcome. Among the means used to exclude them were loyalty oaths, often including the phrase "I am not a member of the Communist Party or any other organization which…" It became glaringly obvious that employers, in particular universities, would shy away from hiring anyone who might be attacked as a Communist; a reputation as a student radical was thus enough to make one a bad bet for an academic job; so student radicals became (in a few short years) very scarce. University administrators would occasionally say, if asked, that there were no Communists on the staff; but they hoped they wouldn't be asked. The FBI and the Red Squads of state and some local police forces kept files on thousands. They had a reputation for exceeding legal restraints in interrogation and for keeping very dubious material in their files; later research bears this out. They cooperated (when it suited their own agenda) with employers who were cleansing their staffs. This put them in an ambivalent relation to the federal government in particular. The FBI's J. Edgar Hoover, while nominally responsible to the Attorney General, sometimes cooperated covertly with Congressional exposés of government agencies.

Most universities wouldn't even let left-wingers speak on campus under auspices of a student group! Paul Robeson, Howard Fast, and Dirk J. Struik were among those banned by administrations in the early 1950s. By the late 1950s, the invitations had dried up.

It was further established that one could be imprisoned for Communist Party activity itself, at least if one were a leader: the Supreme Court upheld in 1951 the conspiracy convictions against the CP officers under the Smith Act. The government maintained concentration camps in which it could incarcerate thousands of dangerous people if it declared a national emergency to exist, and everyone knew whom they considered dangerous. These camps were invented by the "liberal" senators in 1952 in an attempt to show voters that they were just as security-conscious as the Right. But though they originated as a mere tactic, they were not merely on paper: they existed physically. I was told this in casual conversation in 1955 by an acquaintance who was employed at a federal prison — a prison, it happens, where I became an inmate five years later. The story would be better if the guard had looked me up and said hello to me then, but — sorry — we were no longer in touch. I ask you to pause for a moment and think how it felt to be a young instructor in 1952, listening to Richard Milhous Nixon on the radio, hearing him describe the hunt for Communists in the USA as shooting rats in a barrel. It was unpleasant enough, I hope, to the others in the room with me; the unpleasantness had an extra tang for me (guaranteeing me against forgetting the moment), being one of those whose humanity was being denied by the words and the vicious tone.

Meanwhile, dozens of Congressional hearings and a few landmark court cases had set the cameras turning on a new scenario. A Congressional committee would call to the stand four to ten witnesses from a university. Among them might or might not be some "friendly" witnesses, who would answer questions, name themselves and numerous colleagues as Communists, and step down, blessed with the Committee's thanks. Most or all of the witnesses were "unfriendly": that is, they refused to answer, or at least to name fellow radicals. If they refused to answer all related questions, on the stated basis that to do so might tend to incriminate them ("taking the Fifth"), they could not be charged with contempt of Congress; this was confirmed by the Supreme Court in the *Watkins* case in 1952. A steady trickle of unfriendly witnesses took other courses, either not invoking the clause on self-incrimination or applying it selectively, so as to talk about their own actions while refusing to name others. Many of these served prison terms, beginning with Leon Josephson and the Hollywood Ten.

Whether you exposed yourself to prosecution or not, non-cooperation with the investigating Committee made you a good bet to be fired and blacklisted from American universities. The nominal stance of the American Association of University Professors was that mere membership in anything could not properly be the reason for firing a professor. There was a tendency to hedge, and the AAUP suffered a near-total paralysis for most of the 1950s. The Association of American Universities, the university administrations' umbrella organization, on the other hand, said publicly in 1953 that Communists must be eliminated, and that anyone appearing as an unfriendly witness created a presumption of unfitness which required a local investigation. The hunt was on.

Beside hundreds who lost their jobs more quietly, by a damaging letter of recommendation or a tip from the FBI to a department chair or simply by appearing dangerous, there were hundreds of us who fell to the more public auto-da-fé I have described. I wrote an assessment of the damage which was published in 1960; the purge was still going on while I wrote it, and I didn't know I was taking stock at the *end* of a period, but (conveniently for this retrospective) I was. You know when I discovered the period was ending? In spring 1960, in Danbury Federal Correctional Institution, where I was serving my sentence for non-cooperation with the House Committee on Un-American Activities. My Saturday afternoon routine was to lie on my bunk and plug my earphones in to the prison's line playing Pacifica Radio's jazz program. That particular Saturday, Pacifica let the jazz be preempted to play their reporters' tape of the mass demonstrations in San Francisco against the hearings of the House Committee on Un-American Activities. "They'll never be the same again," I said; and they never were. My 1960 article was a snapshot of where the Red-Hunt had culminated.

That article will stand today; there are things I would correct now, but I still recommend it to people. The temptation for me is to use its view of the 1960 future as a checklist to answer the question of today's title. That would be too mechanical. But I do feel that the thirty-three-year-old who wrote that article and heard that broadcast is — if not looking through my eyes today, anyway looking over my shoulder and prompting me. Recalling us, maybe, to questions you would not otherwise have asked; leading, maybe, to answers you wouldn't have thought of.

II

Did the Red-Hunt win?

"You want the short answer?" my late friend Chaim used to say, and if the student said, "Yes," Chaim said, "I don't know." Today's question may not even have any short yes-or-no answer. Let's work toward an answer; there will be surprises on the way.

We can start with a part of the question which does have a short answer. If the core of the Red-Hunt was to drive us out of the universities, the short answer is…

Well, one commonly expressed view is that the Red-Hunt fizzled out. It was an unfortunate incident, a ripple in the smooth current of academic freedom. Some of the Red-Hunt's leaders died in disgrace, and we — we won, or so this view would have it. We have been vindicated by history. Thank you, thank you.

We survivors contribute to this facile, shoddy thinking by being such poor object lessons. I accepted the invitation to speak here today, cheerfully, with the result that now you can see that I am alive and well, flourishing as a Canadian professor. Do I look like a victim? Not terribly. Do I go around constantly complaining that I have been mistreated? No. We won — all right. I remember in 1971 a North Vietnamese saying to me, "We are winning the war, but only in the sense that a small child wins a fight against the schoolyard bully if he is still standing at the end." We won the Red-Hunt the same way: though we suffered casualties we were not wiped out.

A friend whose own experience in the 1950s was far from Left circles complimented me not long ago, "You don't seem at all bitter." Right.

This is partly something true about my feelings: I am *not* bitter in my heart. Then too, it is partly a convention, that people like me shall avoid disturbing the even tenor of their colleagues' days: for those who would not ostracize us as heretics would maybe still ostracize us as embarrassing kvetches. The convention permits us to recall the Red-Hunt in nostalgia sessions once every few years, no big deal, that was the way we were. It's easy for me (not feeling bitter) to go along.

Not today. As an expedient, I appeal first to your human courtesy. It is discourteous to tell us that not much happened, when we are the ones who got the ax! But I am not asking for an apology. I am asking you never to forget again that something happened to academic freedom in the 1950s. I am asking you to think about it in a way that will stay with you in future thinking about the 1990s. I am violating the convention today. This is not a confession that we were really bitter underneath all the while. Maybe, if you like, I just want to remind you how much we have to not be bitter about.

Make no mistake. Though you see the remnants of the former academic Left still, though some of us were never fired (like my friend Steve Smale), though I return to the US from my exile frequently — *we are gone*. We did not survive as we were. Some of us saved our skins without betraying others or ourselves. But let me remind you — almost all of the targets either did crumple or were fired and blacklisted. David Bohm and Moses Finley and Jules Dassin and many less celebrated people were forced into exile; most of the rest had to leave the academic world. A few suffered suicide or other premature death. There weren't the sort of wholesale casualties you saw in Argentina or El Salvador, but the Red-Hunt did succeed in axing a lot of those it went after, and cowing most of the rest. We were out, and we were kept out.

Let me emphasize a distinction. I despise the Nixons and Parnell Thomases who mounted this campaign against the Left. Wouldn't I be justified in resenting also the mathematicians who failed to offer me jobs in the US for the last forty years? (Not including those who did try to get me jobs, but they were few.) Any one of them might have valid reasons to prefer somebody else to me, fine, but a blacklist consists of everybody not making an offer, and that's what happened. Those who don't make an offer *are* the blacklist. Now I have often been in good-sized mathematicians' parties in which most of the mathematicians present were people who had failed to give me a job. "We're hiring the best young PhDs we can get," one of them told me years ago — period. These are not my enemies. This is my community, and I don't have any trouble living in it. It is the great academic center; it is not the Nixons and Parnell Thomases. I'm glad I get along with those who implemented the blacklist, but — it is not required that I, or you, pretend that they did not.

There is a certain cautious willingness nowadays to recognize the existence of our pariah group. It's really quite gracious that a university which fired Lee Lorch invited him back for an honorary degree; the administration recognized somehow that he deserves it, and that they were an appropriate body to bestow it on him. Not to gainsay that, I record for proper perspective that the encomium did not say they were sorry they had let him go. It's also quite gratifying that the Academic Senate of the University of Michigan, which more than acquiesced in my firing in 1954, unanimously asked the Board of Regents in 1989 to do something to atone. Not to deny my good feelings about that, I record for proper perspective that the Board of Regents didn't.

There was amusing discussion at the University of Michigan about what would constitute appropriate compensation. At least it amused me. What might they give, back pay? What would that mean?

I had another life, yielding me satisfactions and enough salary to pay the bills. In 1954, I was a scientist four years past my PhD, and the Regents' decision was to extinguish (it seemed) my professional future. What could they do now to restore to me thirty-five years of that life? If it could be done, I would refuse. The life I had is *my life*.

(Some of you know the great poem by Anna Akhmatova, "Menya kak reku." I can say it in the original, or in my translation, but I'm not so good at saying it without weeping, so I'm just making this point in my own words.) It's not that I'm all that pleased with what I've made of my life, yet I sincerely rejoice that I lived it, that I don't have to be Professor X who rode out the 1950s and 1960s safe in his academic tenure and his virtuously anti-Communist centrism. (I guess I won't substitute a name for *X*.)

This is a deeper, less placid sense in which I am not bitter.

III

Whatever compensation any of us got for the injustice (and a few did get a lot of back pay), it would be only a gesture, because the main damage was not to us. We survived, more or less, most of us. What became of *you*? "You," here, means those who hung on and constituted the American universities and reproduced your kind for the following academic generations.

I argued in 1960 that you could not afford to keep out those that had been expelled, that you had to make the effort to take us back. To let the anathema against us stand, I argued, would be an announcement to all comers that dissent was not protected in the universities; and the essence of the university, the confrontation of ideas, would be undermined. Well, you didn't take us back, and most of you didn't try. Has my baleful warning been justified by events? Did you suffer the consequences?

At first sight, definitely not. The campus Left, nearly extirpated by 1955, rose from the ashes by 1961. Protests against the Committee on Un-American Activities (already mentioned); the Fair Play for Cuba Committee; direct action against segregation; marches against nuclear weapons. The next few years saw the Port Huron Statement and militant action against the war in Vietnam. Not only did challenge return to the campuses without us, it came before we had even caught our breath! To be sure, the ideological catch-words were not always ours, and the style was often not; but that may have been an improvement.

Here's another way the 1960s utterly confounded my 1960 foresight. With many Left intellectuals having been expelled from faculties, before or during the 1950s, and with many of those who remained adopting such good disguises as conservatives that there was no difference — I expected that, unless the expulsions were revoked, the next generation of intellectuals would be very conformist indeed. Instead, by 1970 there were dozens of young academic leftists making their way into the universities, some forbidden lines of analysis had been revived, and controversy flourished.

I no more predicted the New Left than Richard Nixon did.

To be sure, some of the Old Left were active, even central, in the New Left, both in the political organizing and in the intellectual revival. (My friend Carl Braden, who bridged the gap, used to say, "There's no Old and New Left, there's only the Left.") I *said* the Red-hunters hadn't caught us *all*. Some of us whom they did catch and expel were still able to lend a hand from Canada.

Still and all, the movement of the 1960s was mainly the work of a corps of newly arrived leftists, from Bettina Aptheker to Martin Luther King Jr. to Carl Oglesby to Angela Davis to Noam Chomsky to Mary Gray… I'm happy to be proved dispensable in this way. We had been defeated, but the spirit of dissent was not stamped out. New dissenters appeared. What lasting difference did our defeat make?

The most obvious thing is that certain words were not said any more in polite company. I deliberately included two Communists among the new leaders I named just now, and I could have included others, but let's face it—the Port Huron Statement dissociated itself from the Marxist parties (even the Socialist Party which was its grandfather), and the pacifist-anarchist-voluntarist strain in the movement ran strong. It was attractive partly for its strengths, which were real, but partly because it was so distinct from the philosophy of the Communist Party. Communism remained part of the discourse of the 1960s Left partly because of the impulse to rebel: A young radical might say "I am a Communist" in the same spirit as he would burn the flag, or fly the flag of the Vietnamese NLF. (Especially likely if the young radical was an *agent provocateur*.) The words that had been excluded from polite conversation reappeared as cries of rage. Again, that's not all bad: they should be.

On the whole, though, when the Red-Hunters disposed of us they nearly silenced advocacy of socialism as we understood it. We had been circumspect about advocating socialism during the World War II coalition period too, and didn't rev up our publicity for it properly in the lull after the War because the focus was on the new UN and hopes for nuclear disarmament. During the Red-Hunt the subject became almost taboo.

With "socialism" and "communism" established as outlaw terms, the Right has proceeded to try to make "liberal" and "secular" and "pluralist" outlaw terms too (for some jobs even today, you may flunk your job interview if you say "he or she").

I'm approaching the final point, maybe the most difficult point, of this talk, and I want to be sure to state things carefully. I will argue that something has been lost, but I have stipulated that openness to innovative thinking about society was not. Already in my 1960 essay, I said that repression does not target original thought, it targets already established heretical movements, which are not experimental but codified. If it succeeds very well in punishing heresies, it may in a next stage punish originality. And in the population, fear of uttering such a taboo word as "communism" may become general paralysis of social thought. This stage was not fully attained. I have also stipulated that what was done to the Left ideas was not to drive them completely underground. Marxist scholars still hold conferences publicly, and if they are professors (many of them are not, please note), they may even include their Marxist works on their résumés seeking promotion or fellowships.

What has happened is that the center of intellectual discourse has shifted, so that some opinions generally regarded as possible in the 1930s are forgotten as possibilities. I don't want to exaggerate, but I think I see this effect; I think it is a loss; and I think the Red-Hunt contributed greatly to it.

It's not just a matter of stale ideas losing appeal. That happens from one generation to the next, inevitably and not always predictably, even without help from any repression. To explain what I mean by the shifting of the center, let me digress to an example where the center of discourse has shifted in the other direction: racism. Racist theory, in the contention of ideas. What do I mean when I say the center has shifted, for the better?

Not that racism has no advocates. It has a few, and they get cushy grants from the Olin Foundation and a notably good press. But some of the things that one might say as a matter of course a hundred years ago would now sound disreputable. Talk of "lesser breeds," say (just think that Rudyard Kipling used that phrase in an *anti*-imperialist poem). They don't have reputable replacements, either: it's not merely the terminology that has changed but the conceptual starting point.

This parallel I'm drawing won't help my argument unless I show you that changing the center changes results. It does. Here's a startling but typical example. Sir William Herschel, praising the mathematical tradition in Sanskrit, described it as closer to European mentality than to the cannibals of West India. This, remember, is an unusually sympathetic and cultured observer speaking, who has studied the early Hindu manuscripts, understood them, and respected them. Yet his conclusion was an anthropological absurdity: mathematics has no negative correlation with cannibalism; indeed when we survey practitioners of human sacrifice, the all-time champions may have been the priests of Meso-America, who were the mathematicians of their time. How was such a fine observer as Herschel led to nonsense? By the practice of rating all cultures on a scale of closeness (in his eyes) to his own: by

Eurocentrism. He had nothing to say about cannibalism; he was only using it as a tag for distance from — distance below — Europe. Just having the wrong center caused him to say nonsense. A century of anti-racist scholarship since then has not ended the dialogue, but has moved its center to where such a person would not make such a blunder.

In the same way, feminist criticism has moved the center of discourse forward.

In political economy, I'm afraid motion has been (by my standards) negative — so much so that ideas which were on the agenda a hundred years ago and sixty years ago have dropped out of memory because they are too far from the new center of discourse. In the old days, in any debate on taxation, everyone was implicitly aware (even those on the other side of the debate) that sales taxes are "regressive" in the sense of taking most heavily from the poor; that it may be more just to take more from the rich so as to reduce inequality; and that such "progressive" taxation may stimulate the economy because the very poor can't buy goods and the very rich don't use much of their wealth to buy goods. This philosophy was not refuted in the 1950s, not nominally being the target of the purge of the 1950s. But as the agenda was cleansed of "our" issues — economic justice and people's control over the economy — the center shifted so far in the capitalist direction that certain ideas became almost unthinkable. They remain rather more comprehensible, even to the lay electorate, in Canada, a country which, nota bene, refrained from having a Red Scare in the 1950s.

Another example is state religion. The state religion of the USA if there had been one was Christianity. It was understood (from 1787 to 1950) that the decision had been made *not to have one*, and why. Americans who wanted to have things like prayer in the public schools continued to want them, but discourse presumed the secular philosophy. How different since the Eisenhower years! The established religion is Judeo-Christianity (or church-of-your-choicism)—progress, no doubt, but still excluding Islam and Buddhism; and it is established. Much discourse obliterates all memory of the concept of disestablishing religion. We freethinkers are treated as merely a minor sect (and a rather malodorous one).

By now, some of you may reasonably have begun to find me too peevish. Am I saying my ideas have lost out *only* because they were maligned and repressed? Didn't they lose out because we, and especially the Soviets, made such an unpersuasive case for them? Aren't I being an awfully poor loser? Can't I see myself that some of my ideas have been disproved by events since 1945?

Of course the world is wide and deep; to find all the causes of conservative gains we would look beyond the intimidation of the 1950s. I won't try; I won't start to; not in this talk. Of course I'm not saying that I and all the others who were fired were right all the time. We were partly right but not perfect, as were many others you can think of. What I am saying is that our questions were ruled off the agenda or ghettoized, and the irrational Red-Hunt largely did it.

Yes, I've reconsidered my credo, yes, I've repented my errors. Listen—I've repented dozens of errors you don't even know about, errors that Richard Nixon and Arthur M. Schlesinger Jr. would never have thought to accuse us of. (List on request.) Being a butt of diatribes prods one to reconsider one's credo *more* than the "safe and sane" do. But *why only me*? The establishment was doing terrible things, bombing Japan, raping Vietnam — why don't the smug centrists try some self-questioning too? They can see differences within the consensus; a viewpoint outside the consensus they can't fathom.

I ask you to listen to us. Don't accept us back into the fold on the assumption that we've seen we were wrong to stray. If you score our reasonableness by our closeness to the present bipartisan center of discourse (and by the way, we may not score very high), you'll be making a mistake parallel to scoring a culture by how close it is to the European! (Euro-centrism…centro-centrism?) Don't do it.

Not only were a number of *us* driven out of the American academic scene, some of our *questions* were driven out. Don't deprive the next political generation of our questions.

INTERVIEW

"'Trying to Say Something True': The *Paradoxa* Interview with Chandler Davis" first appeared in *Paradoxa: Studies in World Literary Genres* Volume 18 pp. 49-80 (2003). Guest eds. Josh Lukin and Samuel Delany. It is reprinted here thanks to *Paradoxa's* generous policy of allowing its authors to retain the rights to their work.

"TRYING TO SAY SOMETHING TRUE"

FOR ALL THAT Herb Philbrick led three lives, the indefatigable Horace Chandler Davis puts him to shame, leading at least seven. He is Chan Davis, the writer of a dozen science fiction stories that probe deeply into social and ethical issues; he is the renowned mathematician Chandler Davis, longtime editor of *The Mathematical Intelligencer* and innovator in the theory of operators and matrices; he is an anti-war activist, having coordinated international protests against the war in Vietnam and been a director of Science for Peace; he is a composer, having co-written the music for Theodore Sturgeon's song "Thunder and Roses" as well as more recent works; he is a member of the mighty intellectual family that includes his wife, the historian Natalie Zemon Davis, and his daughter, the literary and cultural critic Simone Weil Davis; he is the author of several acclaimed poems; and he is a lifelong civil libertarian who has organized for freedom of expression in Eastern Europe as well as North America.

In 1953, Chandler Davis was served with a subpoena as a result of his having paid for the printing of a pamphlet critical of HUAC. His subsequent ordeal included the loss of his job at the University of Michigan and a six-month imprisonment in 1960 for contempt of Congress. Blacklisted from full-time academic jobs in the US, he ultimately found employment in 1962 at the University of Toronto, where he continues to work as Emeritus Professor of Mathematics. He and his wife have each written articles and given lectures recounting his case in the context of the Red Scare years.

At seventy-five, Chandler Davis is handsome and vigorous, remarkably well-informed on current affairs and eager to think about the past in new ways, and sufficiently generous with his time to have given an extended interview to *Paradoxa*.

Chandler Davis (CD): In the 1950s I was already on my way out of the science fiction field. But I was extremely involved in the science fiction world from 1943 to 1948. That's a relatively short time. So that my effect on it and its effect on me was really prior to the great days of *Galaxy* and the other things that will be the center of your discussion.

Josh Lukin (JL): Nevertheless, an interview documenting some facts and addressing some issues in your life and writing will be of real value. You are a New Englander originally?

CD: Well, on my father's side, yes. But that's not the reason I grew up partly in New England. I grew up here and there, because my father [Horace B. Davis] was trying to make a career as a professor and to make the revolution at the same time; so he was frequently fired. And we moved to the next job. And it just happened that I spent a lot of time in New England. I lived several years in Bradford, Massachusetts, and several years in Newton, Massachusetts, and by that time I was almost ready to go to college, so I went to Harvard. So you see that it's New England-centered. And the reason I don't have a New England accent is that I learned my English from my mother. She had a Midwestern accent, which I picked up.

I was an undergraduate at Harvard beginning in 1942, when the US was already at war. I supported the war: I volunteered enthusiastically to fight Hitler and was assigned to the US Naval V-12 program, which meant that I stayed at Harvard, but in uniform and under orders. Which meant that I was both able to advance toward officer status and finish my degree. Went to a crash course, US Reserve Naval Midshipmen's School, and got my commission in 1945. And I was on active duty for a year and then was demobilized. So I never went overseas, but I was on a Naval base for a while.

JL: *Andrew Ross has written of*

> *…the flourishing of a political community and a subculture which, in the thirties and forties, had transformed so many thousands of its members' lives and which, in the Popular Front period, had*

*tried to establish deep roots in American political
institutions, cultural traditions, and popular structures of feeling. [*No Respect: Intellectuals and
Popular Culture. *London: Routledge, 1989: 35]*

*What influence did the Left culture of the thirties have
on your life? Was it a big part of your upbringing?*

CD: Yes. For a brief period, we lived in New York, and
then we were surrounded by overt things, and then
for the rest of my childhood, there was a sort of dichotomy. There was the culture that I got through the
Movement connections of my parents, and there was
the popular culture that I shared with my schoolmates.
And there wasn't a real good union of the two, except
in exceptional situations. I was reading the Popular
Front literature — some of it — and the Popular Front
literature did get into the general culture too, you
know. John Steinbeck, and so forth, which not only
Movement people read. The left-wing literature of the
thirties. But for example, my parents subscribed to
the *New Masses*. This was part of my childhood.

JL: *What did the popular culture of thirties youth consist of?*

CD: Well, the Hit Parade. The Hit Parade is a good example because to me there was a strong overlap
between my political interest in recognizing the cultural contribution of black people and the popular
culture of the swing craze beginning in 1936. So I
completely espoused that, including more of an interest in black musicians and more of an interest in
small-group Dixieland, as compared with most of my

schoolmates. But they acknowledged the legitimacy of the Dixieland stuff, so that was an area where there was not a disjuncture. I could bridge the gap: it was both popular culture and Popular Front culture. I didn't mention to any of my neighbors that I read the *Daily Worker*. There was a division there.

I was a great admirer of Paul Robeson, but that wasn't a big thing. But listening to Dixieland music when I could get an occasional good program on the radio was important to me. That was an integral thing.

JL: *When did you encounter science fiction?*

CD: I was interested in the occasional science fiction before 1939. But in 1939, I became an avid reader of *Astounding Science Fiction*, and got to the point of branching out into other magazines. I had read the occasional science fiction novel before then. But mostly it was starting at the very end of 1939: reading regularly, writing letters to the editor, and attending a science fiction fan club in the Boston area. L. Russell Chauvenet, Bob Swisher, Norman Stanley—who lived in Maine but occasionally came down—Art Widner, who was a major force in science fiction fandom some time after that too; Tim Orrok, who was a fringe member but genuinely interested, and there were others. Some people, like Widner, got involved in national fan things. And I did too, to some extent. So I was a serious fan before I started submitting stories.

JL: *One fan historian has characterized you as a member of fandom's Brain Trust.*

CD: Really? I hadn't heard the term. In fandom, the people who would have serious discussions of intellectual issues were Rothman, Stanley, Jack Speer: I was definitely in that group. When I submitted my first story to *Astounding Science Fiction*, Campbell already knew my name.

JL: *You'd been in the letter column.*

CD: Not only for that reason, but he had met me through Swisher. I think that was true of many people who started writing science fiction for magazines quite young, that they were known through fan connections.

JL: *There must have been a sufficiently small community compared to today's...*

CD: That's right. I don't remember what the source of Campbell's personal friendship with Swisher was, but I think it was collecting. Swisher was a great collector, and Campbell appreciated that; and I think Swisher was in touch with him mostly in that connection.

JL: *In your early years as a fan, did you have some contact with New York-centered fan culture, the Futurians and so forth?*

CD: Yeah. Of course, now I think of some of these as old, close friends; but at the time, my connection with them was through things like fan magazines and correspondence. By 1942, I was a regular correspondent of Milton Rothman and several others. Miltie wasn't from New York I guess. But from the Futurian group, Fred Pohl became a friend quite early. I was never a personal friend of Moskowitz. But then when I did spend a little more time in New York, I met Judy

Merril and Ted Sturgeon and Phil Klass. But by that time the Futurians as such were a thing of the past. They were something that I had read about in fan magazines and realized that some people had shared a savvy that I was an outsider to. And their political relations had changed.

At the time that I was close to this group, it was a very exciting intellectual context because of the good communication, the disputation between people whose backgrounds were not necessarily the same and whose opinions about things were not necessarily the same. Judy Merril was in background a Trotskyist, with other interests that took her already outside of that context. Jim Blish was a socialist-pacifist. And those who had been in the CP were not anymore. I was.

People were friends of Dwight Macdonald: I met Dwight Macdonald and Nancy in that social milieu. They of course had several different positions but were very close to some of the pacifists. Phil Klass of course was Hashomer Hatzair, whose camps he had attended fully expecting to "make aliyah" and join a socialist kibbutz in Palestine. But he was close to the CP, too. By the time I met him he was still Left but not so Zionist. He was active in what I would consider Popular Front activities.

This was the time when I was entering Harvard, and in my undergraduate career it was the same experience: I met Trotskyists and other varieties of Left intellectuals and found that I was very welcoming to their ideas and very interested in talking with them but at the same time very conscious of the fact that some of my political associates would regard that as quite negative.

JL: *You weren't going to approach these conversations as an ideologue.*

CD: That's right. If I submitted my ideas to discussion by this mixed bag of Left intellectuals, I didn't consider that I was converting the heathen. I considered that I was talking about ideas.

So that was a very important period in my life. It took me from 1939 to 1942 to get into this social group, and after that, from 1942 to 1948 was the time that I was a full member of this group. Of the New York Science Fiction Left Intellectual group.

Some people whom I didn't know that well were still important to me, like Cyril Kornbluth, whom I hardly knew. But I admired his writing, and his opinion was important to me.

JL: *Many professors cite Dwight Macdonald to justify their contempt for popular culture. What was his attitude toward all this science fiction going on?*

CD: That would have been a good question to ask him, but we didn't. And Jim Blish and Virginia Kidd and I, for instance, did take serious culture seriously, too. It's a good question: what was our relationship to popular culture as such? Now this was the time of formulation of Sturgeon's Law, you'll remember. Sturgeon was challenged, not by Dwight Macdonald but by Respectable Suburbanites: "Do you really read that stuff? Isn't most of it crap?" And he said, "Ninety percent of everything is crap," and that's the context in which Sturgeon's Law was created.

JL: *Sturgeon took science fiction with a remarkable degree of literary seriousness.*

CD: Sturgeon and Bradbury were people who really tried to watch their prose. Sturgeon also took John Campbell-type science fiction as a vision of the future quite seriously. Maybe he was ashamed of it later — although I never knew Sturgeon to say that he was ashamed of anything he'd done — but he might have been embarrassed after the fact: he wrote a little piece which appeared in *Astounding* soon after [August 1945], exulting at the vindication of science fiction which the construction of a nuclear bomb represented. Well. I considered that somewhat wrong. Campbell obviously didn't. Campbell published it as if he were endorsing it.

Worries about nuclear weapons appeared before, in "Solution Unsatisfactory" by Heinlein, under the name of Anson Macdonald. And after Hiroshima, first in a story by Sturgeon —

JL: *"Memorial"!*

CD: Yeah. And then a story by me, and then a couple more. So that simply regarding this as a great triumph of science fiction over the unimaginative was a short-lived thing. But it was a reaction that Sturgeon had. And which I had, too, for a couple of days. I became a strong anti-nuclear peacenik on reflection. But my first response was, "Heyyy, we did it!"

The other thing that's wrong with it is that John Campbell didn't make the bomb. And Robert Heinlein didn't make the bomb. So there's a little bit of a misattribution there.

JL: There have been in more recent years people who have claimed to have drawn their inspiration for weapons work and military campaigns from science fiction.

CD: H. Bruce Franklin has written of that in a couple of books.

JL: Did he write in War Stars *of people who derived their military technophilia from science fiction?*

CD: Great book. I don't know for sure, but I think it quite likely that it's true and that he said it.

I, in retrospect, am sorry that I didn't declare myself a conscientious objector. Not at the beginning of the war, because if you are ever going to use military force for anything, that was a situation in which I would happily do it: I was wholehearted about that. But once I knew about the destruction of Dresden and the other massacres of civilian populations by the allies, I think the ethical thing to do would have been to declare myself a conscientious objector. Which Robert Lowell did, and a few other people did. But it didn't occur to me at the time, even though I had some Quaker ancestors. Knew a few conscientious objectors. And after the war, met some people in the science fiction community who had as socialist-pacifists spent years in prison. So at that point, realizing that I recognized and that I respected their decision, I had the possibility to re-examine my own.

JL: *In May 1946, you broke in. You had the cover story in the same issue of* Astounding *in which Phil Klass made his debut.*

CD: Of course I didn't know I was going to make the cover. At the time, I was a committed fan; I was in the Navy; I had written and submitted a couple of more or less juvenile stories, which Campbell had rejected with very kind letters. Personal letters. I was working on an article about the work I was doing for the Navy, but, not surprisingly, this was not approved for release by the Navy. This was Naval mine countermeasures. It's interesting stuff, and it's not classified anymore; but it's not surprising that the Navy routinely forbade me to submit that.

But then I sent ["The Nightmare"] in, and Campbell was enthusiastic. I don't like the story very much any more. But the things which Campbell liked in it were mostly things that were genuine virtues, I guess. I think that Campbell accepted as legitimate and dramatic the magnitude of the danger of nuclear war. And he accepted the genuineness of the threat of nuclear terrorism.

The reception of the story was very good, and I was very pleased with the cover. I'd tried to write a story on the citizen's responsibility to curb our own government, that wasn't very good dramatically and didn't make very much splash, but Campbell happily accepted it. Campbell accepted all my stories for the next year or two, I think.

JL: *Isaac Asimov talks about when he first joined the Futurians and then went to Campbell and naively began regaling Campbell with all these wonderful Marxian ideas that he'd gotten from them, which Campbell obviously was not amenable to. Did you encounter political friction in your first dealings with Campbell?*

CD: No. No. Later. At the early time, the astonishing thing — and I've discussed this with Bruce Franklin and of course with my old friends — was that socialist ideas appeared in *Astounding Science Fiction*, the author being not Asimov or Pohl or myself but Robert Heinlein. Of course Heinlein, having a rather elitist mindset which came out in other things he wrote, wrote about socialism with somewhat of an authoritarian side to it. But stories which I think of especially are "Coventry" and "If This Goes On —," which are essentially militant socialist.

JL: *"If This Goes On —" certainly posits a small elite...*

CD: Yeah. And *Sixth Column* is, like "If This Goes On —," about the good of the people being in the hands of a secretive elite. So that if he'd been there in 1917, he would certainly not have supported Kerensky; he would have been a Bolshevik. Now, I didn't know Heinlein personally; but he was very important to me, an important source of ideas, and I thought about what he wrote (I hope I was supposed to. He wrote very fast, but I think that he considered himself at that time at least a writer of ideas, as I did). Heinlein was raising things that we Reds didn't raise, even though they were more our natural topic. He really brought ideas out. Of course, he also brought out ideas of eugenics and things which I had a different attitude toward.

JL: *It became evident in the late forties that he'd become a Rightist.*

CD: Yes, quite militarist. And this ties in somewhat with the earlier Heinlein in "If This Goes On—." But he's *hard-boiled*. He's always hard-boiled even in the earlier things; so the sentimental, quietist things that you can find in Sturgeon or even Bradbury you don't find in Heinlein.

I think to a certain extent it was compartmentalization, that there were some things that we might talk about with our fellow Marxists that we weren't able to trot out for the general public. I can't read my own mind; it's too long ago. But if we get to 1946 and we talk about "The Nightmare" and "Memorial" and these other stories, at that time my main political concern was international control of atomic energy. And support for the UN. And these were left-wing causes which Campbell supported. Or at least was not opposed to. Campbell was quite pro-UN! And not until the following year would I feel that I was at odds with any part of the core science fiction establishment.

And of course, the international control of atomic energy was spiked from both sides, and ceased to be an issue. In 1948 I was enthusiastically propagating the Stockholm Peace Pledge—No First Use. The US was against it and the Soviet Union was for it. Therefore it was a Communist petition. Well, sure it was a Communist petition. I was a member of the Communist Party again at that time. And so there was at that point no conflict in my political thinking. The Party position and my position, with its science fiction and pacifist inputs, were not in any conflict at this point, in supporting the Stockholm Peace Pledge. I wouldn't have *considered* asking Campbell to sign it. But only one year earlier, I would have assumed that Campbell was in support of the Baruch plan for international control of atomic energy.

JL: *Phil Klass has written that Sturgeon served as a mediator between him and Campbell, between a number of people and Campbell. Did you have such a relationship with Sturgeon?*

CD: No, I didn't need it. I already had Campbell's ear via Swisher.

One of the things involved there was Campbell's anti-Semitism. Some people, like Isaac Asimov, just ignored it and got along okay. Sturgeon advised Judy Zissman to be Judy Somethingelse when she submitted to Campbell, and she did. And he advised Phil Klass to be something else when he submitted to Campbell, and he did.

JL: *But when Campbell met Klass, he told Klass that he believed Jews were the Superior Race.*

CD: Campbell was nervous about Jews, and Sturgeon just felt, rightly or wrongly, Don't Raise The Issue. I think that Campbell, by the time he met Judy and Phil, knew that they were Jewish. But Sturgeon might have been right, that it was simplifying life for them.

JL: *It was clear that Campbell had problems about race from his dealings with Chip Delany in the sixties — his refusal to publish a novel with a black spaceship captain.*

CD: Yeah, Campbell was a racist. His thoughts were confused on that. I talked to him a great deal over the years 1941 to 1948. He was quite a believer in genetic determinism, much more than I ever was. I was more interested in eugenic ideas then than I was later, but Campbell still more so; and he was more than open to the idea that the whites and maybe especially the Jews were somewhat superior to the Yellow Races and much superior to the Africans. And in *Beyond This Horizon*, I think it is, the superindividuals of the future have names, some of which sound Jewish. So it's clear that Heinlein is suggesting — and Campbell, I'm sure endorsed it — that if we just have the cream of the cream, some of them will be Jews. And he can feel that, and be anxious about the quality of Jewish intellect. And that's the way he was. And this led to the end of my friendship with Campbell.

It was autumn 1949. We were in the habit of corresponding freely with each other, and he said some stuff that I didn't like; and I said to him, "Now listen here," and "Don't you see that there's a problem here," and he wrote back and said something which still sounded nasty to me. Now he didn't know at that time that my wife was Jewish; he knew that a lot of my friends were; but he was writing to me in a way that he wouldn't have to somebody he knew to be Jewish.

And it was too creepy.

So I wrote him more sternly than I ought to have, I guess. He accepted a couple of stories after that. But we never exchanged a friendly letter after that.

This was the same year that I wrote an article which appeared in the Vanguard Amateur Press Association, which included a lot of the Futurian gang—Damon Knight, Jim Blish, Virginia, Doc Lowndes, and so forth—in which I said, speaking as one science fiction author to others—because I think that a lot of the fans in this organization were also professionals, people who weren't necessarily prolific authors but were professionally in the field—and I said, "It's not satisfactory for all the characters in stories obviously to be white and to have Anglo-Saxon names."

JL: *You made that evident in the protagonist of your very first story: Ciccone is not an Anglo-Saxon name. Neither are the characters in "Blind Play" or "Share Our World."*

CD: Yes, I was doing that systematically. And later on, Hollywood began doing it systematically, too. But at the time I wrote this article, in 1949, it was still common for authors, even if they were German-Jewish refugees like Eando Binder, to let their heroes be white and have English names. And I said, "The future's not going to be like that." And, "Even the present isn't like that." Mix 'em up. This was the main message, but I said some other things, which were potentially more controversial. I also acknowledged problems with the treatment of women in science fiction stories, but suggested that perhaps science fiction was somewhat ahead of the other pulp genres in its women characters. But I said look, you may have a character named Selmer Hirshman in present fiction, and that's fine; but in the future things were going to be more mixed up, and you might maybe have Christine Hirshman in the future.

JL: *Hymie Kelly.*

CD: Yeah. And furthermore, if you have a character who is Italian or Jewish, don't have them speak with exactly the stereotyped accent that they're supposed to have if they have that name. And I said, even a sympathetic story like "Trouble with Water" by H.L. Gold bothers me, because the characters are presented in the form of butts of racist gibes.

JL: *Music-hall caricatures.*

CD: Yes. Of course, Horace didn't agree with that. And Isaac Asimov didn't agree, and he pointed out that he'd made his character in *Second Foundation* escape suspicion as the mastermind by having him speak in dialect. And of course, I had noticed that he had given him a particular idiolect, but he said, "I just had him speak like my father." That was cute. But it's not really germane. He was just thinking about a conversation around the dinner table when he was growing up, and he thought that he'd give Preem Palver a Brooklyn Yiddish accent without labeling it as such. It's an interesting anecdote.

The piece got a certain amount of disagreement, a certain amount of discussion, and obviously interested people. I wasn't the only one who was calling for this at that time, but I was ahead of my time.

Unfortunately, the example that I chose for a hard example to tie the thing together — maybe I should have had five instead of just one — but I had one, which was by L. Ron Hubbard. Of course, L. Ron Hubbard, who was not known to me personally, but was known to a lot of my friends personally, wouldn't stand for that; and so he struck back.

JL: *He put you into a story.*

CD: Yeah. But he didn't really put me in a story: he had the story all finished, and the Bad Guy was supposed to be Swedish. And he changed his name to Chan Davies and made him a Communist. And this was transparently tacked onto the story afterward, because there was nothing about Communism in the story. Just a way of sneaking in a little slander. It happened that I was in the Party at that time. I think I was in the Party from very late 1943 to the time I went into the Navy, December 1944; and I think I was in the Party again from Spring 1947 to summer 1953. So that's not very long — seven years. But it didn't make any difference that I was in the Party, because he didn't know I was; and it was something that could damage you, to be called a Communist. And in principle, it was something you could collect damages for. Obviously, I wasn't going to go to court. So —

My agent at that time was Fred Pohl. And Fred Pohl wrote to the editor of the journal, which was *Fantastic*

Adventures, and said, "Look, it's no big deal, but this is, um, unethical; and wouldn't it be appropriate for you and the author to, um, enclose a note in an early issue of *Fantastic Adventures*, saying that you regret the, blah blah, and the similarity of the name, blah blah blah"?

So the editor wrote back and said, "Oh, come on: you can have as nasty a character as you want in a story named Ramón Chandler, and Raymond Chandler is not going to complain." Of course, he thought of Raymond Chandler because of the similarity in our names; but his point was simply that he didn't have to publish an apology and he wasn't going to. And that was the end of that. It might have been Howard Browne; I can't remember

[*Howard Browne is said to have had the most fiercely anticommunist of editorial policies and to have often had Raymond Chandler on his mind—JL*].

Once again, the politics of this kind of antiracism are quite accommodating. This was a reasonable thing that I was advocating. It was not a very militant thing. But it was completely wholehearted. In other words, a complete consonance between the militant side of my political thinking and the reformist, accommodating side.

JL: *At the time you wrote "The Nightmare," did you feel with respect to nuclear proliferation that, as the story says, "the truck was big and it was going too fast," or did you feel that was merely a potential for the near future?*

CD: Oh, no. I was scared. And I remarked in 1986 that, looking back forty years, if you had told me that we would escape a world war, I would have believed you, and I would have said, "Oh good." But if you had told me that we would arm to the teeth, and have forty years of violent hostility, and still not have a nuclear war, I would have said, "Ridiculous." I thought it was nuclear disarmament or die, in 1946.

JL: *You wrote that in your essay, "The Purge."*

CD: That's right.

JL: *Your second story in* Astounding *followed hard upon: "To Still the Drums" in October '46. It alludes to an author named E. Phillips Oppenheim. What was he known for?*

CD: *The Great Impersonation.* Great book. I recommend it. It's a thriller, but it's a good one.

JL: *The story includes the line, "no nation puts weapons like these into production unless it expects to use them. Offensively," which ties in to the observation you just made, that you were so astonished that the US hadn't.*

CD: Yeah. And it still is ridiculous to have these weapons if you're not going to use them offensively. And the contradiction is a hundred million dollar scam.

JL: *There's a good deal more money involved than that.*

CD: Yeah. And it's preposterous. And very dangerous.

JL: *The story's "radar-rocket-atomic bombs" were a good approximation of what we ended up making.*

CD: Yeah.

JL: *"The Journey and the Goal" (Astounding May, 1947)*
is a story containing a secret political organization
with a cell-system that keeps its members only par-
tially informed. There's something of an atmosphere of
paranoia and pursuit, as in "To Still the Drums."

CD: That's right. I don't think it's a good story. It's not a
good story dramatically, and it's not well-written. And
even if the framework of the story had been good, in
order to write it properly from a literary point of view,
it would have to have been three times as long.

JL: *It ends kind of abruptly.*

CD: Yeah. I regard that as a flop.

JL: *But there are some attempts at irony which you would*
develop in later years to good effect. And there's also
the line which the protagonist delivers toward the end:
"No resentment at all." That's a statement of an ethical
strand that runs through a lot of your writing.

CD: You mean non-grudge-holding.

JL: *Yes. Opposition to* ressentiment. *The idea that, yes, we*
have these goals, we want to see them achieved, but
they do not depend upon our humiliating our oppo-
nents or perpetuating our enmity. In your September
1999 letter concerning the case of Dr. Chun, you said
in effect, "We want restitution for Dr. Chun — we don't
particularly need an admission of racism on the part
of the university or an admission that they promoted
scholars less qualified than he."

CD: Yeah, that's correct. That's a correct association.
You're right.

And I was right in "The Journey and the Goal" that living a long time at reduced gravity makes you weak. Otherwise I don't think that was a very exciting story.

JL: *Then you came out with a story that turned out to be very popular, "Letter to Ellen." Why was it a big hit?*

CD: Well, it's a good story. Campbell liked the story very much, and he proposed a switcheroo, in which the lady is also a constructed genome. I said, "NOOOO!! You miss the point!"

JL: *He wanted a Fredric Brown ending. Were human beings in fact thought at the time to have forty-eight chromosomes, as it says in the story?*

CD: Yeah.

JL: *Were discussions of bioethics and biotechnology rare in science fiction at that time?*

CD: Yes. But as I say, there was more interest in eugenics among the science fiction people than among the general population. And Bruce Franklin, again, has tracked that more than I have. But it's definitely so; there was interest.

JL: *That comes out dramatically and pervasively in "The Aristocrat" (October 1949), which also takes a dig at the Heinlein small-elite story.*

CD: That's right. It's an anti-elitist story. I don't think it's terribly well-realized. I don't know why I never wrote on a large scale. "The Aristocrat" is called a novelette, but it's pretty short, considering the kind of canvas it pretends to work on. I think that my better stories are all stories which were naturally short. I don't know why this is, but I never felt comfortable expanding. Although I started novels a few times.

JL: *You and Borges, right?*

CD: Yes, well, but Borges knows what he's doing.

JL: *Then you broke out of the Campbell field with "Blind Play" (Planet Stories May, 1951).*

CD: I suppose Campbell must have rejected it. At this time, Pohl was already my agent, and he just sent 'em around any place. Maybe Jerome Bixby was the editor who bought that.

JL: *Your determined avoidance of Anglo-Saxon names even extends to the ship,* Tang Chuh-Chuh.

CD: Yes, I do that a lot. Did anyone tell you the story of A. Bertram Chandler? Chandler resolved sometime in the forties that he was going to get a hammer-and-sickle onto the cover (of *Astounding Science Fiction*). And he did. He had a story in which the ship of the future was a Soviet ship and had a hammer-and-sickle on it. I don't know if he had to whisper in the ear of the cover artist in order to do it, but he slipped that past John. But that was just playing games. This was not. And one of the characters was mixed, was said to be part Malgache and part Brazilian. That was a routine thing.

And of course, the point of "The Individualist" [*the story's original title—JL*] was ideologically committed and slightly wrong. It's not true that arrogant individualist types don't remember about social networks; they do. They take advantage of them. So in some sense the plot is nonsense.

JL: *But among the people who preach Libertarian doctrine…*

CD: Yes, some of them do forget about social arrangements.

JL: *"It had never occurred to him that even when he was alone, as thoroughly alone as anyone can ever be, his life could depend on dozens of other people." Over the past ten or more years, that's become quite a popular religion in the US.*

CD: You mean, intentionally and systematically ignoring your interconnectedness. Yeah, that was the point of the story; and I didn't think that was terribly successful either.

And then I had "The Statistomat Pitch," which I did like. And that attracted no attention. I gave it to a few friends, just to make sure somebody read it.

JL: *The line in "Blind Play": "There were no homestead farms to be settled by lonely pioneer families." Is that a jab at the Heinlein ethos, with its pioneers and freeholders?*

CD: Well, it's a reminder that you have to reject a certain image, yeah. I don't know that it's especially Heinlein. Somebody I like very much, in some ways even better than Heinlein, is Robinson Jeffers. And he has this ideal, very strongly, of living alone. So I can appreciate it and respond to it, and at the same time answer it.

JL: *Nineteen-fifty-three was when your troubles were starting, and your father's as well.*

CD: That's right. My father's testimony was in 1953. My subpoena was in 1953, and I had a lot of postponements. So I didn't testify until 1954. Ellen Schrecker chose to spend a lot of time discussing my case in *No Ivory Tower*, and she mentions my father at less length. And I think we're also both in David Caute's *The Great Fear*. But he gets so *many* things wrong: Ellen is much more reliable.

JL: *Most of these books discuss you and your fate at greater length. What happened to your father after Kansas City?*

CD: That's interesting. There's no reason it shouldn't be remembered. He was fired, and Ralph Spitzer was fired. Spitzer was young and a famous scientist, so he just went off to Canada. And my father didn't know what to do for a job. He did odd jobs for a while, and then he tried something which I did not try when I was blacklisted; I don't know whether it would have worked for me. He went to primarily black institutions in the South.

JL: *Well, Lee Lorch tried that.*

CD: Yeah, Lee Lorch had a very successful though brief career in black institutions. My father did pretty well also. He taught in Benedict College in Columbia, South Carolina. And he was redhunted out of there by this Senator or somebody who thought he would make political capital, and he went to Shaw, in Raleigh, North Carolina. That's where he was living when my mother died. And after that, already past retirement age, he became the Dean of Social Sciences at the University of Guyana, in Georgetown, Guyana. And he stayed there as long as the left-wing government stayed in power. And then when the CIA-supported regime took over, they turned out most of the higher appointees; the university was not destroyed, but it was seriously crippled. After that, he still taught for several more years on a contract basis, one year at a time. Mostly at Hofstra.

He was really a labor historian; but due to the historical accident that, when he got his degree in the 1930s, there was no such field as labor history, he was called an economist. And some of his writings are what we would still call economics today. But it was more labor history.

And at the end of his life, he wrote about the Marxist tradition. He has three good books, which not too many people read: two of his own about the history of Marxism and nationalism, and one that he edited and wrote an introduction to, of essays by Rosa Luxemburg on nationalism, which had not previously existed in English, and which had not been much read because the original language was Polish. That was in the latter part of his career, post-retirement; like me, he was not washed up at sixty-five.

JL: *"Share Our World" was your last appearance in* Astounding. *A multi-ethnic spaceship crew with a large number of principals in the cast, not just a small group of Leaders. In which the scientists record their*

*observations in a medium that would be a hypertext
today.*

CD: That's right, and little did I know what a headache
jpgs and pdfs and the like would be!

JL: *How did it get past Campbell, with its alien species being a good deal quicker on the uptake than the human
beings?*

CD: He didn't have a thing against that. "The Touch of
Your Hand," by Theodore Sturgeon, has mystical
aliens who just happen to be able to neutralize anything you throw at them. In that case, they're sympathetic. But there are also stories by Kuttner and
others where aliens are superior. Heinlein's "Goldfish
Bowl." Cleve Cartmill. [*Subsequent research reveals
"The Touch of Your Hand" to have been published by
Horace Gold, not Campbell — JL*]

JL: *But Asimov and Klass, among others, write of Campbell
having given them trouble over stories with superior
aliens.*

CD: That's interesting. But contradictions are what life
is made out of. As in the case of Campbell's attitude
toward Jews, there's something contradictory there.
The end of the road in the case of my contact with
him was that the anti-Semitism prevailed. But I think
there was a logical contradiction which was never resolved in his thinking.

JL: *Perhaps several.*

CD: Yeah.

JL: *Then you became a satirist. No doubt as a consequence of what you were going through in life.*

CD: No. "The Statistomat Pitch" was written earlier.

JL: *But it only appeared in 1958.*

CD: That's important. Pohl was having a terrible time selling my stories. Some of them he didn't like, and I guess he didn't try; he just sent them back and said, "No, this isn't good enough." But some of 'em he really liked, and he had a hell of a time marketing 'em. And I think I accused Horace Gold—which is awfully impolitic if I did—of being afraid to accept stories from me. But privately, Fred certainly said that people were afraid to accept stories from me. I don't know whether that began before my case became public in 1954 or not, but "The Statistomat Pitch" was written before 1954. And it's important that it was, because what it's satirizing is something with which I was much more familiar after 1954.

After I was fired in July, 1954, I thought, "Well, I don't know what I'll do for a living now, it'd be pretty hard to get a professorship without leaving the country, and I don't want to leave the country. I have a court case which will take a year or so to get rid of (ha!), and so for now I don't want to leave the country." Of course, I didn't know it was gonna take all those years. "But I can always write science fiction." And I sat down, and quickly wrote—I forget in which order—what became "Adrift on the Policy Level" and "The Star System." And they didn't sell. And you left out "Last Year's Grave Undug." It was written earlier;

it was essentially completed before my father's case, and definitely completed before March 1953.

JL: *There are ways in which that was eerily prophetic too.*

CD: Y'uh-huh. But that was of its time. See, that was my attitude then. Not necessarily later. So I was very sorry that it didn't appear until later. But it was on the market before my case was public, for sure. "The Statistomat Pitch" I think may have been as well. But Fred, privately, was saying even before my case was public that people were afraid to touch me, and I think it was true.

"The Statistomat Pitch" went to *Infinity*. Larry Shaw, I think. And that was, of course, you'd think no problem. It was taking a satirical knock at something which a lot of us felt positive about, but which had its downside; and I think it was a very legitimate story. But not terribly read. And I should think that not only Larry Shaw but Doc Lowndes and Jerry Bixby and a lot of other editors at the time would have liked it. And I think it's strange that it was hard to sell, but it was.

And the way in which it was anachronistic is this: after I was blacklisted in 1954, I looked around for jobs. And one of the things that I advertised myself as, was someone who sort of knew something about and could find out more about and could become expert at mathematical models in the social sciences. So I was dealing with people who were making pitches like this. I'd had some contact with the field, but I hadn't had any contact with the hucksterism of the field at the time that I wrote the story. So that's the anachronism I'm talking about.

So then I sat down and wrote these two good stories, which I think are among my best. One about salesmanship predominating over the technical feasibility of a project ["Adrift on the Policy Level"], and one about gender roles ["The Star System"]. And Fred tried and tried to get somebody to take them. And finally he put them in his own magazine, when he briefly had one, *Star*. And that spun off into a series of anthologies, and those didn't get many readers. But in the case of "Adrift on the Policy Level," it was picked up by anthologists right and left. And the other one was not.

I wrote each one in a week. With all the faults that they have, they're good stories. I could have sat down and written another one as good the next week. And I didn't know yet that the stories wouldn't sell. But I decided that I was not going to be a science fiction writer at that point. Because I decided, "Even if I can continue to do this, week after week, that's not what I want to do." And it was a turning point, because I might have decided, "Yeah! This is what I want to do! This is working nicely!" Cause it *was* working nicely! And Poul Anderson did. He kept on writing up a storm, year after year. And… I didn't.

Maybe Fred can explain that, but I can't explain it.

And I told Fred at the time, I said, "Look, I can see that being a professional science fiction writer is very nice, and it's something that I could do; but I'm not gonna do it."

I want to tell you about the most significant interaction between me and Fred Pohl in our life, for which he's never apologized. *Without telling me*, he rewrote both stories. "Adrift on the Policy Level" he rewrote in trivial ways. He gave it the title "Adrift on the Policy Level," which was better than the title I gave it. And he introduced a couple of good lines, and he introduced one stupid line, which I succeeded in getting anthologists to take out again. And I left in Fred's other improvements. So on that, he has nothing to apologize to me for except not telling me.

JL: *That's the Horace Gold method of editing. Gold made drastic changes in stories without telling the authors. I think Phil Dick, among others, stopped writing for him on account of that.*

CD: That's interesting. Because he certainly published some beautiful stories, and maybe some of their virtue was owing to him. But in the case of this re-write by Fred, the one thing he put in that was utterly wrong was wrong in the same way that the proposed snappy ending for "Letter to Ellen" was wrong. That is, it was a little gag that was out of character. So I took that out, and it's essentially a better story than the one I wrote.

Then the other one, the sex-roles one, Fred loused it up royally. And I told him so. And he, as I say, never apologized. He may have felt it was weak in some ways; maybe it was weak in some ways; but he loused it up.

In 1959, Judy Merril was compiling the best science fiction of 1957 and let me know that she was giving an Honorable Mention to "It Walks in Beauty." And I said, "You know, it was better before Fred rewrote it." And she said, "Oh, good: well, let me see the original version." So I gave it to her. And she read it, and she said, "You're right. It was better before he rewrote it." But that doesn't appear in the anthology: she still left it as Honorable Mention. And she doesn't mention that if you want to see it right, you can get it from the author.

So I was sorry she didn't include it in the Best of 1958, because it would've got some readers. And as it is, it got essentially none. A couple of times I got it on the reading list of Peter Fitting's science fiction course here at the University of Toronto. The first time, we had a little discussion of it in class; the second time, they didn't pick up on it particularly. So I still feel that it hasn't got read.

JL: *They're both powerful pieces. "It Walks in Beauty," as it appeared in* Star Science Fiction, *still packs quite a wallop. Along with "Adrift on the Policy Level," it has a very substantial sociological side to it.*

CD: That's right. It's a serious story. It's done tongue-in-cheek, but that doesn't mean I'm kidding. Among other things, I think it's one of the first appearances in print of the emotional problem of homophobia. Because, although there are no homosexuals in the story, the principal character's rejection of his own sincere feeling for somebody who he now learns is not supposed to be acceptable as a love-object…

JL: *Yes! That's the affect there. That is what Eve Kosofsky Sedgwick would call homosexual panic.*

CD: That's right. That's right. I think that's the first appearance, at least in a prominent way, of that emotional problem.

JL: *We-e-ll, Sturgeon comes close, in his two gay stories…*

CD: That's right, that's right! Sturgeon was very interested in that. Did "The World Well Lost"…

JL: *Nineteen-fifty-three. And according to Frank Robinson, Howard Browne was so appalled by that story that he called all the other editors and asked that Sturgeon be blacklisted from the magazines. Which is what Howard Browne was like at the time. His third detective novel seethes with homophobia, which he apologized for in a preface to it forty years later.*

CD: Oh really? That's interesting. "The World Well Lost" is in some ways a beautiful story. And it's a beautiful title, which doesn't go with the story. That's sort of too bad. He should have saved that title for another story. It was his own title. I read it in typescript. I should have told him.

There were stories about sexual tolerance in this period. There was "Venus and the Seven Sexes," much earlier. No homosexuality, but it was inviting exploration of sex images, in a very tongue-in-cheek way, that was not threatening.

And there were several other things about sexual danger in the fifties. I would say that in the same category, in a way, was "No Woman Born" by C.L. Moore. There was one earlier one that wasn't so good, [Lester del Rey's] "Helen O'Loy." Because it wasn't evoking a genuine emotional problem. You could say that "Venus and the Seven Sexes" wasn't either, but I took that as opening up the question of sexuality and thereby confronting people's sexual fears.

JL: *Well, it's about media stereotypes of what sex would be, which has something to do with "It Walks in Beauty."*

CD: Yes. But "No Woman Born" is a beautiful story. And there's a question of the aesthetics of sex. And I think that's opening up real problems.

JL: *The whole Organization Man sociology that informs "Adrift on the Policy Level" was big in that decade. As was, by the end of the fifties, the sociology of the emotions, which has a lot to do with the way the protagonists of this story are treated, or manipulated.*

CD: About the same time was "The Luckiest Man in Denv" by Simon Eisner, who was Cyril Kornbluth. That's a very good story. And I think that some of the issues in "The Statistomat Pitch" and "Adrift on the Policy Level" come into that. It's dramatically much more stark. This is an anti-hero.

JL: *Kornbluth — or the Kornbluth-Klass-Sheckley Jewish Schadenfreude group — did great things. Kornbluth, Klass, and Sturgeon wrote the great Red Scare science fiction stories. Kornbluth in 1958 wrote "Theory of Rocketry," about a student who, for his own advancement, gets his professor caught up in a HUAC-like web of political persecution.*

CD: I should have read that. Of course, by 1958, it's not surprising if I didn't, because I was reading less. I didn't go to a world science fiction convention between 1951 and 1989. I was out of the science fiction world, relatively speaking. I still read some, and I was in touch personally with Judith Merril and Virginia Kidd and Fred Pohl and to a lesser extent Theodore Sturgeon. Phil Klass. I was still interested in science fiction, but more at arm's length.

JL: *Merril also seems to have been someone who was eager to engage in conversation not from an ideologically-bound or proselytizing point of view. And not from an exclusionary point of view either: she was friends with* Cordwainer Smith, *for Heaven's sake, who couldn't have been close to where she was, politically.*

CD: Yes, that's right. The question of having some conservative people in the science fiction world as well — it's always been true, not only Campbell. But Judy was more interested than I was in mysticism. I had a false identification of mysticism with supernatural religion. She was interested in ancient philosophies, as was I. But I had a rationalist bias, which at that time already put me in a rather different direction from her. That…changed later. The radicalism from which she started was Trotskyist. But where she went from there was the counterculture, including its interest in mysticism.

JL: *Does that connect with Campbell's psionic program?*

CD: I wonder. See, I was shocked and horrified by Dianetics. And I think that most of the rest of this gang were too. Dr. Winter and Campbell espoused Dianetics, and otherwise it was sort of an embarrassment for many people in this science fiction pro group.

JL: *But Merril was interested in ESP and the Rhine experiments...*

CD: That's right. And I was impatient with that. First when Campbell did it occasionally. I discussed it in many letters and fan magazine articles with people, and I remained sort of averse to all that.

An over-simple dichotomy, which I was prey to in the period 1946-49 or so, was *Unknown Worlds* and *Weird Tales* represented the wrong side. They were representing fuzzy mysticism. And irrationality. Now of course, that's not fair, because things which present themselves as hard science fiction are sometimes fuzzy Freudian sentimentality or whatever, too. And sometimes fantasy is as hard-edged as any "Campbell Science Fiction Story." A story like *We* by Zamyatin: I don't know whether you should call it fantasy or science fiction. It's social criticism in a world that does not pretend to be a future projection. So I don't make that dichotomy any more. I think it's a false one.

I still read some science fiction in the late fifties, and I loved some of the stories I read. I had a little bit of trouble with later developments in science fiction, partly because they were vague, impressionistic, and mystical. And I continued to see some stuff that I just loved. But the main thing is that my life wasn't re-volving around it any more. I had many friends.

JL: *By the end of the decade, the big community around you was the mathematical community.*

CD: Oh yeah, sure. But that was true before 1954, too. In fact, it was more true before 1954, because I had this period of isolation from 1954 to 1957 — 1956 any-way — when my connections to the mathematical world were attenuated.

There's a gap that I can't very well fill, in my account to you, between late 1954, when I decided that I was not going to be a full-time science fiction writer or anything close to it, and 1968 when Judith Merril came to Toronto on her way home from the 1968 Chicago Democratic Convention, and we had a long talk about how crummy the world was. Between '54 and '68, I've just given you scraps of contact with the science fiction world, and haven't really given you much of a picture of my relations to it, which were certainly not trivial.

So in '68, Judy, with whom I was not out of touch, was protesting the war in Vietnam outside the Democratic convention, and so was I; but we weren't there at the same time. We didn't see each other there. However, we both were very happy to have done it. I came back to Toronto, and she, by prearrangement, stopped off with her daughter and her daughter's boyfriend, and visited us, in Toronto, en route back to New York. So we had a long talk about everything and politics and the US, and she began her decision to move to Toronto at that time.

JL: *At the end of the 1950s—you wrote it in '59, it appeared in '60—your essay on your experience came out, "…From an Exile." It makes a distinction between professional dissenters and amateur dissenters, and expresses the hope that*

> *…diverse parties should dwell side by side, not with the tolerance of indifference, but embattled and cherishing each other; each should know that in its quest, the contest with those who disagree will bring faster progress than would an unobstructed route.*

CD: Yeah, that's a sentiment that draws from the experience of Greenwich Village in the 1940s.

JL: *It's an ambitious goal.*

CD: Yeah, but ya gotta.

JL: *One reads of some fierce academics on the far right…*

CD: They might not be the people that I would choose to talk to. I think there are some people that are very hard to talk to. But you don't ignore them, or suppress them either.

A better example than we usually choose, when we're discussing this, is something that I mentioned earlier to you: genetic determinism. Which has been a right-wing lie and associated with terrible crimes. But the biological facts are complex. Genetics determine *something*. This is something the complexities of which I've been insisting on since I was a teenager, and which I've discussed with a great many people, with an assortment of different biases. And I've been very interested to see what people said who came down on what I would regard as an oppressive side of some political issues.

JL: *Very explicitly oppressive, as some of Heinlein.*

CD: Yes, certainly. Once again, I don't think you expect people to be consistent, and I don't think that everything Heinlein wrote is consistent with everything else that Heinlein wrote. But if I were to say, "Oh well, I can't talk to a eugenicist," then I would be refusing the enlightenment which could be obtained from listening to some intelligent, sincere people, who believe some of this stuff. I guess I don't know that there is as much to be learned from people who know that what they're saying is crap. I mean, obviously, you also have people who promulgate a racist theory which they know is not factual. And maybe there's not much to be learned from them. Right? But people who are trying to say something true…you can probably learn something by talking to them. Anyway, I've often tried. One of the members of the Brain Trust was racist, and in some sense Heinlein was racist. And I patiently and inquiringly pursued dialogue on these things.

JL: *You wrote, "One professor tried to write a book on the exiles, but became one before it was finished, which seriously impeded its progress. We exiles have been systematically studied, sometimes misleadingly, by a few novelists."*

CD: The professor was Arthur Davis. No relation. He finished the book eventually: it's a good, good book. The novelists I identified in a later lecture. *The Groves of Academe* by Mary McCarthy. Terrible book. *Silas Timberman* by Howard Fast. As my friend Ray Ginger, a first-rate US historian, who was in those years sharing the life of an exile from academe enduring Madison Avenue, said, "He knows not whereof he speaks." *The Searching Light* by Martha Dodd, which is a good book. Martha Dodd knew whereof she spoke, but it was a little bit obfuscatory, because she wrote it as if she were presenting characters she knew. And she was presenting a more typical academic freedom situation than her own, which was, you know, an Ambassador, as an unusual case. So it wasn't as good as it seemed to be. The Howard Fast was intermediate in quality: it wasn't an abject, squalid thing like *The Groves of Academe*, but it wasn't a good book either. Mary McCarthy has written a lot of good stuff, but *The Groves of Academe* is Really BAD.

And the fourth one was *Faithful Are the Wounds* by May Sarton. Now that was a good book. It's not terribly well-written, and it's not terribly revelatory; but there again, she was writing about F.O. Matthiessen, and she knew whereof she wrote. And she's a decent person. So there's a lot to be said for the book.

Of course, there's some pretty good nonfiction about the era. You know I like *No Ivory Tower* by Ellen Schrecker. Another book which does include me but is mostly about cases rather different from mine is

Red Scare by Griffin Fariello. That's a good book. It's got a different focus. And there's a lot of interesting sidelights.

A book which I like pretty well, which most people haven't read, is *The Survivor* by Carl Marzani.

JL: *Recent years have also seen a flood of right-wing revisionist books about the Red Scare.*

CD: Well, right. There are books attempting to show that the Rosenbergs were guilty as charged, and books attempting to show that Alger Hiss was guilty as charged, and this and that, this and that...

JL: *I.F. Stone and Albert Einstein have also been implicated...*

CD: Haha. Yes. I was never a student of the spy accusations. It was interesting to me years after to realize that some of what Whittaker Chambers said may have been true. Because Whittaker Chambers was so obviously spouting lies and half-truths at certain points, that it was really startling to realize that some of the things he said were true, too...

JL: *Ellen Schrecker accepts the idea that Julius Rosenberg committed espionage of some sort...*

CD: He seems to have. And of course, Whittaker Chambers was talking about Alger Hiss and J. Peters, and now it appears that J. Peters may have existed. It's sort of interesting. However, there's another variable, which is important in the life of people like me, which is not what the present debate focuses on.

I think that we should have said already in 1953 — as I did say, starting fifteen years after that, but I didn't say then at all; I didn't even take account of it — that there could have been a person who spied for the Soviets with the motivation that Julius Rosenberg was said to have had. Part of the indignation that people felt in 1953 was, "How dare they suggest that someone so much like me spied for the Soviets? Why, I would never spy for the Soviets!" Well, it's perfectly true that Julius Rosenberg was very much like me. And it is perfectly true that I would have refused if I had been asked to spy for the Soviets. But! It would require only a small amount of self-examination of my experience in the Movement to realize that there were some people who would cheerfully have spied for the Soviets, on the same basis that Julius Rosenberg was said to have. And the fact that the evidence against him was not very convincing doesn't alter that. So that I feel that it's too bad that we didn't think this through and have a different social stance. Toward the spy accusations in the Red Hunt.

Now sure enough, it turned out not very long after Julius Rosenberg was arrested, and I guess before he was executed, that Klaus Fuchs had spied for the Soviets, with the same motivation that Julius Rosenberg was said to have had. But Klaus Fuchs wasn't interesting to the redhunters. Julius Rosenberg, they loved *him*: He was an American Jewish Communist. And Klaus Fuchs unfortunately wasn't Jewish and wasn't American. So he was useless! He wasn't what they wanted. And then it turned out, many years later, that Ted Hall and a friend of his had given the Soviets information still more valuable than what Klaus Fuchs did, which in turn was *much* more valuable than what Julius Rosenberg may have. And their motivation was similar too.

They were both Jewish.

But they weren't members of the Communist Party.

So they were useless.

And the present retrospect on this is so poor, because the official position is that we couldn't reveal about Fuchs, and especially Hall, we couldn't reveal it without admitting that we were breaking the code. But that's not the real reason. The real reason was that they loved Julius Rosenberg. He was a New York Jew member of the Communist Party: that's what they wanted.

JL: *The people on the other side at the trial were New York Jews as well, weren't they?*

CD: Yeah, that's right. It was sort of a Jewish monopoly.

A lot of this has been said, but what people don't say — and I'm bringing it up *because* it's what people don't say — is the distinction between proving that Julius Rosenberg did something, which I think was not terribly well done, and as to his wife, not done at all, and conceding that it was a conceivable scenario. And I know a lot of people who would have been willing to hand stuff over to the Soviets if asked at the time, my goodness! And what Al Slack did, I *would* have done! Al Slack, with whom I was in prison for a few months in 1960, was asked by a Russian naval attaché to go to the patent office and copy out some patents for him. The Soviet Union was an ally, Slack was sympathetic to Bolshevism; and it seemed to him perfectly reasonable to go to the patent office and copy this stuff out. He knew why the Soviet naval attaché didn't want to do it: he knew he'd be shadowed, and he didn't want American counterintelligence to know that the Soviets wanted that patent. But the patent was on the public record [*and had been for over thirty years — JL*].

So the righteous indignation which greeted the spy accusations was partly wrongly based. Well. I wish that was the only mistake I ever made in my life.

It's true that the Rosenberg case stinks, but not for that reason.

JL: *And what would the ideal stand have been for the Left to have taken?*

CD: In the first place, they didn't cause the war in Korea; they didn't betray their country. If they did exactly what the prosecution said they did, what they did was share some information with an ally. It's illegal, but it's not causing the deaths of millions of Americans. Furthermore, it's being used to draw conclusions which are false. I think we could have said that, and some of it we did say; but it would have been stronger if our position had been clearer.

JL: *You wrote that "Radical students felt a bread-and-butter pull toward politically neutral vocations." That's what "The Great Fear" means, doesn't it? A campaign of intimidation that, according to Ellen Schrecker,*

333

deprived the country of a huge segment of the discourse that could have done it some good.

CD: That's right. That's very important.

JL: *You wrote, "We do not accept the fate of a pariah group. Most of us yearn for the masses, for the mainstream, and lack the patience to guard a peculiar flame through generations of persecution." Your father can be credited with having guarded that flame, as a labor historian.*

CD: That's right. It is true though that some people, including myself, felt a little more comfortable when associated with massive institutions. That's only part of what I'm saying in that quote, but that is one thing that's true. I was always embedded in some huge organization, whether it was the US Navy or a university. Until 1954—then I was suddenly cut loose. As I say, I might have become a science fiction writer at that point. (I don't know what I would've done, unless Fred'd had better luck selling my stuff. Maybe I would've gone to a pen name the way the blacklisted screenwriters did.) If I had done that, I would have been living in a way which was familiar to Fred—when he wasn't editing for a big company, which most of the time he was—and familiar to my friends, who spent many years not being taken care of by a large organization. I didn't have that experience. So when I settled down again, in 1962, it seemed like a more normal way to live, to me. And I continued to do so for the rest of my life.

That's not exactly the same as the point that I'm making there, but it's similar. That some people's personalities are more congenial to living in a self-employed way, with a less clear reference group.

JL: *Much later, in "The Purge," you wrote of your eight-year struggle,*

> *A broadening time. The experience of marginality is good for the soul and better for the intellect. And throughout, the joy of watching my children grow; always mathematics; always political struggle. My political activity in 1954-1960 was mostly surrounding my court case. I fumed, even more than before, that defense of civil liberties was pre-empting all my energies though it was only one of the burning issues. After my release from prison, it was relaxing to go on an anti-Bomb march with my wife again. (435)*

CD: That's right. That passage about the experience of marginality expresses my true feelings.

In the collection of my poems, *Having Come This Far*, is one I wrote in 1961, not long after I did time, admiring and half-envying the civil rights movement defendants going to jail ["On Bail (Wisconsin, 1961)"]. It ends, "During my thirty-five years of un-earned happiness / A generation of heroes has gasped and died." Some of my friends said, "Why should YOU feel like that?" I note that Don West, who would seem to almost anyone to have taken his full share of lumps, wrote a poem when my friend and his, Carl Braden, was going into prison, expressing chagrin that he, Don West, was not doing the same.

JL: *"Last Year's Grave Undug": what's the source of that title? It sounds like it comes from a line of iambic verse…*

CD: Yes, and it sounds like a line that might've been written by a Modernist poet in the twenties. But it's not a quote: I made it up. I think that's a very good story. I don't know why I was able to write such a good story so young. I'm not *sure* it's a good story, but I *feel* it's a good story. And I commented in later years to Judy and Virginia — and I've said this in print too — "The reader may wonder which of the young men the author identifies with: the answer is, both."

JL: *You wrote that in "The Purge."*

CD: Yeah, but that idea doesn't originate in "The Purge": that idea originates in conversation with my friends.

JL: *Most of our good ideas do.*

CD: Yeah. I wrote a poem, which is also one of my best poems, about 1964, in which I said the same thing. It's the pariah and the safe-and-sane resident of the Establishment, confronting each other. Judy and Virginia hashed it out, between themselves, "Which one is him?" And the answer again was both. Note the dates. I wrote the first version of the poem in 1960, before I had again a secure job; the final version in 1964, after I did. In any case, even in 1960, I already felt both the vantage of the allrightnik comfy in the arms of the establishment and that of the pariah — as Judy and Virginia figured out when they read the poem.

NOW I FACE YOU
How many must it have been,
                              how many midnights
were you out there, before you breached the wall,
before our invitation, belated, grudging.
Your earnest focus on such meager bread
did not make us unable to love you, but
to see you. Now I ask, Were you cold out there?
And now I ask, How many midnights was it?
Now that we're face to face, now I wonder.
With nourishment like that — how does hate grow?
In width, to fill your view, invisible
itself while through its screen you're seeing
all this knob-jawed life? Or just in density,
puckering into a white-dwarf cocksure core?
How many was it? How far can you count?
                              (Don't count
the nights, but what counts: separate spurts of gall.)
I wonder do you lose sight of clean-slate zero.
Once past omega, you can not count backward.
I wonder has it a negative, that number.
Now that we're face to face, now I ask you.
That's not to say I'm not afraid of you;
you chill me through. Not to run away from you
is all the charity I have to offer.
Not that you've asked for it, or anything.
I tell you what: I swear that if you wept
I'd match your weeping.
                              Not that you've asked for it
1960-1964[1]

---

1   "Now I Face You" first appeared in *Canadian Forum* and was reprinted in *Best Poems of 1965: Borestone Mountain Poetry Awards*
(Pacific Books, 1966).

JL: *That's the Chandler Davis ethos. You have to be able to put yourself in the other's place in order to see your interactions as other than dichotomous, good-and-evil confrontations.*

CD: That's right. But that makes it sound as though I identify with one of them but have some empathy for the other. Whereas when I say that in "Now I Face You" I identify both with the speaker and with the pariah, and that both the young heroes are viewpoint characters in "Last Year's Grave Undug," I mean just that.

There were other post-Nuclear Armageddon stories which were circulating at the time that I wrote it, some of which were published, and it seemed as if it might be publishable; but its content was clearly anti-Cold War. So you may say that people were afraid of it. But the other stories that Fred had difficulty placing for me were troublesome because of my being a pariah. In other words, they were pieces that you could imagine his being able to place if he were to say, "Oh, these are by an unknown science fiction writer whom Virginia and I happen to have discovered."

And once "Last Year's Grave Undug" appeared, nobody attacked it as Communist propaganda. Obviously, some people must have disagreed with it.

JL: *Perhaps the people who disagreed with it were smart enough to realize that if they styled it Communist propaganda, they would be putting themselves in the position of the villain in the story. Who also seems to be an exemplar of the individualist pioneer ethic.*

CD: But so are the heroes. In "Last Year's Grave Undug," it's a question of taking refuge from the cities.

The danger of the survivalist ethos is something that I never have confronted. I think it is dangerous, and I think it's interesting that some nuts, right-wing and other, identify with survivalist science fiction. Another impact that science fiction has had…

JL: *There are Nazis who write survivalist science fiction…*

CD: Yeah. But I mean, the science fiction from my time has this theme; and I think it appealed to some people, to some right-wing people…. Some of the science fiction of Rugged Individualist Capitalists from my period, the time that I was paying most attention to it, sounds suitable for Ayn Rand; and in fact, Sturgeon did love *The Fountainhead.*

JL: *There were a lot of contradictions in that man.*

CD: Yup. Yup. We had a vigorous, vigorous correspondence about it. I couldn't stand it.

JL: *Not a lot of Sturgeon's fiction would give one the impression that…*

CD: That's right. It's surprising.

JL: *You published a story in 1970 that has a very Sturgeon-esque feel to it: "Hexamnion."*

CD: Yeah. I wrote two other stories [since the fifties], which I think were good. I thought so at the time and still think so. "The Names of Yanils" and "Hexamnion." That's the order in which I wrote them. "The Names of Yanils" was accepted by Harlan Ellison and then never published, so that had only marginal publication *[twenty-five years after it was written — JL].* And "Hexamnion" had the same problem of people not wanting to touch it; people still didn't want to publish a story by me. Of course, Harry Harrison was very happy to publish it, but it didn't get very many readers.

I think it's a very good story; I think it's well imagined. Fred, or somebody in that gang, pointed out that the ethics of subjecting the kids to this artificial environment, without direct contact with adults, was dubious, and I agree; and I agree that I didn't think about that when I wrote it. I was creating an artificial given, like H.G. Wells. I was saying, "Now suppose, suppose such-and-such" and then we run with it. But my supposition concealed an ethical difficulty, which I concede. But I would have been happy if that had had more notice.

And "The Names of Yanils" is another case of writing something as a short story because I never unlimbered myself to write longer stories very well. I think it goes okay as a sort of compressed novel, but that's what it is: it's like a digest.

JL: *Inasmuch as its power depends on the irony, the compactness helps.*

CD: Yeah, that's right: it brings the ending closer to the beginning. That's what I said to myself when I was writing it, that it was snappy and ironic. My sister is an anthropologist, and I admire her very much; and I care about her reaction. And her reaction was that my not being an anthropologist didn't hurt me, that I had a pretty good anthropological sensitivity. But she still didn't like the story.

JL: *You have an anthropologist sibling just like Phil Klass did.*

CD: We've noticed that similarity.

JL: *"Hexamnion" is striking because it's another no-villains story. In fact, that's part of its theme.*

CD: That's right. But this criticism, which may have come from Fred Pohl, would say that the villain is the institution that put them there.

JL: *"To consider it was not so hard; but to rest easy on such a conclusion with nobody to support it was very hard."— "The Names of Yanils." That's the isolation of the heretic.*

CD: And that's why I say that it was a compressed story. Because I take it through stages. And each stage cannot be understood without the stage before. And if that's the case, and if I'm going to write it in that small number of words, I have to rely on a great deal of agility on the part of the reader, because the context at the beginning of the story is not the one by which to judge the end of the story.

JL: *And you have to write it in epigrammatic lines like that one.*

CD: That's right. And of course, I'm not the only one who's ever written such a story, but it's an uncommon genre, to write that elliptically. I'm talking about condensing the generations and specifically, that plot turns are done in a very small number of words.

JL: *It's among your darkest stories. It has the flavor of some of the satires of Klass and Kornbluth…*

CD: Yeah. There is no escape. Certainly, there's no escape.

JL: *It presents the deterioration of a society without using the gimmick of a cataclysm, a catastrophe…*

CD: That's right. Nor a malevolent force. The society is not oppressed by any force trying to deprive them of their customs or their food.

The particular point I was making, nobody else made — being trapped by tradition. It doesn't mean that the tradition was wrong. But you can still be trapped. And I don't think people usually say that.

JL: *Trapped by the outward forms of tradition, and losing the content…*

CD: Yeah. And I think that it can happen in the real world, and that if it happens in the real world, it's not noticed. So I think it's a story that says something that I wish would be received, and I'm sorry that more people didn't read it.

Unfortunately, a lot of the things in literature which end up with a trapped feeling do so on the basis of some dystopias: that the system is oppressive. And this story attempts to say something different. You're trapped. But — the tradition with which the story opens is oppressive in the way tradition is supposed to be oppressive: it's obscurantist. And tyrannical. I guess it's a no-villain piece in the sense that where they end up is not willed. There is no Bad Guy who willed the trap at the end.

JL: *But it's a no-hero piece. There's no Campbellian figure who uses his ingenuity to find a way out.*

CD: And maybe that's one of the reasons for not writing it at greater length. You would not have been able to do without an even more resourceful protagonist. I have resourceful protagonists, you see, but they are trapped anyway. In this story, I have honest people doing their best, limited by the society in which they find themselves. In a larger scope, just in terms of number of words — not in terms of number of centuries, but a larger framework — I might feel I'd have to have a character with greater insight.

JL: *Even in the great Naturalist novels, there's usually someone, however marginal, who has some of that insight. Even* Studs Lonigan *has Danny O'Neill.*

CD: Who has a perspective on it. But *Journey to the End of Night* by Céline…

JL: *Okay, okay.*

CD: I guess the trapped feeling in my story is dependent on the successive protagonists being as aware as it was possible for them to be in the context which they had.

JL: *Did Harlan Ellison commission you to write a bleak story?*

CD: No. I wrote the story because it was in my soul. And Virginia liked it, and several people liked it. And then Virginia, who was my agent at that time said, when Harlan Ellison gave everybody the opportunity to pull out, "Don't pull out: it couldn't possibly appear in a better place than *The Last Dangerous Visions.*" So I left it there. This was '76 maybe.

JL: Only a few people pulled out.

CD: That's right. If a lot of people had pulled out, then he would have been able to publish the remaining ones.

JL: He would have had a manageable volume, yes.

One of the reasons that "The Names of Yanils" is important is that it depicts a situation in which a whole way of thinking can be obliterated. We've seen that in our history, how a formerly vibrant discursive space can be shrunk very small. How an idea can be reduced to a media caricature.

CD: Phil Klass was once talking to somebody about the Civil Rights Movement in the sixties, and he said, "When I was a Freedom Rider in the early fifties—" And they said, "You mean sixties," and he said "fifties." The Negro Congress had demonstrations, and everyone got the shit beaten out of them—I don't know if Phil ever got the shit beaten out of him—but they started ten years before the famous ones started, and some people were present at both.

My sister had exactly the same conversation in a class she was taking as an older graduate student at the University of California in Berkeley. She said, "When I was arrested in a demonstration against discrimination in hiring in 1949—" They said, "You mean 1969"; she said, "I mean 1949."

JL: Racial discrimination.

344

CD: Yeah. She was arrested outside a store in Boston, where she then lived, which wouldn't hire black people. So she and Phil Klass both had this experience of having been in the Movement before it was known to exist. Of course, it was for the same reason: it was because the Movement prior to the New Left, which means in effect prior to 1960, was redbaited, not out of existence —

JL: *But out of history.*

CD: Yeah. To the point where people felt that they could dismiss it, because "Oh well, it's just those Communists." And of course, some of us *were* Communists.

JL: *Where else were you going to find an association that took all of those stands back in that time?*

CD: That's right. So there were these actions, and they were protests against lynching, protests against discrimination, protests against segregation — they took place in the thirties too, and many thousands supported them. When they took place after the Red-Hunt began, after 1947, the numbers were smaller, and not only because the numbers were smaller but because people were afraid to acknowledge connections with the Communist Party, they were written out of history. Even the ones that were organized entirely by Trotskyists were written out of history.

JL: *It happens. Chip Delany, Terry Gilliam, Tom Tomorrow (Dan Perkins) have written of peace demonstrations in the fifties, sixties, and nineties that were attended by thousands of people and were reported in the press as having involved a few dozen.*

But in the case of the Civil Rights Movement, it begins getting some attention in the forties, when historians have to explain why Strom Thurmond broke with the Democratic Party. Something made an impression on Truman in his first term such that he would talk about these issues.

CD: Yeah. That was a striking thing, that at the same time as, apparently, a swerve to the Right, segregation in the armed forces was very largely discarded.

JL: *Thanks to some black activists who got Truman's ear.*

CD: That's right. That was an advance, in that respect. And Brown vs. Education happened in that era.

JL: *Some people have said that Truman only addressed civil rights issues and labor issues because [Henry] Wallace brought them into the conversation.*

CD: Certainly Wallace brought them into the conversation. But that wouldn't have been a reason for Truman to bring more than superficial attention to them. And in some areas, he made no progress; but in the military, he did. It was quite striking, and it was important.

One of the things on which I'm active now is organizing a conference to discuss the defense of civil liberties in Canada. Which has been the subject of some pretty good conferences, and one good book. But the conferences that have taken place invited almost no defense lawyers. It's a way of minimizing the problem, not to listen to the people who experience the sharpest form of it.

Canada introduced, at the US Government's behest, extreme measures withdrawing the right to counsel, withdrawing this, withdrawing that, immediately after September 11. And this was opposed by the Bar Association and everybody else, and ran into trouble in the Senate. But essentially, it was written into law; and they haven't begun applying the worst provisions yet. So the Establishment would like to say, "Well, we're just ironing out the details," so it's necessary to expose the fact that the whole program is wrong. It requires a lot of work.

The Davis family home on Shawm Hill, by Quentin Brown, 1986

Afterword:
Alternatives to Reverence

Josh Lukin

> I do not transcribe these lines so that the reader
> may revere them.
> — Jorge Luis Borges, "On Oscar Wilde"

I

Hagiography is hard to avoid with a figure who combines a history of suffering with admirable artistic, scientific, and political accomplishment; but it's a very risky approach to a person — not least because of the perils of disappointment. What happens when the idolized figure is wildly mistaken? A worshipper can become bitter and disillusioned for decades. But to find a more democratic way to appreciate a Chandler Davis, one might have to rethink what "mistaken" means, or what constitutes a nonauthoritative truth. To my surprise, J.M. Cameron, whose Olympian pronouncements I ridiculed in "The Untimely Rhetoric of Chandler Davis," offers some ideas that could democratize the reading process.

Cameron as early as 1955 was trying to address how readers could admire powerful authors without feeling obligated to submit to their authority: he wrote of Hobbes, Pascal, Rousseau, and others that their work featured "the co-presence of logical incoherence and a felt power to illuminate political relations" (83) and tried to account for their appeal and utility by citing how, despite their shaky arguments, their work effected "connections of aesthetic appropriateness" (81). He extended these concepts in "Poetry and Dialectic," a 1961 speech he gave in his native UK, in which he tries to defend "poetic" or literary truth.[1] In the final third of the talk, Cameron compares the literary expression of feeling to our vocabulary of sensations:

> How do I learn to identify one of my sensations as a pain? ...to say that the word "pain" has a meaning is to imply that it is a unit in the public language...we could not learn to identify and describe our sensations and emotions through introspection alone... I now go on to say that understanding what it is we see or feel is necessarily connected with being able to give some account...of what this is. It is not that we first understand and then articulate our understanding

---

1 David Lodge has written, "Cameron's conclusions do not differ widely from those of other modern literary theorists and aestheticians. What is interesting is the route by which he reaches these conclusions, which enables him to formulate them in a particularly persuasive and precise way" (2002, 39-40). But Lodge's analysis of Cameron has in fact indicated that what is interesting is his *motives*: Cameron's taste is so catholic that his attempts to determine what distinguishes poetic discourse, unlike those of many mid-century critics, are not placed in the service of a drive to exclude certain authors or texts from the field of the literary—quite the opposite.

> through a conceptual scheme. Such an articulation *is* understanding. (142-3)

Hence poetic discourse expands our vocabulary, in a manner analogous to our knowledge of individual words and concepts, by offering us articulation-cum-understanding of various hitherto uncommunicated aspects of the human condition,

> and just as a concept is not a picture of reality which gets its sense from that slice of reality it pictures, but an instrument of understanding, so that truth belongs to the concept only in the act of judgment, in the same way the poetic representation finds its truth in its proved capacity to further our understanding of ourselves and our society. (146)

Cameron says little about the potentially radical effects of expanding one's poetic vocabulary. But the "capacity to further our understanding" that he attributes to literature embraces the opening of conceivable alternatives to our own worlds and perspectives. And a model in which literature expands one's imaginative repertoire, as opposed to one in which an author unveils hidden truths, can avoid placing authority in a subject-who-knows. It simply adds to our armamentarium of thought, leaving the choice of appropriate armaments up to the reader. As Cameron suggests later in his speech, finding a poetic articulation of a condition does not, or does not only, elicit our admiration for an author; it enriches us and offers us a sense of personal efficacy, or distinctiveness. Many personal essays about the experience of reading discuss how liberating that discovery can be.

Adrienne Rich's great "poetry is not a luxury" essay, "Blood, Bread, and Poetry: The Location of the Poet," traces its author's evolution from indoctrinated reverence for poetry to the experience of poetry and political essays as concretizing her inchoate discontent with the status quo and offering connections to others with the same impulses: she moves from having "believed that poets were inspired by some transcendent authority" (44) to "I don't know why I found [Baldwin's] words encouraging—perhaps because they made me feel less alone" (50) to "breaking the mental barrier that separated private from public life felt in itself like an enormous surge toward liberation" (56). This journey shows how, once one admits the ubiquity of the political (which Cameron, recall, believed could be excluded from some arenas), the insight that feelings are not individual, private, and self-generated, and Cameron's extension of that insight to explain how poetry can affirm our need for a sense of individuality while drawing us together, are empowering discoveries, which have been made repeatedly by sensitive artists.

By regarding literary discourse as a way of adding to our imaginative vocabulary, we might avoid the risks that put us in peril of treating a literary work's argument as authoritative. In the case of Chandler Davis, poetic truth and persuasive rhetoric sometimes go hand-in-hand: even when he is explicitly making a factual argument, Davis shows a gift for placing "these words in this order" (Cameron 1961, 145) in a memorable and powerful fashion to articulate a common feeling. Teaching Kleist's

"Earthquake in Chile" early in 2009, I found myself asking my students if they found the idyllic scene of mutual aid among the earthquake survivors at the story's midpoint to be credible; when they said they did, I burst out with, "Yes! 'PEOPLE CAN PULL TOGETHER.... It even feels good!'" The point was not to invoke the passage or its author as evidence; but Davis had given me a perfect articulation, and an initial understanding, of the feeling I derived from the scene in Kleist. That statement about mutuality is subject to claims about its veracity in a way that many lines of poetry are not (does each man indeed kill the thing he loves? Do all examples really show the infinite task of the human heart? Are bits of our love in fact moldering in the Lost and Found offices of bankrupt railroads? When they're human to police, do they invariably rough up lesbians?);[2] but it also works as a poetic representation.

II

The obvious objection to judging well-crafted literary discourse according to whether it gives a reader an understanding-articulation of a shared feeling is that any number of well-articulated feelings can be destructive to ourselves and our society, particularly if regarded as contributing to our understanding of that society. The criterion doesn't tell us whether, upon reading Kornbluth, we should feel a sense of solidarity ("Hey, I'm not alone in my feelings

2 Assertions made, respectively, by Oscar Wilde in "The Ballad of Reading Gaol," Delmore Schwartz in "For the One Who Would Take Man's Life in His Hands," Marge Piercy in "Night Letter," and Muriel Rukeyser in "What Do We See?"

of frustration and misanthropy!") or alienation ("Hey, I'm validated in my belief that most people are stupid!"). I take Cameron's speech to be neutral on propositions like the second and only interested in propositions like the first. Because his approach does not consider the validation of beliefs, it offers a strategy for connecting with writing (or an explanation of how we already connect with writing) in which we find the argument mistaken or repugnant. There are many students of literature (it's probably evident from my interview with Davis that I was one) who are tempted to write off certain gifted authors on the grounds of their toxic social values, and some could benefit from Cameron's strategy.

Because the approach to poetic truths outlined in "Poetry and Dialectic" can be an alternative or a supplement to judgments that involve a work's political value or propositional accuracy, does that mean it's an apolitical approach? Not at all. Firstly, it disentangles potential confusion between being persuaded by a proposition and connecting with a feeling. It's not unusual for a reader to mistake the first response to Kornbluth for the second: indeed, much political mobilization relies on equating shared feelings of discontent, disgust, shame, or anger with sympathy for a demagogue's propositions. Secondly, expanding one's imaginative repertoire with a vocabulary of shared feeling is an important step in understanding the limits of the dominant ideology. "The Names of Yanils" and "Adrift on the Policy Level" suggest that it's quite possible for a feeling, like an idea or a practice, to be invalidated and marginalized by societal pressures. Adrienne

Rich implicitly connects the three kinds of invalidation in a 1999 interview:

> Antifeminism was central to the right-wing "family" strategy, but so was the defamation of every past social justice movement. I recall in England Thatcher's dictum "There Is No Alternative." Here too, particularly given our history of anti-communism and anti-socialism, the possibility of an alternative has been rubbed out and discredited. (140)

Rich is not only decrying Thatcher's and Reagan's opposition to different practices but their opposition to hope, and to socially meliorative impulses. Collected along with her 1996 essay on "Defying the Space that Separates," with its observation that "We lack a vocabulary for thinking about pain as communal and public" (114), and with the understanding of oppression put forth in "Blood, Bread, and Poetry" — "But in reading de Beauvoir and Baldwin, I began to taste the concrete reality of being unfree…" (51) — the passage contributes to an argument that oppression works in part by exorcising states of feeling as well as historical events and concepts, feelings that literary discourse has unique power to preserve or recover.

So although the criterion of shared feeling, uniquely and powerfully expressed, that enables readers to articulate -understand their own past and future experience, can open us to authors or passages that fail criteria of humane politics or demonstrable accuracy, it is just as important in our apprehension of literary texts that are socially progressive and factually true. Reading, say, Davis's "Hexamnion," we[3] might object to its heteronormativity and indifference to the ethics of human experimentation; if so, our opportunity to connect with the story would depend on the force of its poetic representation. "It Walks in Beauty," on the other hand, manages to depict gender roles that survivors of the fifties can recognize, articulate shared feeling with poetic force, and manifest hope in the face of social injustice. In the process, it also illustrates how Cameron's argument needs to be extended by a post-universalist thinker like Rich. Because "It Walks in Beauty" gives us the conceptual vocabulary to note that at one point in his speech, Cameron turns into Max. He explains that love, by analogy with pain, is a feeling that one cannot misrecognize:

> We cannot mistakenly believe we are in love, though we may be quite mistaken in supposing we love the person we are in love with; but the ability to characterize our own state as one of being in love depends upon our having criteria for deciding when others are in love; and these criteria we get from a particular cultural tradition mediated to us in a thousand different ways. (144)

Has no one in Cameron's world ever decided that the sign "love" did not in fact refer to the feeling s/he'd had, and that s/he had either been misinterpreting or drawing from the wrong aspect of his or her cultural tradition? We can ask that question if we share the sense of possibility that Rich articulated in 1971:

---

3 I'm hypostasizing likely Aqueduct readers here.

> …if the imagination is to transcend and trans-
> form experience, it has to question, to challenge,
> to conceive of alternatives, perhaps to the very life
> you are living at the moment. You have to be free
> to play around with the notion that day might be
> night, love might be hate; nothing can be too sa-
> cred for the imagination to turn into its opposite
> or to call experimentally by another name. (21)

Only with that kind of flexibility can one comprehend a Max who says, "It isn't *natural* to love anybody except the most beautiful woman you've seen, obviously" and recognize the perplexity expressed in that statement as akin to the feelings of a homophobe, or indeed to feelings one might have had when confronted with a novel cultural practice.

Even if Cameron could not live up to the implications of his argument for the necessity of literature, he still provides a fine explanation of an adaptable tool, one which is necessary in a time when some prominent scholars reduce literary works to refutable propositions. As Virginia Kidd and Judith Merril discovered, one often can't do that to a Chandler Davis poem or story; indeed, "Shooting Rats in a Barrel" and "The Purge" also contain moments where Davis argues with himself, leaving readers who seek authoritative dicta unable to determine what side to take. But the taking of sides is not always the point: some of Davis's stories and essays rely on poetic force to evoke the understanding that—to put it in propositional form—"This state of feeling, or sequence of feelings, is possible and even common." A criterion for artistry *and* for radicalism in such a tactic is whether the statement is necessary and unusual: the pedagogy of feeling to which we are subjected every day by the clichéd and conservative discourse around us does not need more literature to reinforce it. Andrea Hairston has written, "Repetition is meaning. What we hear endlessly, goes without saying—is learned." We need the tools to unlearn it, or to find affirmation of what we rarely hear validated; but we aren't blessed with authoritative guides or methods for determining where poetic truth appears, or what manifestations of poetically shared feeling "further our understanding of ourselves and our society." We must fall back upon our own rational faculties and our own moral imagination, with curiosity and compassion fueling our drive to connect with others. Perhaps all examples do show the infinite task of the human heart.

Works Cited

Borges, Jorge Luis. 1946. On Oscar Wilde. Trans. Esther Allen. *Selected Non-Fictions*, ed. Eliot Weinberger. New York: Viking, 1999, 314-316.

Cameron, J.M. 1955. Justification of Political Attitudes. *The Night Battle*. Baltimore, MD: Helicon, 1962, 76-98.

——. 1961. Poetry and Dialectic. *The Night Battle, 119-149.*

Hairston, Andrea. 2010. "*Afrika Solo.*" *Ambling Along the Aqueduct.* Aqueduct Press. February 20, 2010. Blogpost. February 21, 2010.

Kleist, Heinrich von. 1807. The Earthquake in Chile. Trans. David Luke. *The Marquise of O—and Other Stories*, eds. David Luke and Nigel Reeves. London: Penguin, 1978, 51-67.

Lodge, David. 1965. *Language of Fiction: Essays in Criticism and Verbal Analysis of the English Novel*. London: Routledge, 2002.

Piercy, Marge. 1971. Night Letter. *To Be of Use*. New York: Doubleday, 1973, 6-7.

Rich, Adrienne. 2001. *Arts of the Possible*. New York: Norton.

———. 2001. Blood, Bread, and Poetry: The Location of the Poet. *Arts of the Possible*, 41-61.

———. 2001. Defying the Space that Separates. *Arts of the Possible*, 106-114.

———. 2001. Interview with Rachel Spence. *Arts of the Possible*, 138-145.

———. 2001. "When We Dead Awaken": Writing as Re-Vision. *Arts of the Possible*, 10-29.

Rukeyser, Muriel. 1973. What Do We See? *Breaking Open*. New York: Random House, 6-7.

Schwartz, Delmore. 1938. For the One Who Would Take Man's Life in His Hands. *Selected Poems: Summer Knowledge*. New York: Doubleday, 1959, 54.

Wilde, Oscar. 1898. The Ballad of Reading Gaol. *Selected Essays and Poems*. London: Penguin, 1954, 229-252.

Acknowledgements

"Critique & Proposals, 1949" first appeared in Vanguard Amateur Press Association.

"...From an Exile" first appeared in *The New Professors*, ed. R.O. Bowen (Holt, Rinehart, & Winston 1960).

"Violence & Civility" first appeared in *The New York Review of Books* Volume 15, Number 5: 24 September 1970.

"The Selfish Genetics" was published in the University of Toronto *Varsity* in 1979. The sidebar was printed separately and distributed as a flyer.

"Science for Good or Ill" was published as Booklet 26 in the Waging Peace Series of the Nuclear Age Peace Foundation in 1990.

"Last Year's Grave Undug" was first published in *Great Science Fiction by Scientists*, ed. Groff Conklin (Collier, 1962).

"Adrift on the Policy Level," in a slightly altered version, was first published in *Star Science Fiction Stories* in May 1959. The author's preferred version first appeared in *Above the Human Landscape: A Social Science Fiction Anthology*, eds. Willis E. McNelly, Leon E. Stover (Goodyear Publishing, 1972).

"It Walks in Beauty," in a substantially altered version, was published in *Star Science Fiction* in January 1958. The author's original version first appeared on SCIFICTION in September 2003 and has been bootlegged elsewhere on the Internet. "The Statistomat Pitch" first appeared in *Infinity Science Fiction* in January 1958.

"The Names of Yanils" first appeared in *Crank!* in Spring 1994.

"'Trying to Say Something True': The *Paradoxa* Interview with Chandler Davis" first appeared in *Paradoxa: Studies in World Literary Genres* Volume 18, 49-80 (2003).

Biographies

JOSH LUKIN TEACHES at Temple University, a public university in inner city Philadelphia that serves a very diverse student population, as a contingent employee of the First Year Writing Program. He also belongs to Temple's Interdisciplinary Faculty Committee on Disability. His primary specialty is in noncanonical fiction of the midcentury US; he has also published articles about Alan Moore, Oscar Wilde, and the Black Panther Party. In addition to teaching freshman writing and the occasional literature course at Temple, Josh has given many intramural presentations, on such topics as "Salvation and Decay in Colson Whitehead," "Narrative Prosthesis in Raymond Chandler Films," and "Disability in The Souls of Black Folk." In 2008, The University Press of Mississippi published his anthology, *Invisible Suburbs: Recovering Protest Fiction in the 1950s United States*; he has also published work in *minnesota review*, *The New York Review of Science Fiction*, *jml: The Journal of Modern Literature*, *Anarchist Studies*, and *The Encyclopedia of American Disability History*.

CHANDLER DAVIS, LIKE all the professors at Toronto at the time, was obliged to turn emeritus when he turned 65. He relinquished the teaching role only over several years, and reluctantly. He still has full-time work, regaling mathematicians with T*he Mathematical Intelligencer* (he has been on its editorial team since 1986), and trying to save the world despite itself through well-intentioned bodies like Science for Peace. He calls himself a Once and Future Science-Fiction Writer: still rapt in the promise and menace of the future, but for many years now responding otherwise than through fiction. "The future is my grandchildren's department." "My legacy is a considerable output of mathematics and a modest output of words and activism. All of which I relished."